Praise for *The Innocent*

"Once again, Gabhart creates a story that shines."

RT Book Reviews

"*The Innocent* is another well-crafted tale from the pen of Ann H. Gabhart. With characters that will steal your heart, Gabhart introduces a desperate young heroine who seeks safety among the Shakers during the post–Civil War era and a sheriff determined to come to her aid. A rich and rewarding read you won't want to miss!"

Judith Miller, award-winning author of Refined by Love series

"Another superbly crafted and thoroughly entertaining novel from a master storyteller."

The Midwest Book Review

Praise for *The Gifted*

"Gabhart skillfully elucidates Shaker beliefs while neither proselytizing nor condemning the tradition's practices. Drawn to Gabhart's strong characters as they are pressed to make difficult choices in their lives, readers will appreciate this window onto a different culture."

Booklist

"Impeccable research and moving characters."

RT Book Reviews

The
Refuge

Books by Ann H. Gabhart

The Outsider
The Believer
The Seeker
The Blessed
The Gifted
The Innocent
The Refuge

Words Spoken True

Angel Sister
Small Town Girl
Love Comes Home

Christmas at Harmony Hill

The Heart of Hollyhill

Scent of Lilacs
Orchard of Hope
Summer of Joy

These Healing Hills
River to Redemption

Books by A. H. Gabhart

Murder at the Courthouse
Murder Comes by Mail
Murder Is No Accident

The
Refuge

ANN H.
GABHART

Revell

a division of Baker Publishing Group
Grand Rapids, Michigan

© 2019 by Ann H. Gabhart

Published by Revell
a division of Baker Publishing Group
PO Box 6287, Grand Rapids, MI 49516-6287
www.revellbooks.com

Printed in the United States of America

Library of Congress Cataloging-in-Publication Data
Names: Gabhart, Ann H., 1947– author.
Title: The refuge / Ann H. Gabhart.
Description: Grand Rapids, MI : Revell, a division of Baker Publishing Group,
    [2019] | Includes bibliographical references and index.
Identifiers: LCCN 2018045192 | ISBN 9780800729271 (pbk. : alk. paper)
Subjects: | GSAFD: Love stories.
Classification: LCC PS3607.A23 R44 2019 | DDC 813/.6—dc23
LC record available at https://lccn.loc.gov/2018045192

ISBN 978-0-8007-3627-9 (casebound)

Scripture quotations, whether quoted or paraphrased, are from the King James Version of the Bible.

The author is represented by the literary agency of Books & Such Literary Management.

19 20 21 22 23 24 25   7 6 5 4 3 2 1

To my forever sisters

I

You can't cheat death. We thought we could. At least we hoped we could. That was why I sat in a blue Shaker dress, staring across a narrow table at Eldress Maria in her like garb as she told me about Walter. She had fetched me from the cellars and my duty of peeling apples to lead me to this little room where twice a week she encouraged me to confess my every sin. I was ready enough to do that now. To do anything to block away the truth of her words tearing my heart asunder.

"I am sorry, Sister Darcie."

She did look as though she might be. Actually sorry along with being concerned over how I might react to her news. A Shaker through and through, she was left at a village somewhere in the east when she was eight. A blessing, she claimed. Opened the door for her to a perfect life. Then forty-some years ago when she was twenty-nine, a mere five years older than I was now, she came here to teach the Shaker way to those who joined together to form the village of Harmony Hill. Ever a true believer.

I could not say the same. We were here, Walter and I, merely to escape cholera. To escape death. And then Walter did not. Oh, cholera didn't slay him. But death can come in many ways. Like a steamboat explosion. That is what Eldress Maria said stole Walter from me. He'd gone with the Shakers on a trading trip downriver to New Orleans, picked for that duty because he'd been a river man before we married.

Married. Not something the Shakers recognized. Here in the village, men were brothers and women sisters and never the twain could meet in what seemed a God-ordained relationship to me but sinful to them. Neither Walter nor I believed being man and wife was wrong in any way, but we didn't come here to convert to the Shaker way. We only intended to stay among these peculiar people for a little while. Just until the autumn winds blew away the bad air that brought cholera death.

I stared at Eldress Maria. A tear made a laborious trip down through the wrinkles on her cheek. Whether a tear of sorrow or simply a tear from an old woman's watery eyes, I could not know.

My own eyes were dry. I couldn't take it in. The words hung in the air between us, but I didn't want them to be true. Walter couldn't be dead. Not now. Not before I could tell him my news. My hands slipped under my apron to cradle the small swelling there.

Eldress Maria leaned across the table toward me. I sensed she wanted to hold my hands, but I kept them under my apron. I had no idea how long I could keep my secret hidden as well.

"We do understand this news may be difficult for you,

Sister Darcie, since you are so new to the Shaker way. How long have you been here among us?" Another tear slid down Eldress Maria's cheek. She was not without feeling for me.

"Three months. We came in July." Somehow I managed to push out an answer. Words that didn't matter. Nothing mattered now. Nothing except the baby Walter and I must have made right before we came to this place where marriage vows were negated and marriage beds denied.

I would have told him before he went down the river to trade the Shaker brooms, seeds, and jams. I did suspect I was in the family way back then at the first of September, but we had no way to talk. Not without breaking the rules.

In August I had managed to whisper a word to him during one of those times when we were learning steps to the dances they claim as worship. Dancing for church took some getting used to, but practicing the steps proved useful that day. A stumble here, a misstep there, and I ended up near Walter, close enough to arrange a midnight rendezvous.

I climbed through an open kitchen window and made it to the tree behind the Gathering Family House first. I had no problem sneaking out since the three other sisters in my assigned room were all snoring and sound asleep. And little wonder they snored, with orders to sleep laid out like a corpse in those narrow beds. On your back. Arms down to your sides. The Shakers had rules on how best to do most everything, but a body should be able to sleep however she wanted. How I wanted was to be curled next to Walter. Definitely against Shaker rules.

That night I heard him coming before I saw him, and my heart pounded with as much sweet anticipation as any time during our courting days. We weren't newlyweds. We'd shared four years together before coming to the Shakers, but the separation made his touch that much dearer. That night as I stepped into Walter's embrace and rested my head in that sweet spot below his shoulder, I realized how much I missed Walter's arms around me and his manly smell. And now I must miss them forevermore. At last tears filled my eyes and breath came hard.

"Are you sure he is dead?" I choked out the words.

She inclined her head until I couldn't see her eyes under the brim of her bonnet. I wore a like white bonnet, my copper-colored hair twisted into a braid and hidden beneath it. I had refused to cut my hair like the other sisters, because Walter loved stroking his hands through my curls. I blinked away tears and stared at Eldress Maria.

She played her fingers over the table as though searching for the best answer. When she seemed unable to find it, I spoke first. "Walter was a strong swimmer. He could have made it to the other shore."

Eldress Maria said Walter had been killed when the boilers exploded and sank the riverboat carrying the Shaker traders back to Harmony Hill. Such tragedies were not uncommon on the river. But Walter could have escaped death there the same as we escaped cholera. I was not wrong about him being a strong swimmer. He was strong in every way. He had once carried me across a wide creek as if I weighed no more than a dandelion fluff.

The old Shaker sister looked up at me, her eyes kind, but her words unyielding. "Nay. He did not, much to our sorrow. The other brethren escaped death and brought Brother Walter's body back for a proper burial. Even now, they are digging the grave."

"I want to see him." I needed to let my eyes linger on his face one more time.

"That would not be wise." A frown added yet more wrinkles to Eldress Maria's face. "Brother Bertram says dear Brother Walter was badly burned in the accident."

I started to speak, hope again fluttering awake inside me. Perhaps it could be a different unfortunate victim.

Eldress Maria must have guessed my thoughts because she rushed her words out in front of mine. "But not beyond recognition." She reached across the table and this time touched my arm. "It would surely be best for you to remember him as he was."

I shifted away from her hand, straightened my shoulders, and stiffened my resolve. I would not be denied my last look at my husband. "I must see him."

As she leaned back in her chair, Eldress Maria shut her eyes. I wondered if she was praying or simply irritated at my obduracy. Such mulishness was not admired among the Shakers. That mattered little to me. I would see my husband.

"Very well." The old sister opened her eyes and bent her head in concession to my demand. "Perhaps they have not yet nailed the coffin top on."

I didn't say so as I stood up, but a nail driven in could be prized out.

Almost blinded by tears, I turned from Eldress Maria and made my way out of the room. For a moment I stood in the expansive entrance hall to gather myself. After dashing away my tears, I stared at the two sets of stairs climbing up to the retiring rooms in the Gathering Family House. Here was where I had last seen Walter on the morning he left for the trading trip.

He was at the bottom of the brethren's stairway and I at the top of the one designated for the sisters. The Shakers took no chances of the men and women being close enough to touch, but oh, how I wanted to run after Walter that morning and throw my arms around him. I would have too, if not for Sister Helene grabbing my arm. She had befriended me here in the village and only intended to keep me out of trouble with Eldress Maria.

I did manage to lean over the railing and call to Walter. I cared nothing for the rules then. To be truthful, I cared nothing for them now. Even so, a person must get along wherever she lands, and Walter and I had landed here in this village by our own choice. Wisely, we thought. The Shaker village was never afflicted with the bad air that brought cholera on the summer winds.

"Walter." I had no intention of putting brother in front of his name, in spite of Eldress Maria's instructions that I must. He was not my brother. He was my husband. My beloved husband.

He looked up at me with a smile that I knew lit up his brown eyes even though I wasn't close enough to see the way they sparkled with love. He held up his hand with fingers spread wide. Five weeks, he meant. His promise that in five weeks he would return and we would leave these people and once more be together.

"Too long." I shouted the words and slipped past Sister Helene and down the steps so fast I nearly tripped on my skirt.

The brethren hustled him out the door, and by the time I reached the sisters' door, he was already in the wagon riding away. He waved, a mixture of regret and anticipation on his face. He loved me, but he also loved the river. I was safe among the sisters. The river beckoned him.

Would he have changed his mind and climbed out of the wagon had I run after him to tell him about the baby? That was something I could never know.

Eldress Maria came into the hall behind me. "Worry not about returning to your duties today. You can resume your assigned tasks come morning. Meanwhile, I suggest you consider your good fortune to be here among your loving sisters and brothers at this time."

"Yea." I managed the approved Shaker word of agreement without looking back at her. Instead I hurried out the door into autumn sunshine that did nothing to warm me as I forced my feet to move toward the Shaker cemetery.

I still did not believe it. I did not want to believe it. Walter couldn't be dead. Not now when at last I carried his child. We both so wanted children. A houseful. Boys and girls. Walter worried I was too small to safely carry a child, but my own mam was barely taller than me. She carried four without a struggle, though the birthing of her last one had been hard. It was the cholera in 1833 that took her, along with that last child. Dear Rosie, less than two years old.

I pushed the thought away. I had enough sadness confronting me without bringing up past sorrows.

The stone pathway to the cemetery ran in front of the Centre House, where those truly committed to the Shaker way resided. The three-story building made of stones chiseled from nearby river bluffs normally brought admiration from me, but today it merely looked cold and gray. Everything was cold and gray. It mattered not that the sun shone in a sky the blue of my Shaker dress.

I glanced over at the meetinghouse, its modest wood siding overshadowed by the stone building across from it, and considered stopping to pray. The Shakers did not worship as I, but the meetinghouse was nevertheless a church. I imagined those of the village's ministry watching me from the upper rooms over the church where they lived, isolated and no longer part of the fellowship of the whole.

For the good of the village, Sister Helene told me. "We all have our duties and theirs is to stay separate in order to make fair decisions."

And enforce the rules. I would find little sympathy for my grief among them even were I to enter their church. Best to send up my desperate prayers as I went on toward where Walter waited. In a box. Ready to be committed to the ground. Dust to dust.

Shivering, I wanted to hurry and yet delay at the same time. My steps faltered when I reached the graveyard and saw the great mound of dirt beside a hole.

The three men appeared to be finished with their somber chore as they leaned on their shovels. I knew only Brother Bertram, the very one who had somehow discovered Walter knew the river. Perhaps from Walter himself. That was why Brother Bertram lured Walter into a trading trip.

But it was not his fault.

"Sister Darcie, I don't think you should be here until the others gather to pay last respects to this our brother." That was more words than any Shaker brother had addressed to me in the few months I'd been in the village.

"I want to see my husband before you put him in the grave."

"Here you have brothers, not a husband." The man's voice was kind and lacked any hint of condemnation.

I didn't back down. "He is my husband and I will look at him."

"He was burned, Sister. Badly. Poor man. I was told he might have jumped clear of the boat and been safe, but the sound of a child crying stopped his escape. Instead of saving himself, he went back toward the flames to rescue those he could. More than once, according to the survivors." The brother bent his head and stared at the ground. "He would have made a good Shaker."

"No." I spoke the word firmly, purposely not saying the Shaker word *nay*. Walter would not have made a good Shaker. He was a good husband. My husband. "Where is he?"

"Heaven, I would wager, or moving toward that way. Paradise."

I barely restrained myself from attacking him then, as I'd once seen a raccoon attack a dog that had it cornered. The critter had no hope, but even so, it flung itself on the dog's head. I knew not why I thought of that, except I felt the same desperation. The same impossible lack of hope.

"Is his body encased in a coffin?"

"Nay, not yet. The box is being prepared. Brother Walter's body lies in the wagon yonder." Brother Bertram motioned with his head.

As I moved past him on my mission, he attempted to stop me with words. The same as those Eldress Maria used. "Better for you to hold him in your mind as he was. Not as he is now."

"But I must." I did not slow my steps.

He followed me. When because of my short stature I could barely peer into the wagon where Walter's form was covered with a blanket, he found a block of wood for me to stand upon. Without any more words, he pulled back the blanket.

They were right. Both Eldress Maria and this man next to me. I should not have looked, but it was what I had to do. My last service to my husband, to look upon his corpse with love.

Brother Bertram pulled the cover back over Walter's ravaged face. "He lived for a few minutes after he made it to the shore. Long enough to speak a few words."

I didn't ask, but the man continued anyway.

"He spoke of you. Said to tell Sister Darcie he was sorry."

I stared at the covered form in the wagon bed. "Did he say 'Sister' when he spoke of me?"

"Nay, he did not."

2

I waited beside the wagon until they brought Walter's coffin. I kept my eyes averted as they placed his body in the box. I had seen him in death. Now I pushed aside that dreadful image to think of him alive and smiling. That was how I must remember him.

The men carried the wooden box to the grave as other Shakers filed into the cemetery to see Walter laid to rest. The white bonnets of the sisters contrasted sharply with the black of the brethren's broad-brimmed hats as they took up positions on opposite sides of the open grave.

Sister Helene stood near me but thankfully sensed I could not bear to be touched. Eldress Maria made the laborious walk to the cemetery from the Gathering Family House. Others came whom I did not know. Perhaps they merely wanted a respite from their duties.

I regretted my unkind thought and tried to be glad they were here. But how could I be glad about anything as I watched the men grasp the ropes threaded under Walter's coffin to lower him into the ground?

Elder Jacob, who often spoke at the Sunday meetings,

stepped forward and removed his hat. The other brethren followed suit.

"This brother was only with us a short time, but in that time he proved his worth as a Believer. Diligent in his duties, he embraced the Shaker way of hands to work, hearts to God. A man dedicated to taking up his cross and following the Shaker way."

I bit my lip until I tasted blood. What this man said did not matter. I knew what Walter truly wanted. Hands to work. Hearts to God. That much could be true, but I was treasured in his heart too. We would have left this Shaker village and found our own way with the blessing of the Lord. *What therefore God hath joined together, let not man put asunder.*

"Brother Bertram has told me of Brother Walter's courage in giving his life to save others. Such is the example of Christ. No man can do more. We commit this good man to the earth and free his spirit to live forevermore in the perfect confines of heaven while we continue here to bring like perfection to our village. Such would be this brother's wish for us, were he still among us."

Oh, if only he were. Then I could tell him of the baby and we could walk away from this place to begin the rest of our lives. Now here I was—alone.

Elder Jacob nodded toward a sister and she began singing. The sorrowful tune pierced me.

> "Our brother's gone, he is no more;
> he's quit our coast, he's left our shore.
> He's burst the bounds of mortal clay.
> The spirit's fled and soars away."

ANN H. GABHART

She sang on, each word a stone dropped into my heart. I could barely restrain from clapping my hands over my ears. Then that was nothing compared to the sound of dirt being dropped on the box that contained the man I loved.

He was not there. I believed what the elder said about Walter moving on to heaven. He was a good man who loved the Lord. But I loved him, had rejoiced in being near his earthly body, with his voice in my ear, his lips touching mine. And now that body was being given back to the earth. Was it any wonder a wail of grief rose within me to clog my throat?

I could not watch more. Each shovelful of dirt falling into the grave would have been the same as falling in on me, stopping my breath. I had to think of the baby. I could stay there and sink at these Shakers' feet or I could run from their presence. I chose to run.

Sister Helene moved to follow me, but Eldress Maria put out a hand to stop her. For that I was grateful. I wanted no company. At least none that could be.

They say the Lord walks beside us through our deepest valleys. That he is with us even when we are too distraught to know his presence. I don't doubt the truth of what they say or that the Lord was beside me when I ran from Walter's grave. At the same time, I had never felt so alone. Achingly alone. How could I feel any other way with Walter gone?

I made it to the orchard before my insides revolted. Afterward I leaned against the rough bark of an apple tree and was glad for the nausea that proved I wasn't alone. Not completely. I carried new life within me.

"Walter, you would have been such a good father." I whispered the words on the wind. Perhaps they would carry to heaven.

21

I walked on then. I had no desire to go back among people. Better here among the trees. My foot kicked an apple hidden among the grass. A windfall missed when the apples were gathered. Not many were left behind. The Shakers were thorough. I had helped with the apple picking the week before, when even the smallest apples were put into the baskets. Those too small to peel could be pressed into cider. Naught was wasted.

This one didn't go to waste either. I brushed away a yellow-striped bee attracted to the apple's bruised side and, without bothering to so much as rub it off on my apron, took a bite. The crisp tang of the apple cleansed my mouth.

I wandered on, paying scant attention to my direction. All I knew was that I went away from the Shaker village. After crossing a pasture, I stepped into another stand of trees, not fruit trees this time but hardwoods. Some had been harvested by the Shakers, who were continually building something. Harmony Hill was a thriving community with huge houses like the brick Gathering Family House where Walter and I had been given beds on opposite sides of the wide hallway. The rafters and underpinnings of the three-story house surely came from trees such as these.

After I ate around a wormhole to finish off the apple, exhaustion fell over me like a shadow, and I sank down on the stump of what had once been a majestic oak. The rings adorning the stump gave testimony that the tree had stood in this place long before the first settlers came from Virginia. But now the tree was part of some Shaker building. Perhaps the meetinghouse. Perhaps the Gathering Family washhouse, where I spent hours last month in laundry duty until my back ached so much I struggled to sleep.

If not for the many baskets of dirty dresses, shirts, sheets, and more, the chore would not have been that daunting. The Shakers used horsepower to pump water into a holding tank and then piped water to the houses. At the washhouse, they even had large drums of sudsy water where the clothes were churned without the need for washboards and paddles.

My new duty of peeling apples was less strenuous, but tiresome in a different way. I looked down at my fingers darkened by the apple juice. I didn't mind working. I never had. Walter admired that about me. He said I would tackle anything.

Perhaps that was because he first met me tackling the impossible. That day he was an answer to prayer. Only later did I realize what a wonderful answer he was to a prayer I hadn't even known was in my heart.

When the cholera took my mother and little Rosie, I was nine, old enough to be of some use. But not old enough to take my mother's place, or so thought my father. If he had given me a chance, I might have proven him wrong. But instead he farmed me out to Granny and Pap Hatchell, an older couple in our church. Pap gave my father a horse to let me live with them and help Granny with whatever she needed. I was glad to be of value and Pa needed the horse.

The Hatchells couldn't take my younger brothers, Richard and Bertie, so Pa brought them here to the Shakers. They were no longer here. Three years later, after my father found another wife, he fetched them out of the village and they went off to Ohio to start a new life.

He came for me too, but Granny Hatchell needed me. And truth be told, I needed her and Pap. Their place had become my place. Back then, when Pa first left me with the Hatchells, I figured I had ended up better off than the boys who had to live among the odd Shakers. Now here I was in their midst with little recourse for changing that. Life can laugh at us at times.

But I liked living with Granny Hatchell. Oh, I had chores—cleaning, gardening, and such—but what she needed most was company. She was up in years. Twice as old as my own mother, but she had never been blessed with children. She didn't know why the Lord made her barren, but she said it wasn't right to question him. Best to accept the trials that came one's way.

The memory of those words stabbed me now. I had no acceptance of this new trial. I pushed away the now and remembered how Granny Hatchell took me to her heart and made me hers. I loved my brothers, but when Pa came for me, I couldn't leave Granny Hatchell behind. I had moved on from my birth family to a new family. Pa pretended not to be relieved, but I had little doubt he was. I wrote them a few times. Ma had taught me my letters, and Pap Hatchell fetched home books I read to Granny Hatchell to keep me in practice. But I never heard from Pa or my brothers after they left Kentucky.

The years went by. Good years. I grew but not much. I learned to cook and sew and make myself useful to Granny Hatchell. Pap Hatchell had wandering feet. He couldn't stand being cooped up for long. Granny said she never figured out how she actually got him to the church to get married. Maybe it was because she didn't make any demands on him. If he needed to do some walking around, hunting, or fishing, she packed his food in a knapsack and sent him on his way. She didn't complain about taking on the load of the farm until he could stand having his feet under her table again for a spell.

When I asked how come his wanderings didn't upset her, she laughed. "I used to be bothered some, but weren't nary a thing I could do to change John. That was how he was. I knew that when I worried him into marrying me. A body shouldn't be trying to change other folks just to make things more convenient for her."

They had worked all that out long before I lived with them. But then that one summer, Granny had a bad feeling when Pap was gone past sundown. He hadn't asked her to fix his knapsack of food. The next day I went hunting for him and found him on the riverbank a good ways from the farm. I knew he liked to fish there, but Pap had baited his last hook.

He looked peaceful as anything, leaned up against that tree, but he'd done gone on ahead and left his shell of a body behind. Pap wasn't a big man, but no way could I tote him home. Nor could I leave him there. Not after the shadow of an old buzzard sliced across the river water beside us. It might have been just passing by, but I couldn't trust in that. More likely the ugly old bird was headed to fetch his friends. I'd seen what buzzards could do to a cow carcass. A useful service on this earth, but I wasn't about to let them get to Pap.

I sat down beside him to consider my options, much as I was sitting here on this stump in these woods. With his cold hand in mine, I tried to think of what to do. Naught came to mind. I waved away flies buzzing in on Pap and knew things weren't going to take long to go from bad to worse.

I prayed then. Granny Hatchell was a praying woman, and I could almost hear her whispering words in my ear to send up to the Lord. A simple enough prayer straight from one of the Psalms. *I will lift up my eyes to the hills from whence cometh my help.*

Granny Hatchell loved that 121st Psalm. Whenever I read it out loud to her, she would say the words with me. She said the Psalms were songs for the Israelites. At times we would add our own tune to the words. *My help cometh from the Lord, who made heaven and earth.* I couldn't remember every verse, but I did know the Lord promised to be my keeper, my shade from the sun.

I was glad for the shade, for the cool breeze coming off the river and thankful it was September and not July with heat rising from the ground. But none of that changed me needing help. So that was my prayer when I lifted my eyes not to the hills but to the sky.

No sooner had the words crossed my lips than I heard something coming through the woods behind us. I wondered what sort of animal was headed my way to complicate my need. *O, ye of little faith*, I upbraided myself when a man on horseback came out of the trees toward the river.

A strong man from the look of his shoulders. Just what was needed.

Intent on getting his horse to the water, he didn't notice me there. So when I stood up and called out, he jerked around to stare at me.

"I'm in the need of help," I told him. "My grandfather has passed away here on this riverbank and I must take him home for a proper burial." I saw no need in going into the peculiarities of my kinship to Pap.

Walter took in the situation with one glance. That was the kind of man he was. The kind who did whatever needed doing, pleasant or not. The same as he tried to save those people on the riverboat and ended up dead for his caring kindness.

He put Pap across his saddle, and with him leading the horse, we made the long trek back to Granny Hatchell. That gave us more than enough time to get acquainted. He was coming back from a river trip. Had a sister in town. But instead of going on to see her, he stayed to dig Pap's grave and speak what sounded most as good as a preacher's prayer after I read the Twenty-third Psalm to lay Pap to rest.

Walter and I married before the first snow flew that winter. Granny Hatchell claimed she knew we would when she first laid eyes on him. We lived there with Granny, the three of us, happy as larks in a meadow teeming with bugs. We lost Granny Hatchell during a long cold winter three years later and now I had lost Walter too.

I don't know how long I sat on that stump with memories of Walter dancing around me before I heard the crunch of leaves. Somebody was coming through the trees toward me. I didn't get up to run away. A person can't hide forever from what comes next.

3

Sister Helene stopped when she caught sight of me and waited for me to acknowledge her presence. I wondered how she found me, but then eyes were always watching in the village. Watching was an assigned duty, the same as apple peeling or laundry. The Shaker leaders intended to make sure the brothers and sisters abided by the rules to stay apart. Those rules had chafed when Walter and I came to the village, but now it mattered not.

"I am here, Sister Helene." I don't know why I said that, when she could plainly see me there in front of her.

"Yea, I am glad to find you, Sister Darcie. We were concerned."

"Did Eldress Maria send you?"

"She allowed me to seek you out to be sure you were all right." Sister Helene stepped closer but still kept a proper distance. "Are you all right?"

"Yea." I lied. What else could I do? Even if I confessed my heartbroken state, Sister Helene had no power to assuage my sorrow.

"You are very pale." A worried frown wrinkled her forehead. She was a year younger than me, but somehow seemed even younger. Perhaps because she had been with the Shakers since she was a child of five. She told me she could imagine no other life. Wanted no other life. That I could not imagine.

She was plain, but then the Shaker bonnets and wide neck kerchiefs had a way of making every sister plain. I felt plain when I put on the cap that hid my red hair. I had stripped the cap off earlier as I walked across the pasture. Not that I hadn't worn bonnets before coming to the Shaker village. I had. A woman needed to shade her head, but today I worried not about the sun.

I liked my hair free. I had even unwound my plaits to let my curls bounce wherever they willed while I thought of how Walter liked to touch those curls. My hair always made him smile. He'd sometimes bought me hairpins, I think just so he could pull them out and let my hair fall down over his hands.

Sister Helene had light brown hair cut very short to be of little bother when she dressed in the mornings. She often frowned at my hair falling to my shoulders before I stuffed it out of sight under my bonnet. Her eyes were like mine, a mixture. Hers a mixture of green and blue. Mine a mixture of brown and green. Specked with sunlight, Walter said.

I liked Sister Helene. She may have been assigned to me as a duty to bring me into the Shaker fold, but she didn't care for me simply out of duty. Genuine warmth came from her kind heart, as she sincerely wanted to be my sister. So now I was not sorry to see her.

"I was sick earlier." I scooted a bit to the side of the huge stump and held my hand out to her. "Come sit with me."

She looked relieved to be invited near. "I hope you haven't

lost your cap." She perched on the stump beside me, our skirts overlapping.

"Nay." I used the Shaker word. "I have it in my pocket. It may be creased in wrong places." That was the way I felt. Creased in wrong places.

"As long as it isn't lost." Sister Helene's smile looked timid, as though she feared letting it completely win over her face.

"Lost." I echoed her word. "So many things lost."

She put her hand over mine then. "You loved him, didn't you?"

"Very much."

Her next words surprised me. "I have wondered how it would feel to love a man. A husband." When I didn't answer right away, she hurried on. "Such thoughts are sinful and I will have to confess my waywardness to Eldress Maria. Yet I can't seem to stop wondering about such things, even though Mother Ann's teachings are plain. Marriage causes stressful living and not the peace and unity we seek here in our village."

I'd heard much about Mother Ann, the founder of the Shakers, since coming to Harmony Hill. She was the one to decree marriage sinful. The Shakers considered her the female part of the Christ spirit. Their name even represented that. Not Shakers. That was the world's name for them. They did not shun the common name. Instead they accepted the moniker and used it on the products they peddled to the world.

But they began their society in New York as the Believers in the Second Coming of Christ. I didn't believe it for a minute. It mattered not how much Sister Helene or Eldress Maria tried to worm those ideas into my head. I didn't doubt their Mother Ann was a holy woman who knew the Lord and truly believed in what she taught. Nor did I doubt that the fervor of her belief caused her to shake and tremble when she worshiped. Her followers did the same and thus the name Shakers.

I had witnessed such tremors in the Sunday meetings at Harmony Hill, although most of the dances were disciplined marches. Still, at times, one of the believers would be overcome by the spirit to the point of quaking trembles. I never met this Mother Ann. She had passed on into the true realm of heaven many years before, but left behind enough followers to start Shaker communities all across the eastern states, with some in the frontier states, including two here in Kentucky.

The first weeks after I came to Harmony Hill, Eldress Maria had instructed me to read the story of Mother Ann's life to help me accept the Shaker way. I could agree with many of the teachings in the book. The need for generosity, the satisfaction of working with one's own hands to make something useful, the sorrow of riotous living, but the denial of marital love seemed to fly in the face of all that was natural in life.

So now I could have told Sister Helene how very wrong her Mother Ann was about the institution of marriage, but I had no heart for debate. Instead I answered her wondering.

"The love shared between a man and a woman is one of the sweetest blessings the Lord bestows on his people. It is the joy of a sunrise, the beauty of a starry sky, the faithful promise of a rainbow. Two become one forevermore." I stopped, unable to state the one thing that could tear a man and wife apart. Death.

"That can never be in a Shaker life." A timbre of sorrow sounded in her words.

"But if all were Shakers as you say you wish, there would be no babies." My free hand slipped under my apron to touch my midsection.

"You and I both know those in the world will never all choose to walk the Shaker way." She kept her voice low and looked around as if worried a watcher might be listening to her words of doubt. "But should that happen, then the Lord would supply."

Again I did not argue or state the obvious that the Lord had already designed a way for children. Mothers and fathers. Instead we sat silently as the day dimmed among the trees, perhaps each wrapped in our own separate worries. What hers could be, I did not know. Perhaps the wondering she thought would plummet her into sin. I tried not to think at all and be no more feeling than the hard wooden stump beneath me.

After a long while, Sister Helene spoke. "And what will you do now, Sister Darcie?"

I didn't answer her question. Instead I said, "I am with child."

I expected condemnation or at least distress, but instead her face lit up as though I had presented her with a much desired gift.

"Even more I have wondered about a woman bearing a child as Mary bore Jesus."

"Mine will not be a virgin birth." I thought it best to make that clear to one who seemed so innocent of such matters.

"Nay, of course not." She laughed, something I had not often heard her do.

"Will I be sent out of the village?"

"Nay," she said again. "Believers are ever kind to those in

need. You have surely seen that, with the way we feed any who come to us hungry. How we give shelter to those in need. How we took you in when you came among us, even though you lacked belief in our ways."

I could not deny the truth of her words. "Yea," I whispered.

"You must stay with us so that we can care for you." She squeezed my hand.

I had nowhere else to go and months before the baby's birth. By then, perhaps the Lord would provide an answer to the dilemma of being a mother in a Shaker society. I could not, would not, ever call the child within me brother or sister. I would be his mother.

Among those in the Gathering Family, I had noted the longing faces of mothers who had not yet surrendered to the Shaker way for families that separated parents and children. Some need beyond their control must have brought them into the village. Perhaps in time, I would share their desperation, with no way to survive on my own. I thought of my brothers. So many years had passed since I had seen them that they could have forgotten they had a sister. Still, they might take me in, but I knew no way to find them up in Ohio or wherever they may have gone by now.

I couldn't go back to Granny Hatchell's farm. When she died, a nephew I had seen only twice showed up to claim it. I had no legal claim. Walter said it didn't matter. We had each other. We needed nothing else.

I could not dwell on my loss. Best to think one day at a time. The Bible advised such a course. Even the Shakers suggested as much, with their Mother Ann's advice to do their work as if each day would be their last or as if they might live a thousand years. It seemed a strange saying. No one lived a thousand years, but sometimes a day could be one's last.

I stood up to follow Sister Helene back into the Shaker fold to live that one day at a time. A longing rose within me to become a wordless prayer that I would find a way to care for this baby I carried. Surely the Lord would honor such a prayer.

4

"You need a wife. Leatrice needs a mother."

Flynn Keller wanted to walk away from Silas Cox, refuse to listen, but his father-in-law was trying to help. Might even be right. At least about Leatrice needing a mother. So he stood still and let the man have his say. He deserved that much respect from Flynn.

Silas lacked some in size, a couple of hands shorter than Flynn and with no meat on his bones, but that never stopped him. He'd try anything. That was where Lena got it. The sometimes foolhardy try anything. Flynn figured that was how come she married him, a man who knew horses but little else.

Lena loved horses too. Liked riding the more spirited ones Flynn trained, but then she'd gotten on Sebastian before he was fully broken. Not that Lena hadn't lost her seat on horses before. Never stopped her getting right back on. But that last time she must have hit her head. Flynn saw her fall. Carried her to the house. Called in doctors. More than one.

They couldn't do a thing to help her. She never woke up.

Some said it was a blessing when she passed on three weeks later. No blessing to Flynn. He would have sat by her bedside forever with the hope of her coming back to him.

Silas understood. He loved his daughter and grieved over her long and hard. Then last summer when the cholera came through the area, he lost his wife. So he knew.

"Maybe you're the one who needs a wife." Flynn was sorry for his words as soon as the pain flickered across the other man's face. Silas wasn't trying to poke Flynn. He aimed to help.

"That could be. In time. But Beatrice hasn't been in the ground that long." Sorrow darkened the man's eyes. "Lena, God rest her soul, has been gone nigh on two years now. You've got to move on, son. If not for yourself, for my grand-daughter. You can't just let her go wild, and you can't watch her every minute while you work those horses of yours."

Flynn heard the thought behind the man's words. What if Leatrice tried to get on one of the horses without them knowing it? The girl was as headstrong as her mother, even if she was only six. Wouldn't be seven until spring came again. Just this day Silas had been busy about some chore and the girl had gone missing from the house.

They'd found her in the far pasture pulling grass to feed Sebastian, the very horse that could be blamed for her being motherless. Sebastian was long ago trained. A fine horse now. Flynn should have sold him, but Lena had loved that horse. She wouldn't blame him. Flynn didn't blame him, but he did keep him away from the house where he didn't have to lay his eyes on him every single day.

"She knows better," Flynn said. Words that didn't mean much.

"Knowing and doing aren't the same."

Silas looked tired. Things had been hard since the passing of Leatrice's grandmother. She had somehow kept Leatrice in line, unlike the women Flynn had hired since her death. They had been next to useless. A couple of them threw up their hands and gave up the job after a few days. The only one who lasted longer than a week was Irene Black and that had been a disaster.

Flynn pulled in a breath and looked toward the yard where Leatrice was on her swing. The little girl pumped her legs up and back ferociously to go high enough to touch the maple branches with her toes. Her dark hair flew out behind her. She was so like her mother, except for that dark hair like Flynn's instead of Lena's blonde locks.

"You're right." No need arguing with Silas over what was the truth. The only way he could be sure to keep his willful daughter in sight was to rope her like a pony and tie her to his belt. And then he wasn't sure which one of them would be doing the leading.

He spoiled her. But how could he not spoil a child who'd lost her mother? Flynn knew about that. He hadn't seen his own mother since he was a boy. After Flynn's father took off without a word and the cholera epidemic of 1833 stole away Flynn's sister, his mother packed up his younger siblings and headed back to Virginia to live with relatives. His mother hadn't died, but she was gone to him nevertheless. Flynn had made his way, but it was different for a boy of fourteen than a girl of four. Nothing the same about any of that.

Silas was watching Leatrice too. He tensed when the rope caught and popped because she went so high. A laugh drifted over their way. He shook his head and turned back to Flynn. "I hear the preacher and his wife offered to take her as one of their own. Could be you should consider that."

"No." He would not desert his child.

Silas gave him a hard look. "Even if it was best for her?"

"That wouldn't be best. I'm her father."

"I know you love her, son." Silas shook his head a little. "But if she don't get some sense and soon, you're liable to lose her. She's that much like Lena, and we lost her."

"Because she fell off a horse."

"That she shouldn't have been riding. You know it's true, Flynn. I know it's true."

Hot blood flooded Flynn's face. He clenched his hands and tamped down his anger as he spoke his next words slowly, one at a time. "I'm not giving my daughter away. That's the last I want to hear about it, Silas. The last."

Silas didn't blanch. "Could be the preacher wouldn't be right for her anyhow. But that don't mean you don't need to do something."

As if to prove the man's point, Leatrice yelled and jumped out of the swing with it high in the air. Too high. Flynn's breath caught in his chest as she tumbled to the ground and rolled like a stone pitched downhill. Flynn ran toward her, but by the time he was halfway there, Leatrice was on her feet, laughing. She paid no attention to her skinned knee or Flynn as she jumped back into the swing and began pumping it higher again.

Flynn stepped in front of her and grabbed the ropes. "Don't you jump out of this swing like that again. You're apt to break a leg."

"Or my head like Mama." She looked up at Flynn, her

dark blue eyes wide. The girl knew how to keep Flynn from walloping her.

He never liked smacking her bottom anyway. He'd left all that up to Lena or Lena's mother. Now with Silas looking on, he hardened his heart and kept his voice firm. "Or your head."

Tears popped up in the girl's eyes and overflowed down her cheeks. She jumped off the swing so fast it bounced up and down behind her as she buried her face against Flynn's stomach.

Her voice was muffled as her lips moved against him. "I don't want to break my head like Mama's."

"There, there." Flynn smoothed down her dark curls. What else could he do? "You'll be fine. As long as you listen to me and stop doing things that might hurt you."

"I miss Mama." Leatrice sobbed. "And Mamaw Bea."

Whether she was shedding intentional tears to make him forget being upset with her or if the tears were the result of real sadness, it made no difference. Her weeping destroyed Flynn. Something he couldn't fix. He was a man who fixed things. He could take a horse and change every bad behavior, but he had no way to fix a motherless child except, he supposed, what Silas said. Marrying again.

Flynn wasn't ready for that. If he had been, that Irene Black might have already captured him. After the first two women quit and Irene took the job of keeping house, she'd wasted no time letting him know she was ready to marry, but he hadn't been in a marrying mood. Not just for somebody to keep house. He could wash dishes and sweep floors if need be.

Even if he had been tempted to surrender to a marriage

of convenience, he wouldn't have picked Irene Black. Not after he came to the house unexpected one day and heard her telling Leatrice that bears would come eat her if she didn't act right.

The week before, Leatrice had become strangely fearful at night. Flynn thought she was missing her grandmother. But it turned out she was worried about bears eating her while she was sleeping. Flynn sent Irene packing, promised Leatrice what Irene said wasn't true, but to make her feel better, he barred the doors and nailed down her bedroom window so no bears could get near her. That he could fix.

Now he wiped away her tears, hugged her again, and sent her off to gather the eggs. As she headed for the henhouse, his heart felt too big for his chest. He did love that child. Would do anything for her. Maybe he could get her a dog. A lazy, old dog that wouldn't run off with her.

Silas stepped up behind him. "You might think about the Shakers."

Shakers? Flynn didn't know why Silas was talking about them. Flynn did have some Shakers coming to look at one of his horses. While they usually traded with other Shaker villages, some as far flung as Ohio and Pennsylvania, they got a horse from him now and again.

The Shaker village was a few miles away, but near enough to hear their bell tolling when the weather was right. Sometimes he even caught the sound of their singing on worship days. The people had odd ideas about how they thought folks should live, but they were honest and fair in their horse trading. That was more than he could say for some others.

Flynn turned to look at Silas. "You mean to sell more horses?"

"I'm not talking about horses. I'm talking about Leatrice. Those people take in motherless children, teach them how to read and write."

Flynn went stiff. "I know how to read and write. I can teach Leatrice myself."

"I'm not saying you can't, but it would do the girl good to be around other girls her age. Help her learn how to act and all. I've heard the Shakers are good at keeping their youngsters in line."

"They don't have youngsters. They all live as brothers and sisters out there."

"Then their adopted youngsters." Silas was like a cur dog with a bone. Not ready to give up his idea that something needed to be done with Leatrice.

"Leatrice isn't up for adoption."

"Of course not, but you wouldn't have to leave her there forever. Just until things settle down. Until she settles down. With all those sisters watching her, she'd surely stay out of trouble."

"That's crazy talk, Silas. Completely crazy."

Silas shrugged. "Maybe so. You know I just want the best for her. For you too. You could always join up with her."

"Me, a Shaker?" Silas had to have lost his mind.

"Like I said, just for a while. Till Leatrice gets old enough to have some sense. And this way, if you go now, you wouldn't have to give them the farm. You know the farm here is going to you and Leatrice when I die."

"Slow down, Silas. You've got a lot of years left in you."

"Could be. I'm not in any particular hurry to leave this old world." Silas shook his head with a little smile. "But those old Shakers are pretty shrewd. Anybody goes to join up, they add their property right in with theirs, excepting slaves. A body has slaves, they have to set them free on the spot."

Flynn stared at Silas. "I don't have any slaves and don't intend to."

"Well, no, but property is property. They'd likely want your horses. I couldn't claim them as mine. Over there, they own everything together. What's good for one is good for the whole. At least that's what they say." Silas spat on the ground. "Could be some of it's best for the boss Shakers, but the most of them are generous to a fault. Will let anybody come live there as long as they work and stay away from women."

"I'm not giving Leatrice to anybody. Not the preacher. Not the Shakers."

"You're probably right about the preacher, but you should think about the Shakers. The idea come to me while I wasn't able to sleep last night, like maybe the Lord put it there. So maybe you should pray about it. See what the Lord wants you to do."

Silas turned and headed toward the house before Flynn could come up with the right thing to say. If there was a right thing when somebody came up with such an idea. Him a Shaker? He didn't believe any of what the Shaker men he'd dealt with told him about their religion from the belief that their founder, this woman they called Mother Ann, had the Christ spirit. There might not be anything wrong with that. Trying to be like Jesus, but they went a couple of steps on past that with their thinking. They claimed God meant for there to be a female holy person like Jesus and that person was this Mother Ann.

If that wasn't weird enough, they thought a person could

worship by dancing. That went against everything Flynn had ever been taught about church. You danced at the rowdy houses, not at church. Not that doing a jig now and again was all that sinful or sharing some sweet moments arm in arm with the woman you loved was one bit wrong. He and Lena had done some of that kind of dancing. But the Shakers claimed a person could get so filled with the spirit that he would go into trembling fits while whirling around in their dances.

That's how come they were called Shakers. Not what they named themselves. That was something about a Society of Believers, but those who watched them shaking in their worship had called them Shakers and it stuck. While it might have been used with ridicule in the beginning, the Shakers latched on to the name for their Shaker seeds, sweetmeats, potions, and more.

You could depend on Shaker products. Their seed grew. Their cattle looked better than most on the farms around. Could be even their potions would work, although Flynn had never tried them.

And it was a fine thing they did taking in orphans without a place. But Leatrice wasn't an orphan. She had a father. She had him.

5

I kept my baby a secret as long as I could. Sister Helene
knew, of course, and one of the other women in my sleeping
room guessed without being told. Sister Ellie said not only
my morning nausea but also a certain inward look gave me
away. Before she and her husband came to the Shakers six
years ago, she had borne five children.

"Coming here wasn't to my liking, but my Albert was as
sure as I was doubtful," she told me. "Might be fine for those
with no children to claim. But I did miss hearing my own
call me ma after we came among the Shakers."

"What did they call you?" I asked.

"Sister Ellie. Seemed the strangest thing. Children I'd
birthed acting like we had no more connection than you
and me." Sister Ellie shook her head. "Nay, not seemed.
'Twas the strangest thing. The children thought it strange
too. I could tell by their faces. After all, I knew those faces
like my own."

When I asked if the children were in the village, she
frowned. "Only one is still in the Shaker dress. Little Abby.

She wasn't but three when we came here. The others were all older. Soon's they figured they could make their own way, they left this place for more natural living."

"Why didn't you go with them? You could have, couldn't you?"

"I'm not bound here with chains, if that's what you mean, but my man, he embraced the Shaker way full on. Stopped embracing me, if you want to think about it that way. But in my heart he is still my husband. That ceremony our preacher spoke over us had something about whither thou goeth, so must I go. He went here. And there's little Abby too. I can't exactly mother her, but I can keep my eye on her. The others, by the time they left, they didn't really need my mothering. They come back and visit now and again. My eldest girl had a baby with her last time she came."

"Did they let you see her?" I asked.

"Yea, the Shakers are not unkind. They do tell my daughter she should come back into the fold, which I can tell will never happen. Instead my daughter invites me to come away with her." Sister Ellie paused a moment as sorrow mixed with a bit of despair showed in her eyes. She sighed and looked resigned. "I can't go now even if I was willing to break my vows. They wouldn't let my Abby go with me. It's her father's decision that rules on where she must be. I'm not sure she'd go with me if she could. She loves her Shaker sisters. As do I, but there are times . . ." She let her words die away.

I heard the words she didn't speak. I heard them even clearer, now that I carried a baby of my own.

As my shape changed and the size of my midsection could no longer be hidden under my apron, I became something of a pariah among the Shakers. The brethren averted their eyes and sometimes changed direction when they saw me on the pathways. I wasn't sure if I was an embarrassment to their society or a temptation to the memory of how they used to live. Eldress Maria forbade me from joining in at worship times. That was just as well. I had no energy for dancing after a day's work.

She had questioned me for two full hours when she realized my condition. "An example of sinful living," she said.

"I did not know I was with child when we came to the village." I refused to cast my eyes downward as though ashamed of the child growing within me. "Even had I known, you would have surely welcomed one so innocent as an unborn child."

"We turn none away in need, but we do expect those among us to live the Shaker way."

"Yea. I have done so since sleeping under your roof." I had no desire to upset Eldress Maria. Since I had no family to take me in, I needed that Shaker roof.

Eldress Maria didn't dispute my words. I had been diligent in my duties and respectful when she and others instructed me in the Shaker way, although I never gave any indication of belief in their way. Then again, since I had not spoken against their teachings, I suppose silence can be a cowardly way of agreeing. But I was not there to change the Shakers. I was there to escape death, which had run after and caught Walter at any rate.

I kept Walter close in my thoughts as his baby grew within me. I imagined him walking with me, putting his hand on my midsection to feel the baby kick against my skin as though eager to push his way into the world. Him. I was that sure my baby would be a boy. A little Walter. I imagined him with Walter's blue-gray eyes and my red hair. A sturdy little boy afraid of nothing, the same as Walter. The same as me.

Or the way I was before. Now many worries came to mind with uneasy fear trailing after them. What to do? Our few resources had been given over to the Shakers when we came to their village. If I left, those would be returned to me, but I would hardly have enough for a new start. Then came the morning that cramps gripped me.

Sister Ellie frowned when she heard me gasp. Her frown grew darker when she noted blood spots on my nightgown. "How many months did you say you were?"

I counted in my head. July, August, September, October, November, December. "Six."

"Too soon. A baby can come weeks early and survive, but not months early."

"Can I stop it?" My hands clutched my stomach as though to hold the baby in.

"A few early pangs are naught to worry over. If they go away. You should rest until they do. Go to the infirmary and do no work."

"But what of my duties?" I had been assigned to the kitchen where I peeled and chopped vegetables to fill the pots.

"Sister Helene can make your excuses to Eldress Maria. Someone else will take your place."

Sister Ellie looked at Sister Helene, who stopped adjusting her cap to stare at me, her eyes wide with worry. As can be with natural sisters, the three of us had grown so close that the baby no longer seemed mine alone, but in some ways, theirs as well. They had watched him grow to push out my belly, but Sister Ellie was right. I remembered my mother's size before my brothers and little sister were born. My baby needed more time.

So I lay in bed until the pains faded away and no more blood leaked from me.

Yet Sister Ellie continued to watch me with concern. "What has happened once can happen again," she warned.

Eldress Maria said the same, with even more direness. "It can be God's will to take away sin. Our Mother Ann lost four children before the Lord revealed to her the sinfulness of marital life."

"Nay." I sat across from the eldress and denied her words. "The Lord loves all babies."

"Yea, but he can love them even more in heaven where all is good. The babies do not suffer." Eldress Maria narrowed her eyes on me. "Our Lord has many ways of teaching us the lessons we must learn."

Her words were harsh, but I did not protest them. It was near Christmas. A time for peace and for atonement. The Shakers even had a special day for such. A time to ask forgiveness of any they had wronged throughout the year. The mistreated person was to forgive unconditionally in order for the unity of the village to be restored.

So even though I didn't speak the words aloud, I forgave Eldress Maria. She had never carried a child. She could not know the way a baby lived in one's heart long before the first life movements were felt.

After the cramping pains, I was given lighter duty. I spent hours in the sewing room hemming dresses and aprons. I also hemmed small blankets and tiny nightshirts. Nobody said they were for my baby, but the sisters smiled when they handed them to me to do the finishing stitches. Many of them were mothers who remembered a baby growing under their hearts.

January came with cold and snow. My middle grew larger while the rest of me seemed to shrink around it. I struggled to make it to the privy when the pathway was icy. Sister Helene often walked with me, ever ready to grab me if I slipped. She watched me with eyes of wonder, almost as if she could see the baby growing inside me.

"How does it feel?" she continually asked.

I tried to tell her. How the very thought of this baby made my bones soften and my arms eager to feel his weight as he suckled my breast. I did my best to share this journey with her since if she stayed with the Shakers as she thought was her lot in life, she would never know the joy of bearing a child or the sorrow of losing a husband. Both would be lost to her unless she left the village, and that seemed something far from her thoughts. Unlike mine.

Without the baby to consider, I would have walked away from the village. Gone into the town and looked for a job perhaps as a nanny teacher. I could mind children. Hadn't I the same as raised my little brothers while my mother carried little Rosie? But who would hire a woman so near to birthing a baby? None without the bonds of kinship.

My Shaker sisters told me not to think on that. Even Sister Ellie, although a frown did crease her brow from time to time when we talked of spring after the baby came. I knew she was thinking of her Abby who lived in the Children's House with others to watch over her. But surely a mother would be allowed to nurse her baby. I did not ask that question for fear of the answer.

The Shakers had their rules. If they disallowed the relationship between a man and woman, then might they also refuse to recognize the natural bonds of mother and infant? It did not bear thinking upon. At least not during the day when I could keep my hands busy. At night, lying in the narrow bed with my back aching from sitting in a straight chair, plying my needle all through the day, the worry poked at me as I counted the weeks before my baby would come into the world to good or bad. I prayed, silently and fervently. Often I had no words. The Lord knew my need of a place to raise my child.

Sometimes I blocked the truth that he had already given me this place with shelter and food among the Shakers. But I thought of the future and could not help recalling sight of the Shaker children lined up with sisters who weren't their mothers. I prayed for another way.

Sister Ellie understood without my speaking aloud my concerns. She would touch my arm and look into my eyes as Granny Hatchell used to when she was explaining something about life. "Worry not, dear sister. You'll only make yourself ill. Take each day as it comes with the blessings and trials it brings, for the Lord only promises us this day. We can do naught to turn yesterday into a different day, and we know not what the morrow might hold. Simply step out on the day's path with your trust in the one who holds all our days in his hands."

Her words were wise. I did my best to listen. At times, when the baby moved within me, I could embrace the moment and not worry about tomorrow. Other times I was so overcome with grief and anxiety, I could not think of anything except the cradles I'd seen in the Children's House.

No cradles were in the Gathering Family House, where I slept surrounded by women ready to learn the Shaker way or perhaps as trapped as I.

Sister Helene was not trapped. Nothing seemed to truly trouble her. The peace of the Shaker life, she said. Troubles were locked outside the village in the world. All was good here, as much like heaven as humans could make it. She noted my uneasy spirit, but she seemed to float along above it all, much like a fluffy white cloud pushed across the sky by dark thunderclouds. Oblivious to any kind of storm. She would say there was no storm. Not if a person embraced the Shaker way.

Eldress Maria, the leader of the sisters in the Gathering Family house, said the same on the days she heard my required confession of sins. During the week, I gathered these wrongs into a sin sack so I would have something to tell her, even though what I said little mattered. She looked at me and saw worldly sin. The evidence could not be hidden.

Sister Helene had too gentle a soul to see sin in any of her sisters. That was why she was assigned to those of us yet resisting the Shaker teaching. Her kindness and patience made her a perfect teacher. I listened to her words, did my best to abide by the rules she claimed would keep unity in our family. Always step up on the first stair step with one's right foot. Shaker your plate. That meant to eat every morsel you dipped out onto that plate, whether your stomach suddenly rebelled or not. The Shakers probably even had rules on the proper way to lose one's supper, but if so, Sister Helene never shared that one with me.

The Shakers were firm about the need to care for one's body by taking proper nourishment. After all, each person was expected to work. Every day. Except Sunday. Even then there were chores and the dancing worship. The Shakers claimed they were exercising or laboring the songs.

Before I was banned from the services due to my worldly condition, I had seen Sister Helene in the marches stepping to and fro, bowing and bending to the music of the singers. They had no instruments other than their voices. They sang all on the same note for unity and danced the steps practiced in the family houses on evenings during the week. I had practiced the dances, but I never took part in the Sunday worship times.

That suited me. I could do the steps. Small as I was, I had always been light on my feet, but I couldn't wrap my mind around dancing as a way of worship. Never mind that I had read in the Bible about how King David danced in front of the Ark of the Covenant when it was brought to Jerusalem. Those were different times. And a man after the Lord's own heart.

Perhaps I was wrong to judge. Sister Helene did have a glow about her as she danced in the worship times. Others shared that look, but some merely seemed to go through the motions while peering over their shoulders, perhaps for a glimpse of a loved one now separated from them. A few like me checked the little window door where the eyes of those of the Ministry could be seen watching. Ever watching.

So I was happy to have a time of quiet while the others went to the meetinghouse. Even with the windows closed against the winter air, I could hear them singing as they marched in order to church. Two by two. Brethren, then sisters. At the church the men would enter through one door and the women the other. Such was the same at the churches

I attended with my mother and then with Granny Hatchell when she felt up to going. But nothing was the same once the Shakers entered those doors to seek spiritual blessings in a different way, with dancing and whirling. So very different than at my mother's and Granny Hatchell's churches a person sat and quietly waited for the preacher to summon the spirit.

Once I knew the Shakers were inside, I took a chair from the railing where it hung upside down to keep dust from collecting on the seat. The chairs, along with brooms and candles in tin holders and sundry other things, hung out of the way on the railing pegs to make sweeping easier. The Shakers made war on dirt. They even fashioned small brooms with a perfect shape for cleaning corners. They believed good spirits would not live where there was dirt.

I sat in the sunlight, warmed by its trip through the window beside me, and rested my hand on Granny Hatchell's Bible. I had often read to her before the fireplace with its ashes spilling out on the hearth. Pap Hatchell and then later Walter brought in dirt from the fields that had a way of settling into the cracks of the wooden floor. But good spirits abounded in our little cabin. How I wished for a return to that place where order didn't matter as much as love.

Granny Hatchell did love me. I smiled as I remembered her sometimes saying I wasn't big as a minute, but then she'd tell me how I was wonderfully made. That the Lord's hand covered me in my mother's womb. She showed me where it said that in Psalms. I leafed through the thin Bible pages until I found the verse in Psalm 139.

I will praise thee; for I am fearfully and wonderfully

made: marvelous are thy works; and that my soul knoweth right well.

I laid my hand flat on the Scripture, shut my eyes, and dwelled on how my own baby was being fearfully and wonderfully made inside me.

And so I waited.

6

Icy snow stung Flynn's face and the raw wind sliced right through him as he walked to the barn. He hated winter. Had ever since he was a boy.

He'd heard tell of places where it stayed warm year around. No snow. No ice. Said a man near died of the heat in the high summer, but as Flynn clutched his coat closer, he thought maybe he wouldn't mind that trade-off. A fellow could always jump in a pond or river to cool off.

Nobody was going to jump into any ponds around here. They were all frozen over. Another problem. He'd have to break the ice on the pond behind the barn so the cows Silas insisted on keeping would have water. A man needed a milk cow but not a whole field full. Flynn had never taken to cows that gave him blank stares and dug in their hooves and refused to move or threw up their tails to run the wrong way whenever a man needed them to go from here to there. At least a horse could be trained to do what needed doing. But he didn't guess there was any way to train horses to fill their own water and feed buckets.

Flynn looked back toward the house. Through the blowing snow, he could barely see the glow of the lamp he'd left burning on the kitchen table. Surely Leatrice would do as she was told and stay inside. Silas was there with her, but he was showing his age. Yesterday he had nodded off right in the middle of Flynn telling him about the horse the Shakers were coming to get on the morrow.

At least the man hadn't started in again on how Flynn should take Leatrice to the Shakers. The child was nigh on seven. Plenty old enough to do what he said, whether or not he was watching her every minute. By the time Flynn was seven, he was already working with his pa every day, with no time to get into mischief. He had even less time after his pa rode off to town one day when Flynn was twelve and never rode back home.

Nobody knew exactly what happened to him. Flynn figured he just kept riding west. He'd been twitchy for a while, ready to cuff whoever was closest if the least thing went wrong. Flynn, his ma, his sister and little brothers had been staying out of his way when they could, but none of them expected him to just ride off without the first goodbye.

His mother hung onto the farm for a while, but then the cholera came in. Took Flynn's sister in two days. Lillie was a year younger than Flynn and as pretty as her name. Losing her broke Flynn's ma. Turned her eyes back toward Virginia. Flynn refused to go with her. By then, he was as strong as most men, and he intended to be where his pa could find him if he ever came back to Mercer County. That was so he could beat the living daylights out of the scoundrel the next time he laid eyes on him.

Not that he ever got the chance. Life moved on. His pa

had moved on. But Flynn wasn't about to move on when it came to Leatrice. No way would he ride off and leave her behind. He aimed to make sure she didn't have to come up hard the way he had.

That didn't mean she shouldn't learn some women ways when she got older. Cooking would be good. Neither he nor Silas could do much more than stir up a pot of beans. He did miss Ma Beatrice's cooking.

Those sisters over at that Shaker village could cook. He'd taken a meal there now and again when he traded horses with them. He'd heard they had a good school too. Maybe they would let Leatrice come. Just by the day. The girl was anxious to learn her letters, and while he had told Silas he could teach her, a man didn't have time for everything.

It was some warmer in the barn. Leastways the snow wasn't stinging his cheeks and the horses in the stalls put off some heat. The horse the Shakers wanted stuck his head out of his stall and nickered. Flynn got him cheap because he had a sore foot. People lacked patience in working with horses. They were ever ready to push aside the old and find something new. As if a new horse couldn't step on a sharp rock and get a sore foot too.

"Ease down, Jack. I'm coming." Jack didn't have a name until Flynn got him. Not everybody bothered giving their animals names, but Flynn believed horses liked being called something other than "horse."

The Shakers named their animals too. Even their herd bulls. Called one of them "Shaker," so Flynn had heard. Seemed a strange name for an animal they brought over from England to improve their herd bloodlines. Those Shaker brethren must have a sense of humor, even if Flynn never noted it when dealing with them. They seemed ever serious minded. Made Flynn wonder how they turned free enough to shake and twirl in church.

He shook his head at the idea of dancing in church as he filled Jack's feed cradle with hay. He'd make a fine horse for the Shakers. A willing worker. That was what those Shakers wanted from man or beast. Workers. Not a bad thing. Working. Come tomorrow when the Shaker men came for Jack, maybe he'd ask them about school for Leatrice and whether they would teach her without trying to turn her Shaker. He had no desire for Leatrice to become one of those Shaker sisters, spending her last years in a Shaker rocking chair with no children to bring her joy.

By the time he finished with the horses and milked the cow, the snow had stopped and the sun was out. He squinted as he stepped out of the barn into the sunlight glancing off the snow. Lena would have been running around in it, loving the ice glittering on the branches. She could find the beauty in everything. Maybe if she'd still been there with him, he could see the beauty too. Instead he simply felt the wicked cold.

He started to the house with the pail of milk when he remembered the other cows. He took the milk on to the house and set it inside the back door. He had half a mind to holler at Silas to go see to the cows, but Silas had been coughing some at night. Better for the old man to stay in by the fire.

After hitching up his old mare, Blossom, Flynn threw hay down on the sled and found the axe. He pulled his hat low to shade his eyes from the sun glaring off the snow. Blossom knew the way. He didn't have to guide her.

He was almost to the gap into the cows' pasture field when he heard a loud cracking sound. The ice on the pond breaking. One of the cows must have stepped out on it. That was all he needed—to have to pull a cow out of the pond. He muttered about the stupidity of cows as he unhooked the wire gate.

Another cracking sound and then a shriek jerked his head up. Cows didn't shriek.

Flynn's heart did a funny jump.

Leatrice was out on the ice, right in the middle of the pond. The deepest part. The weakest ice. Cracks ran away from her feet. Silas was at the edge of the pond, ready to go after her.

"Wait, Silas."

The man looked around at Flynn with wild eyes. He didn't have on a coat or hat. Must have run outside looking for Leatrice. At least Leatrice had on her coat and boots. Not that they would do anything but drag her down faster if the ice broke.

He did his best to keep panic out of his voice. "Leatrice, stand still."

"The ice is cracking, Papa." She stared toward him.

Silas moved to step on the ice again. "She's going to break through."

"Stop. You'll just fall through with her." Flynn kept his voice firm. He slipped off his coat and wool scarf. But even tied together they weren't long enough to reach Leatrice. He had his axe, but no trees were near the pond. He couldn't chance leaving her to find a pole. If the ice broke and she went under it, all might be lost.

"Scoot your feet toward us, baby." She wasn't that heavy. Maybe she could make it.

But the ice gave way. With another shriek, she fell in. Flynn could hardly breathe until her head popped up out of the water as she frantically clawed at the ice around the hole.

Flynn went down on his stomach to scoot out on the ice. He threw the scarf tied to his coat toward her. It missed by inches. He could feel the ice shifting under him, but he kept inching toward her. He'd get to her or die trying. "Hold on, baby. I'm almost there."

Silas grabbed Flynn's ankles. He was on his belly too, making a rescue chain. Flynn slung the scarf toward Leatrice again. This time she grabbed it.

"All right. Climb back up on the ice." She tried, but the ice broke again.

"Don't let go." The ice cracked under him. He jerked the scarf to bring her close enough to grab her arm as the ice broke and dumped him into the freezing water. But Flynn didn't go under. His feet touched bottom. He picked up Leatrice and tried to move forward, but the ice was thicker closer to the edge of the pond. It gouged his chest and held him in place.

Flynn gently put Leatrice down on the ice and slid her toward Silas, who grabbed the girl and pulled her up on the bank. They were both safe, if looking frozen. His own legs were losing feeling, but he'd been cold before. Many times. He banged his fist down on the ice that groaned but didn't crack.

"Get my axe off the cart." Everything was slowing down for Flynn until he seemed to be somewhere else watching a man like him in the water.

When Silas scooted the axe toward him, the screech on the ice brought Flynn back to what needed doing. He grabbed it before it slid into the water. No problem then slamming the axe-head down and cracking a path through the ice. With water streaming off him and his shirtsleeves freezing in the wind, the thought crossed his mind that at least the cows had their open place to drink. If his face hadn't been frozen stiff, he might have smiled.

Not that there was anything to smile about. Silas had his arms wrapped around Leatrice, but he was shaking more than she was. Tremors shook Flynn too as his teeth rattled together. He looked behind him and stepped back into the water.

Silas cried out. "What are you doing, Flynn?"

Flynn almost laughed. Silas must think the ice had done something to his head. Maybe it had and that was why he kept thinking about smiling when absolutely nothing was funny.

"Got to get my coat." He snagged the sodden mess and pulled it out. A man needed a coat.

He threw it on the cart, then grabbed Leatrice and sat her in the hay. Icicles clattered together in her hair. He thought he might have to pick up Silas too, but on his second try, the man managed to crawl up beside Leatrice.

Leatrice started to say something, but Flynn stopped her with a look. She knew better than to go out on that ice. They could have all drowned. Might yet die of pneumonia or lose toes and fingers to frostbite. He walked alongside Blossom, urging the mare to move faster through the snow toward the house. When Silas started coughing in the cart, he could hear Leatrice talking to him, but Flynn didn't look back. He needed to focus on getting them next to a fire.

Inside, Silas huddled by the fireplace, an odd blank look on his face while Flynn poked up the coals. Sparks flew up around the log he dropped down into the fire.

Leatrice hadn't moved since Flynn carried her in and set her down. "I'm sorry, Papa." Her teeth were chattering so much she barely got out the words.

"Sorry don't do much." Flynn narrowed his eyes on her. "Get those wet clothes off, every stitch."

He fetched two quilts out of the bedroom. Quilts his mother-in-law had spent many winter hours crafting. Dry, warm quilts. He draped one around Silas's shoulders. "Best get those wet shoes off."

Silas nodded and worked on the knotted string. Flynn started to do it for him, but Silas waved him off. The man was right. He needed to tend to Leatrice, dripping next to the fire and looking as if she had forgotten how to undress. Flynn kicked off his own boots. Water spilled out on the floor. He'd worry about that later. He yanked off his socks, then gently pushed Leatrice down in a straight chair to get off her boots. He grabbed a towel out of the cupboard and briskly rubbed her skin dry after he pulled off her woolen stockings, her coat, and the rest of her clothes, down to bare skin. He wrapped her up in the warm quilt.

"Sit there and don't move," he ordered.

"My toes hurt." Tears rolled down her red cheeks.

Flynn didn't let her tears move him. "So do mine. So do your grandpa's. Be glad they're hurting. That means they might not fall off."

More tears floated in her eyes, but she didn't say anything else. The icicles had melted in her hair, and Flynn wrapped a dry towel around her head. Silas was coughing again.

"You'd best find some dry clothes, Silas."

"I'm not the only one. You better do the same."

"True enough." Flynn stared at Leatrice. He wanted to

rub her feet, but instead he glared at her. "Can I depend on you to sit there like you are told?"

"Yes, Papa."

She sounded so small and contrite then that Flynn almost relented. But he didn't. At least not completely. He did let his voice gentle a little. "Rubbing your toes might help them not hurt so bad."

In his bedroom, he stripped down to the skin and pulled on dry clothes. He stared at his wet shirt and pants on the floor. He had hoped to put off doing laundry until the weather moderated. But he couldn't wear pond-water clothes and neither could Leatrice. He'd go hug her now. He couldn't be too mad to hug her. Not when he almost lost all chance to hug her at all. Shivers ran through him again at the thought of her in a cold box in the ground the way Lena was.

Silas was coming out of his room at the same time as Flynn. Another coughing fit had hold of him.

"Are you all right, Silas?" Flynn asked.

"I'm about froze, but I'm breathing."

Next to the fire, Leatrice sneezed.

Silas looked over at her. "We're all still breathing. The good Lord must have been watching over us."

"We need somebody watching over us," Flynn muttered.

"That's the truth." Silas turned back to Flynn. "Something needs doing before we end up burying her like we did Lena."

"I'm not going to let that happen."

"You won't aim to let it happen any more than you aimed to let Lena fall off that horse." Silas jerked the quilt closer around him and shuffled toward the fireplace. He was coughing again before he got to his chair.

Leatrice looked at Flynn. She was still shivering. Not like

before, but little shivers that had her huddling deeper in the quilt. She looked like she wanted to say something but was afraid Flynn wouldn't want to hear it. She sniffled and a new tear rolled down her cheek.

Flynn could only keep his heart hardened toward her for so long. He picked her up and held her, glad to feel her heart beating against his chest. The cows could wait for their hay.

Silas leaned closer to the fire to drop another log in. In silence, they watched the flames.

7

Flynn was up early the next day since the Shakers were coming for Jack and those people never waited for the sun to get started. The few inches of snow would be no hindrance to them. Silas was in the kitchen ahead of him with the coffeepot already hanging on the hook over the fire. Flynn cut a chunk off the loaf of bread on the table and poured a glass of milk.

"You did a lot of coughing last night, Silas. Maybe you should go see the doc."

"No need in that." Silas shrugged off Flynn's words. "I'll be right as rain soon's I get some coffee down me."

Flynn doubted that, but it was useless arguing with the man. "Best put a little of Ma Beatrice's tonic in it for good measure."

"I don't reckon we got none of that left." A frown deepened the man's wrinkles as he turned away from Flynn. "Not much of nothing left around here. The girl still sleeping?"

Flynn nodded. When he peeked in at her, she had looked so warm with the blanket pulled up to her chin, he didn't have the heart to rouse her out of bed. Her eyelashes lay softly on her cheeks as her breath whispered in and out. When he thought about how he could have lost her the day before, a giant fist squeezed his heart. But could be that taught her a lesson. The night before, she had said she was sorry so many times, he was ready to forbid her to say the words again. She'd put actions to her words by carrying a drink to her grandfather and wrapping a blanket over his knees.

Silas was the one unable to shake the chill. The man's hands trembled as he filled his coffee cup. Flynn pretended not to notice.

"The Shakers always pay in cash. We can lay in some supplies." Flynn opened the cupboard and stared at the shelves. No crocks of pickles or cloth bags of dried apples. They had saved some of the late apples and pears, but they were gone now. On Christmas, they'd eaten the last of the blackberry jam Ma Beatrice had made before the cholera got her. At least they still had her sourdough starter and Silas had figured out how to make a passable loaf of bread.

Onions and potatoes were in the root cellar. And turnips. Flynn hoped never to eat another turnip, but with winter hard down on them, they had to eat what they had. Thank goodness, a few of the hens were still laying. Enough for them to have eggs most mornings. He could set some snares for rabbits. They'd be winter poor, but rabbit hash might be a good change from beans and those turnips.

"Best get one of them Shaker sisters to cook it for us," Silas said.

Flynn didn't know if he was serious or not. "I don't think they hire out, but maybe I can barter for some of their fixings."

Silas gave him a hard look, as though their troubles were past words. Somehow Leatrice falling through the ice had gotten to be Flynn's fault. Maybe it was. Same as Lena falling off that horse. Leastways, the cholera couldn't be laid to his blame. But he did miss Ma Beatrice. She had been the one to hold them together after Lena died.

He pushed all that out of his head as he pulled on his boots that had almost dried out and headed for the barn. He needed to be clearheaded to deal with the Shakers. They were fair and honest traders, but shrewd, nevertheless.

Brother Andrew and Brother Hiram showed up an hour later. The two men sat straight on the wagon seat with their like hats and coats. If a man didn't know better, he might think they were actual brothers instead of merely Shaker brothers. A youngster who didn't look to be much older than Leatrice rode in the back of the wagon. While the older Shakers kept their eyes straight ahead as they pulled up to the barn, the boy was trying to look everywhere at once.

When Flynn caught his eyes, the boy lowered his head, but not before Flynn caught his grin. For some reason that made Flynn feel better about the Shakers. He'd begun to wonder if these men ever smiled, but they might wonder the same about him. Smiles hadn't been too common lately around this farm.

"Good day to you, Mr. Keller," the older Shaker said.

Brother Hiram did most of the talking while Brother Andrew checked out the horse. Flynn wasn't sure why the boy was along. Perhaps simply as a pleasure jaunt. He'd heard the Shakers now and again had shucking bees and picnics.

Flynn and Lena had taken sandwiches in their saddlebags and ridden to the river once. One of those golden times when the sun shone brighter and the breezes blew cooler. Maybe he should take Leatrice on a picnic. Silly to think of that now, with snow cold against his boots. But the boy in the wagon made him think of fun. He considered reaching down for a snowball to toss toward him.

Instead, he shoved his hands in his coat pockets still damp with pond water. He was liable to catch pneumonia yet. "The horse is ready to go. A fine workhorse."

Brother Andrew climbed down from the wagon. The boy started to climb down too, but a glance from Brother Hiram stopped him.

"It won't hurt anything for him to come in the barn." All three of the Shakers looked at Flynn as if he'd spoken out of turn. Maybe he had. He lamely added, "If he wants to."

Brother Andrew nodded at the boy, who was out of the wagon quick as a water spider moving across a pond. Flynn needed to quit thinking about ponds.

Flynn led the man and the boy into the barn. Brother Hiram stayed on the wagon. He'd be the one to make the final deal once Brother Andrew determined the horse was sound. Flynn brought Jack out of the stall. The Shaker ran his hands over the horse, picked up each foot, stared into Jack's eyes for a long moment and then pulled back the horse's lips to examine his teeth.

Finally, after taking another walk all the way around the animal, he said, "If Brother Hiram is in agreement, we can make a deal."

"What about little brother here?" Flynn motioned toward the boy. "He have a say?"

Brother Andrew's lips didn't turn up, but he had a smile in his eyes. "Yea, all are equal in our village. So what say you, young Brother Brody?"

The boy put his hand on the horse's nose. "He looks to be of fair stock."

"Got a fine velvety nose, does he?"

The boy didn't try to hide his smile. "He does, Brother Andrew. A good breathing nose is important in a working horse."

"So it is, young brother. So it is."

Flynn handed the rope to the boy and let him lead the horse out into the sunshine. "I named him Jack, but you can change his name if you want."

"Nay. Jack sounds a good name for a horse," the boy said.

Outside, after they made the deal, Flynn said, "Will you take him now or do you want me to bring him to your village later?"

"We can tie him to the back of the wagon," Brother Hiram said.

But even after the horse was tethered to the wagon and Brother Andrew and the boy were back in place, the Shaker didn't flick the reins to start his horses moving.

"Is there more I can do for you? Your horses need water?" Flynn asked.

"There is something. You have a reputation for healing horses," Brother Hiram said. "A convert has brought a horse into our village that hangs his head and refuses to work. We've tried several treatments but nothing works. We thought perhaps fresh eyes might see something we missed. We will pay you for your time."

"I can't guarantee anything." Flynn met the Shaker brother's steady stare.

"Your honest effort is all we ask."

Flynn thought of the food he might get in barter for working with the horse. A perfect solution to their empty cupboards. But then he looked toward the house. He couldn't expect Silas to mind Leatrice all day with how sick he was.

"I can't leave my daughter today."

"Bring her along," Brother Hiram said. "Some of the little sisters can keep her company while you work with the horse."

Flynn hesitated. He could imagine Leatrice climbing the Shaker fences and paying no mind to anyone. "That might not work."

Brother Hiram gave him a curious look. "Why? Is your daughter ill?"

"Not sick, but sometimes ill behaved. Things have been rough for her since her mother and grandmother died."

"Worry not. We deal with many motherless children at our village and teach them proper behavior with loving care."

"So I've heard." Flynn had to wonder if the Shaker had been talking to Silas.

After he promised Brother Hiram to come look at their horse later, he watched the Shaker wagon out of sight. This was surely an answer to their need for supplies, but Flynn wouldn't mention it to Silas yet. Best wait until he had the food in hand. He didn't like rushing into things without proper thought.

That was one of the ways he and Silas were different. Silas didn't have patience to wait for things to work out. Even for something as common as building a fence, Silas would jump in and set the posts without considering the lay of the land. He wanted it done. Flynn liked things done too, but the right way saved work in the long run. So he thought things through to make sure he hadn't missed something. He'd learned that working with horses. A man got a better horse if he took time to figure out the animal.

While he didn't know whether he could judge what problem the Shakers' horse might have, he liked the challenge each new horse brought. Could be the Shakers felt the same way about the young people they brought into their villages.

So he'd go to the Shaker village and take a look at more than their horse, but first he'd have to get up some wood for the fireplace. He hitched Blossom to the sled and headed to the back pasture to work up a tree felled by a storm.

He was loading the wood on the sled when he spotted Leatrice headed toward him. She was so small making her way through the snow. She might have looked older to him if Lena had been able to carry another child to push Leatrice out of the baby spot. Instead Lena hadn't been able to hold onto the babies they started after Leatrice, losing them before she got much more than started along the birthing trail.

Silas must have sent Leatrice out to help Flynn. That was good. The girl needed to do her part. Not that she could do much, but she could gather up the smaller pieces.

"Don't be mad, Papa," she said when she got near enough.

Flynn leaned on his axe. "Why would I be mad?'

"Grandpa told me to wait at the house until you got back, but I was afraid I'd forget what he told me to tell you."

So Silas hadn't sent her. "Is something wrong with your

grandpa?" Flynn looked across the field toward the house, but he was too far back on the farm to even catch a glimpse of smoke from the chimney.

Leatrice shook her head. "He left."

"Left?" Flynn frowned. "Where did he go?"

"I don't know. Said to tell you he might be gone a few days. That he had to do something." Leatrice's bottom lip trembled. "Did he leave because I was bad and made him sick?"

"No." Flynn laid the axe aside and gathered Leatrice close in a hug. "You didn't make him sick."

She pulled back to look up at him. "He got cold because I went out on the pond. He kept coughing before he left."

"He does have a bad cough. Could be he decided to go to the doctor and stay there for a while to get better."

Flynn said the words, but he really had no idea what Silas might be up to. Maybe he had taken one of his cows to town to trade for supplies. Or he could have decided to check out the Shakers himself. Flynn couldn't imagine that, but the man had his own mind. Whatever he was doing, it was his business.

"Will he come back?" Leatrice mumbled the words against his coat.

"Of course he will."

"Mamaw Bea didn't."

"Well, she couldn't, sweetheart. She had to go on up to heaven to be with your mama."

"Sometimes I wish I could go to heaven to see them. I miss them."

"I miss them too. But it's not time for you to go to heaven. You've got things to do down here." Flynn took off his glove and stroked her hair. She hadn't worn her hat. "Aren't your ears cold?"

"A little," she admitted. "I couldn't find my hat. It may be in the pond."

"Well, that could be. We'll have to get you a new one, but until then you can wrap this scarf around your head." He picked up the wool scarf he'd pitched on the sled after he'd warmed up sawing wood. She let him wrap it around her head. "There, now maybe your ears won't freeze and break off."

"They wouldn't really, would they?" Leatrice's eyes got wide as she touched the scarf covering her ears.

"No." Flynn laughed. "They'd just feel like they might. Come on. You can help me load the wood and then ride to Harmony Hill with me."

"Where's that?"

"Not so far. It's where the Shakers live."

"Grandpa says the Shakers sing and dance in church. Nobody ever dances when we go to church."

"That's for sure. I don't think our preacher would be in favor of that."

"Then why do the Shakers dance?"

"They've got a different way of doing things."

"Mama liked to dance. She danced with me sometimes." Leatrice swayed back and forth. "I liked that."

"She danced with me sometimes too." He picked Leatrice up and swung her around. "She'd want us to keep dancing."

Leatrice giggled. "My feet are supposed to be on the ground."

"Not in this dance." He swung her higher in the air before he set her down. "But now we've got to dance this wood up on the sled so we can go visit those dancing Shakers."

"Will I see them dance?"

"Probably not. I think they only do that on Sundays."

After the wood was ricked on the sled, Leatrice climbed on top of it and they headed to the house. Bread and milk would have to do for their meal before they headed to the Shakers. But supper might be better if he could trade them out of some applesauce and jam. Maybe a pie.

He hoped Silas would find a good meal in town.

8

Flynn was always a little agog with wonder when he rode into Shaker village. The great buildings of brick and stone seemed to belong somewhere other than in the middle of farmland. Maybe in a city somewhere or across the sea, but here the buildings stood, built by the Shakers' own hands.

Flynn had built a few things. A barn, a chicken house, a shed, but never anything like these houses with their three stories plus basements and attics.

When he rode up to the hitching post in front of the Trustee House where business with those outside the village was carried out, Brother Hiram was waiting. They must have been watching for him.

"Mr. Keller, thank you for coming." The man didn't quite smile, but his eyes lightened as he looked at Leatrice wedged in the saddle in front of Flynn. "And your daughter too. I have sent for a young sister to attend to her while you work with the horse."

Leatrice shrank back against Flynn. He gently pushed her away to dismount, then lifted her down. She had been excited about coming to see the dancing Shakers, but the sight of Brother Hiram's solemn face had dampened her enthusiasm.

"Ah, here's Sister Faye now." Brother Hiram gestured toward a young sister in a hooded cape hurrying toward them.

When she stepped up beside them, she smiled and held out her hand to Leatrice. "Come, little sister. You must be cold after your ride here. Some warm cider will chase away your shivers."

Leatrice hesitated. "I'm not your sister. I don't have any sisters."

Sister Faye's smile got wider. "We are all sisters here. So today you can be a sister too." Leatrice still hung back, so she went on. "Only for a little while."

When Leatrice looked up at Flynn, he nudged her toward the girl. "Go. You'll be fine."

"Very fine. Perhaps you would like to try on a cloak like mine." Sister Faye swished her cloak to make the fabric rustle.

"I might." Leatrice let go of Flynn's hand. "Will you show me how you dance?"

"Yea, I can teach you a few steps." She led Leatrice along the stone path between the buildings. Leatrice didn't look back.

"Worry not," Brother Hiram said when Flynn watched her out of sight. "She will come to no harm here in our village."

"I know. Actually, I have wondered if she could attend your school here."

Brother Hiram bent his head in a half nod. "That could perhaps be arranged, especially if you would join with us."

He looked over at Flynn as they walked toward the barns. "You would make a good Shaker."

"What is a good Shaker?" Not that he planned to be one, but a man like Brother Hiram made him curious. He looked as if he should be working a farm alongside ten strong sons. Instead here he was, a Shaker.

"One who takes up his cross and follows the Shaker way of unity and peace. We give our hearts to God and work with our hands for the good of all. We leave behind the stress and conflict of earthly love in favor of heavenly love for our sisters and brothers. Such is a better way."

Better for whom, Flynn wondered, but he didn't voice the words. "Were you married before you came here?"

"Yea, I did commit the sin of matrimony."

Flynn frowned at his words. "Surely marriage isn't a sin."

Being married to Lena was the best thing that had ever happened to Flynn. Their union had not been a sin. Were Lena still living, he couldn't imagine giving up that husband-wife relationship to instead think of her as his sister. He would have broken down every Shaker door that tried to keep him from her. The Bible plainly said a man should cleave to his wife.

"Such a life can be hard for one from the world to imagine, but once a man accepts it, nothing can disturb his balance."

"Nothing?"

"Yea, nothing." Brother Hiram lifted up the wooden board that held the barn door shut. "Pity a horse cannot learn the Shaker way."

Flynn held his tongue, but he did wonder how the Shakers would replace their old horses if they had no new foals. The Shaker way went against nature.

The Shaker barn was well built and the breezeway clean. While a few horses nickered at them, the horse in question stood with his head drooped down and paid little notice even when they stopped at his stall.

"He nibbles at his feed but not as he should."

"Has he been exercised?" Flynn studied the horse.

"Yea. A boy leads him out. The animal shows no lameness when he moves."

Flynn stepped into the stall. The horse did raise his head a bit to eye him before drooping again. Flynn ran his hands along the horse's withers and down his legs. He picked up each foot and checked for something that might cause the horse pain.

With a hold on the halter, Flynn lifted the horse's head. His eyes didn't look glassy or sick. Instead they looked flat, as though he had simply lost interest in any kind of horse business.

"How long has he been here?"

"A few months."

"Like this the whole time?" Again Flynn ran his hand down the horse. He could feel the animal's ribs, but he was far from a skeleton. His muscles rippled under Flynn's touch, and from the look of his teeth, he wasn't an old horse.

"Somewhat."

"Have you not used him at all? To pull a wagon or to ride?"

"Not to pull a wagon. We feared this horse would not do his part and put a heavy strain on the others in the team. We tried to use him to power the water, but he refused to do his duty there. We don't mistreat our animals, but they must work."

"What did he have to do to power the water?"

"We pump water from springs into a water house, then feed it via gravity through pipes to our houses. Horses power the pump by walking in a circle."

"So boring work."

"Many chores are boring for man or beast but necessary. Even a horse must do its share."

"True enough." Flynn stroked the horse's nose and the animal perked up his ears.

"He's a fine-looking horse," Brother Hiram said. "But he must work to have a place here. We have no need of pets."

"Have you asked his owner about him? How the horse was before coming here?"

"Sadly, the brother who brought the horse was killed in a riverboat accident." Brother Hiram leaned on the stall door. "Can you fathom the horse's trouble?"

"I can't be sure seeing him only this once, but my guess is he's missing something from before he came here. His owner or a stablemate perhaps."

The Shaker looked far from convinced. "You think an animal can be sad so long? He has many stablemates here in our barn."

"True." Flynn stroked the horse's neck. "But sometimes horses form an attachment with something other than a horse. Perhaps a dog or a goat. Even barn cats."

"We have no barn cats."

Flynn looked around. "What about mice?"

"We catch mice in humane traps. Then we release them far enough away to no longer be a bother to us."

Flynn looked at Brother Hiram, sure he must be joking, but the Shaker wasn't smiling. The more he knew about these Shakers, the odder they seemed. Dancing in church.

Thinking marriage a sin. And now catching and releasing mice.

Flynn shrugged off the Shaker oddities. He wasn't there to judge them. He was there to help this horse in front of him. "I can take him to my farm to work with him. In exchange for some dried apples or applesauce. A few jars of strawberry jam would be fine too. Any food fixings you have in plenty."

"Yea. Such a bartering deal sounds reasonable." Brother Hiram inclined his head a bit. "Come with me back to the Trustee House and we'll write down an agreement."

"If you think that necessary." Flynn stroked the horse's neck one more time before stepping out of the stall.

"Best to have things plain so there can be no misunderstandings." Brother Hiram led the way out of the barn where he looked up at the sky. "We will have one of the sisters bring you supper while you wait. Our dinner bell will be ringing soon."

"I should get my daughter then."

"Worry not. The young sisters will see that she is fed. She will be happier with them than waiting with you."

He didn't know how the Shaker knew what would make Leatrice happier, but he kept his peace. A good Shaker meal sounded better than the pot of beans waiting at home.

Brother Hiram escorted him to a room in the brick Trustee House and lifted down a straight-back chair from pegs on a rail that ran all around the room. The pegs held more chairs turned bottoms up, as well as candleholders and brooms. A small iron stove with a narrow pipe straight up through the ceiling generated enough heat to take the chill from the room.

"Take your ease. I will check with the trustees about our agreement and bring you supper." Brother Hiram went out, shutting the door behind him.

Flynn didn't sit down. Instead he crossed the room to look out at the walkways cleared of snow. The garden plot on the other side of a plank fence was plowed, ready for spring planting. A few Shakers moved purposefully along the paths toward their destinations.

It was good to have a purpose. Since Lena had passed, he'd sometimes felt as though he was drifting. At those times he remembered how his father had drifted completely away from his family. Flynn wasn't about to drift away from Leatrice. Nothing, not adventure, love, riches, was as important as being a good father.

At the thought of Leatrice falling into the pond, he closed his eyes on the peaceful scene outside the window. Could it be that he wasn't that good father? That he wasn't taking proper care of her?

Flynn opened his eyes and looked back out at the buildings. Sturdy and strong. Warm. She would be safe here. But he couldn't give her up. Maybe he should consider marrying again the way Silas said, even if his heart felt as cold as the icicles on the pump handle in the Shaker yard. He blew out a breath, glad to hear the door opening to let him escape his thoughts.

A woman in Shaker dress followed Brother Hiram into the room. Even before she was near enough for him to see what was on the tray she carried, his stomach growled at the delicious scents.

"Sounds as if we are just in time, Sister Darcie." Brother Hiram actually smiled.

"Yea." The sister set the tray down on a small table. "Is there anything else you need?"

Flynn wasn't sure if she was addressing him or the Shaker brother. She looked tired and little wonder. She was obviously far along with carrying a child. That wasn't something he expected to see at the Shaker village with their celibacy rules. Perhaps those rules were sometimes bent.

9

I had to smile at the man's eagerness for the food. Brother Hiram's lips even lifted a bit. I bent my head to hide my own smile. I feared Brother Hiram might report I was being too worldly to Eldress Maria. That thought boosted my smile as indeed my very shape shouted worldliness. A shape the stranger did note. His face registered surprise at seeing an expectant mother in Shaker dress.

My smile did not linger. My feet hurt and my back ached. While I did not mind working in the kitchen, it was tiring. I had been moved from the sewing room to the kitchen in a rotation of duties. At least the eldress had instructed Sister Reva, the one in charge of the Gathering Family kitchen, to assign me the easiest chores.

That was why Sister Reva sent me with the food to the Trustee House. "Walking shouldn't be that hard on you."

I wondered if she had ever carried a child, for I never noted sympathy for my condition in her words, but that didn't trouble me. Sisters Ellie and Helene were ever ready to ease my burdens. Sister Helene would slip from her bed after the candles were snuffed out to massage my feet. I told her not to, that she needed her rest, but she persisted. I wondered if she imagined that was what a husband might do for his wife.

I knew not whether that was so. I couldn't remember my father being extra attentive to my mother. Her baby-carrying months seemed no different than other months, simply something ordinary. Of course, nothing was ordinary about a woman in Shaker dress carrying a baby.

I had asked Eldress Maria if other women had come into the village in the family way, but she considered my question sinful curiosity I should strike from my thoughts. Much was expected to be cast from one's thoughts in this staid village.

I continually reminded myself I was blessed to be here after Walter died. But I could not shake the feeling that if we had not come to the village, Walter might be the one massaging my feet at night.

To keep such thoughts at bay, I studied the man who appeared to be awaiting some word from Brother Hiram before eating his meal. A big man, he was strong across the shoulders as my Walter had been. He looked directly at me and I again lowered my head. But not before I saw something more than curiosity in his dark brown eyes. A deep sadness lay there that I recognized, since the same sort of sorrow lurked within me.

Brother Hiram stepped between the man and me. I was surprised to hear him saying my name yet again.

"Quite the coincidence, Mr. Keller, but Sister Darcie was once wed to the man we spoke of earlier."

My eyes flew up to the man's face. What did he know about my Walter? But before I dared speak, Brother Hiram went on.

"The one who brought the horse in question to our village and had the misfortune to be on the riverboat when the vessel's boilers exploded."

Misfortune. The very word made me want to scream, but my months with the Shakers had drilled some restraint into me. At times, I wondered if I even remembered the woman I used to be before I slipped on the Shaker dress.

"A tragedy." The man turned his gaze from Brother Hiram to me. "I am sorry for the loss of your husband, ma'am."

The sympathy in his voice touched something deep within me, as though he understood that I'd lost half of myself when I lost Walter. Two become one. The Bible stated that plainly.

Tears knotted in my throat and all I could do was nod. I kept my head bent low to hide my face under my bonnet brim. At times, a bonnet could be useful for more than protecting one from the sun.

Brother Hiram was speaking again. "Yea, a sorrow. But I was thinking more of the problem with the horse."

That made me frown. How could any kind of problem with a horse matter more than the loss of a good man like Walter? But the Shakers were ever practical. Walter's horse was a fine animal. Sawyer. An odd name Walter pulled from his river days. A sawyer was a downed tree floating under the water with a branch now and again breaking the surface to warn a river man to be watchful. Not that Sawyer had ever given Walter trouble. I couldn't imagine what problem Brother Hiram might mean.

When both men looked toward me as if expecting me to speak, I asked, "Is something wrong with Walter's horse?"

Brother Hiram's eyes sharpened on me when I did not say

Brother Walter, but he did not change my words. Instead he merely explained. "The horse appears to have no will to work."

"Is Sawyer ill?" The thought of Sawyer being unwell brought a new knot of tears to my throat. Sister Ellie had warned how carrying a child could turn one's emotions on end. That was certainly true on this day for me.

"He gives no sign of a physical ailment or soreness in his joints." The man spoke. "He seems sad."

"Sad?" Such seemed a strange thing to say about a horse, but then Granny Hatchell was fond of saying there was more to animals than we could know. All at once a sweet memory of a dog I'd once had popped into my mind. That dog had a way of reading my thoughts. More tears pricked my eyes. I needed to harden my heart. Ring had been gone far too many years for tears now.

"Yea, a bit odd," Brother Hiram said. "But perhaps you can help Mr. Keller in his quest to know more about the horse."

I looked at the man. "What do you want to know?"

"Did you have other horses in your barn or lot?" The man appeared to have forgotten the food behind him as he considered Sawyer's problem.

"We did not. Why do you ask?"

"Horses are herd animals that often get lonely without other horses around. Did that appear true for your horse? Sawyer, you say."

"Yea, Sawyer." I considered his question. "Lonely? In what way?"

"Was he unsettled in the barn? Anxious when other horses passed by? Off his feed?"

"I never thought him unsettled, although he did whinny at times, but don't all horses?"

"They do, but if you pay attention, you can sometimes tell what the horse is trying to tell you when it neighs." The man's brow wrinkled, as though working through a complicated puzzle. "So he never seemed unhappy in your corral?"

I supposed horses could be a puzzle. Lately everything had been a puzzle to me. Everything except this baby I carried. He was pure love. My life after his birth—that was the puzzle.

But I had no answer for the man's horse puzzle. "Walter never mentioned any such problems." I tried to think back. "He did sometimes laugh about how he would find our cat perched on the edge of the stall close to Sawyer's head. Walter claimed they were telling each other secrets."

Another smile came to warm me. I should purposely bring up more sweet memories to get me through the dark days of missing Walter.

"Where is the cat now?"

"We took it back to the farm where we used to live. The Shakers did not want it here."

"It could be Sawyer wanted it."

Brother Hiram spoke up. "Surely you don't think the absence of a mere cat would make a horse so despondent."

"Perhaps." The man looked over at Brother Hiram. "Perhaps not. I said I'd take the horse to my barn to work with him, but I think now I should come and work with him here."

"Will you bring a cat with you?" Brother Hiram raised his eyebrows.

"Just any cat wouldn't do." The man smiled and shook

his head. "If the lack of his cat friend turns out to be his problem. It could be something else, since a horse can't tell you where it is hurting."

"Yea." Brother Hiram rubbed his chin. "Very well. Come at your convenience, but if after a few visits, no improvement is shown, we will, of necessity, get rid of the horse."

My heart sank at his words, but I knew better than to speak. Sawyer was no longer mine. Since all was owned in common here, we had given him over to the Shakers when we came into the village. We did receive the promise he, or a horse of like value, would be returned to us should we leave. If only we had ridden Sawyer out of the village before that ill-fated trading trip.

The man spoke up. "Don't worry, ma'am. I feel confident I can help Sawyer."

"Thank you." I dared a smile at the man, even though I sensed Brother Hiram's disapproval.

"You may wait in the hallway for the tray after Mr. Keller eats, Sister." Brother Hiram waved me toward the door.

I was glad to be away from Brother Hiram. To him, I surely represented all the Shakers intended to close away from their lives. The very evidence of marital union so forbidden here.

I leaned against the stair railing. The double spiral staircases here in the hallway wound around and appeared to almost float up to the higher floors. I admired the curving banister and the steps somehow anchored to the wall, even though they appeared to be suspended in air.

But in spite of my admiration, right then I was merely relieved I didn't have to climb the stairs to deliver food to any other visitors. Were it not for Brother Hiram apt to come out of the room to see me, I would have sunk down on the bottom step. The day had been long, and then with the fresh sadness bearing down on my spirit from the talk of Walter's horse, my knees wanted to give way with me.

When the front door opened, the chatter of young girls' voices distracted me from my weariness. A good sound, but not something I heard often, since the Shaker children were gathered in a separate house. Two girls came down the hallway toward me. One in Shaker dress I had seen at the Sunday meetings before I was banned from going. Sister Faye had sweet eyes that carried a smile. She, like Sister Helene, appeared to be happy among the Shakers.

The child with her was much younger and not in Shaker dress. Her dark brown hair was in need of a comb. Her coat was well worn and knees peeked through holes in her stockings. She carried a new cape and some stockings the Shakers must have given her.

The Shaker girl stopped in front of me. "We are looking for Sister Leatrice's father. Mr. Keller. Have you seen him?"

"He is here, having his meal and talking with Brother Hiram." I pointed toward the room.

"Then we should wait until he comes out." Sister Faye frowned.

"Is something wrong?" I asked.

Sister Faye glanced back toward the front door. "I need to get back for worship practice."

"I will be here until Mr. Keller and Brother Hiram come out." I peered down at the younger child. "I can keep Sister Leatrice company."

"Oh, that would work wonderfully well. Sister Corinne does not like us to be late." Sister Faye hugged the young girl. "It was good to have you as a sister today. I hope you can come live with us someday." Then without waiting for the child to reply, she hurried up the hall and out the door.

The child watched her before she turned to me. "I'm not really her sister. But she says everybody here is a sister. So I guess you're a sister too."

"I suppose I am. A Shaker sister. I once had a sister and two brothers before I came here, so I was a sister then too. Darcie is my name." I don't know why I told her that, but I liked separating myself from being only a Shaker sister. The neck kerchief felt heavy on my shoulders. A burden I wished to shed.

"My name is Leatrice, but I don't have any sisters or brothers. My mother died."

"I'm sorry." And I was. I knew the sadness of losing a mother.

"She fell off a horse and hit her head on a rock." The little girl's lips trembled. "Sometimes I can't remember what she looked like."

I reached for her hand. "You must have been very young when she died."

"I was four. My mother loved me very much. Mamaw Bea said so." More tears gathered in her eyes. "Then Mamaw died last year. Of the chol'ra."

Since I knew nothing to say in the face of such a load of sadness for one so young, I put my arms around her. Cholera always struck the countryside with sorrow. That was why Walter and I had been so determined to escape it, which this child's grandmother had not. It could be I was wrong in thinking we might have avoided death if we hadn't come here. Instead it might be both of us would be laid to rest by now instead of only Walter. As much as I missed Walter, I could only be glad that wasn't so with the new life growing within me.

A dear life, just as this young girl was a dear life.

"Sometimes we must be strong," I whispered into her hair as I held her close.

"My papa is strong. He takes care of me." The child pushed away from me. "He kept me from drowning."

"He did?"

"I did something bad." Leatrice hung her head. "I just wanted to skate on the pond, but the ice broke. It was really cold."

I put my fingers under her chin and lifted her face up. "But you're all right now."

"My grandpa keeps coughing. He might die too. Because he got cold trying to help me." Her wide eyes were the dark blue of a late evening sky.

While I wanted to ease her worry, I had no idea whether the man would die or not. I thought to hug her again, but she seemed to need words more than hugs. "You can pray he will get better soon."

"Will you pray too?"

"I will, young Leatrice. For your grandfather and for you. Will you pray for me too?"

She nodded then. The next instant a door opened and her father and Brother Hiram came out into the hallway. I squeezed the little girl's hand one last time, then slipped behind the men to fetch the tray to carry back to the kitchen.

As I went out a side door, I looked toward the front of the Trustee House where the man and the child were leaving. They would be riding home in the dark, but the child looked safe and secure in the saddle in front of her father.

My child would never rest in the arms of his father. Never be able to depend on his strength to get him through troubles. He would have no father, just as the child Leatrice had no mother. It was foolish to war against what could not be changed.

As I walked through the gathering twilight, something inside me seemed to shift as my baby's tiny feet beat against my belly. I would not forget Walter. I could never do that, but perhaps I needed to release him to heaven and dwell on the happy days we had shared, of which there were many. Those I would number and save to tell his child when the time was right.

10

Leatrice was full of talk about the Shakers as they rode home. "They spun wool into yarn on this big wheel with a pedal to turn it. The wool came from their sheep. Why don't we have sheep?"

"We have horses."

"The Shakers do too. Horses and sheep and chickens and cows. They even have cows that pull plows. Sister Faye said so and I don't think she ever tells stories." Leatrice twisted around to look up at Flynn. "Our cows can't do that, can they?"

"No, that takes special training." Flynn had no desire to train cows. "I'll stick to horses."

Leatrice settled back against Flynn. "Well, I wish we had sheep. They let me feel the wool. It was soft."

"My mother used to spin wool," Flynn said.

"Did your mother die like my mother?"

"Not like your mother, but she died a few years ago."

"Were you very, very sad?"

"I hadn't seen her for a long time. Not since I was thirteen."

He tried to shift her thinking away from mothers. "They were nice to give you a cloak."

She had the dark blue Shaker cloak wrapped around her. The air had turned colder after the sun went down.

"They gave me stockings too. Because my knees were peeping out of the ones I had."

"That was kind." The child did need new clothes. So many things Lena's mother took care of that failed to cross his mind. Maybe that was where Silas had gone. To town to take care of some of those things.

At least he did have supplies for their bare cupboard. One of the Shaker women had been waiting by his horse with cloth bags packed with jars cushioned with beans and dried apples. An excellent trade for his time today.

"Did you like the Shaker girls?"

Leatrice nodded her head against his chest. "They were nice. The next time I come they say I can sweep. They like to sweep. They showed me a dance where they pretend to sweep away bad things. Do you think they can really do that?"

"Maybe not bad things that happen but bad things they are thinking."

"Am I bad, Papa?" Her voice sounded small.

He tightened his arm around her. "No, Leatrice. Sometimes you do things you shouldn't, but you aren't bad. You're one of the best things to ever happen to me."

With a sigh, Leatrice relaxed against him as they jogged toward home. "I like being a best thing. Was Mama a best thing too?"

"She was."

For a moment, Leatrice was so quiet Flynn thought she'd fallen asleep. But then she said, "That woman in the hallway back there said she lost her mama to the chol'ra like we lost Mamaw Bea. Does everybody lose their best things?"

"Not everybody and not all the best things. I still have you."

Leatrice kissed his hand on the reins. "I'm glad."

By the time they got to the house, she was so sound asleep she barely roused when Flynn carried her inside to her bed and pulled one of Ma Beatrice's quilts over her. The house was cold since Silas was still gone. As Flynn fished coals out of the ashes to build up the fire, he thought about the warm Trustee House with that iron stove.

The old cow was mooing, ready to be milked. The hens had gone to roost without any feed and the horses in the barn would have to wait for morning to get their stalls cleaned. It didn't take long for a man to get behind on his chores, but the Shaker food made the afternoon away from the farm well worth it.

With enough time he'd figure out something about the horse, but if the Shakers got impatient, he'd trade for the horse and bring it home. That way he wouldn't have to think about that Shaker sister's sad eyes when Brother Hiram talked about getting rid it.

She was unhappy over more than a horse. He knew that. Her husband gone. A baby on the way. Straining against the hold of the Shakers. Flynn shook his head. He had no way of knowing that. Her tired look probably had more to do with her condition than Shaker life. He was the one imagining living in the Shaker village as less than good, but he could be completely wrong. The many hands to do the work had to be good.

Right then, he wouldn't mind a brother sharing his chores. At least when he did get through at the barn, the kitchen would be warmed by the fire. A second supper sounded like the very thing to finish off this day. He wouldn't worry about Silas. He'd come home when he was ready.

Flynn didn't go back to the Shaker village the next day. He had to catch up on his work at the farm. Besides, he was keeping an eye out for Silas, but another night came without his father-in-law showing up.

After the morning chores were finished on the third day, Flynn banked the fires in the fireplaces and left Silas a note in case he came home and found them missing. Leatrice was excited about going back to the Shaker village, even though he warned her the Shakers might not have time to entertain her every day.

"Sister Faye said I could come be her sister anytime. Remember, she's going to let me sweep the hallway and stairs. They have lots of stairs. They have to have two. One for the sisters and another for the brothers. I don't know why, do you?" Leatrice's forehead wrinkled as she thought about that while wrapping the Shaker cloak around her shoulders.

"It's just their way." Flynn wasn't ready to explain why the Shakers went to such lengths to keep the men and women apart. Leatrice wasn't anywhere near old enough to know what being celibate meant.

When they got to the village, Sister Faye did come and collect Leatrice again. Same smile. Same welcome. Flynn made his way to the barn where Brother Andrew pointed out one of the calmer mares. Flynn took both the horses out into a corral to see if a bond might form between Sawyer and the mare. The day was cold, but the sun was shining. Snow remained in the shadows. He didn't try to make Sawyer do anything. He just watched the horses.

The mare paid neither Flynn nor Sawyer much attention. She merely seemed glad to feel sunshine on her back. Horses needed fresh air the same as people. Winter had a way of dragging man and beast down. Flynn thought of their house, always closed up in the winter with the smell of smoke from the fireplaces and the windows covered with blankets to keep out the cold. Dark. Depressing.

Funny how he hadn't noticed that while Lena was living. She brought sunshine in every season. He supposed Silas felt the winter drear even more than he did. Silas had been under the weather so much during the cold months that he had hardly left the house where sad memories must assault him on every side. Maybe that was why he had escaped to town. But something about the man being gone so long worried Flynn. He'd have to ride into town to look for him if Silas didn't show up soon.

One thing at a time. Tomorrow was another day. The old farmer he'd lived with after his mother went back to Virginia tried to teach him that. To do what was in front of him without looking past it. If a man tried to live in tomorrow, he'd never know the satisfaction of a good day's work.

Later, back at the farm while doing his evening chores, Flynn wondered if that was how the Shakers tried to live. He thought back to the conversation he'd had with Brother Andrew earlier that day before leaving the Shaker barn. Flynn told Brother Andrew he didn't know how long he might need to work with Sawyer.

The man looked at him with calm eyes. "All a man needs do is tend to the task given him. Our Mother Ann instructed us to do our work well with the idea that we might die on the morrow or as though we expect to live ten thousand years."

The Shakers had some odd ideas. Nobody lived ten thousand years. Not even Methuselah in the Bible who, according to Scripture, lacked a few years making a thousand. Of course few really expected to die on the morrow either. But that could happen. Had happened to Lena and her mother. Could happen to him, and then what would become of Leatrice?

No reason to worry about that. He was healthy. He could handle whatever came his way. Hadn't he already? His father deserting him. His mother leaving him. Lena dying. Ma Beatrice taken by the cholera. He'd handled it all. Silas's warning that something might happen to Leatrice sneaked into his thoughts, but Flynn pushed it away. He'd keep her safe.

Ma Beatrice prodded him then. At least her memory did. She was always asking the Lord's help and guidance and told him he should do the same. She quoted him a verse after Lena died. Something about the Lord being a present help in times of trouble. But that he needed to ask for that help.

Ma Beatrice believed in prayer, even though it hadn't saved her from the cholera. Then again, when she knew she was dying, she had looked toward heaven where she said she'd see Lena again. Perhaps that was how the Lord had helped her.

Before he went in the back door of the house, he bent his head. He was willing to give prayer a try, but he had no idea what to say. He'd heard preachers claim the Lord already knew what a person needed. If that was so, why hadn't God known he needed Lena and kept her from hitting her head? Why was there even a terrible disease like cholera?

"Dear Lord, help me." Help him what? Who knew what dangers and troubles might be lurking in the road ahead.

He'd best think about right now, not ahead. "Help me be a good father and keep my little girl safe."

He remembered again how his heart had almost stopped when she fell through the ice. "And thank you for keeping her from drowning in the pond the other day."

He raised his head then and looked up. He wasn't good at prayer words the way Ma Beatrice was, but when he saw those stars spread across the night sky, he could feel the Lord's presence even more than when he was sitting in a church pew. He might not understand everything that happened, but he could be sure the Lord put those stars in the heavens and made the grass grow in the springtime. One day followed another, and whatever happened, a man had to handle it.

"Amen." He sent the word skyward without worrying about what more he should say. The Lord did know. Hadn't he already supplied food from the Shakers? With the promise of more in the days ahead for a few hours working with a horse. And if he kept taking Leatrice with him, she might learn a little discipline too. The Shakers seemed to have discipline corralled.

II

Sister Ellie kept telling me the nausea would ease, but here I was in my eighth month and the smell of breakfast cooking still made my stomach heave.

"If you're going to lose your breakfast, find a bucket to do it in." Sister Reva scowled at me when she turned from the skillet over the fire.

She had little sympathy for my churning stomach, only concern for her clean kitchen floor. She took the Shaker rules of cleanliness seriously and perhaps all the other rules as well. That could be why she had no welcome for me in her kitchen. I couldn't say she totally lacked compassion. She often gave me chores I could do sitting, and she never asked me to bend over the fire to stir the pots. She may have been concerned I'd catch my apron afire since the baby's growth was pushing my skirts away from my body. My increased girth was making everything more difficult and draining my energy.

That could be, Sister Ellie warned, because I took little out on my plate at mealtimes. At the Shaker table one had to eat whatever one dipped out on her plate, and since I never knew when the nausea might hit, I dipped lightly. While I had not heard it spoken, I had no doubt there was also a rule against fleeing the table to lose whatever one had already eaten.

I tried to summon up a pleasant look as I handed Sister Reva the diced potatoes for her to dump into the skillet, while bracing myself for the sizzling release of more grease into the air.

Sister Nila, the other kitchen help, dared a small smile. She was young, not yet twenty. A pretty girl who had confided in me she couldn't imagine being a Shaker forever. She had little worry about that, since I had noted a few of the Shaker brothers letting their glances linger on her as she set the bowls of food on their tables. Once she chose one to return his look, she would have a way to go from the village and start a new life.

No such door was open for me. Even the most wayward Shaker brother would surely think twice before making eyes at one so heavy with child, no matter how fair of face he might think me. Besides, my heart still mourned Walter.

I returned Nila's smile before I answered Sister Reva. "I have eaten no breakfast to lose. The smell of cooking is upsetting my stomach."

Sister Reva made a sound. Perhaps of disgust. Certainly not of sympathy. "I don't know why Eldress Maria did not let you stay in the sewing room."

"She could not know I would have trouble with the cooking odors."

Sister Reva sighed. "I suppose not. She has ever been with the Shakers with little experience of childbearing. I tried to tell her, but she is very firm on rotating the duties to keep the workloads fair."

"You never work other duties, do you?" I tried not to swallow in order to keep the sickness at bay, even as I glanced around for that bucket Sister Reva had told me I should find.

Sister Nila grabbed an empty wash pan to hold out toward me. I placed it in the chair nearest me.

"That is because being head of the kitchen is my duty. And you as a helper are my duty too. I do not mean to be unsympathetic for I know the upheaval in your stomach, but the work must be done to get meals on the tables."

"So you have borne children?" I hoped if we talked of things other than food, I might yet control my stomach.

"Nay, but I saw my mother carry ten babies. I took care of enough babies to last me a lifetime. Coming to the Shakers was like moving into paradise."

"You do not like babies?"

"I did not say that. I loved every one, but even a saint would get tired of dirty bottoms and runny noses after a while." Sister Reva shook her head a little. "And no one ever accused me of being a saint. My mam used to say if the babies were my own, I would not tire of caring for them, but I noted she often left them with me and spent much time in the garden." She turned and stirred the potatoes into the grease. "Yea, I've never regretted not finding out if my mother was right."

I put my hand over my nose and tried not to breathe in the smell.

Without looking around, she heaved another sigh. "My mam had the sickness all nine months with some of hers. I never understood why she kept having them, but she was fond of saying the Lord sent every woman the children she should mother. I made sure he sent me none."

right for him. That was not riding a horse off into the unknown. Here with the Shakers was where I must stay for now.

"One day at a time," I whispered. "Let me not look ahead but trust in your providence, Lord. Just as you provided manna for the Israelites one day at a time, you are providing food for me and my child. Forgive me for worrying about the morrow and help me be glad for the day."

I said the prayer and meant every word, but worry for the future wriggled down and made a hard knot below my heart.

The sound of a door opening awoke a bit of panic in me. Could I have lost track of the time and the breakfast hour was already over? The Shaker brethren would not be glad to find me out of my place in their barn. At least I would have something to confess to Eldress Maria when next she asked me to list my wrongs.

I gave Sawyer a last pat and checked for the nearest door in hopes I could sneak out without being seen. Not that I could move that fast, but perhaps I could move that quietly. Sawyer nickered as I stepped back from his stall, but that wasn't what stopped me from making my escape. Instead it was a girl's voice where a child did not belong. Just as a sister should not be in this place where the brethren worked.

"Papa, why can't I go look for Sister Faye? I know which house is hers. The Shaker children all live there together."

"Surely with some older sisters," the man said.

They had not seen me yet, but I recognized the man and the child from when I had carried a meal to the Trustee House for him and the girl had told me of her sorrows.

No doubt it would be another sin to confess to Eldress Maria, but I stayed where I was by Sawyer's stall. The girl saw me first.

"Hello." Her smile lit up her eyes. She was a beautiful child, and I thought of her poor mother who wasn't getting to see how she was growing. "Are you feeding the horses?"

For her that seemed a natural thing, as she had probably helped her father feed their animals.

"No." I saw no reason to abide by the Shaker rules with their nay saying with these two from outside the village. It was my morning for rebellion, however slight. "I came to see Sawyer. He used to be my husband's horse."

"He looks glad to see you." The man stopped a respectful distance away and looked from me to the horse. "Have you come to visit him before now?"

"I have not. I thought he would be fine with the Shakers, but then you and Brother Hiram said something was wrong with him."

Before the man could answer, the child spoke. "Horses can't get chol'ra, can they?"

"No." The man put his hand gently on the girl's head. "Sawyer may just be lonesome. Some horses miss their former owners when they come to a new place."

"Poor horse." The child looked from Sawyer to me. "Why doesn't your husband come see him?"

The man started to speak, but I held up a hand to stop him. "Worry not, sir. I don't mind answering her question. My husband died."

"The chol'ra?"

"No, an accident."

"Did he fall off a horse like my mother?"

"A different kind of accident. On a riverboat."

The child was satisfied with that. She had seen death. "I'm glad he didn't fall off this horse. That might make Sawyer even sadder the way Sebastian is back in that field by himself."

I caught the flash of pain on the man's face. The child—I remembered Leatrice was her name—had told me she was four when her mother died. So years had passed since his wife died, but from the look on his face the sorrow was still fresh. He was the sad one. Not the horse.

Would I be the same even after years went by? I sneaked another look at him as he spoke to the child. "Enough about that. Sebastian is fine and Sawyer here will be fine too after I work with him."

"Papa knows how to make horses right." Leatrice looked around. "But I'd rather sweep floors than sit in a barn." She wrinkled her nose and stared up at her father. "Please let me go find Sister Faye. She told me I could come anytime." Her bottom lip jutted out a bit.

"You can't go wandering around the village by yourself." The man frowned at her.

"I'd be good. I promise."

"Leatrice." His voice carried a sound of warning.

I needed to leave the barn anyway. I had already broken too many of the Shaker rules. Eldress Maria would be aghast. So I smiled at the child. "If your father permits, I can take you to the Children's House."

"Please, Papa," the child pleaded.

I could tell by his face he did not like to refuse her anything.

"If you're sure it's not a problem for you." His gaze flashed to my middle and as quickly away.

"No problem at all." I turned my smile toward him, then touched Sawyer's nose in farewell as I thought of all the times Walter had surely done the same.

"Perhaps you should come back to visit the horse again," the man said.

"I doubt that would be permitted," I answered with regret.

"I understand," he said.

Perhaps he did, although I wondered if anyone could understand life in the village if he had not lived it. Certainly I had not expected it to be thus, with every moment of my day arranged by others. I held my hand out to the child.

She came readily enough as he called after her. "Don't get into trouble."

After we were out of the barn, I asked, "Do you get into trouble often?" She had told me about falling through the ice on her pond.

She sighed. "I do. I don't aim to, but Grandpa says I forget to use my head sometimes."

"My mother sometimes said the same about me when I was your age." I smiled. "It gets easier to figure out what you should do and what you shouldn't as you get older." I gently squeezed her hand.

"I can stay out of trouble here. With Sister Faye taking care of me."

"It's good to have somebody take care of you."

"Mamaw Bea used to tell me the Lord would always take care of me. I guess he did when I fell through the ice. But he didn't take care of Mamaw Bea. She died."

"I'm sorry." Those two small words weren't enough. The child needed more. "The Lord helps us in different ways. Sometimes he wraps his arms around us and takes us to heaven to be with him."

"That's good, isn't it? To be in heaven." She sighed. "But I wanted her to stay with me. And my mama too."

I gently touched her forehead with the tips of my fingers. "They will always be with you here in your memories." I moved my hand to her chest. "And in your heart."

She hugged me then as well as she could with her small arms and my large middle. With no more words necessary, we went on toward the Children's House.

12

Flynn watched Leatrice leave with the woman. He hadn't expected to find one of the sisters in the barn and certainly not that sister in her condition. Finding out the horse could be sick must have made her want to see him for herself. That showed she cared. Flynn smiled. People should care about their horses.

The animal must care for her too. He still had his head out over the stall door, peering after the woman. Horses sometimes followed Lena around a pasture like puppy dogs, anxious for a word from her. Lena did love them, but at times, she could be impatient if they didn't do what she wanted.

This Sister Darcie appeared to have plenty of patience as she walked away with Leatrice. Heaven knew a person often needed a double dose of patience to deal with his child.

He had been surprised that morning when Leatrice was so eager to come back to the village. Not that she had a choice. With Silas still gone, she had to come with him. He was getting worried about Silas. That was why he had come to the village early, so he could ride into town later to look for him.

Leatrice would have to go then too. He wasn't about to

leave her alone to get in trouble. At least here in the village she had eyes watching her while he worked with the horse.

He'd heard that eyes were always watching in the village to prevent furtive meetings of men and women in the shadows. Of course, rumors swirled about the Shakers. Some said they kept the young people captive or that the elders had multiple wives instead of sisters. Plenty of others claimed their dancing worship was far from holy.

Flynn put no stock in any of those tales. The Shakers he knew were hardworking, decent people who chose to live a different way. Not how Flynn wanted to live, but then he had not thought to remarry after he lost Lena. So maybe he was more like the Shakers than he was ready to admit.

Perhaps Silas was right that he should have looked for a new wife by now. He didn't deny he was lonely at times or that Leatrice needed a woman in her life to usher her through girlhood. Perhaps that was why she hadn't complained when he roused her before daylight to come to the Shaker village. She got to be with other females here. She had quite happily taken Sister Darcie's hand and left with a bare glance back at him.

What would it be like to leave her here the way Silas had suggested last fall? He didn't want to think about that. Leatrice was his daughter and she belonged with him. But what if living with him wasn't best for her? He shuddered, remembering the pond ice breaking under her feet.

He shut away that thought and turned his attention to the horse in front of him. While he might not be able to solve every problem, he could generally figure out how to fix a horse. Sawyer was showing more life. Head up. Eyes watching. Tail doing a slow swishing dance that meant he wanted to move. Maybe instead of a cat, all the horse needed was a visit from the woman. Brother Hiram would probably chase him out of the village if he suggested letting the woman keep visiting the barn.

Not that she looked like that would be easy for her right now. She wasn't far from birthing her baby or he missed his guess. An expectant mother was not somebody he expected to see at the Shaker village. Seeing her in a horse barn was even more surprising.

"We best stick with the plan of making friends with yon mare, Sawyer." He stroked the horse's neck before he led him out of the stall.

Out in the corral, Sawyer trailed the mare around. A good sign, but at the same time, the way the horse moved made Flynn suspect he might have stomach trouble. Horses could be fragile. A pebble in a hoof, a sore on their hock, even a bad tooth could take one down.

Stomach problems were sometimes the worst. If he still had that suspicion when he next worked with Sawyer, he'd suggest the Shakers add some cider vinegar to his feed and give him more time in the pasture to graze on the winter grass.

After he brushed the horse and put him in the stall, Flynn retrieved his own horse and led it through the village. He wasn't sure how to find Leatrice. He should have asked one of the men in the barn to point out the Children's House.

Sounds of commerce came from every building. Hammering. Sanding. Wood being split. A blacksmith hammer rang down on a piece of metal. The Shakers believed in work. Whatever the season. Whatever the weather. Behind the houses, hens cackled to announce their eggs. A cow bawled for her calf.

A few sisters were hanging out clothes, but he didn't ask

them about the Children's House in case the sisters weren't supposed to speak to strangers. But then Sister Darcie had shown no hesitation to talk with him earlier in the barn.

He wondered about Sister Darcie. She didn't seem to belong among the Shakers and not just because she was carrying a child. He didn't know why he thought that. Perhaps because of the sorrow he saw in her eyes. She was an attractive woman even with the cap hiding all but a few strands of her hair.

Lena had never taken to wearing bonnets, much to her mother's distress. Ma Beatrice worried Lena would freckle, but she never did. This Sister Darcie on the other hand had a scattering of freckles across her nose, even with the bonnet shading her face from the sun. The copper-colored hair peeking out of her cap would be to blame for that.

As if he had called her up by his thoughts, Sister Darcie stepped on the pathway alongside the road a few yards in front of him. She could point him toward the Children's House. He called out to her. "Sister Darcie."

Not hiding her surprise, she turned toward him. "Mr. Keller, did you want to speak to me?"

"Sorry to startle you, ma'am, but I'm looking for Leatrice. If you could point me in the right direction, I'd be grateful."

"Yes, of course." She gestured on up the road. "The Children's House is two buildings down."

Her face was flushed, whether from exertion or because of him, he wasn't sure. She had seemed comfortable talking to him in the barn, but now she appeared to be uneasy.

"Thank you. I didn't mean to cause you trouble." Flynn looked around to see if he had drawn attention or disapproval from any nearby Shakers. They seemed to be alone on this area of the walkway. "Is it breaking rules for you to talk to me?"

"I'm sure it's not recommended. I have not learned all the rules." She breathed out a little sigh. "But don't concern yourself. The Shakers are kind. Even to one in my condition." She gently touched the front of her dress. "They know I have nowhere else to go." The sorrow in those words showed on her face.

"I am sorry," Flynn said.

"So am I, even when I should be grateful."

"Grateful?"

"For their kindness. For having a table to put my feet under. A widow without property or family has few choices." She shook her head a little and smiled. A genuine smile that erased the weariness from her face and lit up her eyes. "But forgive me. You didn't stop me to hear my worries."

He wasn't sure what to say to that, so he merely nodded to acknowledge her words.

That seemed enough for the woman as she went on. "Your daughter is a lovely girl. Someone at the Children's House will fetch her for you." She looked up at the sun. "You have a few minutes before the bell for the midday meal rings."

She turned toward one of the houses.

He called after her. "Sawyer did well today. I think your visit made him better."

"That is good to know." She smiled over her shoulder at him, then lifted her skirts a bare inch and hurried on up the walkway to disappear around the side of the brick house.

For a moment, he stared after her. Something about the woman drew him. Perhaps because he knew she'd lost her husband and now faced delivering a child alone. But she wasn't alone. She would have many sisters to aid her. Yet she looked so lost somehow.

He had probably looked the same after Lena died. It took a while to adjust to being alone again after being joined by love and marriage. As he moved on toward the house the woman had pointed out, he wondered if he had adjusted even now. Nearly three years had passed. When he again thought of Silas telling him he should remarry, he couldn't keep from smiling. He was certainly in the wrong place to wife hunt.

Leatrice wasn't happy when she came out to where he waited. "We were lining up to eat. They were letting me go in their eating room instead of them just bringing me a plate like the first time we were here. Sister Faye told me I would have to Shaker my plate."

"Shaker your plate?" Flynn mounted his horse and then pulled Leatrice up in front of him. "What on earth does that mean?"

"Sounds funny, doesn't it?" Leatrice leaned back against him. "But Sister Faye said it just meant I had to eat everything I put on my plate. I was hungry so that would have been easy. Now I don't get to eat anything."

"Don't pout. We'll find something at the house. Then we need to go find your grandfather."

She twisted around to look up at him. "Do you think he got sick and can't come home?"

He tightened his arm around her. "I don't know. But it could be he'll be there when we get to the house."

"I don't want Grandpa to die."

"No need borrowing trouble. Your grandpa is probably fine." At least he hoped so.

When they rode over the hill, Flynn was relieved to see smoke rising from their chimney. Silas must be home.

At the barn, he slid off his horse and lifted Leatrice down. "Looks like your grandfather is here." He turned the horse into the corral. He'd brush him down after he fixed Leatrice something to eat.

As she ran on ahead, Flynn trailed after her, smiling at her eagerness. She was through the door before he was halfway across the yard. Then when he reached the porch steps, she burst back out of the house as if hornets were after her.

"Whoa." He caught her and held her in front of him. "Slow down. What's going on?"

She stared up at him with wide eyes. "It's her. She's in there."

"Who's in there?"

"That woman. The one that said bears were going to eat me."

"Bears are not going to eat you." He shouldn't have let her go ahead of him. Maybe the woman, Irene Black, had bad news. Why else would she be there after he told her not to come back? "Is she alone?"

Before she could answer, Silas stepped out onto the porch.

"What's the matter with you, girl? Running out of the house like that." Silas frowned at Leatrice. "You know Miss Black."

"Not Miss Black anymore." Irene was behind Silas with a smile on her face that Flynn didn't like. "Isn't that right, Silas?"

Flynn put his hand on Leatrice's shoulder and held her next to him as he looked at Silas.

"That's right," Silas said.

"Well, tell him." The woman reached for Silas's hand and gave it a little shake. "Oh, if you're too shy about it, I will. Silas and I got married yesterday. I'm Mrs. Cox now."

Flynn wished he could believe she was lying. If only. Instead he had the sinking feeling she was laughing at him.

He turned to glare at Silas. Did the man not know how this woman had treated Leatrice? "What have you done?"

Silas didn't back down as he narrowed his eyes and stared back at Flynn. "What you should have done months ago. Got married."

"Till death do us part." Irene touched Silas's cheek. "For better or worse."

Flynn knew which that was going to be. Worse. But nothing he could say would change things now. Silas had made his bed. He'd have to lie in it, comfortable or not.

Flynn managed a smile. "Well then, I guess congratulations are in order."

Silas nodded shortly. He didn't exactly look like a happy newlywed. But some wrong choices weren't easy to undo. Silas would have to figure out that problem. Flynn had to think of Leatrice and make sure the woman left his daughter alone.

As if she read his thoughts, she held out her hand toward Leatrice. "Come on, sweetheart. I'll fix you something to eat. I'm your grandmamma now."

"No." Leatrice jerked away from Flynn and ran toward the barn to no doubt climb up into the loft to hide out with her cats.

"Why don't you go on inside?" Flynn told Irene. "I'll get Leatrice and we'll come eat."

"It appears you do need a few minutes to teach your child

some manners." Irene shook her finger at him, but kept her smile. "We've got stew and cornbread. And I made some fried pies out of the Shaker applesauce I found in the cupboard. They do make good applesauce. You'll see. You'll be glad I'm here."

For a few minutes after the door shut behind her, the two men looked at each other without saying anything. Finally Silas spoke. "She told me she and Leatrice got along and she didn't know why you sent her packing back last year."

Maybe he hadn't known. He was still grieving Ma Beatrice then. "It would have been good if we'd talked first. Unless you love her."

"Love takes longer than a weekend. Truth of it is, she was willing and we need help out here to keep things going. I aimed good."

Flynn let out a slow breath. "I know you did, Silas, and maybe it'll work out."

"I'll make sure she steps lightly around Leatrice."

"And I'll tell Leatrice she has to be respectful. But I don't think she'll ever be ready to claim her as a grandmother."

"She can call her Miss Irene."

"That should work."

Silas shoved his hands in his pockets and looked at the door. "Leastways, she can cook. She helped me pick out some supplies."

"We needed them."

"I was mighty tired of beans every meal."

"I understand." Flynn smiled at the man. What else could he do? This man had taken him to his heart when he married his daughter and been a father to him. "How's your cough?"

"Better except at night. Irene is going to fix me up a tonic."

"That might help." Maybe the woman would be good for Silas. He could only hope that turned out to be true. "I'd best go talk to Leatrice."

"Don't fuss at her overmuch. Some things take getting used to."

Leatrice wasn't the only one who needed to get used to Irene in their house. Flynn would have to do the same, and maybe Silas too.

13

The winter days passed. Snow, cold winds, clouds, or sun, no matter the weather, I wanted each day to linger. I was in no hurry for my time of confinement. As long as I held my baby within me, I could not be separated from him. But the nausea stayed with me, making mealtimes difficult.

"You won't have energy to bring this child into the world if you don't start eating more," Sister Ellie fussed. "Birthing babies is no easy task. A woman walks through a dangerous valley anytime she brings a baby into the world."

I hadn't dwelt upon the ordeal of bringing a baby into the world. I merely feared what might follow the birth of my child since I could not ignore the lack of cradles in the Gathering Family House. I did not speak my fear of being parted from my baby aloud to Sister Ellie. She knew without words between us. I simply promised, "I will eat."

But then when food was in front of me in the Shaker eating room, I could only nibble.

Sister Ellie would not be defeated. She rashly broke the Shaker rules by pirating out biscuits and cheese or whatever she could fit in her pockets, for she somehow guessed my appetite was better at bedtime. Perhaps she heard the growling of my stomach in the night.

Sister Helene knew of the smuggled food but turned her head. For her to follow a tainted path to trouble by breaking rules was surprising. That proved she too worried about me, and her concern was even more vexing since she knew so little of childbirth.

However, she knew well the story of Mother Ann and how she had four babies who all died at young ages while Ann Lee lived in England. This Mother Ann believed their deaths were God's way of convincing her to live a celibate life. Those who followed her were required to shed what the Shakers called the sin of matrimony in order to join their society. I didn't believe any of it.

The Lord who lived in my heart loved me. He loved my baby even as he was formed in my womb. The Bible promised that, but Sister Helene had lived the Shaker way. She had come to this sterile environment as a young girl and knew little of the creation of life, other than the hatching of chicks and the freshening of a mother cow when a calf was dropped.

I, at least, had been with my mother when she birthed my brothers and sister. I knew what to expect, even though, as Sister Ellie warned, every woman came to childbirth alone. Each delivery was a unique experience.

"My first was many hours of pain," Sister Ellie told me. "My second came quickly with ease. Such a gift that was. I was sure those to follow would be the same, and it was so for the third boy. But the fourth, another boy, was turned the wrong way. If the old granny my husband fetched to assist me hadn't guided other such babies into the world, I would have lost that one and perhaps died myself. The last, dear Abby, was born after the others were well beyond their baby years. She came easy enough, but then I struggled to find my feet again."

Sister Ellie gave me a hard look before she went on. "And that was in spite of never neglecting my nourishment. I knew to eat not only for my baby but also for myself. A mother must stay as healthy as possible in order to nurse her baby once he is born."

She had brought me a hunk of cornbread and a slice of apple pie wrapped in her handkerchief. I had managed the pie, but the cornbread needed milk to make it go down. I nibbled at it and considered her words. We perched on the edge of my bed, speaking quietly to keep from disturbing the other two in the room already asleep, although I wondered if Sister Helene only pretended sleep. If she let us know she was awake, she would be conflicted about the need to chastise Sister Ellie for breaking the rules. Eldress Maria gave her the duty of instructing us in proper Shaker behavior. The other, Sister Genna, kept to herself.

I barely kept from choking as I swallowed the cornbread. Sister Ellie produced a small jar of water from the folds of her nightdress. I wondered if she had sewn extra pockets into the garment.

I gratefully took a drink and then stared at the remaining hunk of cornbread in my hand. Sister Ellie was right. I did need to preserve my health in order to properly mother my child, but would I be given that choice?

"Will I be allowed to nurse my baby?" For the first time, I spoke my fears aloud.

Sister Ellie looked puzzled. "The baby must be fed and such is the natural way."

"Little is natural here. At least among the people." I stared down at the cornbread crumbling in my hand. Unshed tears clogged my throat. "I suppose calves are not separated from their mothers before their time."

Sister Ellie's face softened as she wrapped her arms around me. "Nor will you be separated from your baby while he needs the food you can provide. I am sure of it."

"I see no cradles here."

"True. They may move you to the Children's House for a time."

"And when that time is through?" I wiped away a tear that escaped. "What then?"

Her eyes moistened like mine. She knew the answer, had felt the sorrow with her own dear children, but did not want to speak it aloud. Instead she said, "Look not too far ahead. Best to take each day as it comes."

"Yea." But I felt the days counting down.

"Be glad for this gift of motherhood." She hugged me again and whispered in my ear as though she too worried Sister Helene might be listening. "We will pray for a better way for you when that time comes."

"I am praying."

She leaned back and I could see the worry on her face in the moonlight sliding through the window. "Are you still having those pains in your back?"

"Some. Nothing I can't bear."

"At least the eldress let you change from kitchen duty. She should forgive you from all duties until after your baby comes." Sister Ellie squeezed my hand. "I will see if Sister Helene will ask Eldress Maria to allow you to rest."

"Nay, don't do that. I don't mind the duty of hand lettering the seed packages. Eldress Maria said that perhaps I had found my best talent for the Society. Careful script."

After Sister Ellie returned to her own bed, I smiled as I remembered how surprised the eldress had been when I told her I could read and write.

In the days that followed, printing the planting instructions on the seed packages proved an easy duty. I worked alone so if my back stiffened and ached, I could stand and walk about a bit. I think the eldress was glad to hide me away from the other sisters. Many of them looked at me with the same sympathy as Sister Ellie and perhaps regretted the lost joys of motherhood.

At times when I peered out the room's window to rest my eyes from the printing duty, I watched for the child Leatrice and her father. I wondered if he still worked with Walter's horse but dared not go back to the barn.

After that morning when I had strayed from the Shaker rules, Eldress Maria made it clear my visit to Sawyer was a serious infraction. She had known about my transgression even before I made my confession to her. When I asked how, she said such was not my concern but that nothing happening in the village could remain hidden.

I knew about the watchers, those stationed in high windows to make sure all went about their duties without wandering onto paths of sins, but I had assumed even the watchers went to the meals when the bell rang. Obviously, I was mistaken.

Eldress Maria had let me know I was in a precarious position. Those who didn't follow the rules could be asked to leave the village.

"We would hate losing you to the world. We want to embrace you as a dear sister, but as a sister you must abide by our rules. Without such discipline, we cannot have unity." Her frown had deepened as she spoke.

So I had bent my head and murmured the expected words of contrition, even as I prayed for forgiveness for my duplicity. Unity. The only ones I felt sure unity with were the child within me and the husband lost to me.

When the pain of that loss threatened to overwhelm me, I imagined Walter smiling down on me from heaven. He would want me to find a way to be happy. But what way that could be I did not know except I was sure I could find no happiness separated from my child.

When that worry came to mind, I remembered Sister Ellie's whispered words to pray. So I did. Granny Hatchell had taught me prayers offered in faith were answered even when the answers might not be what you expected. The Lord's ways were not man's ways. Or Shaker ways, in my mind.

I was not sure why I continued to look for the child, Leatrice, and her father. But once, while I was still working in the kitchen, I had been almost sure I saw the child with Sister Faye. I was headed to the privy, something I had to do often as the weight of the baby increased. The child I thought might be Leatrice was wearing a Shaker cloak such as she had worn on the morning I ushered her away from the barn, but it could have been another little sister since I didn't see her face.

Another time, after Eldress Maria gave me the lettering duty, I was positive I saw the girl's father riding Sawyer past my window. He stepped lively, and my heart was glad for the horse that Walter had loved. I wished I could run out and stop the man. Speaking with him in the barn about Sawyer that day and then taking his daughter's hand in mine had somehow lifted my spirits. A proof the world went on in its normal way outside the village.

I felt sequestered in the small room that served as Eldress Maria's place to hear the confessions of those in her charge. She gave it over to me for the working hours of the day while she was about other duties, for the elders and eldresses worked with their hands the same as novitiates such as I. Sister Helene said the eldress wove perfect baskets and never dropped a seed when she was filling the seed packets.

The Shakers sold thousands of these seed packets here in the near neighborhood and as far away as New Orleans and the western territories. Each day I was given a stack of the packets already partially printed on a hand press but needing an extra line of planting instructions. For the cabbage seeds, *Sow in early spring.* For other seeds, *Plant after the danger of frost is past.*

Before the eldress assigned me the duty, she had asked me to print out the alphabet. She studied my lettering and nodded that I passed the test. Her smile was genuine and not one I often saw. I was a continual cross for Eldress Maria to bear. Not only did she sense I lacked proper belief in the Shaker way, my condition made her uneasy. Yet she tried to be kind. She *was* kind. I reminded myself of that often. The Shakers were all kind. They worked at practicing kindness the same as they worked making chairs and brooms or packaging seeds.

Were I widowed without the blessing of approaching motherhood, then I might have settled into the village life with ease and enjoyed sharing chores and duties with the sisters. Even the songs and dances of the Shakers were not all that difficult to embrace. Sister Ellie said I was fortunate that what was called the Era of Manifestations was dying out. For several years the community had experienced an odd period of visions and visitations from heaven.

My doubt must have shown on my face, because Sister Ellie merely smiled and went on. "It was a strange time for sure. Sister Faye claimed to go up into heaven and walk all around. Others said the spirits came to dance with them."

"Did you dance with them?"

"Nay. Even when most of those at meeting seemed excited and able to see those from the heavenly realm, I saw and felt nothing."

"Did that upset you?" I asked.

"Not at all. I have no wish to see spirits. Eldress Maria said, and rightly so, that I must not be open to receive spiritual gifts. It is true that I have ever been practical in my thinking, so the steadiness of life here suits me. At the same time I do miss my own kitchen, and it is a sorrow not being the one to tuck my Abby into bed each night."

"Perhaps we should pray for you to have another way too," I told her as we walked to the privy after the morning meal on a late February day that had early spring warmth in its sunshine. No one was near enough to overhear us.

"A way is open to me with my oldest daughter." She sighed. "But I hesitate to take it and leave Abby and my husband behind, even if neither of them seems to note me as mother and wife. I little know what to pray."

"Perhaps peace with your decision," I suggested. "Whatever path you decide to walk."

"Yea. A heart torn two ways knows no joy." Sister Ellie looked away at the trees across the pasture behind the privy and then back at me. "For now, I am glad to be here so I can be a sister mother to you during this time."

"I don't know what I would do without your help. And prayers."

"We will continue to pray for answers." Sister Ellie put an arm around me and I leaned into her strength. "And for an easy birth. How much longer do you think?"

"Four weeks to make nine months." I did not tell her about the pains pulsing in my back. Surely that was from sitting so long at my lettering duty. "Will they call for a doctor when it is my time?"

"We have a Shaker doctor here. Sister Lettie. She is very old but has healing in her hands."

"Will she know about babies?"

"Yea, I'm sure she does. Besides, as long as all is well, I could help usher your little one into the world. The Lord intended such to be a natural process."

"So it was for my mother." I paused to stretch my back. The pain was still there. "I am anxious to hold my baby in my arms and see his face." I stroked the baby moving under my skin as I spoke my next words barely loud enough for Sister Ellie to hear. "But I am afraid."

She hugged me once more. "Yea, that is only natural with a first child. But dwell on the truth that many, many women have gone through this birthing experience. With the Lord's help, you will be fine." She leaned down to peer into my face, a smile on her own. "If you remember to eat enough."

"I will eat," I promised. "But how will I know when the time has come?" I was with my mother during her confinements, but I was so young then. I remembered her hours of laboring to push out the babies, but I didn't remember the beginning.

"Your body will tell you. There will be pain." Sister Ellie's smile disappeared. "You cannot bring a baby into the world without some suffering, but I will be there to hold your hand and Sister Helene will send up sincere prayers."

"I am blessed with sisters." And that I said with complete honesty. If I could not be in my husband's house, then here was a good place for me.

14

I should have told Sister Ellie how much my back was hurting. But that wasn't where labor pains grabbed my mother.
I did know that. Plus I had to consider the four more weeks
my baby needed to grow. Early babies struggled to thrive. I
did not want my baby to have any reason to struggle.

But what one wanted did not always happen. I remembered the early pains and how Sister Ellie had told me to lie
still and rest so they would go away. They did go away then,
with only vague twinges since. But nothing was vague about
the pain attacking me now. Nor did it matter how still I lay
or what position I curled into on the bed.

The pain slid around from my back and grabbed my belly
with dreadful claws before it eased. I tried to count the minutes, but I was very tired and dozed off before the dreadful
tightening that meant another pain was taking possession of
my body. I tensed even as the memory of the midwife granny
telling my mother to take slow breaths to relax came to mind.
Once the woman had her singing hymns.

I considered humming a tune to help endure the pain. But

what I really wanted was for them to slide completely away. To wait yet a little longer, but the pain grabbed me again. Instead of a song, a groan escaped my lips.

Sister Ellie was beside me in an instant. She must have been sleeping with a mother's ear, listening for my least sound. Hadn't she claimed happiness at being my sister mother to help me through this time? Perhaps because she had missed being there for her daughter when her grandchild was born.

She put her hand on my stomach. "Are you having pains?"

My breath caught as the pain strengthened its hold on me so that I could do no more than nod.

"A strong contraction from the feel of it," she said. "How often?"

The pain slid away like a leaf thrown in a brook. I pulled in some air. "I don't know. I tried to keep count but I must have fallen asleep for a few minutes." I reached for her hand. "Will these ease and go away? It is still early."

"Nay, I think early or not, your time has come. We need to run for Sister Lettie."

"I don't think I can run."

Sister Ellie smiled. She had not lit a candle, but the moon sent light in through the window. A ghostly gray light that made me shiver.

Sister Helene came to stand at the end of my bed then. "What is wrong?" She wasn't particularly tall, but she seemed to tower over me, her face in shadows.

"The baby is coming," Sister Ellie told her.

"Now? Are you sure?" Sister Helene twisted her hands together. She seemed even more fearful than I. "What must we do?"

"Worry not, Sister. Your job will be to pray for our sister and her baby. I will rouse Sister Genna to fetch Sister Lettie."

Sister Ellie left my side then and I felt strangely bereft without her hand in mine. I tried to sit up to keep her in sight and perhaps keep the fear at bay, but moving brought on a new pain. One not quite so fierce but fierce enough. I fell back on the pillow.

Sister Helene moaned as though the pain had grabbed her as well. Even in the dim light I could see her wide eyes and the way her hands trembled as she clutched her nightgown.

As the pain eased, I thought to comfort her. "I will be fine. This is as it's supposed to be."

"It does not seem right," she whispered.

"But it is the way of nature ever since Eve was tempted in the garden."

"Yea." Sister Genna, aroused from sleep, frowned down at me. She had already slipped on her dress and was tying on her cap. "In pain you shall bring forth children."

Sister Genna and I had not formed the sister feelings that I shared with Sister Ellie and Sister Helene. She kept to herself, rarely speaking when in our retiring room. She had come into the Shaker village shortly before Walter and me. Sister Ellie tried to draw her out, but every question was answered with a curt yea or nay. The words from the Bible just now spoken were the most I had heard her say at one time.

"Have you been through this pain?" I asked.

"Yea. Twice. All for naught." The sorrow in her voice made me forget my pain for a moment.

Sister Helene looked at her. "Why for naught?"

"One never drew breath. The other took a fever and died before his first birthday."

"I am sorry." I put my hand on the bump that was my baby, while Sister Ellie knelt beside me and squeezed my other hand.

"Nay, it was God's will. At least that is what the Shakers say." Sister Genna leaned down to pull on her shoes. When she straightened back up, her face was set as she stared at me. "Time will tell God's will for yours."

Sister Helene tried to put her hand on Sister Genna in sympathy, but the woman shrugged her off. "I will fetch the Shaker doctor. You best tell the eldress to unlock the door. They keep us locked in, you know."

"Yea, she is right. I will go." Sister Helene followed Sister Genna from the room.

A new pain gripped me. Tears slid down my cheeks. I wasn't sure if the tears were from the pain or the worry of Sister Genna's words. God's will. Had it been God's will that Walter was on the steamboat to die? Was it God's will that I was here in this Shaker room with nothing to look forward to except working with my hands and being separated from my child? If my child lived. I had worried of many things, but not about my baby dying.

"Oh, dear God," I whispered as the pain eased. But I knew not what to pray next. For God's will to be what I willed, but how could I be that bold?

"Block Sister Genna's words from your thoughts. Some babies do not survive the perils of birth, but many more do. This baby will." Sister Ellie leaned close to look directly in my face.

"How do you know?"

"I feel his strength under my hand. He is anxious to get out into the world. Small, perhaps, but full of courage like his mother."

"Thank you, Sister Ellie. You are a heaven-sent blessing. If I don't make it through the birth, I want you to know how much you mean to me."

Sister Ellie shook my hand as if to shake away my words. "Nay. I'll listen to no such talk as that."

A spasm fiercer than those before seized me and I gasped.

"Scream if you must." Sister Ellie gripped both my hands as though to give me her strength.

But I pressed my lips together and did not let out the scream that gathered with the pain. What would all the sleeping Shakers think to be awakened with screams? I had heard a few of them shout in their worship before Eldress Maria banned me from the meetings, but screams in the night would not be welcomed.

Then Eldress Maria was standing over me. No, looming over me. The candle she held threw shadows across her face so that I could not see her clearly, but I heard disapproval in her words. "So it is her time. I thought she lacked a month yet."

Sister Ellie answered. "Babies sometimes come early."

"She needs to be in the infirmary. Not here." Eldress Maria stepped to my side and held the candle higher. "Can you stand, Sister Darcie?"

"Yea." I claimed I could with no idea whether that was true or not. Perhaps when the pain ebbed I could.

An older woman hustled up then. "Give the poor girl room." She moved in front of the eldress. "I will decide if she must be moved."

Her face was lined with wrinkles, but there was kindness in her eyes. She smiled at me. The first smile I had seen since the pain took me over. "All is going to be well, young sister."

"It will be as the good Lord intends." Eldress Maria softly spoke the words behind her. They sounded like a prayer.

"Yea," Sister Lettie agreed. "And he generally intends new life to come." As she talked, she was feeling my stomach, probing along the lines of the baby. "How are the pains, dearie?"

"Stronger with each one," I said.

"And how long have you been suffering?"

"Her back was paining her before the evening meal," Sister Ellie said when I hesitated.

I looked at her. "I did not tell you that."

"You did not have to. I saw the way you moved."

"Never mind that." The old woman put her hand on my forehead. "Just say if it is so."

"Yea, pains have settled in my back all day." I could feel the approach of another contraction. I didn't know whether to run toward it or try to push it away. I gripped Sister Ellie's hand until it must have hurt, but she made no complaint.

"Easy, little one," Sister Lettie said. "Let the pain roll over you. Accept it, for it is what will bring your baby to you."

"We should take her to your infirmary in the Centre House." Eldress Maria had moved back to the foot of the bed. Shadows darkened the wall behind her. Tall shadows nearly to the ceiling, moving in dreadful dances that seemed to mock me as the contraction seized me. I shut my eyes and tried to do as the old Shaker said. Embrace it, for without the pain my baby could not be born.

"Nay, she is too far along to move. This room will serve well. We need hot water and towels. And more candles."

I heard her instructions through a fog of pain.

"Sister Ellie can see to that," Eldress Maria said.

Sister Ellie started to stand, but I gripped her hand with all the strength I could muster. I did not want her to leave my side. Someone who truly loved me and who had walked this path before me.

"It's all right, Sister Darcie. I will return." Sister Ellie stroked my face with her free hand and tried to pull her other hand from mine.

"Nay." I held her hand as though my very life depended on her staying beside me. Somehow I felt it did, reasonable or not.

The Shaker doctor motioned Sister Ellie to stay where she was. "Eldress, get someone else to heat the water. This sister seems to be needed here."

"But that is foolish. You are here with her." Eldress Maria sounded cross.

"Foolish or not, it is how it will be. There are many other sisters in this house who can be of help."

"I know what is needed." Sister Genna slid into view beside Eldress Maria. "I can boil the water. Sister Helene can help."

"But I am praying." Sister Helene's voice sounded timid, a bit shaky. "For our sister and the baby."

"Pray as we walk." Sister Genna's voice was as firm as the sound of her footsteps going out of the room.

"Go with her," the eldress said. "You need not be witness to this."

"Yea," murmured Sister Helene, ever obedient. As she followed Sister Genna from the room, I wanted to call after her to not forget the prayers. But I stayed silent.

"It is a natural part of life," Sister Lettie said quietly.

"Not a Shaker's life," Eldress Maria said.

"Many who are Shakers have borne children before they came into the Society. Your own mother suffered these birthing pains giving you life, Eldress." Sister Lettie stroked my belly as she talked, her voice calm and soothing. "Even our Savior had an earthly mother."

"But that birth was miraculous. A virgin bearing the son of God."

"Yea, miraculous it surely was," Sister Lettie said. "And we cannot know for the Bible does not tell us if Mary had to suffer the same birthing pains as other mothers in the world. Perhaps our Lord's birth was as amazingly singular as his conception. Or it could be Mary suffered the same as any mother to bring him into this world. Be that as it may, this young sister is beset with birthing pains, and we must do everything we can to help her."

Her voice settled down over me like a soft blanket. With the pain receding, I attempted a smile. "Thank you."

"Just relax, little mother. We must be patient and allow your baby to come in his own good time."

"He's early," I said.

"How early?"

"Four weeks as best I can figure."

"Do not concern yourself," Sister Lettie said. "Let us bring the baby out into the light and then we will keep him warm and healthy."

"Or not. The Lord may take the baby as punishment for wrong thinking." Eldress Maria leaned toward me. The candlelight made her shadow waver on the far wall.

"Now, now." Sister Lettie glanced up at the woman. "We must dwell on the good, not the bad."

I shut my eyes to keep from seeing Eldress Maria's frown.

I didn't think she was being intentionally cruel. I thought instead she merely had no notion of how I already loved this child. As Mary surely loved Jesus. As Sister Ellie had loved each of her children. As she still did, even though separated from them. I was far from alone in birthing a beloved child.

Yet even though countless women had traveled this path before me, each had surely felt alone in spite of those around her. Husbands could not birth the child. Nor could sisters. Even those sisters, like Sister Ellie, who had brought children into the world.

I surrendered to the pain then. Floating with it. Absorbing it. Wondering if I would survive it. But I continued to breathe as the pains grew closer together with barely time to catch my breath and recover before the next one roared toward me. I entered another dimension. Voices continued to echo in my head. Sister Ellie's whispers. The old doctor's words as she spoke of the birth of Jesus.

If Mary felt such pain, I was sorrowful for her.

15

The night went on forever. The pains crashed over me one after another. Sister Ellie stayed by my side, speaking Scripture now and again. Sister Lettie massaged my abdomen and assured me all was proceeding as it should. If Sister Helene or Eldress Maria stayed in the room, I couldn't see them. I imagined Sister Helene on her knees praying for my baby, or at least I thought of that when the pain wasn't blanking out all thoughts. Sister Genna surprised me by gently bathing my face and then rolling up the cloth for me to clamp between my teeth as I fought against the need to scream.

At daybreak when the rising bell rang through the village, I was not sure I could survive another contraction, but then Sister Lettie said my baby's head was crowning. "Just a few more pushes, dearie, and you can rest."

My mind was ready to refuse, but my body had no choice except to push. Sister Genna and Sister Ellie raised my shoulders up and held me to give me a bit of extra strength.

"Good, young sister. The sweet head is in my hands. Plenty of dark hair," Sister Lettie said. "Only a little more now."

I cried out then with another push. Whether it was a cry of pain or victory, I was not sure, but my body felt a release and I knew my baby was no longer hidden within me.

Eldress Maria's voice came from somewhere in the room. "You are disturbing the peace of the morning."

"Worry not, Eldress," Sister Lettie said. "We have reason to celebrate. A new little sister is here."

A girl. I had been so sure I carried a boy but I felt no disappointment. A sweet girl child to hold and love. I fell back against the pillow, joy overcoming my weariness. But then all was quiet. Too quiet. I pushed up off the bed again to look. Beside me Sister Ellie held her breath and a tear slid down Sister Genna's cheek as she stroked my hair.

Breaking the silence, Sister Helene sounded fearful. "Is she supposed to be blue?"

"Nay," Eldress Maria said. "Such is the result of sinful living." She did not sound jubilant, but sad.

"No." The word exploded out of me as I pushed up higher to see my baby. She was too still, too small, too gray.

"Breathe, sweet child," Sister Lettie whispered as she flipped the baby over in her hands and thumped her back.

"Please. Please." I sent the frantic words heavenward. The thought of losing my baby before I could feel her warm breath on my cheek was too horrible to contemplate.

Please, Lord, forgive whatever wrongs I've done and let my baby live.

I didn't really believe the Lord would punish my wrongs by not letting my baby draw breath, but at that desperate moment I was not thinking clearly. Instead Eldress Maria's words were shattering my heart. *The result of sinful living.* My love for Walter and his for me had not been sinful, but my baby lay without moving in Sister Lettie's hands.

Sister Lettie blew softly into my baby's face and then massaged her back. I dared not think of the seconds passing as I willed my breath into my baby's lungs. How many seconds would be too long?

Sister Ellie gripped my hand and I knew she was praying as fiercely as I. Then into the silence came a weak cry like that of a young kitten.

"Yea, sing to us, baby sister." Sister Lettie stroked the baby's back and the cry became stronger.

Sister Ellie cried out hallelujah and Sister Genna actually laughed. But tears flooded my eyes and sobs choked me.

"There, there, young sister," Sister Lettie smiled at me. "Your little one lives. Let your tears be those of joy."

And they were. Joy and thanksgiving. I fell back on the pillow and Sister Genna handed me a cloth to wipe my face. When I seemed unable to do so, she took the cloth from me to gently pat my face.

"I am glad," she whispered and somehow I knew she was thinking of her own lost babies.

Sister Lettie wrapped the baby in a towel and handed her to Eldress Maria, who was beside her. I tried to get up to take her from the woman, but Sister Lettie pushed me down. "You have more work to do, my sister. You can hold your baby soon enough, but first we must finish here. You must pass the afterbirth."

She began massaging my abdomen, and my body obliged, even as I kept my eyes on the eldress. I was surprised to see her face gentle as she looked down at the bundle in her arms. And then she sang a few words to her. "'Tis a gift to be simple. 'Tis a gift to be free."

As if she regretted her tender thoughts, she looked up and held the baby out. "This child needs cleaning."

Sister Genna stepped away from my bed to take the baby. "Yea, I can do that." She glanced back at me. "Worry not, I will take great care with her."

"I know you will." I looked at Sister Genna with new eyes. Before she had seemed to want to stay aloof, but perhaps I had been too wrapped up in myself to note her loneliness. The three of us—Sister Ellie, Sister Helene, and I—should have opened our arms and ears to her and not let her shut us away. Now this little child, my baby, had brought her into our circle.

Sister Lettie patted my legs as she positioned me after pulling away the towels she had placed under me on the bed. "You did well, young sister. Very well."

My eyes went from her kind face to Sister Genna, who wrapped my baby in a neck kerchief and brought her to me. "Here, mother. See your child."

Tears threatened to overflow my eyes again as I reached for her. I had never seen anything more beautiful than the baby's sweet round face. She let out a new wail, stronger this time.

"That's right, little sister." Sister Lettie laughed. "Let us hear what you have to say." She came to look down at us. "Do you have wraps and nappies for the dear one?"

"Yea, in the bureau's bottom drawer. I was allowed to make some when I was in the sewing room." I didn't look up at Sister Lettie. I could not take my eyes off my baby. I touched her cheek and she turned toward me.

Sister Lettie laughed again. "A good sign. She is already

hunting for her nourishment, but rest a few minutes before you try nursing her. Cuddling is what you both need right now."

"What are we going to do?" Eldress Maria spoke up. "She can't stay here."

"What do you mean, Eldress? Where else would she stay?" Sister Lettie sounded puzzled.

"In the Children's House."

"Nay. Not yet. This seems the perfect room with three sisters more than willing to tend to the young sister and her baby. One of the brethren can fetch a cradle for the room." Sister Lettie stroked the baby's head.

"I will have to ask permission of the Ministry." Eldress Maria sounded hesitant.

"Do not concern yourself. I will do so for you. They will agree this is best for our new sister." Sister Lettie smiled at me. Her smile got wider as she pulled back the kerchief around the baby to look at her. "Do you have a name for her, young sister?"

I did not, for I had been that sure of having a son. A son named Walter. But the sweet bundle in my arms deserved a good name, and one came to mind without me searching it out.

"Anna Grace," I said. Walter had told me his mother's name was Anna. While I never met her, I loved her son and was grateful for the woman who raised him.

"A fine name." Sister Lettie nodded toward Sister Ellie. "Let your sister there take sweet Anna Grace and wrap her in something soft from those things you have ready. This kerchief is too stiff. Then you can let her nurse. The mother's first milk is important to a baby's health."

With some reluctance, I surrendered Anna Grace to Sister Ellie. Sunlight was filtering through the window and I wanted to continue to study my little one's face in the morning light.

Sister Genna had already found the bundle of clothes, and she and Sister Ellie hovered over Anna Grace, cleaning her little bottom and wrapping her in a soft diaper. I watched from my bed. Sister Helene edged closer to watch too. She seemed unsure of what to do. She was usually the one leading us, telling us the rules and what was expected, but she had no idea what to expect with a baby in the room.

Eldress Maria was not as hesitant. "The bell for the morning meal will ring soon. We need to be about our morning duties."

Sister Helene looked even more conflicted. What could she tell us to do? I certainly had no energy to rise from my bed for any sort of duty other than holding my newborn. Sister Ellie and Sister Genna paid Eldress Maria no mind and continued to fuss over Anna Grace.

"Indeed, such duties are important and necessary," Sister Lettie said. "But there are times when duties must be adjusted to allow for the unexpected, Eldress. This day you and I and Sister Helene will go about our regular duties, but young sister here will need the help of one of her sisters. Sister Ellie and Sister Genna can share the time of care."

"We should just move her to the infirmary." Eldress Maria was frowning. "That would cause less upheaval."

"Upheaval is good for the soul at times." Sister Lettie's smile stayed steady. "The young sister and our new baby sister will be fine here."

"If you insist it must be so." Eldress Maria gave in, but I

feared I might pay the cost later. She was not one who liked her authority challenged. Even so, I was glad to stay here with Sister Ellie and Sister Genna, who had stepped out of her lonely isolation to assist me in my time of need. Now she swaddled my baby with gentle care before she handed her back to me.

"She is beautiful," she whispered. "From her head to her toes." She pulled back the blanket to reveal Anna Grace's sweet toes. My heart swelled with love at the sight of their perfection.

"But she is very small." Sister Lettie sat down on the edge of my bed. "An early baby needs extra care. You must be sure to feed her as often as she will eat and keep her warm. After her struggle to come into the world, we don't want to lose her now."

"How do we keep fevers away?" Sister Genna's words chilled my heart.

"We don't. We have found no medicinal herbs to stop fevers. All we can do is pray the Lord will put a protective hand over this baby and give her the grace to grow in health. Grace, something we all need in plentitude." Sister Lettie wrapped the blanket back around Anna Grace's toes. "Now let us see if she has energy enough to nurse, young sister, although she looks ready to sleep. That's something you both must do today. Rest." Without taking her gaze from Anna Grace, she said, "We will need that cradle this morning, Eldress."

"I will see to it." The eldress took one look back at the bed. For a few seconds, she paused and I thought she might come closer to better see the baby. "Come, Sister Helene. We have work to do to make up for these others."

"Give me a moment." Sister Helene turned from the door

and came to my bed. "I rejoice breath did come to your baby." She leaned over and kissed my forehead, then kissed her fingertips to touch Anna Grace's cheek. "She will be a wonderful sister, just as you are."

I thought to contradict her words. Her sister, perhaps, but my daughter. But I kept my peace. It was not a time for disputes. For now, Anna Grace would be near me and that was an answer to prayer. For now.

Sister Ellie's thoughts must have been the same, for she leaned near me. "A prayer answered. Rejoice in that and worry not about the days beyond."

Sister Lettie heard her words. "Rejoice in the gift of each day given to us. Good advice, Sister. And what a gift this is. To have the chance to bring a new baby into the world after all this time with the Shakers."

"Have none before come into the village in the expectant way?" I asked.

"None while I have been doctoring here," Sister Lettie said. "Now let us see if your little one is a natural at getting her meals or if she will need coaxing."

She did need a bit of encouragement to latch onto my nipple and even then sucked only a few minutes before she fell asleep.

"Let her sleep, but wake her in an hour if she hasn't already roused and feed her again. She is very small. Not even five pounds or I miss my guess. But I have faith she will thrive under the gentle care you and these, your sisters, will give her." Sister Lettie stood up. "Now I, the same as Eldress Maria, must be about my duties. Plus if I have the time right, the morning meal bell will be ringing at any moment." Sister Lettie sent another firm look my way. "You are very thin, young sister. A proper Shaker takes care of her body and you have double reason to do so now."

"Should I get up and go to the eating room?" I wasn't sure I could, but I was ready to try if the old doctor said I should.

"Nay. You must stay here and rest. Best to stay off the stairs and use the chamber pot for a few days. I will come back later to check on you. Meanwhile these two sisters will assist you and bring your meals." She wagged her finger at me. "No cabbage. A nursing mother must eat with the sure knowledge that her food becomes baby's food, and cabbage, although a perfectly good dish for our table, is not on a baby's menu."

"I know what is good," Sister Ellie said. "I nursed my five babies. So I will see to Sister Darcie's morning meal and then go to my duties. Sister Genna can stay. I have laundry duty, which would mean extra work for my other sisters if I do not do my part, while Sister Genna has been working in the sewing room. Perhaps she can bring some new cloth here to our room to fashion into more diapers."

"Is that all right with you, Sister Genna?" I didn't want her to feel pushed to do anything she did not want to do. "I can stay by myself."

"Nay, not on this day," Sister Lettie said. "Your sisters have worked things out. Accept that, young sister."

I bent my head. "Yea."

After Sister Ellie and Sister Lettie left, Sister Genna took Anna Grace and fixed her a warm place on Sister Ellie's bed beside mine. Since the beds were on wheels to allow easy cleaning under them, Sister Genna scooted the bed close to mine.

"There, you can watch her while I take the dirty linens to the washhouse."

The bell for the morning meal rang then.

"Go get your breakfast too. I'll be fine until you can return." I reached for her hand. "Thank you. I don't know what I would have done without you and Sister Ellie."

"Nay, you would have come through it anyway." She shrugged off my thanks.

"Not as well without my sisters."

"Yea." Her face softened as she looked from me to the baby. "It can be a good thing to have sisters."

She picked up the towels and sheets and was out the door. I could hear the Shakers on the stairs and gathering on the floor below to go in to their morning meal. There they would kneel by their chairs for a moment of silent prayer and maintain that silence even after they sat at the tables. The only noise would be chairs scraping against the wooden floor as the Shakers sat down and spoons clattering as portions were dipped out of the serving bowls. At times the sound of my own chewing had seemed loud in the silence. Eating was serious business for the Shakers, and now it needed to be the same for me so that I could feed my baby.

I wished for a drink of water. I was weak and sore, but the journey through the birthing valley had been worth it. I watched my baby's chest rise and fall and thought of Walter then. How I wished I could see him holding this precious child.

"She will be strong like you," I whispered into the air over my baby's head.

I could almost hear Walter's words coming back to me. *"It's your strength she needs."* He had often said I reminded him of a hummingbird, tiny but forever busy about what must be done.

But now I lay still, glad to be alone with my baby and thankful a cradle would be brought into this house where there were no cradles. I had no reason to look further ahead than that. Each day would bring new prayers for this, my daughter.

The door opened and Sister Helene carried in a tray.

"Breakfast cannot be over," I said.

"Nay. I had no appetite, so I went to the kitchen to get your food." She set the tray on the floor.

"I am very thirsty." I was glad to see the glasses of water and milk on the tray.

"Sister Lettie said you would be. Are you able to eat? You had a terrible night."

I sat up and looked at my baby once more before I scooted my feet off the side of the bed and turned my back to her. I would hear her if she whimpered. Sister Helene handed me the water and I drank it all. I should have sipped the water. It landed hard in my stomach, but I managed to keep it down. When she handed me my plate, I was slower eating the eggs and biscuits. The stewed apples flavored with cinnamon were the best thing I'd tasted for days.

"Thank you for this, but I thought Sister Ellie was bringing my food."

"I told her I would so you would not have to wait." Sister Helene looked down at her hands. "That is not the only reason."

"Oh?"

"Yea. I want to apologize for not being a better help to you."

"I don't know what you mean." I wished for another serving of the apples.

She fiddled with her apron, folding it in pleats and then smoothing them out. "Your pain frightened me. I wanted to bury my face in my covers and block my ears to keep from seeing or hearing." Her face was contorted with the effort to keep back tears.

I put down my fork and touched her cheek. "Worry not, Sister. Birthing a baby is a raw experience. You did not fail me. I felt your prayers."

"I did pray. Fervently when it seemed the baby might not pull in breath." She lifted her head to peer over at Anna Grace. "I wanted to do a whirling dance when I heard that first sweet cry."

"You can do such a dance for Anna Grace at the next meeting."

"I do not know if that would be allowed."

I smiled. Sister Helene did not want to stray from accepted behavior, but then here she was skipping the morning meal to come to me. My pregnancy had been a challenge and, at the same time, a wonder to her.

Anna Grace began fussing. I looked back to see she had freed a hand from the blanket and waved it back and forth. I swiftly finished off the last of the eggs and almost held up the empty plate to prove I had indeed shakered my plate. The thought made me smile again. This day with Anna Grace's cries in my ears and the promise of a cradle for our room, everything made me smile.

"Would you pick her up and bring her to me?" I asked.

Sister Helene's eyes widened. "I fear I might hurt her."

"Nay. Just slide your hands under her and be careful to support her head." I remembered my mother telling me the same when I first picked up one of my little brothers.

She did as I said. Then she held her for an extra moment, even though Anna Grace was still showing her unhappiness. "She is so tiny and yet complete in every way. My sweet little sister."

She gently settled the baby in my arms and Anna Grace quieted at once when I put her to my breast. I stroked her cheek and she began to nurse. It was good to have sisters but even better to have a daughter in my arms.

16

APRIL 1850

Every morning when Leatrice got up, she felt under the feather tick on her bed to be sure the pillowcase stuffed with a dress, a shift, drawers, and the Shaker stockings was still hidden there. Wrapped in the middle of the clothes was her mother's gold pin, shaped like a horse's head, with a pearl where the eye would be.

Her mama had loved horses. Leatrice liked horses too, but at the same time they scared her when they snorted and threw up their heads. Papa said that's when they were feeling their oats. Nothing to worry about as long as she kept out of the way. She didn't want to be afraid of horses. She wanted to be like her mother. Not afraid of anything. That was why she did things that scared her sometimes. To prove she wasn't afraid even when she really was.

She was scared of that woman too. Papa said she had to call her Miss Irene and be nice, but that woman wasn't nice. Even if she did smile and pretend she was, whenever Grandpa was around. The woman smiled at Papa too, but Papa didn't like her. Leatrice knew he didn't, but he couldn't make her leave since Grandpa married her.

Papa said marriages were forever. At least until somebody died like her mama had. Or like Mamaw Bea had. Leatrice's heart hurt when she thought about Mamaw Bea. Even more than when she thought about her mama. After Mama died, Mamaw Bea took care of her. Before Mama died too. Mamaw was the one who held her and told her Bible stories about Jesus.

Sometimes when Leatrice had a hard time going to sleep, she remembered those stories. Her favorite was about the boy who gave Jesus his lunch of two fish and five loaves and how Jesus made it enough to feed thousands of people. Leatrice liked to count the number of baskets left over on her fingers. Mamaw Bea said she had to count all her fingers once and then two of them twice.

Leatrice sometimes wondered if the boy with the lunch was running away because something was wrong at his house. Then when he met Jesus, that turned things around for him. Mamaw said meeting Jesus changed everything around for a person and that it would for Leatrice too when she got old enough.

She didn't know how old she needed to be. She'd turned seven two weeks ago. That was old enough to be ready for things to change around. At least to make that woman be gone. But she was still here. Sitting in Mamaw's rocking chair. Pretending to like Grandpa. Looking up from one of her books to smile at Papa.

"I can teach Leatrice to read," she told Papa last night after supper. "The poor child shouldn't grow up ignorant."

Leatrice wasn't ignorant. She knew lots of things, but Papa gave her a look that said not to talk back.

"I've been meaning to teach her myself, but there's always too much to do." Papa acted like he wasn't sure what to say next. "What do you think, Leatrice? Do you want to learn to read?"

That was a hard one for her. She wanted to know how to read. Really, really bad, but she wasn't about to let that woman teach her anything. "Sister Faye said I could come to their Shaker school to learn to read."

"No telling what else you might learn there." That woman laughed. "Dancing and having fits and calling it worship. Saying they're all sisters and brothers. Anyone who believes that is daft in the head. No telling what goes on over there."

Leatrice wanted to say she was wrong, but sometimes it was better to stay quiet. That's what Sister Faye had told her at the Shaker village when Papa worked with their horse. Sometimes she wished she could go back to the Shaker village to get away from that woman who acted like Mamaw's chair was hers now.

Sister Faye said the Shakers always had room for another sister. But Leatrice didn't want to leave Papa. Or her grandpa either. He had this awful cough. She heard him in the night. Coughing and coughing.

That woman fixed him tonics, but they must not be good like the ones Mamaw Bea made. He didn't get better. Leatrice didn't like to think about when Grandpa's cough got worse. That was her fault. Going out on the pond to skate. Making him get too cold.

She hoped Grandpa didn't tell that woman what she'd done. No telling what would happen then. That woman would probably lock her in the cellar again the way she had the first time she was there. Before her grandpa married her. Snakes and spiders hid in the cellar. Leatrice didn't see any, but she felt them watching her in the dark. She screamed and screamed, but Papa and Grandpa were off in the field. That woman always let her out before they came back. Then she told Leatrice bears would come eat her if she told her father about being locked in the cellar.

Her father did find out about the bears, but Leatrice never told him about the cellar. Just in case that woman was telling the truth about the bears. Papa said she wasn't. But then he nailed the window shut in her room and never took out the nails. Maybe she should ask him to now, in case she had to climb out the window to run away. If things got too bad.

So far things weren't that bad. She went to the barn and played with her kittens. She felt safe up in the loft with Papa in and out of the barn with his horses. That woman didn't like barns. Leatrice might never have to run away, but just in case, her bundle was ready. She wondered if she could wrap one of her kittens up in the bundle too if she had to leave, but then she remembered the Shakers didn't have pets. Not even kittens.

Every morning when Flynn got up, he wondered if this would be the day he would have to take Leatrice and find another place to live. It had been over two months since Silas had brought Irene Black home as his wife. Flynn didn't hold that against him. The man was doing what he thought best for Leatrice. He hadn't realized that just any woman couldn't come into the house and make a difference. Especially that woman.

Silas was still coughing at night and couldn't shake the ague that beset him from time to time. He seemed so low, Flynn hesitated to do anything to make the man feel worse. Instead, Flynn kept Leatrice away from Irene.

He let Leatrice know she had to mind her manners around Irene. That took some convincing and more than a week of plates carried to the child in her bedroom, but eventually they got to the point where they could sit down at the supper table together. They didn't have to worry about breakfast, because Irene wasn't an early riser. And the midday meal could be packed out to the barn or wherever Flynn was working.

Breakfast was the best time. Leatrice fried their eggs and Silas always said they were the best he'd ever eaten, no matter how they came out of the skillet. Then he'd slice a piece of the bread he'd made, drizzle honey on it for Leatrice, and tell her the honey was what made her so sweet.

"I like doing it," he told Flynn about making the bread. "Irene cooks plenty of other things. You have to admit we're eating better now."

Flynn did have to admit that. The woman was a good cook, and she kept the house swept and ready for company. Not that they had company. Irene was continually complaining about being isolated here on the farm, but then the woman complained about everything. Especially about Silas. He kept his silence, but Flynn had to wonder if he and Leatrice were the only ones sorry to be sharing a house with Irene.

But what could the man do? He'd married her. Some things had to be accepted and that was that. At the same time, Flynn couldn't ignore how things might go from bad to worse to make him need somewhere else to live. With money he had set aside and a loan from the bank, he could get a place. But he didn't feel right leaving Silas. The man was too weak to even cut wood for the fire. No way could he keep up the farm.

That was why Flynn was glad to hear about a place not far up the road for sale. It wasn't much of a farm. Only ten acres, but it had a house and a barn. The house's roof leaked and the windows were boarded up. But the barn was in fair shape. He could fix up the house and build corrals. He'd never been afraid of hard work. Best of all, he'd be close enough to help Silas.

The only thing holding Flynn back was telling Silas. The man wasn't well. Irene made him a special tonic, but he kept getting worse instead of better. Flynn couldn't help wondering what she put in that tonic. Whatever it was, it wasn't helping.

But he had to admit Irene did take care of Silas. She made sure he sat near the fire and wrapped blankets around his knees. And she acted sweet as sugar to Leatrice, but nothing about her rang true to Flynn.

Leatrice didn't warm to her. The child stiffened, as though poised to run, every time she was near the woman. Sometimes Flynn had the same urge to escape when the woman smiled at him. Not the right kind of smile, and she had a way of stepping too close in the kitchen. But it was a small room. A brush against him as she moved about the table didn't have to be intentional. That was what he tried to believe.

Even so, things couldn't go on the way they were. Leatrice begged him every morning to go back to visit the Shakers.

But a man couldn't just show up at their barns without a reason to be there. He'd finished with the horse Sawyer. Had him back to being a useful animal.

Thinking about the horse brought to mind the woman he'd seen in the barn that one morning. She had looked burdened down not only by the child she carried but also by the sadness of losing her husband. He understood that kind of burden.

At least she didn't have to feel the guilt that could rear up in Flynn when he thought about Lena. He should have kept it from happening, but it did no good to dwell on that. What had happened couldn't be changed.

Moving to a new place might be good, even if leaving behind this farm he'd come to feel of as his own wouldn't be easy. Roots were hard to pull up when a man loved the land he walked across. But saplings could be transplanted and Leatrice needed a change. He sometimes heard her talking to the kittens in the loft, and while he couldn't make out the words, she didn't sound happy. Not since Silas had brought Irene home.

Still, he put off telling Silas, even after he made a deal for the Harley place. He could wait a little longer until Silas felt better.

But things changed the night he came in late, after checking on a mare ready to foal. The day had been warm with a summer feel. If the weather held, he aimed to head over to the new place and work on the roof. Silas wouldn't have to know where he was and Leatrice could go with him. Maybe she'd think it an adventure, like going to the Shakers.

In the house all was quiet with everybody abed. Some embers glowed in the fireplace and he knelt down to add a log to keep the fire going till morning. Could be while he was down on his knees, he should ask the Lord for help with how to tell Silas about his new place. Flynn didn't pray enough. Hadn't ever prayed enough. But that didn't mean he didn't think he should. A man ought to pay attention to what the Lord had in mind for him.

When he lived with the McEntyres after his mother left for Virginia, he liked sitting at the table with them while they read the Bible and prayed. Ma McEntyre could pray up rain in the midst of a drought. She prayed about everything and never failed to pray for Flynn. Sometimes he wondered if she kept praying for him after she went to live with her son. He always hoped so.

He smiled as he remembered those prayers. "Help this boy do right." "Keep him on the right paths." "Forgive him when he does wrong 'cause he's just a boy." "Thank you, Lord, for sending him to us."

She'd prayed the day Pa McEntyre fell off the barn roof, but not what Flynn expected her to pray. While Flynn checked to see if the old man had survived the fall, she looked up and said, "Lord, if'n you is ready for Pa, then I ain't gonna stand in his way to move on to paradise."

Flynn had wanted to stand in his way. He wanted the old man to keep drawing breath, but instead Flynn had dug his grave. He remembered Ma McEntyre's prayer while Lena lay dying, but he wasn't about to pray the same. He didn't care how ready the Lord might be for Lena. He wanted to hold her with him. But she had died anyway.

Flynn bent his head as he knelt there, but no prayer words came to mind. Ma McEntyre had tried to teach him about praying. "You don't need no fancy words, son. The Lord, he knows what you need. You do right and he'll take care of you."

He did try to do right. Not cheat anybody. Give an honest day's work to earn his hire. He'd been faithful and cleaved to his wife without wayward thoughts. He went to church on occasion. Maybe not often enough, but no church was all that near and horses needed feeding on Sunday the same as any other day.

"But I could've done better than I've done about that." He whispered the words into the dark. Once he started, words did come to him. "Help me figure out the best thing to do, Lord. You see and know everything. Future and past. Help me with the now."

He paused a minute and then mumbled, "Amen." He'd once heard a preacher say the word *amen* meant so be it. That when a person said amen after a prayer, it meant he was ready to accept whatever answer the Lord might send down, whether it was what he wanted or not. What other choice did a man have?

He could almost see Ma McEntyre frowning at him for thinking that. Her words whispered through his mind as though she were right beside him. *The Lord's answers are not just the best answers but the only answers.*

"But what about him taking my Lena?"

Bad things happen. That's when you have to depend on the Lord to help you through.

"Help me through." He didn't know whether he was just echoing what he was imagining Ma McEntyre telling him or sending another prayer heavenward.

With a sigh, he stood up. Time to shrug off problems and get some sleep. In his bedroom, the curtains were pulled tightly together over the window so no moonlight slipped into the room. He felt his way to a chair to take off his boots. He hung his pants on the back of the chair and pulled off his shirt.

He had the odd feeling he wasn't alone in the room. All that thinking about Ma McEntyre, he supposed. The bed creaked when he sat down on it. A hand slid down his backbone.

He jumped up and whirled around.

Irene Black laughed softly. "I've been waiting for you."

17

Flynn grabbed his pants off the chair and jerked them on before turning to face the woman again.

"What are you doing in here?" His eyes had adjusted enough to the darkness to make out her shape under the quilt on his bed.

She raised herself up on one elbow and laughed again. "I think you know exactly what I'm doing in here."

"Get out." He kept his voice low but put force in it. "Right now."

"Come, come, Flynn." She sat all the way up then and let the quilt fall away from her. He was relieved to see she had on a nightgown. "Don't be in such a hurry to kick me out. The old man is sound asleep. I gave him a double dose of my special tonic. So what he doesn't know won't hurt him."

"Out." He pointed toward the door.

"You don't really want me to leave. I know men. They like a woman in their bed."

"Go get in the bed you made when you married Silas."

"He's so old." She stood up and flipped open the window curtains to let in the moonlight. "And sick."

"For better or worse. In sickness and health. That's what you promised, isn't it?"

"I'm not leaving him. I'm right here in his house." She stepped toward him. "He just wants somebody to cook for him and take care of your daughter. For that I should get some kind of reward, don't you think? Something more than sleeping with an old man whose hands can't stop shaking. Poor man isn't long for this world."

He shifted away from her. "Go on back to your bedroom and we'll pretend this never happened."

She stayed where she was, her teeth showing in a smile. "Do you know much about the Bible, Flynn?"

He ignored her question. "I want you out of here right now."

She didn't seem bothered by his words. "In the Bible there's this story about Joseph and Potiphar's wife." Her smile got wider. "I can tell by your face you do know the story. Potiphar's wife liked Joseph and invited him to like her. He was foolish and ran away, but then Potiphar's wife told Potiphar Joseph attacked her. I could do that too. Think of how hard Silas will take it when I tell him you forced me into your bed."

"Tell him anything you like. Silas is no fool. He'll know which of us to believe."

"Are you sure? He may be old, but he's still a man and he knows how a man can be carried away by his desires." She gave him a long look. "I'm sure you know all about manly desires."

"I have no desire for you, Irene. None. If you won't leave, I will." He grabbed his shirt and boots and headed for the door.

"Coward," she whispered behind him. When that didn't slow him down, she went on. "Aren't you afraid to leave me alone with your daughter?"

He stopped and turned back toward her. "You stay away from Leatrice."

"What's she told you?" She laughed yet again. "Surely not that crazy story about bears."

"What about bears?" He wanted to see what the woman might say.

"Oh, nothing." She waved as though to shoo away his question. "Nothing at all. Just a fairy tale."

"Where bears eat little children?" He fixed his stare on her. "Is that the kind of fairy tale you like to tell?"

"You said it. Not me." She shrugged. "The girl needs somebody to tell her something. Silas is right that she needs a mother."

"He was wrong to think that could be you."

"He only married me because you wouldn't. Perhaps in his own misguided way, he was thinking to bring you a wife and your daughter a mother before he passed on."

"Of this you can be sure." He narrowed his eyes and stepped a little closer to her. "I would have never married you. I will never marry you."

Her smile didn't waver. "Men. Such foolish creatures. Unable to realize what's best for them." She reached to lay her hand on his chest. "I could definitely be best for you. In so many ways."

He shoved her hand away and moved back. "Go to bed, Irene."

"You should be saying, 'Come to bed, Irene.' I could make you smile again."

He stared at her without saying anything. He was weary of talking to her. He just wanted her out of his sight.

"Papa." Leatrice called to him from her bedroom door. She sounded very small and frightened.

"The princess calls. Best go protect her from the bears." Irene raised her voice on the word "bears."

He didn't bother responding as he went across the sitting room to Leatrice's door. "I'm here, sweetheart. What are you doing awake?"

"I heard you talking." She peeked around him. "Are bears here?"

"No, no bears." He put his hand on her head. "Miss Irene was talking nonsense." He didn't look around to see if the woman had followed him out of his room. Better to simply ignore her.

"Bears scare me." Leatrice's lips quivered.

"Bears can be scary if you see them and maybe even scarier if you're only imagining them, but no bears are around here. So you can stop imagining them."

"How, Papa?"

"By thinking about something else whenever scary thoughts slip into your mind. Flowers or wading in a creek."

"Or my kittens. I'd rather think about them than bears."

"That's the thing then." He turned her toward her bed. "Now back under the covers. A girl needs her sleep."

"You need sleep too, don't you, Papa?"

"I do. So let's get some snoring going."

"Will you stay with me for a while?" She looked toward the window.

"No bears." He leaned down to look her in the face. "Remember, no bears."

"I know, but I might have a bad dream."

"If you do, I'll be here." He pulled Ma Beatrice's quilt up over her. He ran his hand over the stitching as Leatrice settled on the pillow her grandmother had stuffed with feathers.

A woman did have a way of holding things together. The right woman. Ma Beatrice would be chasing Irene out of her house with a broom. Silas had picked right the first time, but every way wrong with Irene. But this time he hadn't married for love.

No, that wasn't right. Silas had married for love. For the love of this child in front of Flynn. The problem was the man had rushed headlong into marriage without proper thought.

"Is Grandpa all right?" Leatrice's eyes were very round.

"He's asleep."

"I don't hear him coughing. He's always coughing."

"It's good then that he's not," Flynn said.

"Not if he's dead like Mamaw Bea." Her eyes got even wider.

"He's just sleeping." He hoped that was so anyway. Her worries had him wanting to go shake Silas awake to be sure he was all right. Flynn glanced back through Leatrice's door into the sitting room. No sign of Irene. That was good. He didn't care where she was, as long as it was away from him.

"Do you like her?" The child's lips were trembling again.

"Who? Mamaw Bea?"

Leatrice shook her head against her pillow. "Her." She pointed toward the doorway, then clutched the edge of the quilt under her chin.

"Are you afraid of Miss Irene?" Flynn asked a question of his own instead of answering hers. Some things were better not spoken aloud.

"Not when you're with me."

"But what about when I'm not with you?"

She let go of the quilt and snaked a hand out to grab his arm. "Please don't leave me here with her. By myself."

"No worries, little one. I won't." He caressed her cheek. "But what has she done that has you so scared?"

"I don't know." Leatrice looked down at the quilt.

He had the feeling she knew exactly why she was scared of Irene, but he didn't push her to tell him more. "You can stay with me or Grandpa Silas. You don't have to stay with her."

"Grandpa is sick, isn't he?"

"His cough is bad." He had to be honest with her.

"Because of getting cold when I went out on the pond? Did that make him sick?"

"He was already coughing before that."

"Maybe he needs some medicine."

"Don't worry about him." Flynn smoothed back her hair. "Miss Irene makes him tonics."

"I don't think they help." She bit her bottom lip as if worried she'd said something she shouldn't have.

"Why do you say that?"

She pulled in a breath and let it whoosh out. "Don't tell her I told you, but last week when I was filling up our glasses from the water bucket, I saw her mixing some stuff in Grandpa's tonic."

"Stuff?" Flynn frowned. "What stuff?"

"I don't know. Black powdery stuff that smelled awful. She said it was a secret ingredient to make Grandpa better." Leatrice sneaked another look past Flynn toward the doorway. She lowered her voice to a whisper. "She told me not to tell anybody, since secret ingredients won't work if people know about them. But I'm telling you, not Grandpa. So it could still work if she was telling the truth. Do you think she was telling the truth?"

"Maybe."

"I don't think she was. When she wasn't looking, I put my finger in some of the powder she spilled and touched it to my tongue. It was nasty."

"Medicines don't always taste good."

"But this was worse than that. I had to run outside to throw up. When I came back in, that woman laughed like she knew what I had done and was glad I got sick."

Flynn wasn't sure what to say. He didn't want to make Leatrice even more frightened of Irene, but then again perhaps she should be. It could be they all should be. He took Leatrice's hand in his. "But you're all right now."

"Maybe because I threw up." Leatrice blinked to keep back tears. "Can't you make her go away, Papa? Please."

If only he could, but Flynn shook his head. "She's Grandpa's wife. I can't make her leave, but we can find another place to live."

"With the Shakers?" She seemed excited about that.

"No, but maybe you can go to school there."

That made her smile. Flynn smoothed the quilts down over her and kissed her forehead. "Now go to sleep. I'll stay here with you for a while."

"To make sure the bears don't get in."

"I told you no bears." Seemed to him bears were the least of their worries. "Oh, did you happen to see where Miss Irene put her secret ingredient?" Whatever Leatrice had seen, he needed to check it out.

Leatrice nodded. "Up on the top shelf in the cabinet, but

the next morning I got a chair and looked for it before she got up and it wasn't there. I couldn't find it in any of the cabinets. She must have hidden it."

Flynn pushed a smile out on his face. "Well, it was a secret ingredient. Now don't worry. I'll take care of it. You just turn over and go to sleep."

He stroked her back until she was breathing in and out slowly. Then he leaned against her bed and stared at the moonlight coming through her window. He thought about raising the window to let in some fresh air, but then he remembered the window was nailed shut against those bears Leatrice was afraid were coming for her. All because of that woman, as Leatrice called her.

What was he going to do? He thought he had it figured out by buying the house down the road, but if Leatrice was right about Irene's tonic, he couldn't leave Silas alone with her. But then, how could he be sure she wasn't putting that secret ingredient in all their food?

Surely Leatrice was wrong about that. All sorts of roots and herbs went into tonics, many with vile tastes. But whether the tonic was harmless or not, Irene had still been in his bed. He had no idea what she might try next, and in spite of how he said Silas wouldn't believe her if she accused Flynn of attacking her, that might not be true. Whether Silas had just married her for a cook or not, Flynn couldn't be sure the man hadn't developed feelings for the woman.

His head drooped. *Dear Lord, I don't know how things got in such a mess. But I need help to know what to do.*

He raised his head and stared at the window. Maybe he should take Leatrice to the Shakers where at least she would be safe. Just until he got the house at the new place fixed up. Meanwhile he could keep living here with Silas to watch Irene. He could always claim a horse needed extra attention and sleep in the barn. Tomorrow he'd talk to Silas.

***

Something woke Leatrice. When she opened her eyes, it was dark. Even darker than when her father had come into her room. The moon had been shining then. Now the moonlight was gone, but morning hadn't come.

She held her breath and listened for whatever had awakened her. Maybe bears scratching on the window. No, Papa said there weren't any bears. He never lied to her. That was why he hadn't answered when she asked if he liked that woman. He didn't want to say he didn't, but he wouldn't lie and say he did. She knew he didn't like her. She didn't know how Grandpa could like her enough to marry her.

But what if her father just didn't know about the bears? They could be bears that only came around when it was too dark to see them. Would she be able to see them if they were scratching on the window? She pulled in a breath for courage and pushed up on her elbow to look toward the window. Nothing there, but right beside her bed, her father was stretched out sleeping on the floor.

Poor Papa. He couldn't be comfortable on the hard floor. And he didn't have any covers. She had two quilts. As carefully as she could, she put her feet on the floor without touching him. She moved over to his other side before she reached for the edge of her top quilt and pulled it over her father. He grunted a little but didn't open his eyes.

She wanted to tuck the quilt around him the way Mamaw Bea used to tuck the covers around her, but that would be

172

sure to wake him up. Instead she tiptoed around him again and crawled back in bed.

Something caught her eye at her bedroom door. A shadow moved. That woman was in the door. Leatrice closed her eyes as if she hadn't seen her and breathed in and out like she was asleep before she opened one eye a slit. She was still there, probably smiling because she knew Leatrice was afraid. When at last the woman left, Leatrice lay very still and listened. A door creaked open and then closed. Her grandpa coughed.

Leatrice turned on her side where she could see her father. He was asleep, but he'd wake up if something tried to bother her, whether it was bears or that woman.

Then she wondered if that woman had been lurking there earlier while she and her father talked. She might have heard Leatrice tell Papa about the secret ingredient. What if that made the woman put that stuff in Leatrice's food? Or Papa's?

She scrunched her eyes shut tight and tried to remember the prayer Mamaw Bea had taught her. Or maybe it was a Bible verse. Something about how much God loved her. Loved everybody. Maybe even that woman.

The words wouldn't come straight in her head, but she did remember the one Mamaw told her to whisper when she had to go to the outhouse at night. It was scary after dark in the outhouse. Not as bad as the cellar, because nobody ever locked her in the outhouse. She could run back to the house. Mamaw Bea hadn't made fun of her being scared. She'd understood and told her to repeat this verse. *Fear thou not, for I am with thee.*

It was easier to fear not when both the Lord was with her and her father was right there beside her bed.

18

APRIL 1850

I welcomed spring with a lighter heart than I thought possible back when winter darkened my thoughts. Anna Grace was the reason. While I still missed Walter and ever would, I embraced this time of new beginnings and refused to think beyond each golden day.

This day Anna Grace was fussy. I had already nursed her, but she still wanted to sing her unhappy song. Morning was coming, but now night still ruled. I guessed another hour before the rising bell would sound in the village.

We had no clocks. Such were not allowed in the retiring rooms. Time was measured by the village bell. Rising time. Retiring time. Mealtimes. Worship times. But after a while, whether one had a working timepiece or not, a person developed an internal clock that rang different sorts of bells. Such was especially true for a mother with the demands of a nursing baby.

Sister Helene slipped out of her bed and tiptoed across the space between us. "Let me take her." She spoke in a whisper to keep from waking Sister Ellie and Sister Genna. "You should rest a few more minutes before the day begins."

I handed Anna Grace over without hesitation. I knew my child would be held with love. Anna Grace brought joy to our retiring room, even at times like this when she could not settle to sleep. Sister Helene starred in our group at those times by walking the floor with the baby and softly singing Shaker songs into her ears.

"We can't let her cries disturb the others in our house," Sister Helene said.

I knew she meant that, but I also knew she liked the feel of my baby's head resting on her shoulder while she walked back and forth between our beds. She knew which of the floorboards squeaked and stepped over those every time.

Sister Ellie did the same, but I thought Sister Genna stepped on them purposefully. She, the same as I, resisted the Shaker way. We were both captives of circumstances, hers different than mine but no easier to change. Her husband had gone to the frontier to find a new start.

"He insisted he could do that faster without me along. 'You go stay with the Shakers for a few months,' he said. 'No longer than a year and I'll come back for you once I get settled out west.'" Sister Genna had shared her story without tears but not without anger warring with worry in her eyes. "And so here I am. Trapped in this village unless Jeremy returns."

"Perhaps he will yet. Something might have delayed him," Sister Ellie said.

We were together in our retiring room during the time of contemplation before the evening meal. Sister Helene was with Eldress Maria. Sister Genna had waited to tell us her story when Sister Helene was not with us.

"She is kindness through and through, but she believes she must follow the rules. Well, except for Anna Grace." Sister Genna's face softened as she looked at the baby in her cradle. Then her face hardened. "I have followed none of the rules, even to that of telling the truth. The two of you are the only ones I have not lied to."

"What lies have you told?" I asked. "Other than perhaps, the same as I, pretending that you might eventually follow the Shaker way."

"That I haven't done. I am not a Shaker and could never be one. Nay, I told the leaders I was a widow so they would allow me in. They do not like to take only one of a marital union. They advise one to convince the reluctant spouse to come into the Shaker village too or to wait until one can do so. Especially if it is the husband who is reluctant."

Sister Ellie nodded. "Yea, that is true. I was resistant to the point of rebellion when my husband began talking of coming to the Shakers, but a wife is bound to do whatever her husband says." She looked down at her hands to hide the tears that seemed to come more often now when she thought of her Abby here in the Shaker village and her other children who had left. She grieved not sharing their lives the way she wished to do. "Sometimes I think I should have simply refused to come. He is a good man. He might have paid me some mind, but now he is a complete Shaker. He will never leave this place."

"But you can." Sister Genna looked straight at Sister Ellie. "You have a daughter who will take you in."

"But what of Abby? And of my marriage vows?"

"Such vows matter little in this place," Sister Genna said. "Or perhaps wherever my Jeremy has roamed. He might have met a more likely woman. One who could give him living children. One he did not have to travel back to Kentucky to get."

I reached to hold her hand. "It has not been a full year. He might yet return or send you money for a stage to wherever he might be."

Sister Genna's face had lightened a bit. "That is true. It is just that I fear lying and saying I am a widow might dare fate to make it so."

She still had no tears. Her sadness went deeper than that. Sister Ellie and I could do nothing but offer her our love and prayers. Just as the two of them, and Sister Helene too, were offering their love to me and to Anna Grace.

Both Sister Genna and Sister Ellie were rocks for me during Anna Grace's first weeks. Each had nursed babies through various ailments, and even though Sister Genna had lost her little one before he could have his first birthday, she knew much about being a mother.

After Anna Grace's too early entry into the world, we shared many times of worry. Anna Grace was so very small and appeared to have a tenuous hold on life. But we nursed her through every concern. We, because of the love of my sisters. While I was Anna Grace's mother, Sisters Ellie, Genna, and Helene were the aunts and grannies. I did believe each of them would have lain down and died for Anna Grace the same as I.

While not the mother-father family unit I believed the Lord planned for his people in spite of the Shaker teachings to the contrary, four sisters to one little baby seemed a perfect Shaker plan for taking care of an infant. Much better than a roomful of children to one or two Shaker sisters. Not only better for the child, but better for the sisters as well.

We still had our assigned duties in the Shaker village. All had to work with their hands here in order to live the Shaker way. Hands to work, hearts to God. Once I was able again, I was given the task of cleaning in our Gathering Family House. Only on the sisters' side of the house, for Eldress Maria said it would not do for me to carry a baby into the brethren's side.

The duty was not easy. In the retiring rooms, every corner needed dusting and sometimes scrubbing. A dead fly missed and left on a windowsill distressed Eldress Maria and brought a lecture on the necessity of cleanliness.

"We must clean our rooms well, Sister Darcie, for good spirits will not live where there is dirt. Our Mother Ann assures us there is no dirt in heaven, and we want our village to be heaven on earth," Eldress Maria told me at least three times a week.

Often she would tell me the same was true of my heart. "If one is not vigilant, dirty little corners can hide in one's heart. Those must be swept clean before one can become a proper Believer."

"Yea." I always nodded as though I agreed with whatever she said and at times promised to take a mental broom to my heart to rid it of unclean corners and to sweep unclean thoughts from my mind. Not that I had such thoughts. My mind was occupied with how best I could care for my baby.

Everywhere I turned, the eldress seemed to be watching, as though to be sure I properly cleaned every spot in the retiring rooms. At least that was what I believed at first. Then I noted how she would wait until she thought I was too busy sweeping or dusting to notice and surreptitiously reach to caress Anna Grace's cheek or straighten her wrappings.

Sister Genna unkindly said she was probably looking for dirt, but I knew that wasn't so. Anna Grace made Eldress Maria smile, and for the good of all of us, I pretended not to notice. She had the power to send Anna Grace and me to the Children's House, and I had no desire to move away from these sisters who loved us.

I already walked the length of the village to take my meals at the Children's House, since Eldress Maria said I could not bring a baby into our Gathering Family eating room. I could hardly leave Anna Grace alone in our room two floors above. I did not mind the walk or being among the children with their fresh faces. The same as the adults, they were silent during the meals so I could not talk with them.

Sister Corinne, the one in charge of all the children, appeared to be very strict, but the other sisters smiled often and quietly corrected any misbehavior. At times they touched this or that child's shoulder with affection, especially if the child looked sad, for not all the children were smiling. Some looked a little lost, as though they missed their mothers.

Perhaps I merely imagined that loneliness because I worried of what might happen when Anna Grace was old enough to be weaned. I had no idea what age the Shakers might insist that happen. I could have asked Sister Lettie, but I did not. I thought it better to simply embrace the blessing of each day.

Sister Lettie came to check on Anna Grace so often I began to worry something might be wrong. But when I asked, Sister Lettie laughed as only she could. Free and easy.

"Nay, young sister. I just like having my hands on a sweet baby again. You and your sisters here are doing a fine job of taking care of this one." She peered over at me, perhaps aware I did not embrace the Shaker beliefs. "See, it is a good thing to have sisters to help you."

"Yea."

That I could not argue even if I knew that only one of the sisters in my room was a committed Believer. Sister Helene did believe the Shaker way was the only way open to her. No, I said that wrong. She believed the Shaker life was the best way open to her. She did not look at the road out of the village with any kind of desire. She had come to the village at a young age and had grown up in the Children's House the same as the children who sat around me at mealtimes.

When I went to the Children's House for my meals, I kept Anna Grace swaddled in a wrap close to my body and shakered my plate every time. Then I returned to the Gathering Family House to chase every iota of dirt out of the sisters' rooms in order to please Eldress Maria.

This morning Sister Helene walked the floor until the gray light of dawn stole into our room. Then she settled the baby in her cradle just as the rising bell began to clang. I had not gone back to sleep but instead had watched her walk my baby back and forth long after Anna Grace was surely sleeping. I had often done the same for the joy of holding her close, smelling her sweet baby scent and letting her fine hair tickle my cheek.

With the rising bell, we began our morning routine by sharing the small dressing room off our retiring room. A pitcher of water and a bowl let us do our morning ablutions. Plus we had a chamber pot, so we didn't have to make the trek out to the privy during the night hours.

We had no time for dallying, as we all had duties before the morning meal. Sister Ellie had kitchen duty this month, and Sister Genna was weeding the strawberry rows during the day but cleaned two of the brethren's rooms before the morning meal. The weeding was hard on the back, she said, but she liked being outside instead of having laundry duty or candle making. The Shakers had huge patches of strawberries. The sweet jams they made from the berries were delicious on our biscuits.

My duty was to clean our room first. I hurried to empty the slop jar before Sister Helene had to leave for her morning duty. She never spoke about her morning duties, merely saying it was a necessary task. Sister Genna, ever the realist, was sure Sister Helene was one of the watchers in the early morning hours.

"Watchers?" At first I didn't know what Sister Genna meant, but then I remembered Sister Helene's warning that somebody was always watching in the Shaker village to make certain all behaved according to Shaker rules. "Oh, those assigned the duty of keeping an eye on what is happening in the village."

"Yea." Sister Genna snorted. "The elders and eldresses intend to prevent any wrong male-female behavior."

It did not seem a proper job for sweet Sister Helene. To have the duty of watching for misconduct from her lookout post, wherever that might be. Sister Genna told me to look up the next time I was outside, and I would note where watchers could stand in attic windows or even in the roof gables.

"And here in our room," Sister Genna added.

"But Sister Helene loves us," I protested.

"I don't deny that, but not more than she loves the Shaker rules." Sister Genna glanced toward the door to be sure no one could overhear her words. "If you are wise, you will be careful what you say in front of our sweet sister."

"I don't believe Sister Helene means anything but good for us," I insisted.

"I can agree with that. But her idea of what is good and our idea of what is good might be different. Trust me on this, Sister Darcie, and guard your time with your little one by careful rule following. I would greatly miss my little sister should Eldress Maria decide to move you from our room." She had kissed Anna Grace's head before she hurried off to her duty.

I remembered that conversation on this day as I hurried back up the stairs to our room. Sister Helene was dressed with her bonnet carefully adjusted and her cloak around her shoulders, for the air was still cool on this April morning.

She reached down to gently rock Anna Grace's cradle. "Our little sister smiled at me when I tucked her cover around her a moment ago. She will be a wonderful Shaker sister someday."

I did not tell her I prayed that would not happen. I did not wish the Shaker life on my child. Or on me. Instead my curiosity got the better of me. "What duties do you have today?"

"I am assigned to the dye room to ready our yarn for the looms. It is not my favorite task, but that is why we rotate duties. So no one has a duty they do not like for too long. I do like mixing the dyes, but I always end up with blue or brown hands." She smiled at me. "Worry not. I will be sure to scrub my hands before I pick up Anna Grace."

"I'm not worried. I see how you care for her."

"Yea, it is easy to love her. It makes me understand better

the anguish some of the sisters feel when they come into our society and are parted from their children."

"But you still believe the Shaker way best?"

"Oh, yea. It is the only way we can live as they do in heaven. As sisters and brothers. It is as our Mother Ann instructed." Her face softened again as she looked toward the cradle. "But I am glad to be able to help with such a little angel sister."

After she left the room, I picked up Anna Grace and held her close as I looked out the window at the Shakers moving around on the walkways. Like so many ants. All the same with their like dress and bonnets or hats. No, that wasn't true. Each one was different. Just as I was different. All with their own stories and their own reasons to be here. Some because they wanted to walk the Shaker path. Others perhaps like me, with no options other than the Shaker roof.

"I don't know how, but we will find a way out of this place. With the Lord's help," I whispered.

"Have faith in the providence of the Lord." Granny Hatchell's words slipped through my mind.

"I do have faith, Lord. You sent me Walter when I needed him and you gave me Anna Grace when you took him from me. I will wait for your answer."

I put Anna Grace back in her cradle to finish my cleaning before the morning meal. When it was near time for the bell to summon the Shakers to breakfast, I positioned Anna Grace in the wrap to head toward the Children's House. To share in the meal, I had to be on time.

As I stepped out into the hallway, the warbling cry of a baby came to my ears. Not Anna Grace, content next to my breast. Sister Helene appeared at the top of the stairs, carrying a bundle. Her face showed a mixture of relief and distress when she saw me.

"Oh, Sister Darcie. I'm glad you are still here. I feared you might have already left."

Eldress Maria appeared behind her, panting from her climb up the stairs.

"What is it? Do you have a baby?" I asked. That didn't seem possible, but the sounds coming from the ragged bundle were unmistakably made by a baby.

"Yea. I saw him on the washhouse steps and hurried to fetch him. Poor dear."

"On the washhouse steps?" I couldn't take it in, even after she pulled the ragged blanket away from the baby's red face. His little mouth was wide open, with his tongue quivering because of his fearful cries.

"Someone deserted him there." Eldress Maria had caught her breath enough to speak. "Sister Lettie says you can nurse him along with Anna Grace."

Sister Lettie appeared at the top of the stairs then. She fanned her face with her hand. "My dear Sister Helene, there was no reason to run with the child. He is not in imminent danger of expiring. I'm too old to be rushing up these stairs like that."

"But you said—" Sister Helene started, but Sister Lettie waved away her words.

"I said the infant would have a better chance to thrive if our young sister here nurses him." Sister Lettie looked directly at me then. "The poor tyke needs a bath and clean clothes and food you can supply him."

"Yea."

Sister Lettie must have heard the worry in my word. "Never fear, young sister. You will have plenty for your baby and for this poor abandoned waif. Think of how his mother threw him away."

"Nay," Sister Helene said softly. "She did not. She brought him to us because she knew we were kind and would care for him. Perhaps she was like Moses's mother who sent her daughter to watch the basket with Moses to be sure he was all right."

Eldress Maria turned stern eyes on Sister Helene. "Did you see whoever left this baby?"

"Nay, I only saw the bundle on the steps and went to see what it might be."

Sister Lettie clapped her hands as if to dismiss all that. "We can worry about that later. Now we must take care of this new soul. Come, Sister Darcie. Back into your room. Your Anna Grace seems content enough. Let us make this child as content."

Sister Helene laid the baby on one of the beds and peeled back the ragged covers. The baby had nothing on.

"How old?" I placed Anna Grace back in her cradle and grabbed one of her clean blankets out of the drawer.

"Maybe a day. Maybe two." Sister Lettie cleaned the baby's bottom and then rubbed his legs. "He's cold and hungry."

"Here, let me have him." I wrapped the clean blanket around him and put him to my breast. After a bit of urging, he figured out what to do and he sucked eagerly. Poor little fellow. He needed me. "I will take care of him. And Anna Grace."

"Yea, of course you will. Sister Helene can assist you today with bringing water for the infant's bath and the morning meal for you." Sister Lettie looked at the eldress again. "Such can be arranged, can it not?"

"Yea." Eldress Maria agreed, but she looked as if she'd been blindsided by a runaway horse. Two babies in a house where there were to be no babies. But she did not argue with Sister Lettie. Instead, she sighed heavily as she turned to leave the room. "I will have someone bring a cradle. Sister Helene, do whatever Sister Lettie asks of you."

"Yea." Sister Helene was beside me, her eyes fastened on the baby boy I held. She waited until the door closed behind Eldress Maria. "Will he be all right?"

Sister Lettie didn't answer and silence built in the room. The baby stopped sucking, too exhausted from his ordeal to continue. His skin was splotchy red and his little bit of dark hair stuck up in points. His eyes opened just a slit, but he didn't cry, as though he knew his demands would be met. At last.

When Sister Lettie finally answered Sister Helene, her voice was soft. "If the Lord wills it so."

The bell to summon everyone to the morning meal began to chime then. The noise startled the baby in my arms and he opened his mouth to cry. I held him closer. He pushed out a breath and settled against me. Yes, I could take care of two babies.

19

"Why you are so dead set against Irene?" Silas frowned at Flynn. "What's she done besides cook us some decent meals?"

And betray the vows she made to you by sneaking into my bedroom. But Flynn couldn't say that. Silas wasn't ready to hear it. He didn't appear to want to hear any complaint against Irene this morning. He was moving slow, as though he had to think about each step he took. Whatever Irene had given him a double dose of the night before was still working on him.

Silas had come out to the barn to hitch the team to the wagon, so they were away from Irene's hearing and from Leatrice's too. The little girl had climbed down from the loft to retrieve one of the kittens she spotted climbing on the woodpile.

Irene wanted to go to the store. Flynn hoped Silas had money for whatever Irene thought she needed. He didn't like the idea of running up a tab at the store. It was bad enough he now owed the bank after buying the Harley place, but owing for land was different than owing for new hats or buttons and bows.

Flynn bent back to mucking out the stalls. This was about more than the frills a woman might want. He needed to find the right words to warn Silas. That morning, Flynn had been up before daylight. After he stirred the fire to a flame, he lit a taper and searched the kitchen for the tin with the black powder Leatrice had seen. He hadn't found it.

He'd like to believe Leatrice was wrong, but he didn't think she'd made up seeing the black powder. That was why not finding something like that in the cabinet worried him. If it had been there on a shelf, that would mean Irene had no reason to conceal whatever it was. But it was gone.

Or perhaps not gone, just hidden, as Leatrice said. The child didn't like Irene. For that matter, Flynn didn't like Irene. Her coming into his bedroom was reprehensible. Her threatening Leatrice was unforgivable. Her trying to poison Silas was criminal. So even if it did upset Silas, he had to warn him.

Before he figured out how best to say what needed saying, Silas spoke up. "Irene said you'd try to turn me against her. That you'd be jealous."

Flynn set the pitchfork down and stepped out of the stall to look at Silas on the other side of the wagon. "You know that's not true, Silas. I would never do anything to hurt you. You're like a father to me."

"I know." Silas stared down at the ground for a few seconds. "I told her she was wrong. It's just that she's in my ear all the day long and half the night about this or that. Sometimes I think I'm losing my mind."

"That cough is getting you down. You seem to be feeling

worse all the time." Flynn hesitated, but he had to say it. "Could be you might ought to skip that tonic Irene's been making for you and get something at the doctor when you are in town today. I don't think her tonic is helping you."

"To be honest, I've been thinking the same thing. Seems like it makes my legs feel like two logs and my hands shake." Silas held a hand over the wagon to show how it trembled. "I can't hardly do anything anymore."

"Why don't you try it without the tonic for a few days?"

"Irene will get mad if I don't drink it." Silas looked worried.

"Just pretend to and pour it out. She doesn't have to see you. That way you can figure out if you feel better when you don't take it without getting her bothered."

Silas fiddled with the harness he was holding. Flynn was afraid he'd upset the man. But instead Silas looked up, straight at Flynn. "You don't really think she's trying to poison me, do you?"

Flynn hesitated.

Silas's gaze didn't waver. "Tell me the truth."

"I don't want to believe that, but I'm not at all sure she isn't." He'd gone this far. He might as well tell it all. "Leatrice saw her putting something she thought looked bad in the drink."

"A little girl can't know what herbs are good and which ones aren't."

"You're right. But Leatrice is worried about you. She loves you, Silas." Again he hesitated.

Silas stared at him. "Go ahead and say whatever it is you're wanting to say."

"I don't think Irene loves you. I think she's just using you."

"For what?"

"That I don't know, but if I were you, I wouldn't drink any more of that tonic. And I wouldn't let her know I wasn't drinking it. Just to be on the safe side."

"Safe." Silas looked off toward the open barn door. "I grew up here on this farm. Never had any reason not to feel safe. This is home. Always has been, but after I lost Beatrice, it's not the same. Nothing's the same."

"The cholera taking Ma Beatrice was hard. You two were married a long time."

"Thirty some years. She always wanted more children, but Lena was the only one the Lord gave us. And then he took her back too soon. That was hard. Him taking Bea on top of it about took me down. Might have if it hadn't been for you and the girl." He turned back to Flynn. "Bea always said I was too quick on the draw. That I needed to pray things through. Guess as how she was right."

"She was a praying woman." Flynn didn't know what else to say.

"She was that. Said Lena and me kept her in practice. I reckon that was so." A smile touched the man's lips, but he couldn't seem to hold it there. "Not sure even she could pray me out of this mess I brung on us. What do you think needs doing?"

"Hard to say, Silas. You'll have to figure that out." Flynn hesitated, but there wasn't any use not telling Silas. He had to know sooner or later. "But what with the way things are, I think it's better for Leatrice and me to find another place. Fact is, I bought old Jackson Harley's place down the road."

Silas frowned. "That house won't hold the rain off your head."

"You're right there." Flynn smiled a little. "But I'm going to fix it up. That will give you and Irene some privacy to maybe work things out."

"I see. When you thinking on moving?"

"Not for a while as long as you don't run me off, but I am thinking on taking Leatrice to the Shakers for a while. Just until I get the house fixed up. You remember you said I ought to do that last year."

Silas pulled in a breath and let it out slowly. "I guess I did. Thought it was the best for her at the time." He looked toward the field outside the barn again. "I don't know if I've got it in me to keep this place going by myself. I'm getting on up in years and with this cough and all."

"I'm not deserting you. I'll just be down the road. I'll come help you with whatever needs doing every day."

"I always intended the place to go to you and then to Leatrice." He blinked as though tears were pushing at his eyes.

"But you're married now. Irene has a claim on the farm."

He was quiet for a long moment. Flynn was turning back to finish with the stalls when Silas said, "Could be we can figure something out. You get the house fixed and we'll swap farms. You can deed that place to me and I'll deed this one to you."

"Irene won't go for that."

"She'll have to do whatever I say. The man makes the decisions on things like that."

"Maybe we better wait and think about this awhile."

"You mean not let Irene know about it?" Silas smiled, but there wasn't much humor in the look. "You think she might up the poison?"

"I don't have any proof about that tonic. Just a bad feeling. Could be I'm wrong."

"Could be you're not." Silas sighed. "But either way, guess I better get these horses hitched up and get her into town. Else I'll never hear the end of it. I'll check in with Doc Robards while I'm there."

"Good. I'll help you hitch up the team."

They talked about ordinary things, like how the horses looked while they put the harness on them, but under their words, a dark worry lurked. Surely he was wrong about Irene. Just because she threw herself at him didn't mean she was ready to poison Silas. Even so, times were when a man needed to keep his eyes and ears open.

* * *

Leatrice scooted up close to the side of the barn when Grandpa drove the wagon outside so he wouldn't see her there and know she'd heard him talking to Papa. She hadn't meant to listen. After she caught her kitten, she would have headed straight to the loft, but the sun felt so good that she settled down by the barn to play. Muggins liked the sun too and purred while she rubbed him.

At first she hadn't paid much attention to what they were saying. She figured it was about the horses, but then Papa said her name. That got her attention. She kept petting the kitten to keep it quiet so she could hear what they said. It wasn't hard. The cracks between the barn planks let their voices come out plain enough.

Papa told Grandpa about the black stuff. Grandpa didn't sound like he wanted to believe it, but then he'd said poison. Poison. That was what Papa used to kill mice in the cellar.

He was always warning Leatrice to keep her cats out of the cellar so they wouldn't eat the poison and die.

Leatrice held the kitten a little closer. Limp as a rag doll, he almost seemed to be melting in the warm sunlight.

She was still worrying over the idea of poison when Papa said he was going to take her to the Shakers. Not just to visit, but to live. While she'd been begging to go to the Shakers, she hadn't thought about not coming on back home at the end of the day.

But Papa said he had bought a house for them, and that was why he was taking her to the Shakers. So he could get the new place fixed up right. Thinking about moving away from here made her stomach jerk funny. This was her place. Or it had been before that woman came. All of this was that woman's fault.

Leatrice stared across the field toward the house where Grandpa was helping that woman up into the wagon. If only she would ride away and not come back. Leatrice didn't want Grandpa not to come back. She loved him. She didn't want him to be poisoned by that woman. If she went to the Shakers, she wouldn't be able to help him or Papa either. And who would take care of Muggins and the other kittens?

But she could learn to read at the Shaker school. And that woman couldn't put something bad in her food. If she was ready to poison Grandpa, no telling what she might do to Leatrice. Papa must think so too. That was why he kept Leatrice with him all the time. And slept by her bed last night.

She watched the wagon until it disappeared down the dirt road. Maybe that woman would stay in town. She didn't act as though she liked it here since she was always fussing about something or other.

If only things could go back to the way they were. With Mamaw Bea still there. She could teach Leatrice to read, using the Bible the way she said she'd taught Mama. A few tears slid down Leatrice's cheeks. She raised the kitten up to brush them away with his fur. He was so soft.

Mamaw Bea couldn't help her. Muggins couldn't help her. Her feet felt itchy as though she needed to get up and run and run. She could run to the Shaker village. Sister Faye wanted Leatrice to be one of her sisters. She'd smile and get her a dress with an apron and a cap to wear on her head. They'd cut off her hair to make it fit.

Sister Faye had told her that the first day when Leatrice asked why everybody's hair was so short. "So our caps will fit and we can get ready faster in the mornings without having to comb tangles out of our hair. It's a better way. A best way."

Leatrice's hair was always a mess anyway. Flopping in her eyes when she was running. Like she wanted to be doing now. Running. Maybe if the Shaker village was too far, she could just run away to the back pasture to live with Sebastian. The horse that killed her mother. The horse didn't do it. He had bucked or so Mamaw Bea told her, but nothing that her mother couldn't normally handle. It was just one of those bad things that happened sometimes.

Nobody wanted it to happen. Nobody made it happen. It just did. That was different from what that woman was doing. Leatrice was glad Papa had warned Grandpa about the tonic. She stroked the kitten to make him start purring again.

"What are you doing out here sitting on the cold ground?"

Papa's voice made her jump. She hadn't seen him come out of the barn to dump the leavings from the stalls. She tried not to look guilty as she answered him. "It's not cold. The sun's warm against the barn."

He stepped over beside her and put his hands on his hips. "You're right. Before you know it, summer will be on us."

"Is that when the Shakers have school?"

"I think they may be having school right now. You want to find out?"

"I don't want to leave you, Papa."

He looked down at her. "You heard us talking, didn't you?"

She nodded. "I didn't aim to. I was just playing with Muggins here by the barn."

"I see." He looked worried that she was going to cry or something. "You'll like the new place once I get the house fixed up. Until then you can go to the Shaker school."

"But what about her? She might do something bad to Grandpa."

"You heard that too, huh." Papa pressed his lips together a minute before he reached for her. "Come here, sweetheart."

She scrambled up, still holding onto the kitten, and leaned against Papa.

He stroked her head the way she'd been stroking the kitten. "I think it might be better for Grandpa and Miss Irene if we're not here. And Grandpa is right about you not being able to tell what that was you saw the other day. Could have been some kind of herb."

"I guess so." She swallowed hard and must have squeezed Muggins too tightly. The kitten squirmed away from her and landed on the ground on all four feet. He crawled through a narrow opening in the rock foundation of the barn and was gone. Back to the loft, Leatrice hoped. She pulled in a breath and pushed out her next question. "When do I have to go?"

"Soon." Papa sounded like the word was hard for him to say. "But it won't be for long. Just a few weeks until I get the house down the road fixed up."

"Will you come to see me?"

"Of course I will. Whenever I can."

"I love you, Papa."

He picked her up then, the way he used to when she was little, and even though she was big now, he held her as easy as she had held the kitten. "And I love you more than all the stars in the sky, my little one."

Leatrice looked up at the sky where a few fluffy clouds floated in the blue. "I don't see any stars."

"But they are there. Always there the same, nighttime or day, as I'll always be there for you wherever you are."

20

Those first days with the foundling and Anna Grace were draining. The poor baby boy seemed unable to calm for more than a few minutes, night or day.

"Because the poor soul knows he was deserted," Sister Genna said. She was a godsend anytime she was in our retiring room. Even though I held him and nursed him, he seemed to rest best when she cuddled him and whisper-sang songs that had nothing to do with Shakers.

I was excused from every duty except cleaning our own retiring room and hemming new blankets and diapers for the babies. I ate the meals Sister Helene brought to me and took care of the babies. Our room had turned into a nursery.

"I am not sure how long the Ministry will allow this." Eldress Maria looked concerned on that first day. I thought not because she no longer wanted the babies here, but because she did. She even had a rocking chair brought to our room. While we had to squeeze the beds closer together to make room, we did not complain.

The chair was a blessing. One even Eldress Maria enjoyed

when she came to see that I was doing all I should during the daytime while the other sisters were about their duties. More than once with pretended irritation, she picked up Anna Grace when she was fussy while I was nursing the baby boy and settled in the rocking chair that I surrendered over to her. I happily sat in one of the straight-back chairs as I diligently kept my eyes away from the eldress, for I knew she didn't want me to see a tender look on her face. But it was there. I had glimpsed such a look now and again but acted as though I didn't. Babies had a way of softening even the sternest hearts.

Sister Helene was the one who insisted we wait no longer to name the boy. "You named Anna Grace the minute she was born. This poor child is at least two days old and without a name. Brother Baby just will not do."

I had to smile at her on that second night while she took her turn rocking him. We were all thankful Anna Grace slept between her feedings.

"He does need a name." Sister Genna took the baby from Sister Helene and whispered words into his ear that none could hear but the babe. He stopped whimpering to listen.

"Whatever do you say to him?" Sister Ellie asked.

Sister Genna smiled. "Words only he can understand."

"Well, tell him to be quiet when it's my turn to hold him." Sister Ellie yawned and lay down on her bed. "I almost fell asleep while hanging out sheets today."

I looked over at her. She did look tired. "Why don't you go on to sleep? I'll take your turn tonight."

"Nay. Who can sleep anyway with the candles still lit and sisters talking secret words to babies. Next, Sister Helene will be singing 'Come down Shaker life' to him."

"A good song for him." Sister Helene stood up. "Do you want to rock him, Sister Genna?"

"Nay, I like walking, although one has to be careful to stick to the path between the beds." Sister Genna cradled the baby against her shoulder and found the one free path across the room. "I am amazed that Eldress Maria has not sent Sister Darcie to the Children's House."

"She doesn't want to," I said.

"You must see a different Eldress Maria than I do." Sister Genna glanced over at Sister Helene. "Sorry, I don't mean disrespect. It's just that she never sees need to bend any rule."

"Rules should not be bent," Sister Helene said. "A bent rule means nothing and breaks the unity of spirit we must have."

"Yea, Sister Helene." Sister Genna acted as if she agreed, but both Sister Ellie and I knew better. Still, her yea was best for the peace of our room. She switched the subject. "I think you are right about naming this sweet bundle too. And since you found him—you did, didn't you?"

"Yea. Poor little one was left on our washhouse steps."

"Did you have washhouse duty?" Sister Genna was prodding, but Sister Helene didn't seem to realize that.

"Nay. I simply happened to see the babe lying there, or at least I saw the bundle and did not know what it was. But it wasn't as it should be. We do not leave rags on our doorsteps. Everything has a place."

"It matters not how she saw him." Sister Ellie jumped in before Sister Genna could say more. "What matters is that she did and brought him to Sister Darcie. Such good fortune that Sister Darcie can nurse him along with Anna Grace."

"And that Eldress Maria and Sister Lettie allowed me to

do so here with you three to help," I said. "But what about his name, Sister Helene? What would you choose for him?"

Sister Genna had calmed the baby as only she could. She laid him on her bed and pulled the blanket back away from his face. "Here, let us all take a good look at him to see what fits him best." She glanced over at Sister Helene. "Tell us what you think first, Sister Helene."

"A Bible name would be best." Sister Helene studied the baby. "Perhaps Moses who was put in a basket and left where a princess could find him."

"Not Moses." Sister Genna shook her head with firm decisiveness. "None of us are princesses. Think of something else."

"Very well. Moses does seem a big name for one so little, and the Egyptian princess gave Moses that name because she rescued him from the water. That is what his name meant."

"You rescued him from the washhouse." Sister Ellie grinned. "Somewhat the same, but I agree that Moses isn't our baby's name. What do you think, Sister Darcie?"

"I don't know." I said that, although I knew if I were allowed to choose, I would have named him Walter without hesitation. Still, it was better to let Sister Helene decide, since she might never have another opportunity to name a baby if she stayed on the Shaker path, as she seemed determined to do.

Sister Helene breathed out a long sigh. "I want his name to be one that will serve him well as he grows up here in our village to perhaps become a faithful leader."

Sister Ellie spoke up quickly to keep Sister Genna from speaking against that. "That could happen, but if so, it will be many years from now. Think of a name that will be good now while he is a babe in arms and for when he is a grown man. Perhaps a name of one of Jesus's disciples. John. Matthew. Philip. Andrew. Simon. Peter."

"Nay." Sister Helene frowned a bit. "Good names all, but not right for our little brother."

"Perhaps we should let you consider it overnight and decide in the morning." The retiring bell had already rung to signal the need to extinguish our candle and at least try to sleep. We were becoming expert at maneuvering in the room with no light other than whatever moonlight slipped in through the window.

Anna Grace was chiefly my responsibility to comfort during the dark hours since her cradle was by my bed, although this or that sister helped if she was colicky. But with the new baby, things were as they were at first with Anna Grace. Each of us sacrificed sleep to keep him quiet.

"Wait. I have the perfect name," Sister Helene announced. "When you think of brothers, you think of Jacob's sons, and his youngest and most beloved son was Benjamin." She reached to caress his cheek with her fingertips. "Our beloved Brother Benjamin."

"Benjamin it is then. Baby Benjamin." Sister Genna picked up the baby again.

"A good name." Sister Ellie waited until Sister Genna was in the rocking chair and both Sister Helene and I were in bed to snuff out the candle. "A very good name."

"Yea." I yawned, glad to have the name picked. "Wake me when he is ready to eat, Sister Genna."

I was more than ready to settle down on my pillow. Soon enough I would need to wake and nurse one of them. I waited until Sister Helene was in her bed before I curled on my side to keep her from reminding me that lying on my back was the proper Shaker position for sleeping. I thought it best not to keep reminding her I wasn't a proper Shaker. I rather doubted any of us in this room were, except for Sister Helene herself.

Sister Ellie did attempt to follow the rules. She claimed it was a simple thing to remember which knee to bend first in prayer or which foot to properly step up onto the stairs. She never carried her handkerchief in the wrong hand and dutifully attended to the silent prayers demanded in the morning and evening and before and after every meal. I had no problem with the prayers. I needed extra prayer time to beseech God for a way out of the Shaker community.

Sister Genna had no patience for the Shaker way and defied their rules with abandon. She nodded when Sister Helene reminded her of the proper Shaker way to go about one's daily routine, but as often as not, would then step with the wrong foot up onto the stairs or wear her cap a wee bit crooked. She did kneel for the morning and night prayers but confided that she sometimes silently said a nursery rhyme instead of a prayer.

When I asked if she did not believe in prayer, she assured me she did.

"I don't pray only when the Shakers decree I should go down on my knees," she said. "Instead I carry prayers in my heart and mind all through the day. Prayers for Jeremy, and I ask the Lord to help me endure my time among these odd people until Jeremy returns to rescue me. I pray for you." Her face had gentled. "And for Anna Grace. That the Lord will let you continue being her mother."

"I will always be her mother," I said.

"You will. I should have said that the Lord would keep

the Shakers from trying to change that with their ridiculous rules."

Ridiculous rules. I thought of her words now as I tried to block out the creak of the rocking chair and snatch an hour of sleep before time to nurse Anna Grace or newly named Benjamin. How did I, like Sister Genna, end up in the middle of these people? Odd, as Sister Genna said, but good, as Sister Helene continually said.

Granny Hatchell used to say the Lord had a purpose to everything. That even when things went their worst, the Lord could turn it into something good. Perhaps the something good of Walter's death and me trapped here in the village was that little baby Sister Genna rocked back and forth as she crooned in his ear. I could feed him, give him a chance at life. Whether he grew up to be a Shaker leader or if he ran from the village as soon as he was old enough mattered not. I merely had this day I'd been given by the Lord to do whatever needed to be done. I might not be able to look ahead without a tremble, but I could look forward to the next time one of these needed feeding and feel blessed to be a mother.

On the third day, Eldress Maria said I must start going back to the Children's House to take my meals. While this had been easy enough to do with only Anna Grace, it presented some problems with two infants. I didn't think it comfortable or even safe to put both the babies in the wrap. Benjamin was so tiny still.

But one thing I had noted about the Shakers. They were very inventive. If there was a better way to do something, then someone among their number would find that way.

Sister Lettie had foreseen my need and had one of the brothers working on the solution before Eldress Maria said I could no longer eat my meals in our retiring room. By then, after two days of being confined inside our small room other than trips to the privy during the daylight hours, I was ready to venture out again, even if it was only to the silent eating room of the Children's House.

On my hurried trips to the privy, I had left the babies safely ensconced in their cradles. This day when I returned, I found Eldress Maria in our room, holding Anna Grace and rocking Benjamin's cradle.

"We can't let their crying disturb the whole house," she said, even though all the sisters and brothers had gone to duties outside the house except those working in the kitchen or basement, where I doubted they could hear the babies on this second floor.

"Yea, I thank you for your kind consideration."

"These little ones are so blessed," she said. "They can spend their whole lives in our society with nothing but peace and love around them. They will never be assaulted by the tribulations that lurk outside the confines of our village."

"Do you never have troubles here?" I took Anna Grace from her and put her back in her cradle. It was her sleepy time, and I suppose my curious time as I dared to question the eldress. I did not believe no trouble ever visited the village, for I was here among them and troubled about the future. Plus I saw the discontent of Sisters Genna and Ellie. We were surely not the only ones doubting the Shaker way as a permanent path for us.

"None that can't be handled by obedience to the rules

which unite us in love and peace." She sounded sure of her words as she peered down at Benjamin, who was fussing while fighting the air with his tiny fists. "He is so very small."

"Yea, but he is growing. Last night he slept for a good stretch without any of us holding him." I picked him up. "He's ready to nurse."

I left the neck kerchief in place but scooted my dress down in front. I kept it unfastened in the back to ease offering my breasts to the babies. I turned away from the eldress, for she seemed uneasy watching the natural act of a baby nursing. I suppose she might never have seen such, since she was young when she was brought to the Shakers. Plus my baby was proof I had, as the Shakers claimed, committed the sin of matrimony. Not a sin Eldress Maria had to confess.

When the eldress tarried in the room, I glanced over my shoulder at her. "Would you like to hear my confession while he nurses?" With the birth of Anna Grace and now the addition of Benjamin to our room, the normal routine had been upset. Weeks had passed since I had spent time in the small office where the eldress heard confessions.

"Do you have wrongs you need to confess?" She stepped over to stare out the window. The sun shone through the glass to brighten the white of her bonnet.

"Perhaps merely the sin of curiosity." That wasn't my only sin, but the only one I chose to name for the eldress. The desire to leave the village that burned within me would be unforgivable.

She didn't look around. "So what questions bother your mind, Sister?"

"I wonder about your life with the Shakers. Have you never thought of any other way to live?" I expected her to condemn my question, but she did not. Instead she continued to stare out the window until I wondered if she'd heard me.

At last she sighed. "I should simply tell you that curiosity is a sin to be avoided. But avoiding an answer to an uncomfortable question is akin to lying. I have been, nay, I am very happy living the Believer's life here at Harmony Hill, even though I have had my moments of wondering. A wise Shaker eldress once told me that such thoughts are only natural as we determine which path to walk through life. Of course the Lord and Mother Ann lead us to the best ways and it is sinful to pick wrong paths."

I hesitated to ask my next question, but when she looked around at me, she seemed to invite me to speak. "And is the Shaker way the only path that is best?"

A smile touched her lips then, but was so quickly gone I thought I might have imagined it. "The only path for me. A covenanted Shaker is one who truly believes in the unity of life lived as sisters and brothers. I signed that covenant the day after I turned twenty-one. None can sign until that age. That was many years ago and I have not regretted it. Even when a few of those wondering thoughts surfaced in my mind."

Benjamin had fallen asleep and I moved him to a better position in my arms. He was not child of my body, but even so, in the few days I had fed him a bond was formed. A mother love that was not as strong as what I felt for Anna Grace, but a love that might grow to be as binding in time.

"I have many wondering thoughts," I admitted.

"Yea, I know you do. And while I hope you find the Shaker path one you can travel, I see the mother attachment you have for Anna Grace. I have never been with a mother and child as I have been with you. It makes me think of Mary and the baby Jesus and how she pondered in her heart the miracle of his birth and all that happened. I also read in the Bible about how the angel told Joseph to marry her and they then had more sons and daughters. If I dwell on such thoughts, I can let confusion come into my heart."

She shook herself a little, as though that would readjust her thinking. "But here in our Society of Believers, we have a different way. We aim to make our villages places where heaven comes down to earth. To do so, we must live as sisters and brothers the way it is in heaven. Our Lord's teachings made it clear that none are married in heaven. And then our Mother Ann had many visions showing her how our society needs to be in order to imitate heaven."

"Yea, you have told me that."

"So I have. And perhaps you will in time accept our teachings." She did smile this time. "Sister Lettie is bringing you something that will help when you go to eat at the Children's House, as you must, beginning tomorrow. Sister Helene has her own duties to attend to and cannot be forever bringing your food here."

"I don't mind walking to the Children's House."

"Very well." Her smile disappeared. "I am unsure how much longer the Ministry will let you stay here, but for now at Sister Lettie's suggestion and my agreement, they are content to allow it to be so. No one denies that babies need mother's milk."

I kept silent. Sometimes no words were best. She nodded and slipped out of the room. I continued to hold Benjamin until Sister Lettie knocked on my door. When I put Benjamin in his cradle and opened it to her, every wrinkle in her face was smiling and her eyes were sparkling.

"Brother Jonas made this for you." She pushed in a basket on wheels.

"How did you get it up the stairs?"

She laughed. "Brother Jonas carried it, and he will carry the wagon back down to the outside steps where it must be left after you examine it. See, the basket slides off and there is a handle to let you carry the baby down the stairs." She slid the basket off the wagon to show me how it was done. "Brother Jonas is very good at making things."

"Yea, I will be sure to thank him if it is allowed."

"Dear sister, thankfulness is always allowed." Her smile had not dimmed. "And I hear our foundling has a name now."

"Sister Helene named him Benjamin. A Bible name."

"An excellent name for a Shaker baby." She laughed. "My, what a blessing Mother Ann has sent us. Two babies to cheer our hearts and swell our number. And a young sister-mother to care for them. We will labor a thankful dance in our worship time."

21

Leaving the Shaker village without Leatrice wedged in the saddle in front of him was one of the hardest things Flynn had ever done. Not as hard as seeing Lena put into the ground, but that pain had numbed a bit as the years passed. While losing Lena would ever be a stab in his heart, this riding away from his daughter was a fresh, gouging wound.

"Get hold of yourself." He spoke the words firmly. His horse skittered to the side, puzzled by the unknown direction.

Flynn was the one in need of direction. Leatrice was not dead. She was very alive and apt to be happier at the Shaker village than at their house with all the upheaval there. Flynn didn't want to believe Irene might be using poison as a means to whatever ends she wanted, but he feared it might be true. Things were not right with the woman.

Since she waylaid him in his bedroom, Flynn had spent the nights in Leatrice's room. He'd slept in worse places than the floor by his daughter's bed, and nothing was going to move him from there after he'd awakened that first night to see Irene in the doorway, staring at his sleeping child.

He pretended to be asleep and after a few minutes she moved away. Instead of Leatrice, she was probably glaring at him for rejecting her advances. But he couldn't be sure of anything about her except that she had brought trouble to their house.

After he and Silas talked at the barn, Flynn was relieved when Silas carried Irene's tonic out on the back porch. Needed the fresh air, he told her, to make the medicine go down. He had gotten some pills from the doctor. So Flynn wasn't sure whether those or not drinking the tonic were helping Silas, but while he still coughed at night, the man didn't look quite so gray and tired.

That morning when he told Leatrice goodbye, Silas hadn't been able to keep back a few tears, but Leatrice hugged him and came up with the perfect thing to say. "Will you please take care of my kittens until I come home, Grandpa?"

That made Silas smile. "You know I will. How many are there now?"

"Four. Muggins, that's the gray and white one, he's the one to watch. He's always getting into trouble." Leatrice's lips trembled a little, even as she smiled. "Like me, I guess."

"Well, you stay out of trouble over there in that Shaker-town," Silas said. "And don't you ever forget how much your old grandpa loves you."

Leatrice gave him another hug before she ran to the barn to tell her kittens a last goodbye.

Silas pulled his handkerchief out of his pocket to swipe his eyes. "I know I said you ought to take her to the Shakers last fall, but now I just have the bad feeling I might never see her again." He stuffed the handkerchief back in his pocket.

"You don't have to worry about that." Flynn put his hand on the man's shoulder. "They don't keep their children prisoner. Maybe I can bring her home for visits."

"But where is home now? Here or there?" Silas gestured toward the road.

"Home will always be here for us, even after we move to the other place. Nothing can ever change that."

"You're a good man, Flynn Keller. As good a son as I could have ever hoped to have. Lena picked well when she picked you." Silas blew out a breath. "She took after me with rushing headlong into things, but it worked out for her." He had looked toward the house. Irene was nowhere in sight. Probably still sleeping. "Maybe this will work out too."

"Maybe it will." Flynn tightened his grip on the man's shoulder for a moment before he stepped back and called Leatrice.

Leatrice had leaned out around Flynn to wave at her grandfather until they were out of sight. Then she looked up at Flynn. "You won't let him die, will you, Papa? Not like Mama and Mamaw Bea did."

"I'll do my best," Flynn had promised. But would his best be good enough? It hadn't been good enough for Lena. Or Ma Beatrice.

Maybe his best with the Lord's help. That was what Ma McEntyre would tell him. She was always after him to pray about everything. When he confessed he didn't know how to pray, she taught him the Lord's Prayer. *Our Father who art in heaven.*

Flynn had humored the old woman. He was glad enough to recite the Lord's Prayer for her, but he never thought saying the words did much good. The Lord hadn't put any easy roads in front of him after his pa left. He'd had to make it on his own.

But what about finding a place where you were kindly cared for and even loved after your mother went back to Virginia?

Ma McEntyre's voice was in his ear. That was good, he almost answered aloud, but he'd have made it anyway. If the Lord was helping him, then why didn't he help his father stay with his family?

People do wrong things all the time. The Lord doesn't have us on puppet strings. So what about a woman like Lena falling in love with you?

Now he wasn't sure whose voice was in his head, but this time he did softly speak the answer out loud. "I am thankful for that, but if the Lord aimed us to marry, why did he take her away so soon?"

That's something we can't figure out. God's ways are not man's ways. It could be that accidents just happen. It could be that her time had come. We won't ever know the answer until we go to heaven.

"It could be," Flynn muttered. "It could be the Lord is too busy to mess with the likes of me. It could be I'll have to keep on handling things."

It could be that you're refusing to look at things with a clear eye. What about the Lord letting you see Leatrice before she broke through the ice?

This time he knew Ma Beatrice was the one he imagined arguing with him. She had been ever faithful, even through Lena's last days and then her own illness. If only she were still at the farm taking care of things.

But I'm not. I'm not saying you don't still need to handle things, but that handling will go a lot better if you say a prayer or two.

"I did pray. Right before I went in my bedroom and found Irene there."

That wasn't the Lord's doing. His doing was you knowing the right thing to do next. You keep on praying for what to do and help will come.

"Yes, ma'am." He knew it was silly taking part in an imaginary conversation, but at the same time he felt better. As though he still had Ma McEntyre and Ma Beatrice watching over him and praying better prayers than any of his.

He cringed a little, knowing how they would frown at him for thinking that. They'd both taught him that prayers didn't have to be pretty words strung together. Anybody could say a proper prayer.

"Our Father who art in heaven, hallowed be thy name . . ." He kept his eyes open as he spoke the prayer all the way to the end. "Lead us not into temptation, but deliver us from evil, for thine is the kingdom and the power and the glory forever."

He started to say amen, but then kept quiet for a moment as his horse trotted on down the road, no longer bothered by him talking to himself. A prayer rose from his heart. "Watch over my little girl. Let her know I haven't deserted her."

He worried she would think that. After Leatrice went into the Children's House, an old sister stepped up in front of Flynn to say, "It would be best if you gave our little sister time to settle in before you return to visit her."

"I was told visits were allowed." He couldn't remember

213

what the sister's name was, but she lacked the sweet smile Sister Faye had given Leatrice as she led her away.

"Yea, so they are. But in order for our youngsters to settle in and give their attention to learning our ways, it is better if a few weeks pass before family from the world return to confuse them." The sister had smiled then. A very stiff smile. "You have brought your daughter to us for her own good. You said that yourself. I know you wish her to be satisfied and happy here. As she will be, I can assure you."

He stared at the woman with no answering smile, stiff or not. After a strained silence, he nodded. "A week. I'll come back to see how she's doing in a week."

The sister had inclined her head slightly in acknowledgment before she turned to climb the steps and disappear through the same door Leatrice had gone through moments before.

The week stretched out long in front of Flynn. Had he done the right thing?

⁂

Everything was strange. Not at all the way Leatrice thought things would be when she was visiting Sister Faye. Then she hadn't had to worry about all the rules Sister Corinne said she must follow. She tried to do things the way they said, but she couldn't see why it mattered which knee hit the floor first when she knelt for prayer.

She didn't mind the praying rules. She wanted to pray for Papa and Grandpa. She was glad she didn't have to say the prayers out loud, since Sister Corinne told her not to dwell on where she used to live. Instead she was supposed to think about her new sisters. Brothers too, though they stayed on the other side of the hallway. Even when they went to eat, the boys were on one side of the room and the girls on the other.

They couldn't talk while they were eating. Not even to say pass the beans or biscuits. Sister Corinne said the serving bowls were in easy reach, so Leatrice was supposed to keep quiet, dip what she wanted, and then listen to everybody chew. Chewing was extra loud when nobody was talking.

Even after she finished eating and placed her knife and fork across her empty plate the way Sister Corinne said, she couldn't talk. Not until she was out of that room. Even then she had to keep her voice low. No shouting. No screaming. No jumping. No kittens. No Papa.

Leatrice had promised Papa she wouldn't cry, but that first night when all the candles were out and the dark pushed down on her, tears leaked out and slid down her cheeks to dampen her pillow.

If only Papa were sleeping on the floor by her bed the way he had the last few nights at home. With him there close enough to touch, that woman couldn't bother her.

Leatrice wasn't afraid now. She felt safe enough in the room with four other girls and Sister Tansy who made sure they knelt by their beds to pray before they went to sleep and then got up and prayed again before they washed and dressed for school. Sister Tansy was nice. Almost as nice as Sister Faye had been when Leatrice had visited the village. A different kind of nice.

Sister Tansy rubbed her back and sang to her that first night. No songs Leatrice knew. They were Shaker songs. Sister Tansy hugged her too, sort of like Mamaw Bea used

215

to. Not exactly, of course, but close. She hugged all the girls, and when she smiled her teeth showed. Sister Corinne's lips sometimes turned up, but she never showed any teeth. One of the other girls in the room, Sister Mona, said she probably didn't have any teeth. Leatrice didn't know if that was true, but Sister Corinne was really old. Even her hands were wrinkled.

On her second day with the Shakers while Leatrice was lining up to go into the eating room, she saw the sister who promised to pray for Grandpa and then had been at the barn petting her horse. Leatrice forgot about the no-talking rules and ran over to her.

"Sister Darcie." She was glad she remembered her name. "You have two babies."

One baby face was peeping out of a wrap on the woman's chest and another baby was in a little basket. They were so cute. Almost as cute as her kittens back home in the loft. She supposed she shouldn't compare kittens and babies.

The sister leaned over and whispered in her ear. "Shh. We can't talk in here, but after we eat I'll let you hold one of the babies if Sister Corinne gives you permission."

Sister Corinne's name froze Leatrice in place. Even before the old sister rushed across the room to grip her shoulder, Leatrice knew she was in trouble. The woman didn't speak out loud, but her frown said plenty as she glared at Sister Darcie and then Leatrice. Sister Darcie didn't seem bothered by Sister Corinne's hard look. Instead she smiled with a quick wink at Leatrice before she turned to find her place at the table.

Sister Corinne held on to Leatrice's shoulder and propelled her back in line. After they ate, she pulled Leatrice aside to tell her she'd done a bad thing she should confess to Sister Tansy.

Every night before they went to bed, they had to tell Sister Tansy what they'd done wrong that day. That night, Sister Janice, the oldest girl in the room at eleven and the one who smiled the most, went first.

"I had a bad thought." Sister Janice looked sorry about that, but she didn't go on to say what she'd thought or why it was bad.

Leatrice could confess having bad thoughts. She had plenty of them about that woman back at the farm.

The sister named Mona stood up next. Even though she was a year younger than Sister Janice, she was almost as tall but so slim the apron she wore wrapped all the way around her waist. She kept her hands clasped behind her the same as Sister Janice had, except Mona crossed her fingers on both her hands.

"Please forgive me. I didn't straighten my covers when I got out of bed and I ran through the hens to make them squawk."

Leatrice sometimes crossed her fingers when she wished for something good to happen or when she was trying to stay out of trouble by skirting around the truth. Mamaw Bea always knew, but sometimes she slipped things past Papa. Sister Mona, with her sorrowful expression and crossed fingers, must be trying to slip something past Sister Tansy.

When Sister Tansy nodded toward Leatrice to tell the things she'd done wrong, she stood up and put her hands behind her back the way the other girls had. She didn't cross her fingers because she wasn't wishing for anything or telling anything that wasn't true.

"I tore my dress when I climbed a fence. I didn't know I wasn't supposed to climb over the fences to take a shorter way to the privy. I talked in the room where we eat and are supposed to be quiet. I felt mad because I didn't get to hold one of Sister Darcie's babies." She paused for a couple of seconds. "Did I say enough wrong things?"

Sister Tansy put her hand over her mouth, but that didn't hide the smile in her eyes. She cleared her throat. "You don't have to confess a set number of wrongs, Sister Leatrice. It's best to have no need to confess anything, for that would mean you had done nothing wrong."

"I don't think I could go all day without doing something wrong. You have so many rules I can't remember them all."

When Sister Mona giggled, Sister Tansy frowned at her. Giggling must be against the rules too. Then the sister said, "You will remember them in time, Sister Leatrice. Until then, do your best and depend on your sisters to help you. The rules help us have unity of spirit and action."

"Yes, ma'am."

"Not yes, Sister Leatrice. Yea. And nay for no. You must remember that." Sister Tansy fixed her gaze on Leatrice, but even though she was correcting her, her face was kind as she nodded for Leatrice to sit down and let the next girl stand to list her wrongs.

After she heard their confessions, Sister Tansy left them alone to get ready for bed in their white nightgowns. While Leatrice was unpinning the scratchy neck kerchief, Sister Mona sidled over next to her. "Only a silly goose thinks she has to tell everything she does wrong."

Leatrice frowned at her. "I'm not a silly goose."

"You sounded like one. 'I tore my dress climbing a fence.'"

Sister Mona mocked her. "You'd probably tell on me if you saw me climbing a fence, wouldn't you?"

"No. I mean, nay. Why would I?"

"Why? Because you want to be the perfect little Shaker sister."

Leatrice curled her hands into fists, but then she took a breath. She'd promised her father she wouldn't get in trouble. She couldn't break her promise on the second day. "I told my father I would do what the Shaker sisters wanted."

"Why do you care about that? Your father brought you here and left you. Got rid of you, didn't he?"

"No. He's coming back for me after I go to school for a while." She tightened her fists, but she couldn't hit the girl. Hitting somebody was sure to be against the rules.

"That's what they all say. Then they never come back. Ever."

"Leave her alone." Sister Janice stepped between Sister Mona and Leatrice. "You're just trying to make trouble."

"Well, perfect Sister Janice won't ever get in any trouble, will she?" Sister Mona stuck out her tongue at Sister Janice and headed to her bed when Sister Tansy came back in the room.

Sister Janice whispered to Leatrice. "Don't pay her any mind. She doesn't like it here and wants everybody else to be unhappy too."

"Is she right about fathers not ever coming back?" Leatrice didn't believe that about Papa, but he hadn't come to see her yet. She blinked back tears.

Sister Janice hugged her. "She was right about her father. She might not be right about yours. But don't worry about that. You have a new family of sisters and brothers now."

Sister Janice was trying to make her feel better, but a knot of tears still gathered in Leatrice's throat. She knelt by the bed, remembering to kneel on the right knee first. Leatrice bowed her head to pray for her father, grandfather, and Muggins. She didn't pray for that woman who had messed everything up and she didn't pray for Sister Mona.

22

I was surprised to see the little girl, Leatrice. She told me her mother was dead the first time I met her, but her father had seemed to care so much for her, I couldn't imagine him bringing her to the Shakers. Not to leave her. The child had seemed eager to be here the second time I saw her when I walked her to the Children's House from the barn. Perhaps after the grandmother died of cholera, things became too difficult to care for the girl, or it could be her father had work that took him away from home.

I had no reason to worry over why the child was in Shaker dress. Yet I did. I wanted her to be leaning back against her father on his horse. That picture of father-daughter love had stuck with me. I suppose I had let it dwell so sweetly in my mind because my daughter would never know her father.

She did know her mother, and with each day that passed, I prayed we would never be separated. But every time I walked past the meetinghouse, I could almost feel the eyes of the Ministry watching me from the windows in the upper story where they lived. Two sisters and two brothers. Chosen by the Shakers to preserve the unity of the village and make decisions based on the Millennial Laws written by Shaker leaders in some eastern village.

When I first came among the Shakers, Eldress Maria had given me a copy of these Shaker laws. Much was covered in them. What a Shaker could have. What a Shaker could not have. Rules against ornamentation. Rules about behavior. I didn't read any rules about when a nursing baby could be taken from her mother, but I would not have been surprised to know such a rule existed.

Each morning, including this very one, I held Anna Grace close and whispered love into her ear. Then after nursing both the babies and cleaning our retiring room, I loaded sweet Benjamin in his basket, wrapped Anna Grace in the sling next to my body, and set out for the Children's House before the bell chimed to call everyone to the morning meal.

The conveyance Brother Jonas made for Benjamin worked well. A belt held the basket on the cart and then a waist-high handle stuck up in the back. That way I could see if Benjamin was in any kind of distress as I pushed him through the village.

The rocks on the path did bounce the carriage, but Benjamin did not seem to mind. I considered letting Anna Grace ride instead of Benjamin to find out if she would giggle with each bounce. She smiled at everything and sometimes laughed out loud when we rocked her.

Sister Ellie continually said a happy child was a blessing. While she didn't say so, I felt she was thinking of her own dear Abby, who never smiled when she saw Sister Ellie. Not only did she not smile, she didn't seem to even know Sister

Ellie was her mother. She was just another adult sister in like dress to all the other sisters. Abby's smiles were saved for the young sisters who shared her life at the Children's House.

At mealtimes, I watched for Abby so I could tell Sister Ellie about her. I had no trouble picking her out. She was that much like her mother, tall and pretty. Now nine, she seemed well content with her Shaker life. While Sister Ellie was glad of this, at the same time she was sad to think she had lost her daughter. I had no illusions I would not do the same if I didn't find a way to leave the Shaker village before they turned Anna Grace into my sister instead of my daughter.

I did not see that kind of contented happiness on Leatrice's face, but the child was new to Shaker life. Learning the Shaker way was not an easy task. I had struggled often in my early days with the many rules, and I was far older than Leatrice.

To be honest, I continued to struggle with the Shaker life. The fact that I lived in one of their houses, ate their food while only pretending I might someday be a committed Shaker was a burr on my conscience, but what other choice did I have?

Every morning Sister Ellie assured me that if we continued to pray with fervent belief, another way would appear.

That very morning Sister Genna had waited until Sister Ellie rushed out to her duties before she shook her head and said, "Dear Ellie. She believes even after years of no answers for her own prayers. Sometimes a woman must make her own way."

"But I have no way on my own." My heart sank at the

truth of that as I looked at Anna Grace happily waving her hands in her cradle. She would soon outgrow the small bed, and then what?

When she saw how her words distressed me, Sister Genna put her arms around me. "Forgive me, my sister. My bitterness sometimes leaks out when it shouldn't. I do know the Lord can do the impossible. Did not the angel assure Mary of that when she was perplexed at his proclamation that she would conceive and bear a son?"

"Yea, he did." I leaned on this sister who had come to mean so much to me. I had no pretensions with her. Or with Sister Ellie. "While I have never doubted the Lord did the impossible for her, I find it harder to have faith he will provide what seems impossible for Anna Grace and me."

"But miracles do happen." She turned loose of me and went to lean over Benjamin's cradle. "Just look at this sweet miracle right here in our room. A baby boy to love in this barren place." She turned to look at me as I picked up Anna Grace. "And remember when Anna Grace hesitated to take her first breath? How we all sent desperate prayers heavenward?"

"And then I heard her first cry." I cuddled Anna Grace closer to me. "Answered prayers."

"Yea, answered prayers. Perhaps the impossible will happen yet for all of us. Sister Ellie will leave this place and be a grandmother to her children's children. Jeremy will remember he has a wife and come for me. And you will find a way to return to the world with your sweet Anna Grace."

"I know not how that can be, but I do pray for a way." I watched her pick up Benjamin and touch her cheek to his. Whenever she held him, her face brightened with love. "At the same time, even if that miracle did happen, I would hate to leave Benjamin."

"They would never let you take him." Sister Genna kept her gaze on the baby boy. "You've heard Sister Helene. She and Eldress Maria already see him as a Shaker elder someday."

"They cannot know what sort of man he will become. Most of the children brought here do not stay, do they?"

"Why would they? Why would anybody?" Sister Genna frowned over at me and then smiled again when she turned back to Benjamin.

"Many of the Believers seem happy," I said.

"And some of them do not." She put Benjamin back in his cradle and gently tucked his blanket around him. "I'd best be on my way to my morning duty or I'll be in trouble with the eldress. I don't begrudge them my labor. Only my freedom."

"We are free to leave."

"If we have a way." Sister Genna touched her cheek to mine just as she had to baby Benjamin's. "Perhaps Sister Ellie is right and we only need to pray with more fervor. With more faith. But that baby boy over there is not going to grow up to be an elder. He's going to go out into the world and live a full and beautiful life."

A full and beautiful life. That was what I wanted for both the babies I carried into the Children's House. What I wanted for every child here. And for myself. I had expected to have that with Walter, but now I needed to seek out a new way to keep and love his child. But what about Benjamin? I did love him too.

I spotted Leatrice right away with the other young sisters

ready to go into the eating room. I could tell she saw me as well, but she stayed in line. Sister Corinne was watching to be sure she followed the rules.

Sister Corinne, who took her duties very seriously, never seemed pleased to see me come in. I was a disruption to the order she demanded. Perhaps such stern order was needed to keep so many children in line. Anna Grace had ever been a quiet baby and rarely cried during the mealtimes as I kept her cuddled close to me in her wrap. Benjamin was very different. He did not settle easily and often set up a fuss. Comforting him was difficult in the silent dining room, for he seemed to need the sound of a voice to assure him he had not been abandoned yet again.

At the evening meal, I had been forced to carry him out of the eating room in order to calm him. That caused a break in the rules, since I was unable to finish the food I dipped out on my plate before leaving the table. I had no idea which Sister Corinne preferred I do. Finish my meal or quiet the baby. Today I tried jiggling him on my knee while I wolfed down my food. I was constantly hungry now that I was feeding two babies and thankful Sister Ellie still smuggled me an extra biscuit or piece of pie most days.

To let me finish eating now, Sister Tansy lifted Benjamin from my lap to walk him up and down beside the table. Short and dumpy, she bounced when she walked and that not only comforted Benjamin but amused the girls behind her. They knew better than to giggle, with Sister Corinne's stern eye on them, but smiles did slip out. Smiles Sister Tansy returned even though Sister Corinne frowned at her too. I was pleased Leatrice was in her group.

I had no real reason to feel more attachment to Leatrice

than to the other young sisters, but that did not change the truth that I did feel drawn to her. Her sorrow had touched my heart when she had told me about her grandmother dying of cholera and her worry about her grandfather. I had prayed for his recovery as I promised I would. And I had prayed for the girl without a mother, since I knew that sorrow firsthand.

Granny Hatchell said a person couldn't sincerely pray for another without beginning to love them. So it could be my prayers were what awakened and strengthened the affection I felt for this child I barely knew. She too seemed to feel a connection. That might be because I was a familiar face here in the village among so many strangers. Someone she recognized as I recognized her.

That day when I broke the rules and slipped away to the barn to see Sawyer had been a time of despair for me, but talking with Leatrice and her father had lightened the dark sorrow wrapped around me. The girl's chatter about her father's gift with the horses as I walked her to the Children's House had brought smiles. The man's gift must have worked with Walter's horse. I sometimes saw Sawyer running about in one of the pasture fields. His lively canter around the fences showed he'd fully recovered from whatever made him so listless. Another reason to be thankful.

I had not considered it when I saw Leatrice the day before, but it could be her father had joined the Shakers too. Set apart from not only the brethren but most of the Shaker sisters as well while I cared for these babies, I could not expect to see every new convert. But were he here, the Shakers would surely be glad to have him among their number, with his obvious strength and ability with horses.

For some reason that didn't make me feel any better about seeing Leatrice in Shaker dress. Perhaps because even if he was in the Shaker village, he wouldn't be allowed to be the loving father I had thought him.

Sister Tansy returned Benjamin to his basket and led her young sisters out of the room. I followed with my babies. These two would never know their fathers even if they didn't stay with the Shakers. Anna Grace because her father had died and Benjamin because his father had not claimed him. At least that was the only reason I could imagine for a mother abandoning her baby to the Shakers. It was only right that now we were showering him with bountiful love.

That didn't keep him from setting up a wail as I went into the hallway to leave the house and return to my duties in the Gathering Family House, where an overflowing basket of aprons and neck kerchiefs in need of hemming awaited me. Eldress Maria would not understand if I did not finish them today. The woman had no idea how draining caring for two babies could be or how a mother could not always set her own schedule.

I gently swung the basket back and forth, but Benjamin wailed louder. Then as if in support of Benjamin's distress, Anna Grace squirmed in her wrapping and expressed her dissatisfaction too. I dared not look around at Sister Corinne, even though I could practically feel her glare burning into my back.

All babies cry. I knew that and didn't worry about the wails so much as the fear that Sister Corinne would decide my care for the babies was lacking. She might insist on taking the babies away from me.

"Tsk." Sister Tansy stepped up beside me. "The little ones

appear to be unsettled this morning. Such does happen from time to time."

"They will quiet down when I get them back to their cradles."

"Yea." Sister Tansy gave me a thoughtful look. "But your little Anna Grace is growing and becoming a burden to carry along with this little fellow."

"Nay, I can manage with the wagon Brother Jonas made for me. I am stronger than I look." I was barely taller than her.

"I didn't mean to imply you weren't strong, my sister, but sometimes it is good to accept help. That is one of the beautiful things about being a Believer. The fact that we have many hands to help and sisters eager to share one another's burdens."

"These are not a burden." I wrapped one arm around Anna Grace and kept a tight hold on the basket handle with the other. I looked with yearning at the door and wanted nothing more than to escape to the sanctuary of my retiring room.

Sister Tansy surprised me with a gentle look and a pat on my cheek. "Worry not, my sister. I am not taking these from you. I merely want to offer you help."

She kept her voice so low I barely heard her over Benjamin's cries. At least Anna Grace had stopped fussing and was now sucking her fingers, as she often did to calm herself.

"Yea." What else could I say?

She smiled then. "I have two little sisters who would be glad to walk with you back to your dwelling. One you seem to know or who seemed to know you. Sister Leatrice. She is new among us and a bit lonesome for her former home right now. Do you know her?" Sister Tansy raised her eyebrows at me in question.

"Yea, I met her when she visited the village with her father some months ago."

"I see. So you did not know her before you came to our village? Or her father?"

"Nay, I did not." I bounced the basket up and down, and Benjamin's cries turned to whimpers that hurt my heart for him but did not hurt the ears.

"I think it would help her happiness among us to have the duty of accompanying you on your treks to our eating room. She is young, so she best not carry the babies, but she could carry other things you might need or make silly faces to amuse the little ones. Or push your little cart."

"If you can spare her from her other duties."

"Yea, such can be adjusted. And Sister Janice, who has been with us for several years, will go along to help you both, since we cannot have Sister Leatrice alone on the paths here in the village as yet. While it seems simple to go from here to there for us, the paths can be confusing for one so young. It wouldn't do for her to walk you to your house and then you have to walk her to this house and, well, thinking about such makes one dizzy." Sister Tansy wobbled her head back and forth, then smiled. "Do you think having their help might please you?"

"Yea, that would be good." I smiled, glad to accept the company of Leatrice and the other young sister. And very pleased she wasn't suggesting I leave the babies at the Children's House.

Sister Janice, who was nearly as tall as I, carefully carried Benjamin's basket down the steps to the little cart on the walkway. Leatrice, on the other hand, ran down the steps as if she had just been awarded extra play time. I felt somewhat the same. The children cheered up the morning.

"Do slow down, Sister Leatrice." Sister Janice looked at me to make excuses for Leatrice. "I fear she hasn't learned caution yet."

Leatrice stopped at the bottom of the steps to wait for us. "I'm sorry, Sister Janice. But my feet get itchy sometimes and make me want to run. Does that never happen with you?"

"Nay, but I am older," Sister Janice said.

"How much older?" I asked.

"I am eleven, and Sister Leatrice is only just seven." Sister Janice set the basket down on the cart. "Do you want me to fasten the strap?"

"I'll do it." I threaded the strap through the openings in the bottom of the basket and up over Benjamin's middle. Benjamin fussed and Anna Grace giggled as I leaned over.

That made Leatrice giggle too as she hopped from one foot to the other.

I looked over at her. "Are those feet still itchy?"

"Yea. I am sorry." Her head drooped.

I laughed. "Worry not, Sister Leatrice. While our Sister Janice here has control of her feet, I admit that sometimes my feet feel a little itchy too."

Leatrice's eyes popped open wider. "You want to run? With these babies?"

"Nay, not with them. I would fear falling. But yea, there are times when my feet want to walk or even run."

"Then I won't have to quit running when I'm eleven?" Leatrice sneaked a look over at Sister Janice. "I do like to run."

"You don't have to quit running ever. You merely have to learn the proper time for things. A time to run. A time to walk. A time to sit very still." Saying that made me remember the chapter in Ecclesiastes where the preacher named all the many times. *A time to weep, and a time to laugh; a time to mourn, and a time to dance.* So many opposites in that chapter, but so much truth.

Perhaps having these young sisters with me now gave a time to laugh. A time to dance. Even perhaps as the Shakers danced to worship. *To everything there is a season.*

"A time to listen and a time to talk," Sister Janice chimed in. "Sister Tansy is always telling us that one. Sister Leatrice struggles with listening, but she's only been here a few days. I've been here four years."

"Why are you here?" After I spoke, I thought this might be a time I should have stayed silent, but the girl didn't seem to mind my question.

"My father died and my mother married another. He was not kind like my father, but my mother didn't know that until after they married. Worse, he had a son who took pleasure in tormenting me in various ways I prefer not to recall."

"I'm sorry."

"Nay, there is no need for sorrow. Not here in our village where all is good." Sister Janice smiled easily. "I was glad to come to the Shakers and live with my sisters here. I only wish my mother had come with me."

"She did not?"

"Nay. She could not break her marriage vows. The man she married and his son would never be ready to embrace the peaceful life of a Believer."

"Does she ever come to see you?" Leatrice's voice sounded

very small and sad. I thought she might be thinking of her own lost mother.

"She did." Sister Janice's smile slipped away. "But she hasn't been here for more than a year now."

"That man could have poisoned her." Leatrice's words surprised both Sister Janice and me.

"Why would you say such a thing?" Sister Janice frowned. "He was unkind, but I don't think he would have done something that horrid."

I stepped in. "There could be many reasons she has not been here. She could be unwell or tied down with a new baby."

"Or her husband talked of going west. He might not have let her come tell me that, and she didn't know how to write so could not send me word." The girl's smile came back. "It matters not. I am happy here with my sisters and would not leave were they to want me back."

Leatrice did not look convinced, but I distracted her by letting her push the cart. Soon she was smiling again. Even Benjamin stopped crying, in spite of it being time for him to nurse. But I did wonder why a child as young as Leatrice would think someone might be poisoned. I pushed that from my mind and was glad for the happy company of the girls.

Sister Janice carried Benjamin's basket up the two flights of stairs to our room, with Leatrice tagging along behind. When I thanked them, Leatrice grabbed me around the waist and hugged me gently since I still carried Anna Grace. I leaned down and kissed the top of her cap and then stood at the door and watched as they started down the steps.

Sister Janice had promised they would return before the midday meal bell to assist me again. I hurried to peer out the window at the two heading back up the walkway. Leatrice's feet must have been itchy again as she skipped along beside Sister Janice.

This indeed felt like a time to smile. Perhaps even to dance, if Eldress Maria decided I should go to worship times again. Not that I could ever embrace the Shaker beliefs, but dancing could help a person's itchy feet.

23

The days had dragged by until each one seemed a week long. By the third day Flynn was ready to ride back to the Shaker village, but he had given his word to the Shaker sister. Even so, each day he missed Leatrice more, while worry that she might be even half as miserable as he was had his stomach rolling.

At least he hoped the worry was what had his stomach upset and not Irene being more liberal with her special ingredients. But he watched and she dipped out of the same pans or bowls as he and Silas did. The woman wouldn't poison herself. Silas still took the tonic out on the porch to drink. If Irene suspected him of pouring it out, she gave no indication of that, although sometimes Flynn had the feeling she was laughing at them both.

She had not bothered him again. That could be because he was sleeping in the barn. He told Silas he was worried about one of his mares foaling. Silas knew better, but sometimes a man had to pretend things were different than they were.

Flynn had gone to the new place each day to work on the house that was in even worse shape than he'd thought. The roof had to be fixed first, but for that he needed new shingles. He could down a tree and fashion the shingles himself, but if the wood wasn't seasoned, the shingles might curl and the roof would be no better than it was now. Nothing for it but to sell one of his horses and buy shingles in town. After he got the roof fixed, he could start on the floors and walls.

Even working every spare moment between training his horses and helping Silas on the farm, he'd be fortunate to have the house livable by the time cold weather came again.

Five months wasn't forever, but it might feel like forever to Leatrice. And to him. At least she'd get more time for school. And once the week was up, he could go see her so she'd know he hadn't deserted her. The Shakers separated children from their parents. Everybody knew that. It was one of their strange ways. They might be trying to convince Leatrice to turn her back on him.

That worry had his breakfast doing somersaults in his stomach as he hitched his old mare to the sled loaded down with his tools. He'd hauled the shingles from town to the house the day before, and he was anxious to get the roof on. Besides, if he stayed busy, maybe he could keep from worrying about Leatrice. What if she was already in trouble over there? Already needed him?

He pushed the thoughts away. All those Shaker sisters would watch her and not let her get in trouble. At least not dangerous trouble like falling in a pond. No ice now anyway. The day was warm for early May. He didn't think she'd jump into one of the Shaker ponds, but who knew how many other ways she could get in trouble? It probably wouldn't take much to get that old sister frowning at her.

He had to quit thinking about it. Quit regretting taking her there. It was for her own good. She wanted to go to school and she needed to be away from Irene. While she had looked near tears when he left her at the Shakers, she was tough like her mother. She would manage. And he'd go see her when the week was up. Till then he'd work.

He had just torn the last of the old shingles off one side of the roof when he was surprised to see Silas driving his wagon toward the house.

"Need a little help up there?" Silas called after he'd reined in his horses.

"You don't need to be on any roofs," Flynn yelled back. He hadn't forgotten about Pa McEntyre falling off a barn roof. He wasn't about to let that happen to Silas.

"What's the matter? You think I'm too old to be any use?"

Actually he did, but he liked the life he heard in the man's voice. Instead of answering, he peered down at Silas and asked, "What are you doing here?"

Silas clambered out of the wagon to smile up at Flynn. "Irene had a hankering to spend the day in town with some friend of hers. So until time to pick her up, I thought I'd come help you get this old place into shape." He walked over to the house. "But now that I get a better look at it, I'm not real sure that's possible."

"It's going to take some work."

"Looks to me you might best tear it down and start from scratch." Silas stepped up on the small porch and disappeared from Flynn's sight, but then he could see him through the holes in the roof, walking around inside.

Silas called up through one of the openings. "Come on down. I brung you some dinner."

Flynn was ready for a break. With the sun directly overhead, the roof was hot, but at least no rain clouds were in sight. He should be able to get the roof covered before he had to head back to the farm to do the evening chores. Especially if Silas stayed long enough to help hoist up the shingles. That would save a lot of trips up and down the ladder.

Silas handed Flynn a ham sandwich and a fried pie. When he noticed Flynn checking it out, he said, "Don't worry. I bought this in town. Irene didn't make it."

"I was just seeing what kind it was." Flynn took a drink from the jar of water he'd filled up at the well that morning and sat down on the porch steps. At least the rock steps were something he wouldn't need to fix. "Could be I was wrong about that other."

Silas kicked over a bucket for a seat and folded the paper back from another sandwich. "Could be you weren't." He didn't look at Flynn.

"You are feeling better, but that might be because of the medicine the doctor gave you." Flynn took a bite of his sandwich. "Whoever you got this from did a fair job."

"Got it at the tavern. Seemed money well spent. Food a fellow doesn't have to wonder about." He chewed for a minute before he went on. "But you do have to admit that Irene is a fair cook."

"Better than the two of us anyhow."

"That didn't take much, but she cooks up a fine stew."

They ate in companionable silence for a stretch. Silas finished off his sandwich and Flynn offered him his jug of water.

Silas took it and studied the water in the jar for a minute. "You did get it straight from the well, didn't you?"

Flynn knew what he meant. "I told you I might have been wrong about Irene's tonic."

"You might have been." Silas took a swig of water and handed the jar back to Flynn. He wiped his mouth off on his shirtsleeve. "But you weren't."

"What do you mean?"

"Just what I said. You weren't wrong. And it's not just Doc's pills that's got my legs back under me." Silas looked off toward the trees beside the house. "It was the tonic. Or I guess not drinking the tonic."

"You sound awful sure about that. Did you find the can of powder Leatrice was talking about?" Flynn kept his gaze on the man's face.

"Nope. Something worse. I'm feeling real bad about it." Silas looked back at Flynn. "Figured I'd better tell you to see what to do about Leatrice."

"Leatrice? She's away from it all at the Shaker village." Flynn frowned. Silas was talking in circles.

"That's a good thing, I'm thinking." Silas sighed and rubbed his hands up and down his thighs. "But it's that kitten. You know, the one Leatrice asked me to take care of for her. Muggins, wasn't it?"

"I think that's what she said. What about it?"

"Found it this morning out by the woodpile. Dead as a doornail. I don't know what I'll tell Leatrice." He looked down at the ground.

"That wasn't your fault. Kittens have a way of dying or disappearing. Leatrice will understand."

"Well, it was sort of my fault." He rubbed his hands up

and down his thighs again, then looked straight at Flynn and went on in a flat, matter-of-fact voice. "That's where I've been dumping my tonic. I never thought about anything licking it up, especially not those barn cats. The stuff tastes awful. But Leatrice did warn me the gray-and-white kitty was prone to trouble. Guess it found it."

"Could be we ought to be more worried about us finding trouble."

"You mean me." Silas looked off toward the trees again.

"No, us. If you've got trouble, I do too." Flynn watched the man who kept staring off into the distance.

"I'm the one who brung us the trouble." His voice went quieter. "Maybe I should just drink the tonic and let it do its work."

"That's crazy talk, Silas." Flynn grabbed the man's arm and made him look at him. "We don't have to let her get away with this. We can go to the sheriff."

"With what? A dead kitten?"

"Well, you can kick her out. Take her back to town and tell her you're getting a divorce."

"I've heard divorces aren't that easy without proof one or the other has been unfaithful. I don't think Irene has been running off with anybody else."

Flynn could have told Silas about her being in his bedroom, but he thought it best not to mention that. The man already had too much weighing him down. "Poisoning you sounds like plenty of reason."

"If I could prove it." Silas shook his head. "The way things stand right now, if I tried to divorce her I'm thinking the courts would be on her side. She might get enough of a settlement that I'd have to sell the farm. I'm not wanting to lose the farm. It was my daddy's before it was mine, and I aimed to pass it on to Lena and now to you and Leatrice. That's what Beatrice wanted too. She set a lot of store by you, Flynn."

"She was a good woman."

"Yes." Silas slapped his hands down on his thighs. "Anyhow, I've figured it out."

"You can't drink the tonic." Flynn narrowed his eyes on Silas.

"No, I reckon not. Might serve me right for going off half-cocked and marrying Irene, but I'm thinking straighter now. It's like I told you the other day. Once you get this house fixed up, I'll sell you my farm for a dollar and you can sell me this place for two dollars. Sound like a fair price?"

"A little cheap for yours."

"My farm to sell at whatever price I set."

"But, Silas, I'm still not sure about you doing this."

Silas waved his hand through the air as though to shove aside Flynn's doubts. "I don't want to hear it. I've done made up my mind, and if you're worried about Irene, don't. If she raises a fuss, I'll sign this place over to her."

"I doubt that will make her happy."

"I'm not worrying about her happiness. I am worrying some about Leatrice's when I have to tell her about Muggins." He looked worried. "What do you think?"

"Don't fret about that. Leatrice has handled worse sorrows. And by the time she gets to come home, there might be a new litter of barn cats. For now, if she asks about Muggins, I'll tell her. If she doesn't, we'll let it ride until I see how things are going for her at the Shaker village. The other three kittens are still mewing, aren't they?"

Silas nodded. "I buried the gray-and-white one, but the others were up in the loft. I'll have to find a better way to get rid of the tonic."

"You could just tell Irene you don't need it anymore."

"I could, but then I'd have to wonder what she might doctor up next. I figure I'm better off just pretending to sip that tonic and then dumping it. Guess I'll need to cover it up with dirt from now on. Wouldn't want to lose any more of the girl's kittens. She did seem to set store by them. She have cats to play with over there at that Shaker village?"

"They don't have cats. No use for pets, or so one of the men told me."

"They're peculiar, those people. But I hear they eat good." Silas wadded up the paper his sandwich had been wrapped in and pitched it to the side.

"Leatrice won't go hungry. But, Silas, I miss her. I've half a mind to bring her home."

"Best not do that just yet. Give the girl time to learn to read and us time to get this place fixed up." Silas stood up. "So finish eating that fried pie so we can get a move on. I ate my pie on the way over here. Couldn't wait on it."

The work did go faster with Silas tying bundles of the shingles to a rope and Flynn hoisting them up to the roof. He was almost through with the whole side he'd torn off when Silas said he'd have to go get Irene.

"You'll be careful, won't you?" Flynn said.

"You're the one should be careful. The ground's hard when you fall from that high up."

"I mean you need to be careful around Irene. You can't trust her."

"True enough, but I'm thinking she's not the type to stab

a man in his sleep." Silas brushed off his hands. "Fact is, I've been sleeping in the girl's room the last few nights. Irene says my snoring keeps her awake. That's why she has to sleep half the morning away. But I note she hasn't been getting out any earlier since I give her the bed." He brought his eyes back around to look at Flynn on the roof. "How's sleeping out in the barn?"

"Better than sleeping here."

"I reckon so." Silas laughed. "We're gonna fix that. It might take a while, but we can hang on through the summer. So long as we make sure to dip out of the same pot as Irene when we're eating her fine stew."

Flynn watched him drive the wagon away down the road. The man was in surprisingly good spirits for somebody who knew his wife was trying to poison him.

24

By her seventh day at the Shaker village, Leatrice wanted to refuse to wear the cap with its itchy strings tied under her chin and kick off the stiff Shaker shoes and walk home. The shoes didn't have even one scuff, but they weren't all worn to her feet the way her old shoes were. She asked Sister Tansy if she couldn't have her old shoes back, but the sister said they threw them away. The splits along the soles did let in some dirt, but that was no reason to throw them away.

Sister Tansy said she should be grateful for new shoes. So she said "thank you," all polite the way Mamaw Bea taught her, but she hadn't meant it. She should have crossed her fingers the way Sister Mona did when she was confessing the things she'd done wrong.

This morning she looked at the Shaker shoes and couldn't keep from crying. The blisters on her heels were going to hurt when she put them on.

"Don't be such a baby." Sister Mona pointed at her and laughed when Sister Tansy wasn't looking.

Leatrice didn't think about whether Sister Tansy was watching or not. She picked up one of the shoes and threw it straight at Sister Mona. Everybody in the room got real quiet and stared at her. Nobody was smiling except Sister Mona, who twisted her mouth sideways to hide her grin while she pretended she was hurt. She wasn't hurt. Leatrice hadn't aimed to hit her. Well, not in the face. The shoe bouncing off her leg couldn't have hurt much.

She was going to be in trouble. Sister Tansy had a fierce frown as she rushed across the room toward Leatrice. More tears spilled out on her cheeks. She'd promised Papa she'd be good. But he'd promised to come see her. She hoped Sister Tansy would tell her she couldn't stay in the village. Then she wouldn't have to run away. But what if she went home and Papa didn't want her? Maybe he had brought her here to get rid of her the way Sister Mona said.

Sister Janice hurried over to stand between Leatrice and Sister Tansy. "I'm sure she didn't aim to do that. The shoe must have slipped out of her hand."

"She threw it at me." Sister Mona made a face and rubbed her leg. "It hurts."

Leatrice sank down on her bed and stared at her knees.

"Did you aim to throw your shoe at your sister, Sister Leatrice?" Sister Tansy sounded almost as cross as Sister Corinne.

"She called me a baby." Leatrice wasn't going to compound her sin by lying. She peeked up at Sister Tansy. The woman had her fists propped on her hips as she stared at Leatrice.

"So you proved it by acting like one," Sister Tansy said.

"Yea. I am sorry, Sister Tansy."

"Sorry you got caught," Sister Mona said.

"That is enough, Sister Mona." Sister Tansy turned to

look at Sister Mona. When she looked back at Leatrice, her eyes were not quite so stern. "I am not the one you need to apologize to, Sister Leatrice."

Leatrice took a deep breath. She had to do what Sister Tansy said, even if what she really wanted to do was throw the other shoe at Sister Mona. This time she might aim for her face to make her stop smirking behind Sister Tansy's back.

With a quick swipe at her tears, Leatrice stood up. "I am sorry, Sister Mona. I should not have thrown my shoe at you. Will you forgive me?" Leatrice added that last in her sweetest voice because she didn't think Sister Mona would want to forgive her any more than Leatrice was actually sorry. They both should have their fingers crossed behind their backs.

Everybody stopped looking at Leatrice to look at Sister Mona. She hesitated. Sister Tansy tapped her foot on the floor. After a minute, Sister Mona slid her hands around behind her back. "Yea, I forgive you for acting like a baby."

"Tsk." Sister Tansy continued to tap her foot on the floor. "I am not pleased with either of you right now. I think you need more time together in order to form the proper sister bond of unity."

That didn't sound good to Leatrice. She did her best to avoid being close to Sister Mona.

"I'm not sure that would be a good idea," Sister Janice spoke up quickly.

Sister Tansy raised her eyebrows with a look that said silence was all that was expected. "I will determine which ideas are best, Sister Janice. For today, Sisters Mona and Leatrice will sit together at meals and while doing their lessons and will share their duties." She pointed her finger at Leatrice, then Sister Mona. "I do not want to hear of any conflict between the two of you."

When Sister Janice started to speak up again, Sister Tansy stopped her with a frown. "Not a peep. None." She waved her hand at all the girls in the room. "I expect proper behavior from you all. We cannot let conflict or misbehavior find dirty little corners to hide away in our hearts. We must sweep away every wrong thought and deed."

"Yea, Sister Tansy," Leatrice echoed the words with the other girls.

"Which duties will we share?" Sister Mona asked. "Mine or hers?"

"You will take Sister Janice's place today helping Sister Leatrice with Sister Darcie and the babies. That is at every meal, but other than those times, Sister Leatrice will assist with whatever duties you have. If I remember correctly, and I think I do, you are to empty our washbowl water and bring fresh water for our pitchers. Then you are to sweep the schoolroom." She pointed a finger at Sister Mona. "And I do expect a proper job. Sister Josephine found a cobweb in a corner yesterday."

"It was not there when I swept." Sister Mona lifted up her chin.

Sister Tansy held her hand palm out toward Sister Mona. "Nay, Sister, do not compound a shoddy job with excuses. Spiderwebs are not built in minutes. You know our Mother Ann says good spirits will not stay where there is dirt for we can be sure we will find no dirt in heaven."

"Now get dressed. All of you." Sister Tansy clapped her hands together twice. "Sister Mona, fetch Sister Leatrice another pair of stockings. Doubling them on her feet will cushion the blisters."

"Can she not fetch her own stockings?" Sister Mona whined.

"Of course she could." Sister Tansy smiled. "But you as her loving sister are going to do it for her."

Leatrice's heart sank as Sister Mona turned back to the chest to get the stockings. More tears pushed at her eyes at the thought of being tormented by Sister Mona all day long.

Sister Janice gave her a little hug and whispered close to her ear. "She will behave. Sister Tansy will be watching her."

Leatrice simply nodded. She had no choice. What Sister Tansy said had to be done. She blinked away her tears. She wouldn't let Sister Mona make her cry. She'd be strong like her mother. Like her father. That made her feel like crying again. Why hadn't he come to see her?

Maybe he hadn't come because he was sick like Grandpa, but it couldn't be that Papa wanted to be rid of her. She didn't care what Sister Mona said.

Mamaw Bea used to say a day wasn't forever when they had to do something like clean out the chicken house. This day wouldn't be all bad. She would still get to help Sister Darcie. Walking her babies through the village was the best part of the day. She hadn't figured out why Sister Darcie had two babies. They couldn't be twins, since Anna Grace was lots bigger than Baby Benjamin.

The extra stockings did help cushion her blisters, but that didn't keep her from wanting to take off those stockings and shoes and head home barefoot.

When Sister Mona poured the water from the washing basin into a piggin, she splashed some out on Leatrice's feet on purpose. "Now, look what you made me do." She pitched a towel to Leatrice. "Clean it up."

Leatrice mopped up the spill without a word. Then she gathered up the other towels. "I'll take these to the wash-house."

"Not by yourself. A baby like you might get lost."

"Then you better come with me." Leatrice headed out of the room for the stairs. "Since we're sisters."

"You're not my sister. I don't have any sisters."

"We're sisters today. Sister Tansy said so." Leatrice didn't look back. She didn't care if Sister Mona came with her or not. Leatrice knew where the washhouse was. And she knew how to get to the house where Sister Darcie lived. She wouldn't get lost, but right now she wanted to get lost from Sister Mona.

But Sister Mona clumped down the steps behind her, carrying the dirty wash water. Leatrice was happy to get out the door before she spilled it again.

Sister Mona dumped the water in the grass. "Go on and take those towels to the washhouse. Then wait here. I've got to fill the piggin to take back upstairs."

Leatrice looked around. "Where's the well?"

"Don't you know anything?" Sister Mona made a face. "No wells. Water comes in pipes right to the kitchen."

"You're making that up." Leatrice couldn't imagine not having to draw water out of a well or dip it out of a spring or creek.

"Maybe I am. Maybe I'm not. Either way, you wait here till I get back."

"Maybe I will. Maybe I won't." Leatrice got a better grip on the towels and headed for the washhouse. She could look in there and see if Sister Mona was lying. And what did she care anyway what the girl said? She was trying to be mean. She was mean. She probably wouldn't even be there when Leatrice got back, and then she would tell Sister Tansy Leatrice hadn't waited where she was supposed to.

But Sister Mona was sitting on the steps when Leatrice came back from the washhouse. "What took you so long?"

Leatrice didn't answer her. "We need to go get Sister Darcie."

"You're not supposed to tell me what to do. I'm the oldest."

"All right." Leatrice glared at Sister Mona. "Then tell me that we need to go get Sister Darcie."

"I don't guess I need to now." Sister Mona stood up and walked in the wrong direction.

"You know that's not the right way." Leatrice stayed where she was.

"Do I?" Sister Mona smiled over her shoulder at Leatrice. "Are you sure you know how to go?"

"I know the way." Leatrice started down the path toward the Gathering Family House. Whatever Sister Tansy did to her for not doing what she said wouldn't be as bad as putting up with Sister Mona.

She was halfway to the other house when Sister Mona ran up behind her and grabbed her shoulder. "Wait for me, little sister. You know sisters have to help one another and be perfect little angels just like in heaven."

Leatrice ignored her and kept walking.

"I don't think she likes me, Mother Ann." Sister Mona acted as though she were talking to someone else. "You say sisters are supposed to love one another, don't you? She probably doesn't even know who you are, Mother Ann."

Leatrice wasn't sure who Mother Ann was, even though people here were always talking about her. One day at school, some of the girls had played a game they said was Mother Ann in jail. Leatrice wondered why they would pretend their mother was in jail, but she hadn't asked. Everything was just too strange. She certainly wasn't going to ask Sister Mona. Anything.

When they got to the Gathering Family House, Sister Darcie was coming down the steps with her basket. She smiled when she saw Leatrice. She even smiled at Sister Mona. That was because she didn't know how mean she was.

"Hello, Sister Leatrice. I see you have a new companion today. I hope Sister Janice isn't ill."

"Nay, she is fine," Leatrice said.

Before she could say more, Sister Mona stepped in front of her. "I'm Sister Mona and Sister Tansy is making Sister Leatrice and me be together all day because Sister Leatrice threw her shoe at me this morning." She rubbed her leg. "I think I have a bruise."

"Oh my." Sister Darcie's smile didn't go away. "I'm sorry about your bruise, but sometimes one just must throw a shoe."

"I don't think Sister Tansy thinks that is true." Sister Mona frowned a bit.

"Well, it could be that Sister Tansy has never felt like throwing a shoe." Sister Darcie got a considering look on her face. "I'm sure Sister Leatrice was properly sorry."

"I am properly sorry." Leatrice looked down at her feet. She really liked Sister Darcie. She was so pretty and never cross like Sister Corinne. Leatrice wanted her to understand why she had thrown her shoe. "I shouldn't have gotten mad just because Sister Mona called me a baby."

"That's because you are a baby," Sister Mona said. "I don't like babies."

"Come, come, Sister Mona. No need being mean." Sister Darcie's smile turned to a frown.

That made Leatrice feel better. Sister Darcie knew Sister Mona was mean.

Sister Darcie fastened the basket with Baby Benjamin onto the little wagon. He let out a wail and Leatrice leaned down to baby talk to him. The other baby, Anna Grace, made a cooing noise.

"I think she's talking to you, Sister Leatrice. Do you want to push the cart today? I'm not sure he would like to be pushed by Sister Mona if she doesn't like babies." Sister Darcie looked over at Sister Mona. "Why don't you like babies, Sister Mona? Babies are very sweet."

"My mother had a baby. It killed her." Sister Mona spun in a little circle, as though what she was saying didn't bother her at all.

"Oh, I'm sorry. It's very hard to lose a mother. My mother died too when I was a little girl."

"Because she had a baby?" Sister Mona asked.

"Nay. She had cholera."

"Oh." Sister Mona spun around again and made her apron fly out away from her dress.

"And Sister Leatrice knows how sad it is to lose a mother too, don't you, Sister Leatrice?"

Leatrice nodded.

"What happened to her?" Sister Mona stopped spinning. She sounded curious.

"She fell off a horse." Leatrice stared at the cart as she pushed it down the walkway. "Do all mothers die of something?"

"Nay." Sister Darcie's voice was soft. "Not all mothers die. I'm a mother and I'm quite well."

"But something might happen to you," Sister Mona said. "You might die."

"That's true, Sister Mona. We all die sooner or later, but I hope for it to be later so that I will have more time with my babies."

"They won't let you keep them," Sister Mona said.

Leatrice frowned at Sister Mona. "What do you mean? She has to keep her babies."

"Not here. Babies and children in the place where we are. Mothers in other places if they aren't dead. Isn't that the way it is, Sister Darcie?"

"So they tell me." Sister Darcie looked sad.

"Anna Grace and Benjamin will cry if they aren't with you," Leatrice said.

"They don't care if babies cry," Sister Mona said. "Not even if babies like you cry because your father brought you here to get rid of you."

"He didn't get rid of me. He's going to come see me and take me home again after I go to school for a while."

"Did he really tell you he'd come to see you?" Sister Mona grinned like she didn't believe it could be true.

It was a good thing Leatrice was wearing her shoes, or she might have thrown another one at Sister Mona.

"That's enough, Sister Mona." Sister Darcie sounded as stern as Sister Corinne. "If Leatrice's father said he would come see her, then he will."

"Fathers never do what they say," Sister Mona muttered.

"Some fathers do," Sister Darcie said.

"Did yours?" Sister Mona peered up at Sister Darcie.

"It's been a long time since I've seen him," Sister Darcie said.

"So he didn't."

"Whatever he did doesn't matter. Sister Leatrice's father will come."

Sister Darcie sounded so sure, Leatrice wanted to hug her. Then she wanted to ask her when he was coming, but she couldn't know that.

All at once, she heard her name. "Leatrice." And as if Sister Darcie had summoned him with her sure words, there was Papa sliding off his horse and coming toward her. Papa. Really there to see her just the way he had promised.

"Papa!" Leatrice turned loose of the cart handle and ran to him.

25

Flynn couldn't believe his good fortune when he spotted Leatrice beside the road. He had worried the Shaker sister, who wanted him to stay away, wouldn't agree to fetch Leatrice. Not that he would have taken no for an answer. Even if he had to push his way past that old sister.

He'd gotten up while the stars were still shining so he could be at the village before Leatrice would be in school. Now here she was right beside the road with another girl and the woman named Darcie he'd met when he was working with the horse, Sawyer. Odd how their paths kept crossing. She had obviously had her baby. The tired look was gone and a smile lit up her face as Leatrice ran from her side toward Flynn.

That was all he had time to notice before Leatrice jumped into his arms. "Oh, Papa. I knew you would come. I knew you would."

He picked her up, even though she was far from a baby, but he needed to hold her. She looked different in her Shaker dress. Older somehow. Less his. But then he supposed all children got less their parents' and more their own person as they got older. That was as it should be, but he didn't want it to happen in a week.

"I told you I would come."

"But it's been so long." She wrapped her arms around his neck and hugged him tight.

"Only a week. They asked me not to come for a week. One of the sisters said that would give you time to settle in." He set her back on her feet beside him. She looked fine. He'd known she would, but at the same time he'd worried she wouldn't.

"That must have been Sister Corinne." The other girl stepped up behind Leatrice. The girl didn't lack much being as tall as Sister Darcie, who watched from the walkway, still smiling. "She's the one who tells everybody what to do. Sister Tansy does too, but that's just us and not somebody like you from the world."

Saying he was from the world sounded odd to Flynn, as though when he came into the village he entered some different realm. He supposed the Shakers thought that was true. He grabbed his horse's reins and looped them over a tree branch, then turned back to Leatrice. "So who is your friend, Leatrice?"

Leatrice didn't look particularly happy. "Sister Mona. She sleeps in the same room I do."

"Sisters perhaps, according to Shaker rules. Friends, well, that might be more difficult." The girl tapped her cheek with one of her fingers. "Definitely more difficult."

"Mind your manners, Sister Mona." Sister Darcie spoke sharply to her. "You need to come back over here with me."

The girl looked at Sister Darcie. "Sister Tansy said I had

to stay with Sister Leatrice. So I could help her if she got in trouble."

"You'd be the one to get me in trouble," Leatrice muttered before she looked up at Flynn. "Spending the day together is how Sister Tansy is punishing us."

"Not a punishment, dear sister," Sister Mona said. "It's to make us love one another. The way we should as sweet, loving sisters."

"Seems to lack some working." Flynn gave the girl a steady look. "You best do what Sister Darcie says. Leatrice is going to stay with me for a few minutes."

"She'll get in trouble if she misses the morning meal. Even more trouble than she's in now." Sister Mona stepped directly in front of Flynn. "She threw a shoe at me, you know."

Flynn considered the girl. She was definitely trying to needle Leatrice. So he smiled. "Sometimes a person just needs to throw a shoe at something."

Leatrice giggled. "Sister Darcie said the same thing."

"Did she?" Flynn smiled over at the woman. "We must think alike."

"So we must." She returned his smile. "Of course, throwing shoes is not encouraged here in the village. A great many things are not encouraged here in the village." Her smile slipped away as she cuddled the baby in the wrap next to her chest. But the wails of another baby came from the basket.

"Did you have twins?" The woman looked too small to handle two babies.

"Oh, nay." She laughed. "This is my baby, Anna Grace." She pulled back the wrap to show a baby sucking on her fingers. Then she pointed at the basket. "And this is Benjamin. Someone left the poor foundling on the Shakers' doorstep."

"What's a foundling?" Leatrice asked.

"A baby nobody wants." Sister Mona did an odd little twirl. "Something like me, except I'm not a baby."

"This baby is loved and wanted now," Sister Darcie said. "The same as you are loved here in the village, Sister Mona."

Sister Mona did another twirl. "You're just saying that because you think you should, but nobody loves me. I like it that way. But what about Sister Leatrice? Does her father love her enough to take her home?"

"That is not for you to ask, Sister Mona." Sister Darcie grabbed the girl's arm as she spun close to her. "You come with me."

The girl tried to jerk free, but Sister Darcie held her tight. She was obviously stronger than she looked. The baby in the basket wailed louder.

"You can't make me go with you." Sister Mona's eyes narrowed to slits as she stared at Sister Darcie. "You can't hold on to me and push that baby wagon too."

"You're right." Sister Darcie looked calm as she let go of Sister Mona. "That's why you are going to push the cart."

A sly look crossed the girl's face. "But what if I hit a bump and the wagon turns over?"

Leatrice ran to get between the other girl and the cart. "I'll push Benjamin." She looked back at Flynn. "I'm sorry, Papa, but I have to take care of Benjamin."

"Yes, you do." Flynn wanted to grab Leatrice and hug her again. He started to step closer, but with how the Shakers were so diligent about keeping men away from the sisters, he stopped. He didn't want to cause trouble for Sister Darcie. She looked as proud of Leatrice as he was.

"Thank you, Sister Leatrice," she said softly. "Benjamin

will appreciate your care in pushing him, but I'm sure Sister Mona would have reconsidered her thinking."

Flynn was surprised to see a gentle look on the sister's face as she looked at the other girl. He wasn't feeling gentle toward her at all, but then she was just a young girl. Who knew what sort of troubles she'd had to land her here in this place?

"Maybe I would. Maybe I wouldn't." Sister Mona lifted her chin defiantly. At the same time she did trail along behind Leatrice as she pushed the cart up the walkway.

Sister Darcie glanced back at him as she followed them. "I'm sure if you come ask the sisters at the Children's House, they will permit you to visit Leatrice. If you have time to wait until she eats. Sister Mona is right. The Shakers are very strict about mealtimes."

"I'll wait all day if I must." As Flynn untied his horse to trail along behind them, he couldn't help but be curious about how she had spoken of the Shakers as though she were not one of them.

Leatrice wolfed down her food, then couldn't stop fidgeting. She wanted everybody to eat faster. Her father was waiting for her. When they first came inside, Sister Darcie told Sister Tansy that Papa was here. Leatrice kept quiet to listen. She was worried when Sister Corinne came over to hear what Sister Darcie was saying.

"He's not planning to take her away, is he?" Sister Corinne asked.

"That would be something you would have to ask him."

Sister Darcie swayed the basket back and forth to keep Benjamin from crying.

Leatrice wanted to step closer to sing to him, but Sister Corinne wouldn't like that. Not while they were supposed to be silent. Best not to do anything to upset her and make her want to send Papa away.

"Was he waiting for her out on the road?" Sister Corinne didn't sound pleased.

"Nay. He rode into the village as Sister Leatrice and Sister Mona were helping me with the babies on my walk here."

"Yea, the babies." Sister Corinne's frown got fiercer. "I don't know why you gave the children permission to accompany Sister Darcie, Sister Tansy."

"She needs help." Sister Tansy sounded the way she sometimes did when talking to Leatrice and the others in their retiring room. Kind. Comforting. "And it makes the young sisters feel useful. They are useful, are they not, Sister Darcie?"

"Yea. Very." Sister Darcie didn't look around at Leatrice, but Leatrice had the feeling she knew she was listening. "Especially Sister Leatrice. She has a way of making Benjamin stop crying."

"That baby must have the colic." Sister Corinne rubbed her forehead and looked at Sister Tansy. "How long has Sister Leatrice been here?"

"A week today," Sister Tansy said.

Sister Corinne sighed. "I did agree to let her worldly father wait only one week to come back to see her. I suppose I can't deny his visit now. Very well, she may miss the morning school session, but she will have to do extra work to make it up to Sister Josephine."

260

Leatrice hurried back into line before Sister Corinne noticed her eavesdropping. When Sister Mona tried to block her, Sister Janice made room. But now she was stuck in the eating room while everybody kept eating and eating.

At last Sister Corinne held up her hand to signal they should all stand and then kneel beside their chairs for a silent prayer.

Dear Lord, thank you for Papa coming. Thank you for Sister Darcie and Sister Janice. Help me to not throw my shoes at Sister Mona. Amen.

Out in the hallway, Leatrice was glad to see Sister Tansy pointing Sister Mona toward the schoolroom.

Leatrice wanted to run outside, but she kept her feet under control. She didn't want to get in trouble with Sister Corinne. Not today.

As she followed Sister Darcie out the door and down the steps, Baby Benjamin started crying. Leatrice looked out at Papa waiting in the shade for her, but she had to help Sister Darcie.

"I'll sing to him while you fix his basket on the cart." Leatrice leaned over the baby in the basket and sang words she made up. "Sweet little baby, don't you cry."

"Thank you, Sister Leatrice, but he is fine. Really. Babies have to do some crying."

"But he likes me to sing to him."

"He does, but your father is waiting for you." Sister Darcie glanced at Papa coming toward them, leading his horse.

"Papa can walk with us while I push Benjamin. He won't mind." Papa was close enough to hear her then. "Will you, Papa?"

"Will I mind what?"

"Walking back to Sister Darcie's house so I can push Baby Benjamin." Leatrice grabbed the cart handle.

"I don't mind at all." He walked along beside them. "Where's Sister Mona?"

"She had to go to school." Leatrice couldn't keep from smiling.

"You look happy about that," Papa said.

"I am. She's mean." She peeked over at Sister Darcie to see if she was in trouble for saying that, but the sister only smiled.

"She did seem to have a mean streak." Papa slowed his pace to match theirs.

The cart had wheels that rolled easy, but it bumped up and down too much if she pushed it fast. So she went slow, the same as she did on other days when Sister Janice walked with her and Sister Darcie. Then after they helped Sister Darcie carry the babies to her room, she and Sister Janice would hurry down the steps to race each other back through the village to school. With her long legs, Sister Janice always won if she didn't pretend to have a sore foot or something.

Leatrice wondered if Sister Mona would have raced with her. She'd win for sure. Her legs were even longer than Sister Janice's. But then she might lag behind just to make them late and get into more trouble.

"She didn't behave very nicely. I admit that," Sister Darcie said. "But the poor girl has had some hard times. Losing her mother. Thinking her father brought her here because he didn't want her. We can't know if that's true. Perhaps he thought he was doing what was best for her." Sister Darcie looked over at Papa.

"As I did for Leatrice." Papa's smile disappeared. "I want her to be safe and get to go to school."

Sister Darcie seemed puzzled by what Papa said about wanting her to be safe. She didn't know about that woman and her poison tonics. Maybe Leatrice would tell her someday, but now she just said, "But you promised to come see me."

"That was a good promise kept," Sister Darcie said. "But Sister Mona's father has not visited her, and whatever the reason behind her being here, the child feels deserted. That makes her very unhappy."

"So she tries to make everybody around her as unhappy as she is." Now Papa was the one looking puzzled. "Not a very good way to be."

"Not a good way at all. Nor does it excuse her behavior." Sister Darcie looked at Leatrice. "You must not let her torment you without complaint. Tell Sister Tansy if she bothers you. Perhaps in time her anger will lessen and she will embrace friendship here." Sister Darcie slowed her step as though she was in no hurry to reach her house.

"She doesn't want to be my friend and I don't want to be her friend," Leatrice said.

"That is how it seems," Sister Darcie said. "But in the Bible Jesus tells us to love our enemies and pray for those who persecute us. So maybe you and I can pray for Sister Mona."

Leatrice nodded without saying anything. When somebody told you to pray about something, it was easier to say you would and then maybe you would and maybe you wouldn't. She was sorry as soon as she thought that. It sounded like something Sister Mona would say. Leatrice didn't want to be like Sister Mona. So she would try to remember to pray for

Sister Mona, but she wasn't about to pray for that woman trying to poison her grandpa.

"And I will too," Papa said.

That surprised Leatrice. She didn't know Papa prayed. She knew Mamaw Bea did and she figured everybody here did. Except maybe Sister Mona. And the babies. They couldn't pray.

When they reached the Gathering Family House, Sister Darcie unfastened the belt that held the basket on and picked it up. She turned to smile at Leatrice. "Thank you for helping me with Benjamin. And if Sister Mona comes with you again, we'll remember that she's unhappy and we won't let her upset us. Do you think we can do that?"

"I don't know." She didn't want to promise something that she couldn't do.

Sister Darcie laughed a little. "I don't know either, but we can only try." Then she looked at Papa who waited with his horse in front of the house. "Thank you too, Mr. Keller, for walking with us and praying with us." She hesitated as she shifted the basket to her other arm. "And if you say that prayer for Sister Mona, say one for me too that I can stay with my babies."

"They surely won't separate you from your babies." Papa frowned.

"In time they will. It is their way here in the Shaker village." Sister Darcie sounded sad as her smile slipped away. Benjamin began wailing then. "My fussy little boy is hungry."

"Do you want me to carry him up to your room?" Leatrice asked.

"Nay, I can manage today. Good day to you both."

Even after she went in the sisters' door, Leatrice could hear Baby Benjamin crying. "She needs to sing to him."

Papa laughed. "So you have become an expert on calming babies."

"Well, only Baby Benjamin."

Papa stared at the closed door for a moment. "It's nice that you are helping Sister Darcie keep her babies happy. She seems nice."

"I like her. She remembered me from when we saw her at the barn with the horse with the funny name. Sawyer." Leatrice took Papa's hand. It felt rough and strong, just the way it was supposed to. "Is Sawyer all right now?"

"I saw him in the field when I rode into the village. He looked good." He picked Leatrice up and sat her on his horse.

"Where are we going? Are you taking me home?"

"Not yet." Papa didn't look happy about that. "I need to do more to our new house, and I don't think it would be good for you to come home right now."

"That woman is still trying to poison Grandpa, isn't she?"

He didn't answer her. "Your grandpa is feeling better. He told me to tell you how much he misses you. Maybe he can come with me next time I come see you."

"I don't want her to come."

"Don't worry. She won't." Papa's face got hard, the way it did sometimes when a horse didn't act right. He rubbed his hand across his mouth and then was smiling again. "Let's find a bit of shade where Brownie can eat some grass while you tell me what you've been doing."

Leatrice wanted to beg Papa to take her home. She could sleep with her kittens in the loft and stay away from that woman. But Papa would never let her do that. Besides, she hadn't learned to read yet. And maybe if Sister Darcie and Papa both prayed for Sister Mona, she might stop being so mean. Leatrice would pray too, but she couldn't understand why Jesus said to pray for somebody who was mean to you.

26

The days passed into summer. Nothing changed except the weather and how both babies grew. Anna Grace was eating soft foods as well as nursing now. Eldress Maria allowed me to go to the Gathering Family kitchen to prepare her oatmeal and applesauce. Those in the kitchen liked me coming, for I brought the babies with me.

Someone was ever ready to stop whatever they were doing to entertain the little ones. Even Sister Reva, who had been so impatient with me while I was carrying Anna Grace. As soon as I entered the kitchen now, she reached for Anna Grace, lifted her up in the air, and started babbling baby talk. Anna Grace rewarded her with smiles and giggles.

"It is good to have my hands on a baby again," Sister Reva said on a day late in July. "We should have children in every house instead of all set apart. Especially babies."

A different worker, Sister Alice, held Benjamin. The poor baby cried as soon as she took him, but when Sister Alice cooed in his ear, he quieted.

Sister Reva nodded to Sister Nila, who had worked with me in the kitchen months before. "Get the gruel we made for this little one. I think he is hungry." She looked at me. "I know you are doing your best to feed them, Sister Darcie, but two babies are a lot for one as scrawny as you. They could need more. How old is he now?"

She didn't mean the scrawny as an insult, just the truth. I was very thin. Nursing two babies and attending to my assigned duties of cleaning, sewing, or sometimes working in the garden while the babies slept in the shade kept me, as Sister Reva so truthfully said, scrawny. She did not look as if she had ever been scrawny. She was a fine testimony to the goodness of the food she prepared in her kitchen.

"He is a little more than three months if Sister Lettie was right about him being only a day old when Sister Helene found him."

"Sister Lettie is always right." Sister Reva announced it as if that was truth all should know. "And I am always right about food. We need to feed these babies to get them healthy before they have to go live at the Children's House."

I blanched at her so casual mention of the babies being taken from me. I was continuing to pray, each day more fervently, for an answer to the blessing and dilemma of my growing babies. Feeding them porridge or gruel might make that day come faster, but Sister Reva was right. Benjamin did seem hungry, and even Anna Grace had sucked on her fingers more before I started feeding her extra food. She was five months old. Able to sit now, propped by pillows.

Brother Jonas had fashioned a new contrivance for transporting the babies. He bolted a very small cushioned chair to a slightly bigger cart. So now I tied Anna Grace in the cart's chair and carried Benjamin next to my heart. He cried less and Anna Grace laughed more.

Sister Leatrice still came to help with the babies at mealtimes, often alone since she was more familiar with the lay of the village. Occasionally, Sister Janice came with her, and now and again, since that unhappy first time, Sister Mona walked along with us.

Our prayers had not yet made a change in the girl, since she continually tried to upset Sister Leatrice. However, perhaps our prayers helped in a different way, for Leatrice kept her peaceful calm even when I was the one ready to throw a shoe at the girl. I prayed then for a love for the girl that passed understanding.

I knew the Lord could give such love, for I had prayed the same for Eldress Maria, and now I could truly say I was fond of the old woman. That could be, Sister Genna reminded me, because Eldress Maria had softened.

"Perhaps because of prayer," I told Sister Genna.

"More likely because of Anna Grace."

Sister Genna was ever a realist, and of course, she was right. Eldress Maria made some excuse or another to come wherever I was working each day and hold Anna Grace for a while. To let me work, she said, but I saw the way she smiled at my baby girl. Anna Grace was a child ready to reach for anyone to hold her. I tried to be glad about that. I was glad about that. If the day came when they did separate her from me, she would not mourn the same as I. And yet I wanted her to need me, her mother.

As young Leatrice needed her father. He came faithfully to see her, at times bringing along Leatrice's grandfather. When he showed up early enough to catch Leatrice walking with me to the morning meal as he had that first time, I was always happy to see him coming toward us. And not only because of Leatrice. He seemed like an old friend, even though I hadn't known him long.

That first day when Sister Reva spooned the thin gruel into Benjamin's mouth, more ended up on his face and clothes than inside him as he pushed it out with his tongue. But then he rolled a bit of it around in his mouth and swallowed. After that, plenty still spotted his face, but some also found a way to his stomach. The sisters in the kitchen and I cheered him on as we opened our mouths when Sister Reva pushed the spoon toward him as if to help him eat.

Later, after the evening meal, we had worship practice. Eldress Maria had decided I should once more attend the practice times to learn the songs and dances, although I still did not attend the Sunday services. I was just as glad, for I feared drawing the notice of the Ministry elders and eldresses to my babies. I think Eldress Maria felt the same.

On those nights, Sister Ellie, Sister Genna, or I took turns staying with the babies in our retiring room. Not only did Sister Helene not want to miss the worship time, tending to both babies was challenging for her. This night Sister Genna looked up at me from the rocking chair when we came back to the room after the final song was sung and the last dance labored, as the Shakers said. Benjamin slept contentedly against her shoulder.

"Do you think he is sick?" She looked concerned. "He has hardly cried at all."

"Nay, I think he is full. Sister Reva made him gruel. She worried that I didn't have enough milk for him."

"So he's eating solid foods now." Sister Genna looked thoughtful as she studied Benjamin's sweet head. "He could stop nursing."

"Nay," Sister Ellie spoke up. "He still needs to nurse."

"But he could survive with food mashed and fed to him."

"He could, but he won't need to. My milk has not dried up." I took the baby from her and put him in his cradle. Anna Grace was already asleep. The stomping and singing in the room down the hall never disturbed her. But then she had heard it ever since she was born. Songs in the night were as natural as sunlight in the morning to her.

"Where's Sister Helene?" Sister Genna asked.

"She told us she would be along soon. She needed to talk to someone." I sat down on the bed and undid my shoe lacings.

"Not one of the brothers, do you think?" Sister Genna lifted her eyebrows as she untied her apron and hung it on one of the pegs along the railing behind her bed.

"Wouldn't that be the sweetest thing? Our Sister Helene in love." Sister Ellie held her hands over her heart and sighed. Then she shook her head. "But nay, I don't think so."

Sister Genna laughed. "The very idea of one of the brethren making eyes at her would have our sister breaking out in hives."

"You never know," Sister Ellie said. "Love can sometimes sneak up on a person."

"Was it that way for you, Sister Ellie?" I asked.

"Yea. I was so young when Albert came calling. He said he'd had his eye on me at church for some time and was merely waiting until I was old enough to court. He is ten years older than me." Sister Ellie sighed as she sat down on the bed and rolled down her stockings. "He brought me a fistful of daisies he'd picked along the road to my house. He quite knocked the breath out of me. I hadn't even thought

271

of falling in love, but when he smiled at me with those blue eyes, I think I would have taken his hand and walked right out of my house to the preacher's that very day. We had some good years."

"Before the Shakers," Sister Genna said.

Sister Ellie sighed again, a sorrowful sound this time. "Yea, before the Shakers."

"Did you not try to turn him against coming to the Shakers?" Sister Genna asked.

"Yea, but the Shakers came to our house and convinced him the Lord intended him to be a Shaker." She shrugged and raised her hands up and let them fall back into her lap. "Once he believed that in his heart, my words were nothing more than the clanging cymbals spoken of in Corinthians. They meant nothing. I hoped that once we were here and separated from each other and our children, he would miss the love we had shared for so many years, but that did not happen. Perhaps the Lord did lead him here, and I am wrong to still wish for a different way."

"Nay." Sister Genna pulled on her nightgown. "Men get odd ideas sometimes. Just like my Jeremy thinking I couldn't go west with him and sending me here instead. I shouldn't have meekly agreed. That is one thing the Shakers have done for me. Helped me see that what a woman wants can matter. While I don't believe everything this Shaker Mother Ann taught, she had to be strong and vocal in her beliefs to get so many to follow her. Not just other women, but men too."

"It is good Sister Helene is not hearing us talk," I said. "Or Eldress Maria. They might both think I have led the two of you astray, for they know that I have many doubts about the Shaker way."

"In a way, you have changed my thinking," Sister Ellie said. "You brought the babies to our room."

"The babies?" I frowned, not understanding.

"Yea, the babies have reawakened my yearning for a normal life," Sister Ellie said. "A life where I can rock my grandbabies and teach my young daughter how to cook and sew instead of letting others do so. To be a mother again instead of pretending to be a sister." She looked over at Sister Genna and then me. "Not that I haven't loved being sister to you both. And to Sister Helene too, but I need more."

Sister Genna and I both moved over to sit with her on her bed. "You sound as if you have made a decision for change." Sister Genna took her hand.

"Yea. My older daughter is in the family way again. She already has one little one and she needs me."

"What about Abby?" I asked.

"Yea, Abby." Sister Ellie's voice was very quiet. "I got permission to speak with Albert. And he agreed to let Abby go with me should I decide to leave."

"That's good." I looked at her sad face. "Isn't it?"

Sister Genna tightened her hold on Sister Ellie's hand. "Tell us what has your heart so heavy."

"He said she could go with me, but only if it was her choice." Distress was evident on Sister Ellie's face. "A child cannot know what is best for her."

"Have you talked to her?" I asked.

Sister Ellie's head drooped as she stared at her lap. "Not yet."

"They aren't refusing to let you see her, are they?" Sister Genna was tense, ready to do battle with someone, anyone, on Sister Ellie's behalf.

"Nay, Sister Corinne says I may talk to Abby tomorrow."

"Then why the long face?" Sister Genna asked, but I understood Sister Ellie's worry. I had seen young Abby at the Children's House.

"She won't come with me. Not willingly. Perhaps if Albert came too. If we were a family again, but nay." Sister Ellie's voice died away.

"Perhaps you are wrong." My heart was heavy for her.

She slowly shook her head. "I wish I could believe that, but it does little good to refuse to face the truth. My Abby is happy here. Others have replaced me as her mother. She barely remembers me, if she remembers me at all. She was only four when we came." A tear dropped from her eye to land on her hand. She didn't wipe it away.

"We will pray you are wrong." Sister Genna clutched Sister Ellie's hand and reached for mine. "Now. With all our hearts, Sisters."

We bent our heads close together then and silently prayed. I could almost feel their prayers joining mine. I wanted to believe our prayers would be answered, but I think Sister Genna was the only one of the three of us who prayed with belief.

Benjamin started fussing and brought us away from our prayers. Sister Ellie stood up. "Let me take care of him tonight. I might not get to do so again."

"You are leaving that soon?" I asked.

"Yea, Elizabeth's husband is coming to fetch me."

Tears pricked my eyes. "I don't think I can bear to see you leave."

She blinked back tears of her own. "You will be fine. Sister Genna will be here to help you. And Sister Helene too."

Sister Genna picked Benjamin up out of his cradle and handed him to Sister Ellie. "Does she know? Sister Helene?"

"I don't think so. I did speak to Eldress Maria. I had to in order to arrange to see Abby. She is very unhappy with me. Says I am stepping onto a slippery slope to destruction." Sister Ellie sat down in the rocking chair and put Benjamin up to her shoulder, as he most liked being held. "Perhaps I am."

"Coming to this village in the first place was the slippery slope to sorrow." Sister Genna folded the cover back on her bed. "You are doing exactly what you should."

"Even if Abby refuses to come with me?" Sister Ellie sounded lost.

"If she won't go with you, you have lost her already. Staying won't change that." Sister Genna's voice was as sad as Sister Ellie's.

"But she might change her mind when she gets older and want me to be her mother again." Sister Ellie rocked back and forth and patted Benjamin's back. He stopped crying.

"We have prayed that will be tomorrow," Sister Genna said. "But even if it isn't and she doesn't make that sensible decision until later, she can come to you then."

"If she knows how to find me."

"Of course she could find you." I looked up from tucking the blanket tighter around Anna Grace. I rested my hand on her, loving the feel of her chest rising and falling. "You and Elizabeth can come see her. They won't keep you from visiting, will they?" Even though I had been in the village a year, I still did not know many of the Shaker rules.

"Nay. But they would leave the choice of seeing me or not to Abby." She let out a long sigh. "I remember poor Mrs.

York. I know that was before you came among us, Sister Darcie, but were you here then, Sister Genna?"

"I was." Sister Genna shook her head. "The most sorrowful sight."

"What was that?" I asked.

Sister Ellie swallowed hard and new tears slid down her cheeks. "You tell her, Sister Genna."

"Mrs. York's son was here. I don't know if she went through a bad time and brought him herself, or if his father did. Whichever way it was, she obviously loved the boy, and after a time her situation must have improved. She drove a buggy here to see him every day. I never knew if she hoped to take him away with her or merely wanted to see him."

"They wouldn't let him see her?" I frowned.

Sister Ellie spoke up. "They did not forbid her to come. Nor did they forbid the boy going out to his mother." More tears wet her cheek.

"Then why so sad at the telling of the story?"

"They allowed him to go see her, but they did not make him do so," Sister Ellie said. "So he did not."

"Day after day after day, his mother came and waited in her buggy." Sister Genna handed Sister Ellie a handkerchief. "It was dreadful to witness."

"He never went out?" I said.

"Nay." With her free hand, Sister Ellie wiped away her tears even as she continued to rock Benjamin. "Finally one day, Sister Tansy went out and sat with the mother in her buggy for a long time. I don't know what she told the woman, but she didn't come back."

"Is the boy still here?"

"I was never sure which child he was," Sister Genna said.

"So maybe he is, or maybe once she stopped coming, he went to her. I hope that."

"But you don't believe it," Sister Ellie said softly. "Such might be what would happen should I come back to visit Abby."

"You don't know yet that our prayers won't be answered. She may go with you now." Sister Genna pounded her pillow to fluff the feathers before she lay down. "I think Sister Helene is coming. If you tire of rocking Benjamin, wake me."

"You won't leave without telling us goodbye, will you?" I whispered as Sister Helene came through the door.

"Nay, my sister. I will not."

27

"I get the feeling you're avoiding me, Flynn." Irene stepped between him and the door after supper.

"Just busy, Irene. Lots to do."

That was certainly true. He didn't have two free minutes to rub together, between his work with the horses, keeping up the farm here, and working on the house. That hadn't gone as quickly as he'd hoped. Here it was the first of August and he still needed to replace floorboards and rebuild part of the kitchen chimney.

"Surely you have a few minutes to sit on the porch and cool off before you go hide out in the barn. It can't be all that comfortable sleeping out there." Irene fanned her face with a folded paper and led the way out the door. She pushed a chair toward him. "Sit down. Rest a while."

"Where's Silas?" Flynn looked around.

"He took some scraps out to those barn cats. I never knew a man to be so fond of cats." She sat down. "Sit awhile. I promise not to make eyes at you. I just need somebody to talk to."

"You could try your husband." Flynn scooted the chair

away from Irene and sat down. Maybe it was past time for an honest talk.

"Oh, I try him all right." Irene smiled. "I don't think he's enjoying married life. The poor man is too old. Too sick."

"He's better. Not coughing much at all."

"Must be my tonic."

He could tell by the way she twisted her mouth to the side to hide a smile that she knew Silas wasn't drinking the tonic. He pretended along with her. "Could be."

She laughed out loud then. "You men are so funny. I've known Silas hasn't been drinking that for weeks."

"Then why do you keep making it?"

"Got to keep up the farce, don't we? That I'm a loving wife. That he's a trusting husband glad to be married to a younger woman like me. That you don't hate my guts."

"I don't hate your guts."

"You don't like me." She raised her eyebrows as she peered over at him. "Are you going to lie and deny that?"

"I don't lie." Flynn didn't shrink back from her look, but he didn't answer her either.

"You know, I think you think that's true, but everybody lies. Sometimes to ourselves the most. That's how we survive in this life."

"What lies do you tell yourself?" Flynn was suddenly curious about Irene. She was attractive enough if a man just looked at the outside.

"Too many to name." She stared out at the lane in front of the house. "Then again, maybe I've never lied to myself. Only to everybody else." She looked back at Flynn. "I was married before. Did you know that?"

"I think somebody did tell me you were a widow when I

asked around about you last year." That was before he hired her to watch Leatrice when she'd been new to the town.

"Yes, a widow." She let her gaze drift back out to the road. "A widow of my own making."

"So that was a lie? You weren't widowed?"

"No lie. His name was Barton. I ran away from home all the way to Kentucky with him. I doubt my father missed me back in Virginia except maybe for the work I did. My mother died in childbirth. Her seventh baby in ten years. I was oldest and so I became mother. Five younger than me. That seventh baby died along with my mother. Somebody was wanting something all the time. I couldn't even go to the outhouse without one of them tagging along. You'd think that might make me fond of them, but I just wished they'd all disappear. My father acted like he felt the same, except he was ready for me to disappear too."

"So you never liked children."

"So I never liked children." She smiled over at him. "Guess that explains why I had no patience with your Leatrice. Did she ever tell you about me locking her in the cellar?" Her smile actually got wider when he shook his head. "I told her not to or else, but I figured she'd run tell on me anyway. I know she told you about the bears."

"No. I overheard you threatening her with those bears. Don't you remember? That's why I sent you packing." Flynn gripped his hands together. He wanted to chase her off their porch and away from their land, but instead he clenched his jaw and sat still.

"She's such an impressionable child." She shrugged a little. "I suppose I should say I'm sorry, but that would be one of those lies. We're being painfully honest here, aren't we?" When Flynn didn't say anything, she went on. "Anyway, when Barton showed up to help my father clear some land and took a fancy to me, I jumped at my chance to get away."

"You should have wanted to take care of your brothers and sisters."

"Should have? I don't deny that. Want to? I do deny that. I'd done it for five years. It was somebody else's turn. So when Barton was through helping my father, he helped me. Gave me a hand up on his horse. We found a preacher and did everything legal like. I did love that man." She shook her head a little with a faraway look on her face.

"What happened to him?"

"He died."

"I'm sorry."

"I was too when I shot him. Like I said, I did love that man, but as good as he was when he wasn't drinking was as bad as he was when he got hold of some home brew. Made him crazy. I hid from him when I could, but that day he came at me with an axe. I didn't have much recourse except to shoot him."

Flynn didn't know what to say, so he didn't say anything.

"That surprised you, didn't it? Or maybe not." She looked over at him. "Anyway, I used to wonder if I could have just shot him in the leg, but I feared I'd miss. He was wild with the drink and ready to bash in my head with that axe. Wasn't anything for it except to aim for the chest. He was dead before he hit the floor. I wasn't even able to tell him I loved him, but I did cry enough tears to flood that room." She breathed out a long sigh. "I was nineteen."

"I'm sorry." And he was. But that didn't excuse other things she'd done.

"Aren't you going to ask me how come they didn't hang me?" Her smile was back.

"Sounded like self defense."

"I wasn't about to trust a judge or bunch of men on a jury believing that. I was young but I wasn't stupid. We didn't have any near neighbors. Barton liked his solitude. So it took me a couple of days of hard digging, but I managed to give him a proper burying. Then I went to town and told the sheriff Barton had died of cholera. It was the right time of the year for it. Nobody was interested in digging him up to see if I told the truth. Turned out the sheriff had lost his wife the year before and was some lonesome. I lived with his sister for a few months until he deemed it proper for us to marry. I was glad enough he didn't have any children to complicate matters. 'Course I never loved him. Not like I did Barton."

"What happened to him?"

"You mean did I shoot him dead?" She laughed, then gave him a sly look. "Or maybe poison him?"

"I assumed you were widowed again." Flynn didn't smile.

"That I was. But in a natural enough way. The sheriff was old when I married him and lived a sight longer than I thought he would. Anyway, once he was gone, I decided I needed a change of scenery. I wasn't as young as I used to be. I couldn't depend on my looks forever." She waved away a fly. "I hoped to find a man I could love something the way I did Barton. Thought maybe I'd found him when you came along."

"But you hadn't." Flynn kept his voice hard.

"I had." She waved her makeshift fan in front of her face a few times. "You just didn't go along with the plan."

"So why did you marry Silas?"

"I guess that ought to be easy enough to figure out. You."
She smiled over at him. "Silas didn't seem long for this world
with the way he was coughing and all. I figured I'd be here
and one thing would lead to another. A lonely man. An attractive woman. Hasn't worked out quite like I hoped. Guess
my looks are already failing me."

"Your looks were never the problem."

"Oh, does that mean you do find me attractive?" She leaned
toward him.

"No. That means I could never even consider marrying a
woman who wasn't good to my daughter."

She sighed. "As I said, children do complicate matters.
And now I'm stuck out here on this godforsaken farm married to an old man who worries I'm trying to poison him."

"Should he be worried? Should I be worried?" Flynn stared
at her without blinking.

"Could be. I've never had a great deal of patience. I could
poison our stew and we could all die together. Tragic but
romantic."

"You won't do that."

"I won't?" Irene fanned herself and then laughed again.
"You're right. I won't. I'm not too happy with how life is
going right now, but very little is permanent."

"Why don't you leave?" Flynn pointed toward the road.
"You're not happy. Silas isn't happy."

She slapped her hand on her chest in fake surprise. "But
I'm a married woman. I promised till death do us part."

"Then try being a wife to Silas. He's a good fellow."

"But so old. I used up some of the best years of my life
with an old man. I don't plan to spend the few good years I
have left with another old man."

Flynn stood up and looked down at her. "Could be you shouldn't have married him then."

"But he wanted me to so much. Thought I was just what you and that daughter of yours needed. He wasn't thinking about himself at all. Well, except he was tired of eating his own cooking." She smiled up at Flynn. "You have to admit I kept that part of the bargain. I've cooked for him. And nobody has died. Yet."

"Keep it that way." He gave her a hard look before he turned to go off the porch.

"You don't have to keep sleeping in the barn. I won't bother you unless you want to be bothered." She jumped up to put her hands on his back.

"I don't mind the barn." He stepped away from her.

She laughed again. "Maybe you should join those old Shakers over there where you took your daughter. I think you'd fit right in."

"I might. If all women were like you." He didn't look back at her as he went down the steps.

"So have you met one you like?" she called after him.

He kept walking without answering her. Out of nowhere the Shaker sister, Darcie, with her two babies came to mind. She always had smiles for Leatrice. And for him. Without actually thinking about it, he had started timing his visits to Leatrice so that he could see those smiles. If that wasn't the craziest thing. The first woman he'd really looked at since Lena died was a Shaker. The good Lord must have a sense of humor.

Silas stepped up beside him when he got to the barn. "What did she want?"

"To talk, she said."

"About what?" Silas looked out the barn toward the house.

"Her hard times mostly." Flynn picked up the pitchfork to clean out the stalls.

"Yeah, she's told me how things haven't been easy for her." Silas straightened a shovel hanging in the barn's breezeway. "She's right about one thing. I am too old. I shouldn't have tied her to me."

"You didn't force her to say 'I do.'"

"I know, but I didn't aim to ruin her life. Or ours." He stuck his hands in his pockets and stared down at the ground.

"She could leave." Flynn forked fresh bedding into one of the stalls.

"I suggested that very thing to her the other day, but she says she hasn't got anywhere to go. That she's my wife and I promised to provide for her." Silas pulled in a deep breath and blew it out slowly. "I guess I did when I married her and I've always been a man of my word."

"That does muddy the waters." Flynn straightened up and looked at Silas.

"True, but I can clear things up by giving her that place you bought after we trade properties all legal like. Tell you what. How about I ride along with you tomorrow morning to go see Leatrice? Then we can head on into town to take care of the paperwork about the farms."

"I know you say that's what you want to do, Silas, but I don't feel right about such an uneven trade."

"We're trading properties and I don't want to hear one more word against it." Silas stepped closer and poked his finger at Flynn's chest. "It's what I want. What Beatrice and Lena would expect of me."

"But what if I get married again?"

Silas peered up at Flynn. "You got somebody in mind?"

"Can't say that I do, but I might someday. If I did, then whoever I married and her children would have a claim on your farm if you sign it over to me. That's not what you want."

"That's where you're wrong. I think you finding a new woman would be a fine thing. Wouldn't bother me at all. Leatrice could do with some sisters and brothers."

"Slow down." Flynn held up his hand, palm out toward Silas. "I just wanted you to think about what could be. I'm not ready to stand up in front of a preacher with anybody."

"At least you're doing some considering." Silas grinned at him. "Maybe you ought to consider that little Shaker woman we see when we go visit Leatrice. The one with the babies. She's a pretty little thing. Seems to have a real warm smile for you."

"She smiles just as warm at you and Leatrice."

"Maybe at Leatrice. But that's to the good. She appears to be a fine mother to those babies too. My Beatrice was a loving mother like that. I was always sorry we never had more children for her to mother. Then she did get to mother Leatrice. Took up some of the slack from Lena."

Flynn frowned. "What do you mean? Lena loved Leatrice."

"I didn't say she didn't love her, but Beatrice was the one who mothered her. Lena didn't have much patience for mothering. You remember that, don't you?" Silas gave him a curious look. "Or maybe you were too busy with your horses to notice."

Flynn shut his eyes. He did remember. Ma Beatrice was the one who tucked Leatrice in at night and fed her breakfast in the mornings. "Maybe we should have moved out on our own."

"No need thinking about that. You can't go back and do things over. Besides, Lena was so young when Leatrice was born that it could be she wasn't ready to do all those mothering things. Being our only child, we'd spoiled her some. Well, maybe more than some. Who knows? If she hadn't lost those other babies, she might have gotten more into a mother role. Or if she was still with us now."

"She would." Flynn didn't know why he felt the need to defend Lena. If anybody loved her as much as he did, it was Silas.

Silas patted Flynn's shoulder. "I wasn't aiming to make you regretful. Leastways not about something like that. We were all happy with the way things were back then. Lena most of all. She got to go riding when she wanted and watch you with those horses. She did love the horses. And Beatrice loved mothering Leatrice. You know that."

He did know that. "I appreciate all you've done for me, Silas. I can never repay you."

"You already have a hundred times over." Silas smiled. "So how about the two of us go over to that Shaker village early in the morning to see Leatrice and maybe that pretty little Shaker sister too? Then we can go on into town."

"If you're sure."

"I'm sure."

"Leatrice will be happy to see you."

"I like going over there to see her." Silas looked out the end of the barn toward the trees. "It's the oddest thing, but I feel good when I go into that village. Everything seems to calm down inside me, like as how the Lord is telling me to quit worrying and just move along the path, whatever it is, that he opens up to me." Silas looked back at Flynn. "Do you feel that way over there?"

"Can't say that I do." Flynn shook his head a little. "I just aim to see Leatrice. That's all. She told me last week that she was pretty good at reading now. I think she's anxious to come on home."

"Home. That's a fine word, but I've been wondering lately if home maybe has more to do with the people you love than with a place." Silas looked out toward the trees again. "I haven't felt at home since Beatrice died. She was what made this place home for me. That's why it won't matter when we switch places. Trust me. It's the good Lord's plan."

28

Dark clouds blew in from the west on the night before Ellie's son-in-law was to come for her. Booming thunder rattled the windows just after the evening meal. I was glad to be back from the Children's House before the rain, but even inside, the storm's noise so startled Benjamin, someone had to hold him.

Sister Ellie insisted on staying with the babies while Sister Genna and I went to the evening worship practice. She had no reason to practice more of the dance exercises, since Shaker songs would soon be in her past.

We would have rather stayed with her and the babies, but that was not allowed. Neither Sister Genna nor I had any interest in learning the dances or songs of Shaker life coming down to us. We were both ready to walk out of the village with Sister Ellie, had that been possible. But instead we went through the motions of counting our steps and weaving back and forth, being careful to maintain a proper distance from any of the brethren. The lightning flashed through the windows and lit up the intense faces of those like Sister Helene, who did yearn after the Shaker way.

When the session was over, Eldress Maria followed us back to our retiring room to tell Sister Ellie the storm was a sign she was making a terrible mistake leaving the safe shelter of the village. When Sister Ellie refused to listen, the eldress declared she could no longer be called sister.

Sister Ellie did not shy away from Eldress Maria's words. Instead she handed Benjamin to Sister Genna and faced the eldress. "I am glad enough to be shed of the title Sister. Simply calling someone sister does not make it true."

"I fear trials will await you in the world." Eldress Maria spoke softly, her voice sad. "You were a good Shaker."

"I appreciate your forbearance with me through the years," Ellie said.

"Such was merely my duty." Eldress Maria's shoulders slumped as she turned and left the room. I had never seen her look so old.

That night we broke the Shaker rules and let our candle burn down while we talked long after the retiring bell rang. Now and again Sister Helene told us to extinguish the light, but when we did not, neither did she smother the flame. The last few days, she had talked to Ellie until her voice was hoarse to convince her not to leave, but eventually she joined Sister Genna and me as we cried with Ellie and prayed for her to have happiness as the dark hours ticked away.

Abby did not agree to go with her.

"But I did have the chance to tell her she would always be my daughter, and if ever the time came when she no longer was happy here at Harmony Hill, I would welcome her with open arms." Ellie shed fewer tears than the rest of us when she said this. She had already faced the sorrow of leaving her child.

"I am surprised Sister Corinne let you tell her that," Sister Helene whispered.

"She did tell Abby not to listen to one who was stepping out onto a wrong path toward destruction." A smile slipped across Ellie's face so quickly I wasn't sure I had actually seen it. "Perhaps I am."

"Nay, my sister," Sister Genna said. "You will have love and happiness and joy. And someday Abby will come to you."

Sister Helene looked at Sister Genna ready to argue, but Sister Genna held up her hand. "You have had your turn the last two days. Now it is time to give Sister Ellie our love, not our unhappy words."

"No longer our sister," Sister Helene said sadly.

Sister Genna took one of Ellie's hands and I took the other. "Always our sister," we said almost in unison.

"And I yours." Ellie looked over at Sister Helene. "And yours too, my sister. I do appreciate your concern, but I have been here for six years. Way past the time I should have become a covenanted member. I followed your rules, even those that seemed odd. I willingly gave my hands to work and my feet to dance, and long ago before I even knew about this village, I gave my heart to the Lord, but there is much about your ways here that I could never accept."

"If I cannot change your thinking, at least I can pray for you and assure you that you will be welcomed back if you decide to return," Sister Helene said.

Sister Genna started to speak, but Ellie squeezed her hand. "Nay, Sister. Remember your own words from a moment ago. Let us not fuss on this last night together. I am happy to have Sister Helene's prayers."

"I'm sorry our prayers for you and Abby weren't answered," Sister Genna said.

"Not answered as we hoped, but yet answered." Ellie smiled first at Sister Genna and then me. "Abby pulled away from Sister Corinne as they were leaving and came back to hug me and let me hug her. She even whispered 'Goodbye, Mother' in my ear. I will ever feel her in my arms and hear her sweet voice in my ear. That was our prayers answered and a gift I can take with me."

With daylight came the hard parting. The rising bell rang to signal time to be about our assigned chores. The storms had passed in the night, but the day was still gray with clouds. As was my routine, I had fed the babies before the rising bell. On this day, my three sisters were awake with me in these early morning hours. Ellie cuddled Anna Grace while Benjamin nursed and then held Benjamin while I fed Anna Grace.

"I will miss these sweet babies and you, my sisters." She put Benjamin down to embrace Sister Helene and then Sister Genna when they were dressed and ready to be about their duties.

"No tears," she told Sister Helene, but tears streamed down the sister's face anyway as she turned and left.

Ellie smiled then at Sister Genna. "I don't have to tell you no tears. Not our tough and capable Sister Genna."

"I have no reason for tears," Sister Genna said. "It's more a day for joy. I'm glad you are leaving this place. I hope to do the same, and aren't we both praying our Sister Darcie and Anna Grace will find a path out of here very soon?"

"Prayers for you too." Ellie held Sister Genna's hands. "Your Jeremy will come back for you as he promised."

"It's been so long since I've heard from him. He could be dead."

"Nay." Ellie shook her head. "It will be a while before I can stop saying yea and nay. But I have faith your Jeremy is not dead, merely delayed longer than he expected. After all, anything is possible. Just think of my Abby calling me 'Mother' after I thought she'd forgotten my love."

"Then I will have faith too. At least for a little longer." She hugged Ellie again and then was gone. Without tears.

I knew I would not be able to do the same. Tears already threatened to spill out of my eyes as I straightened our retiring room, which was my morning duty. While I swept the floor and straightened the beds we had not slept in, Ellie talked to the babies. Sweet words about how beloved they were and how they were going to grow up strong to follow the Lord's leading.

"And you, Anna Grace, will be beautiful like your mother and someday marry a good man and have lovable babies like you."

I stopped what I was doing and looked at her. "I am not beautiful, but I do think Anna Grace will be."

"Did your husband never tell you that you were beautiful?"

"Yea, but he was looking through eyes of love."

"Is that not the very best way to be beautiful? But you are easy to look at no matter the eyes that see you. That gleaming red hair. Those golden green eyes that see so much more than some can see. Your face that finds a way to smile even in sad moments. But better than how you look is your strength. Whatever happens, you will survive."

"Even losing Anna Grace if they take her from me?" I knew I could not have any kind of smile on my face then.

"Yea, even then should that happen, but it is not going to. You will not let it happen."

"How will I stop it?" My gaze went to my child.

"I don't know the answer to that, but the same as I have faith Sister Genna's Jeremy will yet return for her, I have faith an answer will come for you." She put Anna Grace down and came to stand in front of me. "You will not let them take Anna Grace from you as I let them take Abby from me."

"I want to believe you. I do believe you." I looked up at her since she was taller than I. "But I don't know how I will keep it from happening."

"That's where faith comes in. And continued prayers." She put her hands on my shoulders and bent down to look directly into my face. "And that determined strength you have."

"I am going to miss you so much."

"But you won't be here that much longer and then perhaps the Lord will let our paths cross again. I will keep my eye out for an answer to your dilemma. Perhaps a man in need of a housekeeper or an older woman without family who needs someone to care for her. Perhaps one of our brethren here will take a fancy to you and ask you to leave with him."

"I can't think of loving someone as I did Walter." A tear slipped out of my eye and down my cheek.

She rubbed it away with her thumb. "You won't love anyone as you loved him. If you love again, it will be a new way with a new man. That is as it should be."

"And you? Will you love again?"

"Nay, I am yet married to Albert, whether he wants to be my husband or not. But I will love my grandchildren and my children and the ones they have chosen to love. As Sister

Genna says, it is good. Not exactly as I would want, but good nevertheless."

We embraced then and more tears slid down my cheeks. Her eyes were moist too as she turned from me. She laid her Shaker cap and the neck kerchief on her bed. "I leave these, but I take many good memories of our nights here with these babies. Take care of them and love Benjamin as your own."

"I do already."

"You may have to steal away in the night if you take Benjamin with you when you leave." She said it as if there was no doubt I would leave.

"Sister Genna would be heartbroken if I took Benjamin away from her."

"If you don't, the Shakers will. Keep that in mind, my sister."

Ellie picked up each baby for one more kiss. Anna Grace laughed, as seemed so easy for her. Then Benjamin laughed too. That made Ellie and me laugh as well, for he did not laugh often.

"It is good to leave on a smile." She picked up her bundle of personal things then and without another word was out the door. She had already decided to slip away before the morning meal to meet her son-in-law somewhere on the road outside the village.

I watched from the window as she walked away. She did not look back. I sent prayers chasing after her until she was out of sight, and then I leaned my head against the window and wept. I did not feel strong at all.

When I heard the door open behind me, I pulled myself together and wiped away my tears before I turned. I knew it would be Eldress Maria. She often came into our room before the morning meal. Without saying that was the reason, I knew it was so the babies would not be alone while I carried out the chamber pot and the water from our morning ablutions.

She pretended not to notice my red eyes. Nor did she speak of Ellie, even though she looked at the cap and neck kerchief laid out on her bed. Instead she said "good morning" as usual and picked Anna Grace up from her pallet on the floor. I could no longer leave her in the cradle while I cleaned the room, for fear she would grab the sides to raise herself up and topple out.

"Ellie's gone." I felt it wrong not to speak of Ellie at all.

Eldress Maria frowned at me. "The one of whom you speak is of the world now. Her name will no longer be spoken in my presence until she comes to her senses and returns to us."

I started to say something, but the look she gave me made the words die in my throat.

Her smile returned as she looked at Anna Grace. "How old is our little sister Anna Grace now?"

"Nearly six months."

"The time has passed so quickly." She kissed my baby's cheek and was rewarded with a smile. "You'd best hurry to finish your duties before the morning meal."

"Yea."

I wanted to ask if I could simply fetch food for the babies from our kitchen this day instead of going to the Children's House. I could not imagine eating with the sorrow of Ellie's leaving weighing upon my heart, but I knew the eldress would not approve. Plus, Leatrice would soon be waiting on the steps to walk me to the Children's House. I could not disappoint her, for she looked forward to helping with the babies.

Perhaps this would be a morning her father came. I hoped so, for then I could ask if he had seen Ellie on the road with her son-in-law. That would let me know she was not alone.

That was what I would be if I walked out of the village. Alone.

29

Sister Darcie wasn't at the door when Leatrice got to her house. Leatrice never had to wait for her. Maybe she had missed her, but the little wagon Anna Grace rode in was by the steps. Leatrice shifted from one foot to the other as she watched the door and wondered if she should go inside to see if something was wrong with Sister Darcie.

A few raindrops left over from the storms in the night hit her cap. She should have worn her cloak, but then she would have been hot even this early in the morning. It was summer. August. Sister Tansy told them it was August yesterday.

Leatrice didn't want to be here anymore. She had learned her letters and the secret of how they went together to make words. She could read. Her father could help her with words she couldn't sound out.

That woman was why she was here. She was why Papa was working on a new place for them to live. But Leatrice hadn't thought it would take so long. Not longer than she needed to learn to read. Sister Josephine said she had plenty more to learn. Especially about how to be the right kind of Shaker sister.

She didn't want to be a Shaker. She wanted to go home and see her kittens. They would be cats by now. Kittens grew up fast. Leatrice sighed and sat down on the steps. She didn't care if she did get the skirt of her dress wet and make Sister Tansy fuss about taking proper care of her clothes. Somebody was always fussing about something. So many rules. She wasn't allowed to do this or that. Sometimes she just wanted to go outside and scream.

She was pretty sure screaming was against the rules. At least once somebody got to be seven. Baby Benjamin could get away with screaming, but lately he hadn't cried as much. Sister Darcie said that was because she was feeding him mashed-up food and gruel. Leatrice wrinkled her nose at the thought of eating gruel. She wasn't sure exactly what it was, but it sounded bad. Maybe not as bad as that woman's black secret ingredient, but still not good.

If that woman would just go away, things would be better. The same as if Mona went away, things would be better. Sister Darcie told her to pray for Sister Mona and Leatrice did. But that hadn't kept Sister Mona from doing stuff to make her mad. So far Leatrice hadn't thrown any more shoes at her. So far.

Whenever Sister Mona started bothering her, Leatrice did say a silent prayer. Those were the kind the Shakers liked. She had several for Sister Mona. *Lord, help Sister Mona not be so mean. Lord, make Sister Mona go somewhere else. Lord, make a sweat bee sting Sister Mona.* She said that last one when they were out in the garden. Sometimes it worked and other times the sweat bee stung Leatrice.

Mamaw Bea used to say the Lord didn't always answer your prayers exactly the way you wanted, but that he had a way of making things work out right. If the answer wasn't what you thought it should be, that was the Lord's way of letting you know maybe you hadn't prayed the right prayer.

Leatrice sighed. Her prayers for Sister Mona probably weren't the right prayers. Especially the sweat bee one. But Sister Darcie had said she was going to pray for Sister Mona and so had Papa. Their prayers would be better and Sister Mona wasn't getting any nicer. So what did that mean?

Maybe she'd ask Sister Darcie when she came out of her house. If she didn't come soon, they were going to be late, and being on time was one of those rules they weren't supposed to break. Leatrice had to be in line when they rang the little bell inside the Children's House.

The door opened behind Leatrice just as the big village bell began to ring. Usually she and Sister Darcie were already walking along the path between the houses when that happened.

"I'm sorry you had to wait on me." Sister Darcie hurried down the steps. She had a little blanket draped over Anna Grace's head and Baby Benjamin was trying to kick out of the wrap she had in front of her chest. "I hope it doesn't start raining again."

Sister Darcie wasn't smiling the way she usually was, and her eyes were all red. "Are you all right?" Leatrice asked.

"I'm fine." Sister Darcie gave her a quick hug after she fastened Anna Grace onto the little wagon seat. "We better hurry. Sister Corinne will not be happy if we are late."

"Sister Corinne is never happy," Leatrice said.

"Surely that is not true. Everybody should be happy some of the time."

Sister Darcie didn't look happy at all. Leatrice was pretty

sure she had a tear on her cheek instead of a raindrop. Maybe Leatrice needed to pray for her too. That wouldn't be hard. She liked Sister Darcie. But thinking about praying made her remember Sister Mona again and how just last night she had sneaked over to tie Leatrice's shoelaces together in knots. Leatrice worked out the knots without saying anything, but she wished a wasp would be in Sister Mona's cap.

"Do you still pray for Sister Mona?" Leatrice asked as she pushed Anna Grace down the walkway. They hit a little bump and Anna Grace laughed the way she always did.

"I do," Sister Darcie said. "Do you?"

"Yea, but it doesn't help. She's always being mean to me."

"Have you thrown another shoe at her?"

"Nay, but I want to." Leatrice watched the path. A little bump was all right, but she needed to guide around the big bumps that might make the wagon turn over.

"I don't blame you," Sister Darcie said. "I pray for you too, Sister Leatrice."

"What do you pray?"

"I pray that your father will come to see you. That you will learn to read. That you will have a smile on your face when you come to walk with me. That I can always be your friend."

"You mean sister."

"Nay. I mean friend. But a sister can be a friend too." A drop of water rolled down Sister Darcie's face.

Leatrice was positive this one was a tear. "Are you sad today?"

"I am. One of my sister friends left the village this morning, and I don't know when I will see her again."

"You won't leave too, will you?" Leatrice looked up at her. "And take the babies?"

"Not today," Sister Darcie's voice was very quiet. "But maybe someday."

Leatrice let go of the wagon handle and turned to hug Sister Darcie. "Please don't go."

Sister Darcie stroked Leatrice's head. "Shh, Leatrice. I am still here, and it could be your father will take you home before I find a way to leave. But let this be a secret between us. I would not like to upset Sister Tansy or Sister Corinne."

Leatrice thought of how she was supposed to confess every wrong thing to Sister Tansy, but keeping a secret with Sister Darcie didn't feel like a wrong thing. "I can keep a secret."

"Good." Sister Darcie pushed her away and smiled. "And look who's coming up the road. Your father and your grand-father too."

My little friend's worries turned into smiles. She always sparkled when she saw her father coming. I was glad enough to see him myself. Perhaps because his coming made Leatrice so happy.

Then as we continued on toward him, I knew it was more than her happiness that made my heart beat a bit faster at the sight of him sitting tall on his horse. Perhaps Ellie's words predicting I would again find love had me looking at this good man in a different way.

I pushed the thought aside. He had shown me nothing more than the kind attention he might have afforded anyone with his daughter. The good I felt at his sight was merely my joy for this sweet child Leatrice, mixed with a wish for what could not be, as I imagined Walter, like this man, a loving father to our Anna Grace, had he lived.

When we met them, he dismounted and stepped close to hug Leatrice. Anna Grace waved her hands and made baby noises to get his attention. He laughed and leaned down to her.

"And how is young Anna Grace this misty gray morning?" When she smiled, he went on. "Ah, I can see the weather makes no difference to your happy heart. Your mother has loved you well."

"I have loved Benjamin as well and he cries as much as Anna Grace smiles." I felt a smile curling my own lips.

The grandfather whose name I could not remember slid down off his horse to come over to us. He was a small man next to Leatrice's father and often pale when he came to visit. But today he looked well. "That is life, Miss Darcie. A little laughter. A few tears. We are blessed when the smiles outnumber the tears."

"You are so right, sir." I liked that he hadn't named me sister. I was always sorry when Mr. Keller called me sister.

Mr. Keller looked at me now and I spoke quickly in hopes he would ignore my tear-reddened eyes. "Did you see a woman in Shaker dress on the road as you came to the village?"

"Has someone run away?" he asked.

"She didn't run away. She freely walked out of the village early this morning to meet her son-in-law, but I will feel better to know he came for her."

"We did meet a buggy with a young man and a woman in a blue dress. You remember, don't you, Silas?" He looked at the grandfather, then back at me. "Could that have been the woman you mean?"

"Yea." My smile came easier. "Thank you so much. I hoped if you came this morning, you would see her and ease my worries for her."

"Was there trouble here?" His smile seemed less sure.

"No place is totally without trouble," I said.

"This place seems so peaceful." The grandfather he had called Silas looked around.

"For many it is. They work to make it a heaven on earth. With unity of spirit." I surprised myself by sounding like Sister Helene trying to convert someone to the Shaker life. I had to balance out what I said. "For others the unity is no more than an impossible dream."

"Then why are those here?" the grandfather asked.

"Life can give some few choices." I held my little Benjamin closer and let my gaze fasten on Anna Grace. Three who had little choice of where we were.

"Are you one of those?" Leatrice's father asked.

I raised my eyes to meet his. "Yes." I purposely did not use the Shaker yea. "Yes, I am." I looked away from him at Leatrice. "Come, Leatrice. We best hurry or we'll be late for the meal."

"I'm not hungry. I want to stay here with Papa and Grandpa." She folded her arms across her chest. "I don't want to do what they say anymore. I want to go home." Her lips trembled.

"I can tell Sister Tansy that you are with your father and grandfather." It wouldn't hurt her to miss a meal. Perhaps her father would take her home as she wished. I reached to push Anna Grace the rest of the way to the Children's House.

"Go. Eat." Her father's voice was firm. "When you come back, we will talk."

Without a word, she came back to the walkway and moved in front of me to push Anna Grace. I longed to put my hand on her shoulder to let her know I understood how she felt, but instead I walked silently behind her.

Sister Corinne's frown was fierce when we came into the hallway as the boys and girls moved toward the dining room. Leatrice had carried Anna Grace up the steps, but now she handed her to me as Sister Janice reached to pull her into the line. I waited and went in last. I was thankful Benjamin was asleep next to my breast.

After I tied a towel around Anna Grace's middle to hold her in the chair next to me, I forced down the eggs and biscuits. The babies needed the milk my body made, and as Sister Genna had said, I should be happy for Ellie, not too sad to eat.

After the meal I found Sister Tansy to ask a special forgiveness for Leatrice, who trailed after me, carrying Anna Grace. "Her grandfather is here with her father. Perhaps Sister Leatrice could be given a few extra minutes to visit with him."

"But what of you and the babies?" she asked. "You truly need help with them."

"I can manage." I took Anna Grace from Leatrice and held her on my hip while still holding Benjamin. It wasn't an easy task, but one I could do. Leatrice looked up at Sister Tansy with hopeful eyes.

"I'll help her." Sister Mona slipped up beside us.

Sister Tansy looked at me. "Is that all right with you, Sister Darcie?"

Sister Mona had not come with Leatrice to walk with me for some time, but Leatrice had just told me she had not changed her ways. My arm tightened around my daughter as I looked at the girl.

"Please." She reached for Anna Grace.

"I can carry her to her cart." Leatrice started to step in front of Sister Mona.

I wanted to let her, to turn away Sister Mona's offer of help. But I had been praying for the girl and something in her eyes made me know this was a time to trust those prayers. "Nay, Sister Leatrice. Sister Mona can help me today." I let the girl take Anna Grace.

"Very well," Sister Tansy said. "Go, all of you, but Sister Leatrice, tell your father you must be back to your duties in an hour." She hurried away without a backward look.

Leatrice did look back several times when I told her to go on out to her father.

"I don't think she trusts me with Anna Grace." Sister Mona propped my baby on her slim hip. Anna Grace grabbed hold of the girl's neck kerchief. She was not concerned. She'd known nothing but kindness so far in her young life.

"But I do." I looked directly at Sister Mona. "And even more important, Anna Grace trusts you. See how she's smiling at you."

I prayed as I led the way out the door and down the steep concrete steps. I breathed easier after Sister Mona sat Anna Grace in her wagon seat. I fastened the straps and stepped back to let Sister Mona take the handle.

"Did you think I would drop her?"

"Nay. If I thought that, I would not have let you carry her."

"I could have dropped her." Sister Mona pushed the wagon along beside me.

"But you did not."

She had a sly look as she peered over at me. The girl was

almost as tall as I, but wafer thin. "Would you have cried if I had?"

"Yea, I would be very upset if my daughter got hurt. I love her very much."

"My mother loved me very much, but she died. Now nobody loves me." She looked over her shoulder back to where Leatrice was with her father and grandfather. "I wish she would go away. I don't like her."

"Why?" I shifted Benjamin, who squirmed in his wrap. Cries were sure to follow.

"Everybody loves her. Her father and grandfather. Sister Janice. Sister Tansy. Not Sister Corinne. She doesn't like anybody." She made a face and then looked over at me again. "But you love her."

"I do. Why do you think that is?"

"I don't know." Sister Mona shrugged a little. "Maybe because she is pretty."

"I don't think it has anything to do with how she looks." I wanted to say the right thing to help Mona. "You are as pretty as she is. Especially when you smile."

Sister Mona stopped walking and touched her face. Then she narrowed her eyes and stared at me. "You're just saying that. You don't really believe it."

"I don't say things I don't believe." I wasn't lying. I did think with her light blue eyes, taffy-colored hair, and nicely shaped nose and mouth she had every chance of being a very pretty woman.

"My mother used to tell me I was pretty. Before she died."

"Losing her must have been really hard for you." I kept my voice soft.

"Well, no need whining and moaning about it now. I'll

get by." She had her fierce look again. "I don't care whether anybody likes me or not. Maybe I'll grow up to be like Sister Corinne. She's not pretty at all."

As she started pushing Anna Grace again, I wanted to take the handle from her, but I didn't. I did start walking right beside the wagon. Anna Grace was sucking on her fingers.

"I told you being pretty isn't what makes people like you. Being nice matters more. Much more. And liking other people. Besides, I'm sure Sister Corinne is loved by sisters here, and Jesus loves us all. You. Me. Sister Corinne."

"My mother used to say that. Jesus loves you. Jesus loves everybody."

"Your mother knew."

"Maybe he loved me then. Nobody loves me now." Her face closed up. "That's the way I want it."

I stopped and looked directly at her. "That's not true. You are loved. By Jesus. By me."

"You're lying." She jerked the wagon handle sideways and turned it loose.

Anna Grace let out a frightened cry. If I hadn't been close enough to grab the wagon, it would have toppled over on the rock walkway.

With wide eyes, Sister Mona stared at Anna Grace crying, then looked at me. "Do you still love me?"

Benjamin began wailing too as he always did when Anna Grace cried. I stooped by Anna Grace and caressed her face to let her know she was all right. I wouldn't be able to completely comfort Benjamin until I had him back in the room and out of the wrap. I had no idea how to comfort Sister Mona, but she seemed the one most in need of love at that moment.

I looked up at her. "I don't like what you just did, but I do still love you."

I was a little surprised that I meant it. But I had been praying for the child, and those prayers had put love for her in my heart. My words made her even angrier.

"I don't believe you." Mona's hands were in fists.

I was in a vulnerable position squatting beside Anna Grace, but I didn't move as I continued to look at Mona. "Whether you believe it or not doesn't make it any less true."

She shoved me then, knocking me down on my backside. Again her eyes widened before her face crumpled as she spun around and ran away.

I shut my eyes and whispered a prayer, but I couldn't go after her. I had to care for the two babies the Lord had given me. "Hush, Anna Grace. You're all right. Come, I'll push you now." I scooted nearer to her and kissed her forehead.

She sniffled, rubbed her eyes, and once more sucked on her fingers. Benjamin continued to wail. I was struggling to stand with Benjamin's weight pulling me down when strong hands lifted me up.

Once I was on my feet, Leatrice's father looked down at me with concern. "Are you all right?"

"I am fine. Thank you." I patted Benjamin's back to calm him as best I could and stepped away from the man. I worried what those Shakers I knew might be watching would think of the man helping me.

He stared after Sister Mona. "Is that the same girl who worries Leatrice?"

"She's a troubled child," I said. "She needs someone to love her."

"Don't we all." He turned back to me, his face looking as lonely as I suddenly felt.

"Yea, we do." I took the handle of Anna Grace's wagon and began on toward the Gathering Family House.

"Do you need help?"

"Nay. The house is not far."

He seemed to realize I was uneasy with him so near me. He couldn't know the reason had nothing to do with him but only with those who might be watching. I continually worried that some misstep I made would hurry the decision to take Anna Grace from me.

"I can send Leatrice to help you."

"Really, I can manage. I care for the two of them all the time."

"Your Anna Grace is a beautiful baby," he said, but he wasn't looking at Anna Grace. He was looking at me.

I was captured by his eyes. "Your Leatrice is a beautiful girl too."

It was good Benjamin began kicking against me to bring me back to my senses. I smiled and turned to hurry on to my room. I did not look back, but I had the feeling he watched until I went up the steps and through the door of the house.

30

What was he doing? Staring after a Shaker sister like a love-sick calf. No wonder she practically ran away from him up the steps into her house. Even carrying two babies. That was a big load for such a small woman. A fragile-looking woman. But looks could be deceiving.

"Was Anna Grace all right?" Leatrice tugged on his sleeve. "And Sister Darcie?"

"They were both fine. The other baby was crying."

"Baby Benjamin cries all the time," Leatrice said. "He stops sometimes when I sing to him."

"I remember you told me that once before." Flynn smiled down at her and took her hand. "What do you sing?"

"Silly songs I make up or one of the Shaker songs. Some of them are pretty silly too. 'Sweep, sweep and cleanse your floor.'" She pretended she was sweeping as she sang the words and then giggled. "And some of the others don't have any words that make sense. 'Qui quaw ka treen.' I don't know what it means, but it sounds kind of fun and it makes Baby Benjamin stop crying."

She looked toward the house the sister had gone into. "I

should have helped Sister Darcie. I knew Sister Mona would do something mean."

"Don't look so worried. Sister Darcie said she was all right."

"I like Sister Darcie," Leatrice said. "She's so nice. I don't want her to leave like her sister friend did."

"Oh? Is she planning to leave?"

"Someday, but it's a secret. I wasn't supposed to tell anybody. But she said you would probably come get me first." Leatrice looked up at him. "Can I go home with you now? I know how to read."

"You've learned everything?"

"Not everything, but you promised I wouldn't have to stay here forever."

"And you won't. A couple more weeks."

Her bottom lip jutted out as she blinked back tears.

"Two weeks isn't so much, is it?" When she shook her head sadly, he went on. "Is that girl Mona bothering you?"

"She tries to, but I don't pay any attention to her." Leatrice frowned. "But she shouldn't have tried to hurt Anna Grace."

"Maybe it was an accident."

"She pushed Sister Darcie down on purpose."

"It did look like it, but Sister Darcie didn't seem angry about it."

Leatrice raised her shoulders and lowered them with a big sigh. "She wouldn't. She's the one who said we should pray for Sister Mona back when I got in trouble for throwing a shoe at her. Remember? You said you would pray too. Did you?"

He did remember. He'd even said a prayer or two for the girl before it had slipped his mind. "I pray more for you. Do you pray for Sister Mona?"

"Maybe not the right way. I just pray she'll leave me alone." She looked down. "Sister Darcie probably prays better for her and look what Sister Mona still did." She blew out a long breath. "Sister Darcie says it's because Sister Mona thinks her father doesn't love her. So maybe I should pray she could have a papa like you. Or a grandpa. She might not be so mean then."

"That could be. Right now, we better head over where your grandpa is so you can tell him goodbye. I need to go finish getting that house fixed up."

"Can I take the kittens to the new barn?"

"If you can catch them, you can take them." Flynn put his hand on her shoulder and turned her toward where Silas waited. "Your grandpa says the mama cat looks ready to have more kittens."

"I can take those too." She smiled and clapped her hands together. "I can't wait to see Muggins again."

Flynn started to let that slide. Maybe she would think one of the other kittens was Muggins. But a father shouldn't lie to his daughter. "I guess I should have told you, but Muggins must have eaten something he shouldn't have. Your grandpa found him dead out by the woodpile."

Leatrice's smile disappeared. "She poisoned him, didn't she?"

"We don't know that anybody poisoned anything." That wasn't a lie. He didn't know. Not for sure. Who knew what the kitten had eaten?

"Can't Grandpa make her go away?"

"I've told you that when somebody gets married, it's a forever promise. As long as you both are alive."

"Grandpa doesn't want to be with her forever."

"That's not something you can decide," Flynn said. "Now hush. We aren't going to talk about it where he can hear us. Miss Irene is his wife and we have to respect that."

"Yea, Papa. If you say so."

She ran on ahead then to give Silas a hug. Her saying the Shaker yea sounded strange to his ears. It shouldn't have. She'd been here with them all through the summer. But now she'd asked to come home. Twice. He wasn't going to leave her here through the winter. Two weeks. Maybe sooner.

If Irene didn't forget poison and just shoot them both when she found out about Silas and him swapping farms.

After another round of hugs, Leatrice ran up the Children's House steps, turned to wave, and then disappeared through the door.

"It's been good for her to be here," Silas said. "She's learned some discipline."

"She has." Flynn mounted his horse.

Silas followed suit and let his horse walk up beside Flynn's. "I like it here. I'm thinking on joining up with them once we get the farms switched. I wouldn't want to have to hand over my farm to the Shakers. Like I said, that one's yours, but this other one would be fine."

Flynn reined in his horse to look over at Silas. "You're joking, right?"

"Not at all. I'm not as young as I used to be, but I like gardening and fooling with cows. I'm guessing they could use some of that kind of help. And the eating is good."

"I don't think Irene will go along with joining up with the Shakers." Flynn let his horse start walking again.

"That could be." Silas smiled over at Flynn. "Another problem solved. I've heard tell that when one spouse joins up with the Shakers but the other one doesn't want to, that one can get a divorce in the courts easy as pie. Should work out fine if I put some money in her pockets before I head over here."

"You can't join the Shakers just to get rid of Irene." Flynn frowned over at him.

"I don't see why not. And I wouldn't be getting rid of her. She could come with me. Be Sister Irene. Dance a few Shaker jigs." Silas swayed back and forth in his saddle as though hearing music. "I might even get a little spirit in my feet to do some Shaker dancing too."

"I can't believe you're serious."

Silas's smile disappeared. "I'm tired, Flynn. I messed up marrying Irene. We both know that. This is a way out that seems right to me. These Shaker folks believe in the same God I do. Maybe in a little different way, but I like how they say 'hands to work and hearts to God.' No problem believing that right along with them." His smile came back. "And they know how to cook."

"I don't know what to say."

"Well, that's fine. You don't need to say anything." Silas raised his eyebrows at Flynn. "At least not to me, but maybe you should think up something good to say to the pretty little woman with the babies."

Flynn scowled at him. "She's a Shaker, Silas."

"Unless I miss my guess, I don't think that lady has embraced the Shaker way. But she might think about embracing you." Silas laughed and flicked his reins to move ahead of Flynn.

Flynn kept his horse walking the same pace. He didn't know what to say to that either. But he did look back over his shoulder toward the Shaker village and hoped he'd see that pretty little woman with the babies again.

When I got to our retiring room, I told myself not to go to the window, but my feet didn't listen. I put Anna Grace down on her pallet and hurried to look out. My gaze rested on Flynn Keller hugging Leatrice and then walking her back toward the Children's House.

"Walter, forgive me," I whispered.

There was no denying I was attracted to the man and his kindness. Walter had been gone for almost a year. Not long enough for me to be thinking of another man. My heart was heavy as I turned from the window to nurse Benjamin. Poor little baby. His face was red and damp with his tears. I gently wiped them away and put him to my breast.

A mother has time to ponder while feeding her babies, and as Benjamin suckled my breast, I thought of my Walter. "Oh, Walter, I thought we'd grow old together."

Across the room, Anna Grace had rolled over and over again until she was no longer on the pallet. She rubbed her hands over the floor as though liking the feel of it. Each new thing was a wonder to her and to Benjamin too.

As I stroked the soft hair on Benjamin's head, my guilty feelings eased. New discoveries lay in wait for me as well. I would always mourn Walter and the years together we lost. But life went on. These two sweet babies proved that. Ellie's leaving proved that. Even my attraction to Flynn Keller was a sign of change. And change was life.

That didn't mean Leatrice's father was attracted to me, even if his eyes had seemed to dwell on my face. That could have been my attraction to him playing tricks on me. It didn't matter anyway. He had his life. I had mine. He would soon fetch Leatrice home and I might never see them again.

That thought made me so sad, I turned my mind away from it. I could bear no more sadness on this day. Ellie gone. Mona running away from me. I might have been that child like Mona after my mother died if not for Granny Hatchell. Every child needed someone to love her or him.

"Dear Benjamin," I whispered as he dozed off in my arms. "We don't know your story, but you are loved. Ellie loved you. I love you. Sister Genna loves you the most of all."

That seemed odd when I was the one nursing him, but Sister Genna had taken the baby boy to her heart from the very first day as if she had borne him. After I put him in his cradle and situated Anna Grace back on her pallet so I could do the sewing I had been assigned, I realized I had not included Sister Helene when I named those who loved Benjamin.

I threaded the needle and began stitching the skirt seam. But of course, Sister Helene loved the babies too. She took her turn rocking them and dressing them, but she did surrender them with much eagerness when they began to cry. She worried they cried because of something she did when they merely needed a change, a burp, or an extra cuddle.

Sister Helene worried about many things. She seemed to think everyone's happiness was up to her. Since she had been taught the only good life lay along the Shaker road and she had been assigned three sisters wary of the Shaker way, her forehead was often creased with worry lines.

I finished a seam and examined my even stitches. They would surely pass Eldress Maria's inspection for work as near to perfection as I could do. With so much practice with my needle, perhaps I could make my way as a seamstress when I left the village.

When. Not if. While I repositioned the fabric of the dress to do another seam, I looked over at my beloved daughter. She had fallen asleep with her fingers in her mouth. She looked so peaceful with happiness easy for her right now.

We were safe here. We had no reason to leave for an unknown future yet, but when the time came, we would leave. Even if I had no plan of what next. I would trust the Lord to guide us. Hadn't I just told Mona that the Lord loved everybody? Even her. Even me and especially these babies.

He would show me a way when the time came. Until then I would wait. And pray.

31

"You're out of your mind if you think I'm going to move into that three-room shack down the road." Irene glared at Silas. "This place is bad enough."

They had waited until the day before the move to confront Irene. Flynn figured she knew they were up to something, but not what. Certainly she hadn't expected this. She would expect what Silas told her next even less.

Flynn had already moved all but one of Silas's cows over to the new pasture. He wasn't sorry to see them go. He did keep a milk cow. A growing girl needed milk and butter. She'd need more than that, but somehow Flynn would figure out the cooking.

Now Irene looked ready to throw things, but they were prepared for that. All the butcher knives and iron skillets were hidden away.

Silas smiled at Irene. He'd been a different man the last few weeks. He had it all figured out and nothing anybody said or did was going to change that. "Well, Mrs. Cox, if you don't want to live there, I can offer you a room in a three-story brick house with fine windows and doors."

She narrowed her eyes as she stared at Silas. "Where would an old farmer like you come up with a house like that?"

Flynn backed up closer to the door. Even if no major weapons were at hand, Irene could still find plenty of things to throw. Silas didn't seem a bit worried.

"It's like this, Irene. If you aren't willing to move over to the Harley place and live a married life with me, then I'm thinking on going to the Shakers."

That knocked the wind out of Irene. "The Shakers?" She sank down in a chair beside the kitchen table.

"The Shakers. I've been over there visiting Leatrice, and I kind of like the place." He gave her a direct look. "Seeing as how you seem fond of the celibate lifestyle and are anxious for a bigger house, Harmony Hill fits the bill."

"You can't be serious."

"Serious as a heart attack."

She looked up at him. "I don't suppose you'd want to have one of those right now to make me a widow."

"Again?" Flynn spoke up.

She flashed him a look. "Third time might be a charm."

"Sorry, but the old ticker seems to be humming along pretty good." Silas appeared to be enjoying the whole thing. "Must have been all those tonics you made me."

"Must have been." She shook her head. "I can't believe this. The Shakers!" Then she surprised both of them, perhaps even herself, by laughing. "I think you've outmaneuvered me, old man. Are you really going to join the Shakers?"

"Look, Irene, we might as well be frank with one another." Silas's smile faded away as he sat down at the table across from her. "Neither one of us got what we were expecting out of this marriage. Well, I can't fault your cooking and you kept the house fine, but you weren't ever a wife and I wasn't ever a husband to you."

She looked at him without saying anything.

"I am an old man just the way you say, and I don't want to live my last years with a woman who knows she made a mistake marrying me. If you tell me that's not true and you want to give our marriage a try like I promised when we stood in front of the preacher, then I'll stand by my word."

"I don't know that marrying you was a mistake, Silas, but it didn't work out the way I thought it might," she said.

"I didn't die."

"Since, as you say, we're being frank, that's right. My good cooking got you to feeling better." She did smile a little then. "And the exercise you got going out to the woodpile to dump my tonics."

"The stuff did taste horrible." Silas blew out a breath. "But let's forget all that. Start from here, this spot, this minute."

"I'm not moving to that other house with you, and I'm not going to the Shakers."

"That's plain enough. But the Shakers, that's our answer. I'll join up with them and give them the Harley place. First I'll take you into town and give you the money I've got in the bank. Not a lot but enough to keep you in buttons and bows for a while. I figure it won't take you long to find a better match."

"I'll still be married to you."

"That's the good part for you about me going to the Shakers. There's a law that somebody who's married to one of those crazies joining the Shakers can get a divorce with no problem. You'll be free."

"But you'll be a Shaker."

"That's the good part for me. I hear they eat fine."

"Old men, always ruled by their stomachs." She shook her head again. "But, Silas, I never took you for much of a dancer."

"Could be I just need the right music." Silas smiled. "Those Shaker tunes might be the very thing."

"So you have it all figured out." She looked over at Flynn. "Or is this all your plan, Flynn, to get rid of me?"

Flynn raised his hands up, palms out toward her. "I wouldn't interfere with the relations between a man and his wife."

"He didn't have nothing to do with it." Silas kept his gaze straight on Irene. "So are you willing to go along with it and let us take this easy way out of the mess we're in?"

After a long minute, she nodded. "But you better be generous with the money."

"As generous as I can be." Silas slapped the table with both hands. "Then it's done. Tomorrow Flynn brings Leatrice out and I go in." He got up and did a shuffle step. "I haven't felt this good in months."

"You're one crazy old coot." Irene stood up. "Guess I'd better go pack." She stopped at the door to look back at them. "But don't expect me to cook you any supper tonight."

***

Leatrice tried to keep count of the days since Papa told her he'd take her home in two weeks, but she kept getting mixed up.

"Do you remember which day Papa was here?" she asked Sister Darcie after she lost count.

"I do. It was on Wednesday. I'm surprised he hasn't come

322

back to see you again. That's been almost a week. Today is Monday."

"A week is seven days, isn't it?"

"Yea. Why?"

"Papa is coming to take me home in . . ." Leatrice stopped to think. "Nine days. I'm trying to keep count, but I keep getting mixed up."

Sister Darcie smiled. "That's wonderful. So if you only have nine days to wait, you can count on your fingers." She held up her hands with one of her thumbs turned against her palm. "Each day you can turn another finger down until you run out of fingers. But you have to remember that sometimes people take longer than they think to get things done."

"Not Papa. If he said he'll come, he'll come."

So each day she and Sister Darcie had put a finger down until this morning they turned the last finger down. She watched for Papa when they walked to the morning meal, but he didn't come then.

Sister Darcie hugged her before they went up the steps into the Children's House. "Maybe we got our fingers mixed up."

"I don't think so," Leatrice said. "But the day is not through. Papa will come."

"Yea, he will."

When the noon bell rang summoning everybody to the midday meal, Papa hadn't come. Sister Mona said he wouldn't. She walked with Leatrice to help Sister Darcie. She came with her now at least once every day, even though she never asked Sister Tansy if she could.

Sister Mona had not gotten into trouble for days. Not since she'd shoved Sister Darcie down. Even then she hadn't gotten in trouble, because Sister Darcie didn't tell on her.

Instead she made a point of finding Sister Mona the next day and talking to her. She even let Sister Mona hold Anna Grace. That surprised Leatrice. She would have never let Sister Mona close to Anna Grace again. Even if she was acting better.

Sister Tansy bragged on Sister Mona and said she was finally settling in and being a proper Shaker sister. Sister Mona smiled sweetly until Sister Tansy turned around. Then she stuck her tongue out at her. But Leatrice hadn't said anything. If Sister Darcie wasn't going to tell on her, neither would Leatrice.

Sister Darcie always acted happy to see Sister Mona. She didn't hug her the way she did Leatrice, but she would have if Sister Mona had let her. Leatrice wondered if Sister Mona ever let anybody hug her. She didn't like feeling sorry for Sister Mona, but she did. She even prayed a new prayer for her that she would let Sister Darcie hug her someday. That had to be nicer than praying Sister Mona would go away. Hugs made a person feel better. She couldn't wait to hug her father when he got there to take her home.

"He won't come," Sister Mona repeated a little louder after Leatrice acted as though she didn't hear her the first time.

"He will." Leatrice wished Sister Darcie was still with them so she could make Sister Mona hush. But she had already gone back into her house.

The sun was beating down on them and Sister Tansy said they had to go pick beans. Papa wouldn't know to look for her in the garden.

"Nay, he won't." Sister Mona ran a little circle around Leatrice. "He probably found another little girl to take home with him."

Leatrice put her fists on her hips and glared at Sister Mona. "Why are you so mean?"

"Because everybody thinks I'm mean, so if they think I'm mean, I might as well be mean so they won't be disappointed."

"Sister Darcie doesn't think you're mean. She likes you."

Sister Mona stopped circling Leatrice and started walking again. "Sister Darcie is different. She thinks I'm different. Different good."

"Are you? Different good."

"I can be. Sometimes."

"Well, be that way with me. I'm tired of different mean."

Sister Mona laughed. "Sometimes I like you, Sister Leatrice. Sometimes."

They went straight to the garden patch behind the Children's House. The patch was big and the rows long. Leatrice had already helped pick cucumbers and peppers on other days. But today they had to fill many baskets with beans. It did no good to fuss or ask Sister Tansy to let her go wait on the Children's House steps for Papa.

She looked up toward the sun sliding toward the west. Where was he? He never came this late to see her. She wiggled her fingers. Maybe they had turned down one of their fingers too soon, the way Sister Darcie said.

Leatrice tried not to think about the time passing toward sundown as she pulled off the beans carefully to keep from breaking the vines. Sister Tansy had been very firm about not breaking the vines. But what Leatrice wanted to do was crawl up under the vines and hide until Papa came. He would come. He would.

Then Sister Mona came up behind her. Leatrice grabbed

a handful of beans in her basket. She would throw them at Sister Mona if she said anything about Papa not coming. She didn't care if she did get in trouble.

Sister Mona tapped her on the shoulder. "You were right. Your father is here."

"You're just trying to get me in trouble with Sister Tansy." Leatrice tightened her fingers around the beans.

"You were so sure he would come." Sister Mona gave her an exasperated look. "And now you don't believe me when I tell you he's here. I was just trying to be different good the way you wanted."

Leatrice looked around. She couldn't see anything but bean vines growing up on the poles. "Where? I don't see him."

"That's because you're so short. I can see over the beans." She pointed. "Trust me. He's right over there."

She wasn't sure she should trust her, but she dropped the beans out of her hand and carried her basket to the end of the row the way she was supposed to if it was full. It wasn't full, but that wouldn't matter if Papa was there.

And he was. Just the way Sister Mona said. Leatrice dropped her basket and ran out of the garden. She didn't pay any attention when Sister Tansy called to her. She was going home.

Sister Mona came out of the garden behind her. "See, I told you."

Papa hugged her. "Sister Corinne says she will have your things ready so you can leave." He looked over at Sister Mona. "Hello, Mona. Are you having a good day?"

She did a little spin. "Nay. I don't like picking beans. And it's hot and they won't let us take off these things." She flipped up the corner of her neck kerchief. "I think I might melt."

"What would you rather be doing?" Papa asked.

"Wading in a creek." Sister Mona looked off toward the road. "Going home." She blew out a breath and did another spin. "But I don't have a home. Except here. Where I have to pick beans and not go wading in the creek."

Sister Janice came out of the garden. "So you are really leaving, Sister Leatrice. I will miss you."

Leatrice gave her a hug as tears pricked her eyes. She did want to go home, but she was going to miss some of her sisters here.

When Sister Janice went back into the garden, Papa asked, "Is there anybody else you want to tell goodbye?"

"Only Sister Darcie, but she's not here."

"We can run find her," Sister Mona said. "I'll go with you."

"You'll get in trouble with Sister Tansy." Leatrice frowned.

But Sister Mona was grinning. "Nay. You run first and I'll pretend to be chasing you to bring you back and get you to stay here picking beans."

Papa laughed. "Go. I'll wait for you at the Children's House."

So she took off with Sister Mona running after her. At the Gathering Family House, they stopped to catch their breath.

"I like to run," Sister Mona said. "Makes me forget."

"Forget what?"

"Everything I don't want to remember." Sister Mona looked up at the open windows in the house. "Maybe if we yell for her she'll come to the window and see us."

They yelled, but she didn't come.

"She must be working in one of the gardens like we are," Sister Mona said.

"Yea, she does sometimes. She takes the babies and lays them on a quilt in the shade." Leatrice was disappointed. But Sister Darcie knew Papa was coming today. She would understand. "Will you tell her goodbye for me when you go help her later? You will go help her, won't you?"

"I suppose I can," Sister Mona said.

"And give her this hug for me." She put her arms around Sister Mona and pulled her close in a hug. At first Sister Mona stayed stiff as a tree, but then her arms went around Leatrice to hug her back.

Leatrice ran back through the village to where her father was waiting. He lifted her up in front of him on his horse.

"Are we going to the new house?"

"No, your grandpa traded houses with us. He wanted you to live in the home you know."

"So he won't be there."

"Tonight he will be. He wants to see you, but then tomorrow he's coming to live here at Harmony Hill."

Leatrice twisted around to look up at her father. "Grandpa's going to be a Shaker?"

"He decided he liked it here when he came to visit you."

"What about that woman?"

"You don't have to worry about her. She decided she didn't want to come with Grandpa to be a Shaker. So she's gone back to town."

"But I thought you said marriage was forever."

"It is supposed to be, but sometimes what's supposed to be doesn't happen."

Leatrice leaned back against Papa's chest again. This was what was supposed to happen for her. Going home. But at the same time she felt a little funny inside thinking about not helping Sister Darcie with the babies. Nobody would be there to sing silly songs to Baby Benjamin. Sister Mona wouldn't do that. She probably wouldn't even give Sister Darcie the hug, but Leatrice hoped she would.

32

As the week passed, I missed Leatrice more each day. I had not realized how much I looked forward to our time together. Her laughter with Anna Grace and her silly songs for Benjamin had been a bright spot in my day.

Anna Grace missed her too, looking around each time I fastened her into the seat on her little wagon. She smiled at Mona but without quite the same joyfulness she had done with Leatrice. Mona's smiles were not as ready on her face, and my sweet baby did respond to smiles.

Mona told me Leatrice had gone. Of course, I had been expecting it as I counted down the days with her, but being glad for her, the same as I was for Ellie when she left, did not keep away the sadness of missing them.

I was surprised to see a similar sorrow in Mona's eyes that first evening when she came alone to help me. I was completely shocked when, all at once, she clumsily wrapped her arms around me and squeezed.

Just as quickly she stepped away. "That's from Sister Leatrice. She hugged me and wanted me to pass it on to you. We came here to find you before she left, but you didn't come out when we called."

"I'm sorry. I was picking beans in one of the gardens. Eldress Maria sat in the shade and watched the babies."

"Sitting in the shade sounds better than picking beans." Mona scratched her arms. "I hate picking beans. It makes me itch."

"The vines are itchy, but the beans taste good when on our plate." I smiled at her. "Thank you for delivering Leatrice's hug." I reached out toward her. "Come here. I will give you a hug to return to her in case you see her before I do."

To my continued surprise, she stepped into my embrace with something near eagerness, and I gently wrapped my arms around her while standing a bit sideways to not squash Benjamin. Even so, he was part of the hug and when he cooed, Mona's face lit up.

She scowled to hide her pleasure as she pulled free. "We better go. We'll be late."

Each mealtime since then, Mona came faithfully to assist me. Sister Tansy was aware of Mona taking Leatrice's place, but she made no mention of it. I think she, the same as I, hoped Mona would continue to move away from the anger that so often spoiled not only her days but the days of those around her.

Mona didn't speak of Leatrice again until a week had passed. The August day was sultry hot. With Benjamin a warm bundle against my chest, sweat rivulets slid down my sides under my arms. Even Anna Grace was fussy because of the heat. I would have been happy with a heel of bread and a jar of water in the shade of an oak tree, but instead we walked through the village with the noonday sun beating down on our bonnets.

Mona swished her skirts back and forth to fan her legs. I thought she might do one of her spinning twirls, but she stuck to business and pushed Anna Grace. The movement of the wagon made Anna Grace hush her crying, but Benjamin whimpered in the wrap. Poor baby had to be sweltering. I lifted him out where he could at least get a breath of air.

"It's too hot," Mona said. "They should let us go play in a creek."

"That would be good."

"We could go. Just the two of us." She shook her head. "I mean the four of us."

"We could. But we would have to miss our meal and I don't know where there is a creek."

"I wonder if there is one on Leatrice's farm."

"There could be."

"Do you think Leatrice is happy now?" Mona didn't look at me, but I heard a lonesome longing in her voice.

"I'm sure she is. She was eager to go home."

"But she won't have any sisters there. She might be lonely."

"She has her father."

"Fathers can be very busy," Mona said. "She said he worked with horses."

"True. But she also has her grandfather to look after her."

"Nay." Mona looked over at me. "Leatrice's grandfather came into the village. To live here."

"Are you sure?"

"Yea. I saw him once when he came to visit Leatrice. At meeting, the elder spoke his name and had him stand where everyone could see him. He looked different in the Shaker clothes, but it was the same man. I am very good with faces. Didn't you see him?"

"I don't go to the meetings. Because of the babies."

"That is fortunate for you." Mona made a face.

I couldn't keep from smiling. "You don't like the songs and dances?"

"I don't like anything about this place." She hesitated, then added, "Except Anna Grace. But she's not a Shaker. She's a baby."

"What about Benjamin? He's a baby too." I pulled the wrap up to shield him from the sun.

"He cries too much."

To prove her right, he made a fussy cry and pushed against me. "Poor Baby Benjamin." I rubbed my hand up and down his back. Sister Genna said he cried so much because he was frustrated with being so small. That he wanted to grow faster to be big enough to leave the village. Those were surely her own thoughts as living the Shaker life seemed more difficult for her each day. She often yanked on the collar of her dress as though she needed more air. Perhaps she did, since she claimed the Shaker village was suffocating her.

I too noted that feeling of being trapped with no escape, but each time I dwelt on the memory of Ellie's sure prayers and added my own. The answer would come, Ellie had assured me, but would it be an answer like the one she had received? Not quite what I would want most. But as long as I got to be mother to my baby—my babies—then the answer would be good.

I prayed Mona would find a good answer too, a way to be happy. She bent down beside Anna Grace to point toward a butterfly floating past. Some of my prayers for Mona had already been answered. She appeared to truly love Anna Grace in spite of her angry shove of the cart a few weeks ago.

I flapped the wrap up and back to fan Benjamin and pretended not to notice Mona's smile. She was not yet ready to give up her angry front completely. As I waited for her to begin pushing Anna Grace again, I thought about Leatrice's grandfather joining the Shakers.

I don't know why I was so surprised. I had never exchanged more than a simple greeting with the man. Flynn Keller was the one whose path had continually crossed my own here in this village. His words and smiles were what had cheered my heart.

Mona brought me back to the moment. "Leatrice would like that butterfly."

"Yea. Butterflies are so light and free."

"Do you think we'll ever see her again?"

"Perhaps. I think she lives nearby. So they might come visit her grandfather." Hope of that rose within me and I gave my head a mental shake to stop my foolish thoughts.

Mona was silent as she pushed Anna Grace's wagon. When she did speak, I could tell it was something she had been thinking about for a while. "Did her grandfather have to come to stay in her place? So that she could leave?"

"Nay. We are not prisoners here."

"I feel like a prisoner sometimes."

As did I, but I didn't say those words aloud. "Anyone is free to leave. If they have somewhere to go." I reached and touched her shoulder. "And are old enough to make their way."

"You are old enough," Mona said.

"Old enough but without the somewhere to go."

"Oh." Her forehead wrinkled as she considered that. "So you are stuck here forever."

"I pray not." I kept my voice soft. It would not be good

for any passing near to hear my words. "I am praying for a way to open to me."

Again she considered my words before she spoke. "Then I will pray the same." She looked across the field at the woods in the distance. "Do you think we could go live in the woods? Perhaps in a cave and eat nuts and berries."

I did not laugh, but I could not keep from smiling. "For now we will pray for something better."

I did note how she said "we" and how I said the same in answer. An answer to my prayers had just become even more difficult, but didn't the Bible say nothing was impossible with God? *Dear Lord, let that be true.* I sent the words heavenward and tried to have faith an answer would come for these children and for me.

Two days later an answer came for Sister Genna. She had seemed different for a few days. She kept smiling when she thought no one was watching her. She held Benjamin even when he wasn't being fussy. She got down on the floor to play with Anna Grace, who had started to crawl.

She was joyful. Even when she was holding Benjamin whom she loved, I had never thought her joyful. But now something had happened that she was not sharing with me. At least not yet. I waited, for Sister Genna was not one to be pushed.

On Thursday evening, she came back to the room early from the worship practice. It was my turn to stay with the babies.

"I told Sister Helene I wasn't feeling well." Sister Genna's eyes were sparkling when she came back into the room but not with any kind of sickness fever.

She looked so happy I knew there could be only one reason. "You heard from Jeremy."

"Yea." She did a spin much like the devout Shaker sisters often did in the exercise of the dance. "I got a letter a few days ago. Someone wrote it for him since he does not know his letters. There were few words, but enough. *Be ready. I am coming.*"

I hugged her and we danced in another little circle. Sister Helene would have been proud of us. Or not, since we were celebrating that which was considered sinful among the Shakers. The reuniting of a man and wife.

"So how do you know when to be ready?" I asked as she turned from me to the chest.

"He found me in the garden today and I sneaked away to talk to him for a few minutes before I was missed. He promised to return tonight. At midnight."

"Why midnight?" I frowned. "You could have simply walked away as Ellie did."

"There are complications." She shifted her gaze away from me as if she did not want me to see her eyes.

"What complications?" I asked.

"I will tell you when I am ready to leave." She pulled things from the chest and folded them into a bundle.

I stepped closer. "Those are Benjamin's clothes."

"Yea." She sighed and her shoulders drooped as she turned back to me. "You must understand, Sister Darcie."

I knew her intent. "You cannot think to take him." I turned to pick him up from his cradle and hold him close. "You cannot feed him."

She stared at me. "I cannot nurse him, but I can feed him the gruel and other food. I won't let him go hungry. If needed, I can find another wet nurse."

"I am more than a wet nurse. He is my baby as much as Anna Grace."

"Nay, not as much. You cannot say as much." Her voice was gentle as she stepped nearer and put her hand on the baby's back. "You do love Benjamin. I know you do, but you must know I love him more. He is a gift from God given directly to me, just as your Anna Grace was a gift to you after your Walter died."

I tightened my arms around Benjamin. She was right about Anna Grace being dearer to me than Benjamin. I had to admit that truth. Anna Grace was my child. The visible truth of my love with Walter. But at the same time Benjamin became dearer to me each day. My breast ached at the thought of no longer having him in my arms.

"You can't take him. I cannot let you."

"But you must, my sister." She put an arm around me. "You know this child is not destined to be a Shaker."

"Being a Shaker is not such a dreadful thing."

"If you are not a mother or a baby." Sister Genna gently moved me over to the bed where we could sit together. She did not try to take Benjamin. "We need to talk this through before Sister Helene comes to the room. She would never understand, but you must."

"What is there to say?" I sat him out on my knees and supported him in a sitting position. As his gaze fastened on Sister Genna, he smiled and reached for her.

She lifted him away from me then. "There is always much to say but as much that cannot be said." He grasped the strings of her bonnet, but she paid no mind, although he jerked her bonnet askew. "Even should I not steal him away, they will. You will not be allowed to keep him much longer. Not him. Not Anna Grace."

"Nay, I still have time."

Her gaze on me grew more intense. "A few months at most. You know that is true. It is only because Eldress Maria is so fond of Anna Grace that they have not already moved the babies to the Children's House and only let you come feed them. But soon they will decide they are old enough to wean and they will take them then. Completely."

"I won't let that happen. I will leave first."

"So you might and I wish you Godspeed should that happen, but you would have no claim to Benjamin. They would never let you take him. He is not your child."

"Nor yours."

"Nor mine by birth. But mine nevertheless." She kissed the top of his head. Then she handed him back to me. "Give him to me, Sister Darcie. Let him be my son."

His weight in my arms was so familiar. "Will your husband think you have betrayed him with another if you show up with a baby?"

"Nay. I did not have long with him today, but enough time to tell him about Benjamin. Even without seeing him, he is ready to be his father." She leaned her head over against mine. "Please let this be."

"But he will be hungry."

She reached over and stroked his head. Again he smiled and kicked his feet in pleasure. "I talked with Sister Lettie. Not now, but weeks ago. I didn't know Jeremy was coming, but I wanted to be ready in case those prayers you and Ellie offered up for me brought him back. And they did. For that, I am thankful. You prayed when my heart was too discouraged to hope."

She shut her eyes a moment as if praying right then. I kept quiet and waited.

She opened her eyes and went on. "So I asked Sister Lettie what would have happened to Benjamin if you had not been here already nursing Anna Grace. She told me Benjamin isn't the first foundling taken in by the Shakers. At first they soaked a clean cloth in milk for the baby to suck on. Goat milk is best, she said."

"Does your Jeremy have a goat?"

"Not yet, but we will find one to take west with us. Anyway, Sister Lettie said the cloth feeding did not work well. Nor did trying to spoon the milk into the baby's mouth. But she said thank goodness and Mother Ann—her words, not mine—that Shakers knew how to come up with better ways to do things. She showed me a bottle with a narrow top and told how a leather tip with a hole in the end was tied onto it."

"But do you have such a thing?" I frowned at her.

"I do. I slipped into Sister Lettie's doctoring room and stole the bottle. May the Lord forgive me, but she has plenty of other small bottles should another baby be found on their doorsteps. Then I filched some leather pieces from the cobbler. They were probably too small to have any use for shoes."

"It sounds as if you have it all worked out." I leaned down to put my cheek against Benjamin's baby face. "Except how you will break my heart. To not only lose Benjamin but also you." I raised my head to look at her.

"I know, my sister." She put her arm around me again. "But you would not deny me the happiness of being with my husband." She leaned out to look directly at my face. "Or having my son with me. He is not destined to be that Shaker leader Sister Helene wants him to be. Instead, he will go west and grow up sturdy and strong to live life to the fullest."

"You are my sister and I love you, Genna, but you cannot take him. He is too young." I was sure of my refusal. He was too small to make such a journey.

Her lips tightened into a straight line. "Perhaps you are right. He is very young." She let out a long breath and then reached for him again. "But at least let me hold him a while and then you can feed him before you go to sleep."

She gave in too easily. I knew it at the time. Sister Genna was not one to give up on what she wanted. So I was not surprised when a slight rustle of a skirt or perhaps a blanket awakened me in the dark of the night. Sister Helene softly snored as she slept on. She was a heavy sleeper who rarely awoke even when the babies cried. But I roused at the slightest whimper.

Sister Genna knew that, so I sensed her holding her breath and watching me. I feigned sleep and prayed for guidance. A bit of Scripture came to mind. *Be still and know that I am God.* I did not know if that was the Lord's message to me or not. But in spite of the sorrow swelling in my heart, I did not sit up and sound an alarm. Perhaps I should have. I can never be sure if I did right, but I could not break my sister's heart. So I surrendered Benjamin to Genna.

She came and stood by my bed. "I know you are awake, Sister Darcie," she whispered. "I am sorry, but I cannot bear to leave him. I promise I will forever love him and care for him." A tremble sounded in her voice. "You will always be my sister."

I gave up the pretense of sleep then and stood to embrace her and Benjamin. "And you mine." Tears wet both our cheeks, but for once Benjamin slept soundly.

Then they were gone, out the door like a shadow. I stuffed my fist in my mouth to stifle my sobs and went to the window to watch. I did not know how she would get out of the house, as the door was key locked at night to keep others out or perhaps to keep us within. With her resourcefulness, I had no doubt that somehow Genna had a key to open the door and escape the Shaker life.

I could barely see her dim form move away down the road. I longed to pick up Anna Grace and run after her. Escape into the night as she was doing. But I had no Jeremy waiting for me in the darkness.

"May the Lord watch over you both," I whispered. Then I lifted my sleeping baby out of her cradle and lay back on my bed with her cuddled next to me to await the rising bell.

33

"Why did you not stop her?" Sister Helene was distraught. She may not have been comfortable tending to Benjamin, but she had felt ownership of the baby since she was the one to find him on the washhouse steps.

"I could not." Tears came to my eyes as I looked at the empty cradle. If he were here, I would be nursing him. By now he would be hungry.

"Could not or would not?"

She was as angry as I had ever seen her. Always she was patient and understanding no matter the wrongs I or Genna and Ellie did. She would simply forgive us as she gently instructed us in the proper Shaker way. But now two beds were empty in our room, along with the cradle of the child she hoped would become a Shaker leader. I wished my bed and Anna Grace's cradle were as empty.

"Could not," I answered her, although I supposed would not was as true.

"Eldress Maria is going to be very upset."

"Yea. I too am very upset." I did not speak an untruth. I had already determined that I would not lie. I would admit knowing Sister Genna left. I would not deny seeing her with Benjamin in her arms. Granny Hatchell long ago told me that telling a falsehood or even sidestepping the truth only led to more lies. Best to be truthful and face the consequences for any wrongs done.

"You should have told her she could not take Benjamin."

"I did tell her that," I said. "She pretended to agree, but then she took him in the night."

"Without you knowing?" Sister Helene looked at me with raised eyebrows. She knew how lightly I slept.

"Nay, I saw her leave."

"And did not stop her."

"I could not." I saw no reason to change my words.

She wrapped her apron around her dress and tied it with angry tugs. She frowned at me as she stuffed her hair under her cap. I had not put on my cap as yet, so my red hair curled around my face. "I have always heard redheads could not be trusted."

It was so unlike Sister Helene to say such a thing that I could not help smiling. I turned to keep her from seeing my amusement. Amusement that quickly faded at the sight of the neck kerchief and bonnet left on Genna's bed the same as Ellie had done. Two of my dear sisters gone and this other one angry with me. I looked back at Sister Helene. "I forgive you for your angry words."

Without warning, she put her hands over her face and burst into tears. "I am in need of forgiveness, for I have failed my sisters. Both have deserted the peace and joy of Shaker life to go to the world where sorrow and troubles surely await them."

Or love. But I did not say that aloud. Instead I put my

arms around her. "You did your best to show us the good of life here at Harmony Hill. With love."

"But I failed."

"Nay, love never fails. They simply chose a different path."

She leaned back and looked at me, her eyes awash with tears. "And you, Sister Darcie? Will you choose a different path?"

"Not today."

"But someday?"

I searched for words that would not upset her, but I knew none. "I do not want to be parted from my Anna Grace, as the custom is here in your village to separate mother and child."

"But you won't be separated from her. She will be here and you will be here. Sisters as it would be in heaven."

"I am not yet in heaven. I am Anna Grace's mother. Not her sister."

She shook her head at me. "You still have much to learn about the good of the Shaker life."

"Yea, I suppose I do."

She wiped her tears away with her handkerchief. "I must go tell Eldress Maria. She will need to hear your confession."

"So be it." I turned to finish straightening my bed.

When the door opened quietly behind me a half hour later, I had the room clean and was merely going through the motions of checking corners for dust. Dirt had little chance in this Shaker village with so many hands ready to chase it away. The wrongs they might think lurked in the corners of my heart were harder to sweep away.

I turned to face Eldress Maria. I saw no anger on her face, merely resignation. As was her usual way in the morning, she reached down to pluck up Anna Grace. My little charmer brightened the room with her welcoming smile.

The eldress sat in the rocking chair and waved me to sit on the nearest bed, which happened to be Sister Genna's. I scooted aside the neck kerchief I had not yet folded away, sat down, and waited for whatever might come next.

She rocked Anna Grace and let her play with her fingers without speaking for a span of minutes. Finally she looked over at me. "It has been sweet having the babies here in this house where they are not commonly allowed."

I did not like the way she spoke, as though that sweetness was in the past, but I kept quiet. I had grown fond of Eldress Maria in spite of our prickly start together. Her love for Anna Grace had softened my heart toward her.

"Perhaps I was wrong to allow you and the babies to stay here as Sister Lettie advised. She has always been one to look at the rules a bit differently." She lifted Anna Grace up and let the baby pat her cheeks. "Not that she was not right about it being better for the babies. This one has proven that with her many smiles."

I sensed she wasn't ready yet for me to speak. So I merely smiled even if my heart was far from cheerful.

She sighed. "Yea, better for the babies, but perhaps not better for you sisters. It kept thoughts of the world too strongly in your minds. First Sister Ellie, who had been with us for years, deserted the way."

It was the first time I'd heard her say Ellie's name since she left.

"And now this other one stole away in the night and took that poor little baby boy with her." Eldress Maria's wrinkles deepened with sadness. "I can't imagine what she was thinking with no way to feed the poor babe." She put Anna Grace down on the floor and stared across at me. "I can't imagine what you were thinking to let her take him."

"I told her not to." I met the woman's gaze.

"But you did not stop her."

"Nay, I did not." I looked down at my hands folded in my lap.

"I know you cared for the infant. Do you not fear he will die from hunger without you to nurse him?"

"He has been eating gruel and applesauce."

Again she sighed. "You let your love for your former sister cloud your judgment."

"It is not wrong to love one's sisters." I raised my eyes to look at her again. Anna Grace sat on the floor between us, sucking on her fingers.

"Nay. But it is wrong to encourage one's sisters in sinful actions." She peered over at me. "That is not a proper way to show love."

"If I have done wrong, I ask forgiveness. I lacked wisdom for any other way."

"That is why you should have awakened me."

"Yea." I looked down again. I did not want her to see my stubborn resistance to her words.

She stood, stepped around Anna Grace, and came over to lay her hand on my head with gentleness. "I do forgive you, Sister Darcie. However, I fear the Ministry will not look favorably on this situation. You best prepare yourself."

I looked up at her. "For what?"

"I cannot say, for I do not know what will be decided. They will inform me of any changes they deem necessary." Her shoulders drooped. "We will have to do whatever they say. It could not be to your liking." She dropped her hand away from my head and let her gaze go to Anna Grace. "Or mine. I am sorry."

"How long do I have . . ." I hesitated, then used her words. "To prepare myself?"

"That too is up to the Ministry."

I did not question her more, for I could see she was as concerned as I. Perhaps more than I, since she knew past decisions the Ministry may have made, while I knew nothing about them. They did not mingle with the rest of the Shakers. That was so their decisions could be fair and not biased by close ties to others in the village. Or so Sister Helene had told me.

But what they considered fair and what I might wish could be poles apart. It was time, indeed, to do as Eldress Maria said and prepare myself. Not for the Ministry's decision, but for what I planned to do. I did not want to be like Genna and too discouraged to pray, but my spirits were low as I carried Anna Grace down the hallway to clean another of the retiring rooms that were part of my morning duties.

As I made the beds and swept the floor, Granny Hatchell again came to mind. She had always been sure of the Lord's love and care no matter what happened to her, even when Pap Hatchell died.

I remembered her words to me then as we faced an uncertain future. *"The good Lord knows the way ahead even if we can't see it now. All he expects of us is to take that first step down the road in faith. We don't need to know the end of the road. Just the beginning."*

"But I don't even know which road to step out on," I whispered.

Then as though Genna still stood beside me, I heard her voice in my head. *"Only one road leads out of the village."*

I looked over at Anna Grace trying to pull herself up to the low windowsill. She fell back on her bottom but didn't cry. She scooted nearer the window and reached to try yet again. Again she fell back, but the third time she tried, she made it to a wobbly stand and squealed with delight at being able to see out the window.

If I stayed here, they would take Anna Grace from me, but I would know she was fed and cared for. If I stepped out on that road to leave this place, I had no idea where we could go or what we would eat. I had no money. What little we had when we came to the Shakers last year was given over to them.

Then I remembered, as though someone put the thought in my mind, the Shakers had promised to return whatever we brought with us should we decide to leave as, of course, we had planned to do. Ellie had not taken anything away with her because her husband stayed among the Shakers. Genna would have had nothing as valuable to her as the baby she spirited away in the night. We, Walter and I, had a few coins and a horse.

I might have no choice but to leave Walter here in their graveyard, but I did not have to leave his horse. I could sell Sawyer and use that money to set up a seamstress shop or, failing that, perhaps get by until I could find a position as a housekeeper. It was a first step, but a shaky one.

Mona was waiting for me when I carried Anna Grace outside to go to the morning meal. She jumped up to help carry one of the babies. When she saw only Anna Grace in my arms, she peered behind me almost as though she expected Benjamin to be toddling along after me.

"Where is Baby Benjamin?"

"Sister Genna left in the night and took him with her."

"Oh. Then that is why you have red blotches on your face. You've been crying."

"I am sad. I love Baby Benjamin."

"Yea, I am sad too. Even if he did cry all the time." Her brow wrinkled as she turned to me. "Do you think he will be all right?"

"I pray so." After I fastened the straps around Anna Grace in the wagon, I looked over at Mona. "We can pray for that right now."

She frowned a little. "My head is cluttered with prayers. For Leatrice. For you. Now for Baby Benjamin."

"Nay, Sister Mona. Prayers don't stay in your head. You send them to the Lord."

"Oh." She threw up her hands then, as though pitching them heavenward.

She pushed the wagon while I walked beside her, my arms achingly empty. "You won't need to come at noon. I can bring Anna Grace without help."

She gave me a stricken look. "You do not want me to come?"

"I didn't say that. I like having you with me, but Sister Tansy will no longer think it needed."

"I don't care what they say. I do what I want." She lifted her chin and looked ahead. "Do not think you can get rid of me that easily."

"I don't want to be rid of you, Mona."

"Ever?" She slowed her step and looked around at me.

"Ever. But sometimes things happen that we cannot control." I touched her shoulder.

She didn't jerk away from me as she would have just weeks ago. "Like that sister taking Baby Benjamin."

"Yea. Like that."

She peered up at me as though trying to read my thoughts. "Will you leave in the middle of the night?"

"Nay. I have no reason to sneak away. I can walk away."

"But you said you have nowhere to go."

"That is true, but I may have to trust my uncertain future to the Lord's providence. If they say I can no longer care for Anna Grace."

She was quiet for a moment as she pushed Anna Grace. Then she said, "If you leave, I am going with you."

I didn't say she couldn't. I was already awash in a sea of uncertainty about what might happen next. Instead I pushed a different truth toward her. "They will not let you go with me."

"I told you I do what I want." She spoke with sure determination, as again she lifted her chin defiantly.

34

I spent the day trying to chase away my worry with prayer, but the worry would not be put to rest. I had little hope the Ministry would allow Anna Grace to stay with me in the Gathering Family House.

That afternoon when Mona came before the evening meal, she grabbed me in a hug. I was almost too stunned to hug her back. "Worry not, Sister Darcie. We will figure out what to do."

She was just a child, but even so, her confident words bolstered my courage. "With a strong girl like you helping me, that may be true."

She pulled Anna Grace's wagon around in front of the steps. "I am strong." She stood a little taller while I fastened Anna Grace in her seat. "That's good, isn't it?"

"Yea, very good." I straightened up and smiled at her. "Strong in body and strong in mind." I felt neither, as my unknown future sat heavy on my shoulders and my mind was weary of looking for a way and seeing none.

You lack faith, child. Faith means believing what cannot be seen. Granny Hatchell's words came to me. *Did Ruth know how Naomi would find food when they made the journey back to her homeland of Judah?*

The story of Naomi and Ruth was one of Granny Hatchell's favorites. Perhaps because I had chosen to stay with her instead of going with my father to Ohio. Should I go to Ohio now? That was truly desperation thinking. I had no idea where in Ohio my father had settled or even if he had settled. He and my brothers could be in California by now, drawn there by the prospect of finding gold.

Heading to Ohio didn't sound like a first step of faith, but rather foolishness. Almost as foolish as looking to a child of ten for answers, but she did seem anxious to tell me something.

"What do we need to figure out, Sister Mona?"

"Much, I would think." She began to slowly push Anna Grace down the walkway. "I kept my eyes and ears open today. The old sisters moved beds around in the little children's retiring room."

"They could have been cleaning." I don't know why I kept hoping for a different way here in the village.

"Nay. I overheard Sister Corinne say at least Benjamin wouldn't be coming to keep everybody awake with his squalling." Sister Mona scowled. "I don't like Sister Corinne." Then she looked cheerful again. "But that's all right because she doesn't like me either. Back in the spring, I heard her tell Sister Tansy she wished I'd run away. I didn't, just to spite her."

"Sister Tansy doesn't want you to run away."

"Maybe not, but I doubt she'd cry if my bed was empty come morning."

"You're too young to run away."

"I can take care of myself." The chin went up again. Then she was peeking around at me once more. "But you're old enough to run away. I could go with you to help with Anna Grace."

"I'm not going to run away."

"But what about Anna Grace and them moving her to the Children's House. You know that's what they're going to do."

"I didn't say I wasn't going to leave, but I don't have to run away. I can walk away."

"Oh." Sister Mona was silent for a moment. "Then I can walk away with you."

"I don't think they will let you." In fact, I was sure they wouldn't let her, and tears filled my eyes. I didn't know when I'd gotten so weepy.

"You cry as much as Baby Benjamin." Mona frowned at me.

"I do." I swiped away the tears. "Tell you what. If they will let you, you can come and starve with Anna Grace and me."

"We won't starve." She actually smiled. "Didn't you pray?"

I nodded.

"Then you have to believe." She sounded very sure as she turned to look back down the walkway. "We won't starve."

I didn't say anything more. I'd already tried to push the truth toward her, but she refused to listen. Perhaps she was right. Perhaps the Lord would answer our prayers, although I knew not how.

Eldress Maria was waiting for me when I went back to my room with the news I already knew from Mona. Her lips trembled as she told me what the Ministry had decreed.

"I am sorry, Sister Darcie. We are to move Anna Grace

tomorrow. You will be allowed to go at assigned times to nurse her, but since she is old enough to sleep through the night, you will not stay with her. Those sisters assigned to the Children's House will care for her."

She pressed her lips together and swallowed hard as she looked down at Anna Grace, who had crawled over to pull at her skirt. She could not resist the baby's smile and leaned down to pick her up. "You know this is not what I wish any more than it is what you want."

"I know. You have been like a grandmother to my Anna Grace."

"Nay," she said softly even as she hugged the baby close. "A sister. Always a sister."

"Then a loving sister." I smiled.

Her forehead wrinkled with a puzzled look. "You don't appear to be very upset, Sister."

"I was prepared after your warning this morning." I didn't mention Sister Mona. "I hope you aren't in trouble for allowing the babies to stay here until now."

"I confessed my faulty thinking and was forgiven. I will continue my duty here in our Gathering Family. You must move to a different room and allow Sister Helene new sisters to guide in the Shaker way."

"I will always remember dear Sister Helene with fondness."

Eldress Maria's eyes sharpened on me. "You will still be together in our family."

"I appreciate all you have done for me and for Anna Grace. I don't know what I would have done without your help after Walter was killed, but I won't give up Anna Grace. We will leave tomorrow."

Her arms tightened around Anna Grace as she stared at me. "Where will you go?"

"I do not know."

Eldress Maria frowned. "Surely it would be better to stay here where your child has shelter and food and loving care-takers."

"But you won't let me be that caretaker. Well, you might, but others whose rules must be followed will not. When Walter and I came into the village, we were told we could take away whatever we brought with us if we left. We had only a little money, but we did have Walter's horse, Saw-yer, and his saddle. He also had a rifle. I had my Granny Hatchell's Bible and Anna Grace growing inside me. So tomorrow I will collect those few things and go out to find a new place."

"But you may go hungry." She looked truly worried.

"Do you believe in prayer, Eldress?"

"What a question! Of course I believe in prayer. We here at Harmony Hill pray many times a day."

"Yea, it is easy to silently send up prayers. The hard part is believing those prayers will be answered. I have been praying for months for a way to leave here before I was separated from Anna Grace."

"You prayed wrongly. You should have prayed to accept the Shaker way so you could take up your cross and live a heavenly life with your sisters here."

"Perhaps you are right." I reached and took Anna Grace from her. "But I do not yet believe that. Instead I have faith my prayers will be answered."

Eldress Maria pulled in a breath and let it out slowly. "I see I cannot convince you differently. But I do fear you are headed toward naught but trouble and taking this sweet baby with you."

"If I am wrong, you would welcome me back again into your society, would you not?"

"We would. We welcome many who come to stay during the hard months of the year and then leave in the springtime. Over and over. It sometimes seems wrong to do so, but we are instructed by Mother Ann to be kind."

"I appreciate that kindness and I promise that, should I come back into your fold, I will do my best to live the proper Shaker life."

"Even if you don't believe in the Shaker way?" She raised her eyebrows.

"I cannot promise to believe. I can promise to abide by your rules." I looked straight at her. "But first I am going to step out with faith the Lord will help me find a different way."

"You may be on a slippery path to destruction, my sister." Again she pressed her lips together tightly for a moment before she went on. "But one you seem determined to walk. I will arrange with the trustees in charge of such things to have your horse and possessions here in the morning."

"Thank you."

She did not acknowledge my thanks, but she did look back at Anna Grace once more before she went out the door.

Sister Helene came into the room then, her eyes awash with tears. She begged me again to forgive her angry words that morning. I did without pause, and then we sat together in silence a while before we began to speak of our many times together in the last year.

A knock on the door brought Sister Reva from the kitchen

with a cloth bag. "I hear you are leaving us, Sister Darcie, and taking our baby." She smiled over at Anna Grace, who crawled toward her as fast as she could. Sister Reva often gave her a sugary treat when we visited the kitchen. "Yea, little one, I've packed some cookies and applesauce in here for you." She handed the bag to me. "We would not want our little sister to go hungry."

She picked up Anna Grace and pulled a cookie from her pocket. Anna Grace gave a happy squeal.

I blinked away tears. "Thank you, Sister Reva."

"Mother Ann instructs us to be generous. I will pray for you both." Then she put Anna Grace down and hurried out of the room.

Other sisters came by the room. Some merely to say good-bye, but Sister Nila brought me a silk kerchief made here in the village. "This is all I have, but I have been told such silk kerchiefs are much in demand in the world. If you have a need, you may be able to sell it."

"Nay, I can't take it." I knew how the sisters treasured their silk kerchiefs, a rare luxurious item they were allowed. I handed it back to her.

She put her hands up and refused to take it. "I will get another the next time I work with the silkworms. Keep it for Anna Grace if you never have need to sell it."

Just before the retiring bell, a soft knock sounded on our door. When I opened it, no one was there, but Sister Helene rushed over to pick up a tiny pair of shoes from the hallway floor.

"Oh good. Brother Marcus was able to finish the shoes." Sister Helene handed them to me. "A week ago, Eldress Maria had me ask him to make Anna Grace shoes for when she began walking, but we did not realize we had need for hurry."

The light brown shoes were soft to the touch. "I'm thankful Anna Grace is so loved."

"You can stay among us and let her continue in that love," Sister Helene said.

"Nay, I cannot."

She did not argue, perhaps wanting our last night together to be one of peace.

The next day, I was up before the rising bell as always. Sister Helene and I parted as though this was a morning the same as any other. That seemed better than tears. Too many had already been shed.

Eldress Maria came to hold Anna Grace one last time. Before she left, she said, "May you always remember that here you were loved."

I was not sure if she was talking to me or to Anna Grace.

When near time for the bell to summon the Shakers to their morning meal, I gathered up the bundle of Anna Grace's clothes, Granny Hatchell's Bible, and the sack of food from Sister Reva. So little to go out into the world, but perhaps enough. I tucked the silk kerchief in one pocket. In the other pocket was the money Eldress Maria had laid on the chest without comment. The exact amount we had brought into the village last July. I was not completely without resources.

The Shakers were true to their word. Sawyer was tied to a hitching post in front of the house, with Walter's rifle in a sling hanging from the pommel of the saddle and saddlebags slung over the horse's hips. Mona stood beside the horse. I was both glad and sorry to see her there.

She stroked Sawyer's neck, then looked around at me. "Do you think he will let me ride him?"

"Have you ridden horses before?"

"Nay, but I have done many things that I have not done before." She stepped away from the horse closer to me. "Are you going to take me with you?"

"If they will allow it." I said the words, but I knew that would not happen.

"They won't." Mona shrugged. "They say my father gave me to them. Not you." She did not sound at all concerned as she did a little spin. "So I suppose I must bid you farewell."

I studied her face to discern her true feelings, but I could not. "Come give Anna Grace and me a hug."

She stepped into my embrace willingly enough. I kissed the top of her bonnet. "I will miss you, Sister Mona."

"Will you?" She smiled as she leaned against me to whisper, "Remember, I do what I want." She spun away from me with a laugh. "Goodbye, Sister Darcie."

"Goodbye, Sister Mona," I called after her as she ran away. "I will write."

She didn't look around as the village bell began to ring. I sat Anna Grace in the grass and stuffed my bundles in the saddlebags. The leathery smell brought Walter to mind. He had often brought me little treasures in these very saddlebags. A pretty stone. A swatch of cloth. A few apples.

I smiled at the memory as I picked up Anna Grace. "He would have brought you treasures too, my baby."

I carried Anna Grace and led Sawyer through the village. A few Shakers passed me but kept their eyes turned away as they hurried to their morning meal. I was no longer one of them. I walked on out into the world beyond the Shaker shelter.

"All right, Granny Hatchell, I took that first step," I muttered. "Now what?"

It's not me you need to be asking. It's the Lord.

I was sure those would be her words, were she beside me. I shifted Anna Grace in the swaddling carrier. She had outgrown it, but having her bottom rest in it did give my arms more freedom, even as her weight pulled on my neck. Without a whimper, she dozed off, as was her habit at this time of the morning. She could not know I had no idea where we might find shelter at nightfall.

I looked up and spoke my prayer aloud. "At least give me some sign that I'm going in the right direction."

"Definitely. Without a doubt, the right direction."

The man's voice startled me. I had been so focused on moving forward that I hadn't noticed him there beside the road. The Shaker brother pushed away from the tree he'd been leaning against and stepped toward me. "You do realize horses are meant to be ridden."

The Shaker hat and clothes fooled me for a moment, but then I recognized him. "You are Leatrice's grandfather."

He smiled. "So I am. Silas Cox, Miss Darcie. I beg your forgiveness for using your given name, but in the Shaker world first names seem all that's necessary. It's Brother this, Sister that."

"I'm no longer Sister Darcie."

"So your young friend told me. And I can understand. What mother would ever want to give up her baby?"

"It could be that I should have. I am at a loss as to what to do next." I looked away from him down the road. Sawyer snuffled behind me, impatient with standing still. I walked him to the side of the road where he could nibble some grass. "Other than selling my horse."

"You know Leatrice's father works with horses." The man studied Sawyer. "He worked with this one, didn't he? Some months back?"

"He did. I never heard what he thought was wrong with Sawyer except he might have been missing our stable cat." I smiled a little. "I guess that sounds foolish."

"Not at all." He smiled at me again, seemingly in no hurry to be on about his business.

I frowned a little. "If I may be so bold to ask, were you here waiting for me?"

"So I was. Your young friend, the one who said you were leaving, thought I might be able to help you."

"What friend is that? Sister Mona?" I could imagine no one else.

"I don't think she said her name. But she was very slim, with eyes the blue of her Shaker dress. I think I'd seen her with you and Leatrice. Anyway, she knew about your horse and asked if I thought Flynn would buy him." He smiled at me. "I do think the girl had it all figured out, down to me coming out here to give you directions. She reminded me a bit of myself, although I've been known to make a muddle of things by rushing into something without proper thought."

"When did she talk to you?" She couldn't have had time after I told her goodbye.

"She waylaid me when I went out to the barn this morning to help with the stock. She was very convincing." He laughed. "Trust me, I don't miss meals without good reason."

361

"Are you leaving the Shakers?"

"No, not at all, but since I'm out here on the road, I decided it would be a fine time to go see Leatrice. Maybe Flynn made biscuits this morning. I showed him how before I left, but he could do with a housekeeper. The man can't cook. Can you?"

"I haven't had much practice for a while." Could it possibly be I might find a place to stay so easily? I turned away from that unfounded hope by saying, "But won't you get in trouble leaving like this?"

"I'm new to these Shakers, but I've already figured out they're a forgiving lot. When I go back later today and say I'm sorry for deserting my duties, they'll forgive me and give me more duties tomorrow. Best, I am almost sure they won't break my plate. I do enjoy the Shaker meals." He peered over at me. "Are you sure you've been eating? You're not as big as a minute."

I couldn't keep from smiling at that. Granny Hatchell had told me that so many times. "I eat plenty."

"Hmph." He didn't sound as if he believed me. "That baby of yours has to be heavy. Is she sleeping?"

"She is. Not much disturbs her naps."

"Well, let me give you a leg up on your horse and the two of you can ride while I lead you. We've got a few miles to go if you want Flynn to look at your horse, but we should make it before the sun gets too hot." He looked up at the sky and then bent by Sawyer's side with his hands cupped. "Anchor that baby good and step up here in my hands."

I did as he said and climbed astride the horse. Anna Grace stirred as I adjusted the rifle in its sling and settled my skirts as modestly as I could while Silas considerately turned away.

As he led Sawyer forward, the motion of the horse soon calmed Anna Grace as I held on to the pommel.

I said a thankful prayer for Mona even as my heart was sad for leaving her behind. I should have known better. We went around another bend and Mona skipped out in front of us.

"What took you so long?" She stood in the middle of the road with her hands on her hips and a smile that would have lit up the night better than twenty candles.

Silas stopped Sawyer. "Do we have trouble here?"

I didn't answer him. I kept my gaze on Mona. "What are you doing?"

"I told you I do what I want." She did her little twirl and came closer to us. "And I want to be with you and Anna Grace." She peered up at me on the horse. "You said I could come with you. Did you not mean it?"

"I meant it, but I said if they would let you."

"Here I am, so they must have let me."

Silas spoke up. "I'm thinking you ran away."

"That could be." She put her hands behind her and twisted first one way and then another. "But they are glad to see me gone. I made sure of that."

I was almost afraid to ask. "How?"

She hung her head a little, but I could see her grin. "I kind of tied knots in all their bonnet strings and their apron strings too." She peeked up at me. "And I may have hidden their shoes in the cellar. In the potato barrel. They'll find them soon enough."

"Mona, that was mean."

"It was, wasn't it?" She sounded very cheerful about it. "But Sister Corinne has never been nice to me, so why should I be nice to her. Mostly, I wanted to make sure she would be so glad to be rid of me that she would merely say good riddance to bad Shakers."

Silas laughed out loud. "Looks like we have a traveling companion." He beckoned Mona closer. "Come on, child. Those saddlebags aren't that big. I think you can straddle them and ride behind Miss Darcie."

He boosted Mona up behind me. "You'll have to hang on to keep from falling off." He frowned up at her. "Aren't you the one who tormented Leatrice now and again?"

"Yea." Mona sounded sad, but I couldn't see her face so I wasn't sure how sincere she was. "But I promise never to be mean to her again. Never to be mean to anybody as long as I'm with my new mother." She snaked her arms around my waist and laid her head against my back. "Remember, Mama Darcie, you promised I could come with you and we could starve together."

"No such talk as that." Silas started leading Sawyer again. "Flynn won't let you starve."

Was that going to be the Lord's answer for me? To throw myself on the mercy of a near stranger. With Anna Grace stirring in the wrap in front of me and Mona clinging to me from behind, I definitely needed mercy. Flynn Keller had seemed a good man. My heart always lifted with joy at the sight of him coming on his horse toward Leatrice and me in the early mornings.

What would he think of me, with the baggage I carried, coming on a horse toward him?

35

Leatrice was glad to be home. Really, she was. And very glad that woman was gone. For good, Papa said. But so was Grandpa. Gone to the Shakers. Leatrice missed him. Her father was busy with his horses. He had to be. That was his work, but she needed something to do too. At the Shaker village, she'd been busy every minute of the day.

Papa said she did plenty. She swept the floor and washed the dishes. She fed the chickens and played with the cats. Papa wouldn't let her cook unless he was in the kitchen with her. Those times were good. She could fry eggs and anybody could put beans in a pot and hang it on a hook over the fire. But Papa worried she'd catch her dress tail on fire.

He did promise to get her some books so she could practice reading. She tried to read Mamaw Bea's Bible, but some of the words were too hard. Maybe she hadn't learned as much as she thought she had, the way Sister Corinne and Sister Josephine told her.

She didn't miss Sister Corinne at all. She did miss Sister Janice and even Sister Mona a little. The ones she really missed—so much that her heart kind of hurt inside her chest—were Sister Darcie and her babies. Sometimes Leatrice would sing a silly song to one of her cats and pretend it was Baby Benjamin.

She worried about not being there to push Anna Grace in her little wagon. Somebody else was probably helping Sister Darcie. Maybe Sister Mona. If she was, Leatrice hoped she wasn't being mean. Leatrice could never figure out why Sister Darcie was so nice to Sister Mona when sometimes Sister Mona was not nice at all.

Instead, Sister Darcie kept praying for her. Leatrice did feel kind of sorry for Sister Mona, with no father to love her the way Papa loved Leatrice. So she prayed that someday Sister Mona would have a father who loved her. Leatrice wasn't sure how that could happen, but Mamaw Bea used to say the Lord had ways of working things out for the best.

Last night, Papa had said they would go see Grandpa in a few days.

"Can we go see Sister Darcie and her babies too?" Leatrice asked.

"That would be nice." Papa looked out the kitchen window toward the road, as if thinking about going right away. Then he shook his head a little. "But I don't think the Shakers would allow that."

"We could go early so we could see them walking to the morning meal," Leatrice suggested.

"I suppose so." Papa smiled. "But she might not want to see us."

Leatrice frowned. "Why wouldn't she want to see us? She was always hugging me and she looked happy when she saw you too." She went over and stood right in front of Papa so she could see his face. "You liked her, didn't you?"

"You sound like your grandpa, trying to do some matchmaking." Papa put his hand on her head and ruffled her hair. "She's a Shaker sister, don't forget."

"But she didn't want to be. She wanted to be a mother, not a sister." Leatrice had felt a real yearning then to have a mother again. A mother like Sister Darcie, but some things a person couldn't say out loud. Not even to her papa.

So when she headed out to the barn to look for the mama cat's new kittens, she thought her eyes might be playing tricks on her when she saw Grandpa coming down the road leading a horse. Even though they were still a good ways from the house, Leatrice was pretty sure Sister Darcie was on the horse.

Leatrice jumped up and down and waved before she ran to the barn. "Papa! Papa!"

"No need to shout, Leatrice. I'm right here." Papa didn't like anybody yelling around the horses.

"But, Papa, Grandpa is coming." She did remember to lower her voice. "And he's got somebody with him. I think it's Sister Darcie."

Papa frowned at her. "You must be seeing things."

"No. Come look." Leatrice couldn't wait any longer. She ran out of the barn and up the lane toward her grandfather and Sister Darcie.

***

The girl had to be seeing things. Or maybe playing a trick on him, since she'd talked about wanting to go see Sister Darcie. Either way, Flynn best find out what she was up to.

He put down the curry comb and left his horse tied in the breezeway.

He stepped out into the sunshine. Leatrice wasn't seeing things. Silas was coming down the lane toward the house leading a horse. A horse carrying a woman in a Shaker dress. An answer to a prayer he hadn't even realized he'd been praying. Ma Beatrice said things like that could happen. That sometimes the Lord just knew what a person needed.

Yet even with that thought in his head, he stood still, as though afraid to move while the ground seemed to shift under his feet. Perhaps he was the one seeing things. But no, Silas was helping the woman down from the horse. Sister Darcie's husband's horse. But she had no husband now. And he had no wife.

The girl riding behind Sister Darcie slid off the horse without help. She was light on her feet. The girl who had given Leatrice trouble. But now she and Leatrice were hugging and dancing in a circle, making the horse skitter to the side. Silas grabbed the horse's bridle to settle it down.

Flynn wished his heart would settle down, but it kept beating too fast as crazy thoughts ran through his mind. He had no idea why the woman was here or the girl with her or even why Silas was here. Best not get carried away until he found out what they wanted. But still he stood without moving.

Leatrice ran to him and grabbed his hand. "Don't just stand there, Papa. Come on."

He let her tug him toward where they waited by the house. He had the strangest feeling he was walking through a gateway into a new life.

They all hushed as he stepped up to them. The young girl

slid behind Sister Darcie to peek out at him with worried eyes. Leatrice was watching him with big eyes too, as though she was afraid he wouldn't say the right thing. Whatever the right thing was. The woman gave him a hesitant smile and then looked relieved when her baby cried to take her attention. She lifted her out of the wrap, and the baby's cries turned to happy babbling as she smiled at Flynn. Anna Grace. But where was the other baby?

He spoke to Silas first. "Have you left the Shakers, Silas?"

"Nope, nay. Whatever it is I'm supposed to say these days for no." Silas smiled. "I just walked away this morning for a spell. I expect to have my feet back under their table for the evening meal. We weren't wrong about those Shaker cooks."

Flynn looked at the woman and his heart started beating faster again. "And you, Sister Darcie? Do you plan to have your feet back under the Shaker table this night?"

"No, I have left the village." She looked uneasy as she went on. "I suppose you are wondering why I am here. Why we are here."

"I'm guessing because Silas brought you."

"Well, yes." She turned and gave the baby to the child behind her. Then she straightened her shoulders and looked straight at Flynn. "He said that you might buy my horse. His price might tide me over until I find a way to earn my keep."

"And what way is that?"

"Perhaps as a seamstress. Or a housekeeper." Her forehead wrinkled with a frown. "Not that such is your concern. I merely ask you to consider my horse."

"Yes, your horse. Sawyer." He moved over to the horse, not because he needed to know more about the animal but because he needed time to steady his thoughts. Flynn's hand trembled as he rubbed the horse's neck. He could feel Silas staring at him, but he didn't look toward him.

"Sister Darcie."

"Don't bother her right now, Leatrice." Silas stopped her. "Let's go get a drink and maybe you can dig us up some food. I figure the lot of us missed breakfast this morning except for the baby here."

"But where is Baby Benjamin, Sister Darcie?" Leatrice looked worried.

She turned to touch Leatrice's cheek. "Another sister took him from the village to raise as her own. She loves him very much. Even more than I do."

"Oh," Leatrice said. "Does she sing silly songs to him?"

The woman smiled. "I don't know if they are silly songs, but she does sing to him."

"I wish he was here." Leatrice blinked back tears.

"I know. So do I, but he loved Sister Genna best. That is what we must remember."

Leatrice started to say something else, but Silas put his arm around her to turn her toward the house. "That baby will be fine. Now come on to the house before your old grandpa dies of thirst. Your pa don't need us bothering him while he checks out Miss Darcie's horse."

The girl Mona asked, "Should I take Anna Grace inside too?"

The woman's voice was soft. "That would be good. The sun is hot for her."

"For you too." Flynn glanced around at her. "And for Sawyer. Come on over to the barn." He didn't look back as he led the horse to the watering trough, but he knew she followed him.

After the horse drank his fill, Flynn tied his reins to a hitching post under the oak next to the barn. He went through the motions of checking the horse's legs and hooves and then pulling back his lips to check the teeth, but he wasn't thinking about the horse. He was thinking about the woman behind him.

"He's healthy, isn't he?" she said.

"A very nice horse. I'm glad the Shakers let you have him back."

"Yea. They are not unkind." She stepped over to touch the horse's nose.

"Unfortunately I don't have any ready cash to buy him right now." That much was true. He had spent most of his money on the house Silas had given to the Shakers. Money well spent, since he and Leatrice now had this farm.

She flinched at his words, but recovered quickly. "I see. Perhaps I can find a buyer in the town."

"I'm sure you could, but you have to be careful with horse traders. They sometimes try to get a horse for less than its worth."

"I'll keep that in mind. Thank you." She gave the horse's nose another pat before she turned toward the house. "I'd best go see about Anna Grace so we can head on to town. Thank you for letting us rest here for a little while."

"Wait." Flynn moved in front of her. "So you want a housekeeping job?"

"If I can find one." She pulled in a breath as if for courage. "I know I'm being too bold, but Silas said you might need someone to keep house and watch Leatrice."

"I don't need a housekeeper."

"Oh." Disappointment washed over her face. "Forgive me. I shouldn't have asked."

She ducked her head and started to move past him. Again he stepped in front of her. If she could be bold, then so could he. "I don't need a housekeeper. I need a wife."

⁂

If he had offered me one thousand dollars for Sawyer, I would not have been more astounded. I stared at him, wondering if I'd heard his words correctly, while my heart did a funny hop in my chest. Did he really mean he needed me as his wife?

"You hardly know me," I stammered.

"True, and you hardly know me." He moved a bit closer. "But you need a husband and I need a wife. Sounds the perfect trade to me."

"I'm not a horse to be traded."

He actually laughed. "No, indeed. You are a beautiful woman my daughter already loves."

"It is you who would be marrying me. Not your daughter."

"You stir my heart, Darcie. I believe love will grow where that stirring is taking place." He peered down at me intently. "The question is, Do you think love for me could grow in your heart?"

I placed my hand flat against my chest. "My heart is trying to jump out of my chest."

His eyes were tender on me. "But is that because of joy or fear?"

"Perhaps both."

"Then what do you say?"

When I didn't answer right away, he went on. "I understand this is sudden. If you will stay and consider my offer, I'll sleep in the barn until you're sure of your answer."

"I see. That might be good since you would need to get to know me better as well." I hesitated, but as much as I wanted to agree to his plan, to even perhaps step into his embrace right that minute, I knew I must make him aware of all I brought with me. "I have a baby."

"I am ready to be Anna Grace's father the same as you are ready to be Leatrice's mother."

I breathed in and out. "There is also Mona."

He frowned a little. "Isn't she going back to Harmony Hill with Silas?"

"No. I have promised Mona she can be my daughter."

Flynn frowned and looked toward the house. I didn't turn to look, but I sensed Mona watching us from the porch. "But won't the Shakers insist she come back to the village?"

"I don't think so. My Mona is not an easy child. She thinks they will be glad to be rid of her and I believe she may be right."

"You want me to take in a child who is unkind to my daughter?"

I moistened my lips and said words I didn't want to say, but I could not desert Mona. "She is trying to change her ways, but it is still too much to ask. We will go on into the town."

Again he stopped me. This time with a hand on my arm. "Don't be in such a hurry. You have to give a man time to adjust to going from being the father of one daughter to the father of three."

Such relief and joy swept through me that I lost all constraint and threw my arms around his neck. Thankfully, he accepted my embrace and returned it in kind.

"May I seal our promise with a kiss?" he whispered into my ear.

I kept my arms around him as I leaned my head back to look up at him. "That would seem a good way to begin to know you better."

His lips on mine were soft, not demanding in any way. A perfect beginning.

Epilogue

I did marry Flynn Keller on September 25, 1850, exactly one month from the day that I brazenly threw myself into his arms. He did as he promised and slept in the barn until that day, but we spent time together in the daylight hours to get to know one another.

A preacher came to the farm on that September day. Silas came too from the village and I was surprised to see Eldress Maria and Sister Lettie in the buggy with him. Surprised but overjoyed as well. Eldress Maria's face looked every bit as joyful when Anna Grace reached for her as soon as she stepped down from the buggy. Of course, Anna Grace was the reason she had come to our wedding, an event considered sinful by the Shakers.

Sister Lettie was her usual cheerful self and seemed not the least uncomfortable to be witnessing an exchange of marital vows. They both pretended not to recognize Mona or perhaps they did not, for Mona was much changed by the time the month had passed. Smiles sat on her face more than frowns, and she had added a few pounds to her frame since she was not so ready to miss meals to get into mischief as she had been at the Shaker village. I strictly warned her not to mention Sister Corinne's and Sister Tansy's hidden shoes.

"You know I do what I want." She did her little spin and laughed. "But maybe I will want to do what my Mama Darcie says."

The eldress brought letters from Ellie and Genna that came for me at the village. Ellie's was long, full of many words about her grandchildren and how she continued to pray for me. Genna's was more to the point, just as Genna always was.

Benjamin is sipping the goat's milk from a cup now. He misses you, but he is happy. I am happy. I pray you are free. Your forever sister, Genna.

I could not have gotten a more treasured gift on my wedding day. To hear from both my forever sisters.

I thought of Walter as I took Flynn's hand in front of the preacher. But it was not with regret or sadness. Walter would have been the first to tell me that my love for him was not lessened because I stepped on a new path of love with another.

In the year since then, I cannot say that it has always been easy. Mona is after all Mona, and even natural-born sisters have their times of conflict. But Mona tries very hard and Leatrice does as well. Anna Grace is her continual happy self, so very like Walter always was. She won Flynn's heart without effort. As Flynn won mine.

We added a baby boy to our girls in August. We named him Silas Walter. Had he been a girl, her name would have been Lena Maria. We do not try to forget the loves we had in the past, but we rejoice in the love we share now.

Such are the blessings of being a beloved child of God.

READ ON FOR A GLIMPSE OF
RIVER TO REDEMPTION
FROM ANN H. GABHART . . .

One

Adria Starr didn't want her mother and little brother to stop breathing the way her father had. She wanted to take care of them.

She was seven. That was old enough to do things. She could draw water from the well and carry wood to the stove. She could even run for the doctor, like she did after her daddy came home sick, but a woman answered the door at the doctor's house to say he couldn't come. He was sick too. That it wouldn't matter anyway. Not with the cholera.

Adria had heard her father whisper that word to her mother. Adria didn't know what it meant, but her mother clutched the back of a chair and made a sound like somebody had hit her in the stomach. Then with her eyes too wide, she looked at Adria, and it was like somebody was squeezing Adria's heart.

"Leave." Adria's father told her mother. "Get away from the bad air here in town."

Even before her father quit breathing, her mother started

packing a bag to go somewhere after Adria came back without the doctor. But how could they leave Daddy? Then Eddie got sick. Just like their father. He was only two and he cried until Adria wanted to put her hands over her ears. But when he stopped, everything was too quiet.

They didn't leave. Her mother couldn't stop shaking and she was very sick. Like her insides wanted to come out of her body. She leaned on Adria while she sat on the pot. She told Adria to go away, but if Adria hadn't held her, her mother would have fallen to the floor.

After Mama got through being sick, Adria helped her to the couch and laid Eddie down beside her. Adria kissed his cheek, but it didn't feel right. She didn't look at his chest. She didn't want to know if it had stopped moving up and down. She didn't look at her mother's chest either. Instead she carried the slop jar and basin into the sitting room in case her mother needed them again. Then she got a blanket and curled up on the floor beside the couch.

Her mother didn't need the basin, but Adria did. She must have breathed in that bad air too. After she was through being sick, she lay back down on the floor. The only sounds were the mantel clock ticking and more bad air ruffling the window curtains.

She fell asleep for a while. When she woke up, the clock wasn't ticking anymore. Her father was the one who always wound it. The air had stopped moving too. Maybe the bad air had moved away to another town. But Adria's stomach still hurt. She needed a drink of water, but she didn't think she could get up to go to the kitchen.

Adria reached up toward her mother but stayed her hand without touching her. Everything was so still. Nothing was moving. Usually their house was filled with sound. Eddie jabbering or crying. Her mother singing while she clattered pans in the kitchen. Her father coming in the door from work and grabbing Adria to swing her up in the air and then giving Eddie a turn. She didn't know which of them squealed the loudest.

But now silence wrapped around her. Nothing but her heart beating in her ears. She wanted to ask her mother if the bad air killed everybody, but she clamped her lips together and didn't let the words out. She was scared her mother wouldn't answer.

Adria squeezed her eyes shut. Where she'd been sick smelled bad. Really bad. She pinched her nose to block the odor, but then her breathing sounded too loud, like she'd been running or something. She pulled a pillow over her face.

She hoped it wouldn't hurt if the bad air killed her. Maybe her heart would just stop the way the clock had stopped ticking. She tried to remember whether the preacher ever said anything in his sermons about dying. But most of the stories she could remember were about Jesus feeding people or making them well. Maybe if she prayed, he would make her well, and Eddie and her parents too.

"Please," she whispered into the pillow. She tried to think of more words, but she was tired. So she just said the bedtime prayer her mother taught her. "Now I lay me down to sleep. I pray the Lord my soul to keep. And if I should die before I wake, I pray the Lord my soul to take."

She prayed that all the time, but she had never worried about not waking up. Not until now. What would happen if the Lord took her soul? Would it be silent like now, or noisy? Angels singing maybe. No, that was when Jesus was born.

But heaven might be noisy. Lots of people there, and didn't they say something about crossing a river? She'd seen a river. The water was noisy. She really needed a drink.

The knock on the door made her jump. Her father had said something once about a person knocking on heaven's door, but this sounded more like their own front door. Maybe it was the doctor coming after all. When she pushed up off the floor, the room started spinning, and she cried out and fell back with a thump.

The door swung open and a deep voice called out, "Somebody in here needin' help?"

When the big man stepped around the couch, Adria let out another shriek, but her mother didn't make the first sound. The man stared down at Adria. Sweat made tracks down his black face and he looked like a giant looming over her. She scrambled away from him, but moving made her sick again. She tried to get to the basin, but she didn't make it.

Big gentle hands reached down to hold her. "There, there, missy. It's done gonna be all right." He stroked her hair sort of the way her daddy did sometimes when he was telling her good night.

When she was through being sick, the man wiped her mouth off with a handkerchief and gathered her up in his arms as though she wasn't any bigger than Eddie. She forgot about being afraid and laid her head against his chest. His heart was beating, steady and sure. It was a good sound, and even his sweaty smell was better than the smell from her being sick.

"What's your name, child?" he asked.

"Adria," she whispered, a little surprised the sound came out of her dry lips.

"Adria," he echoed her. "That's a fine name. I'm gonna take you back to Mr. George's hotel where we can see to you."

"What about Eddie?"

"That your little brother there?" The man's voice was soft. "You don't have to worry about him. I'll come back and do what needs doing."

Adria didn't want to, but she couldn't keep her eyes from peeking away from the man's chest toward Eddie beside her mother. He wasn't moving and her mother's eyes were staring up at the ceiling. "What needs doing?"

"Well, it ain't an easy thing for a little missy like you to know, but your mama and li'l brother done gone on to glory. All's can be done for them now is a proper burial. I been doing it for all them that got took by the cholera." He rubbed his hand up and down Adria's back and turned so she couldn't see her mother anymore. "What about your pappy?"

"He died first." Adria pointed toward the bedroom.

The man nodded. "It's a sorrowful thing."

"Am I going to go to glory too?" Glory seemed easier to say than die.

"Only the good Lord knows our appointed time to leave this old world, but I'm thinkin' that you might have to wait a while to see glory. Could be the Lord has more for you to do down here like he has for me."

"What's that?"

"Hard to say. But time will tell, missy. Time will tell. Now you just rest your head down on my shoulder and let ol' Louis take you on up the street. Matilda, she ain't bothered by the cholera, same as me, and she's got a healin' hand.

Me and her, we'll do for you and chase that old cholera out of you."

"I want my mama." Adria was crying inside, but her tears had all dried up. Her eyes felt scratchy when she blinked.

"Ain't that the way of us all. To want our mammies." He carried her out the door.

Night was falling, or maybe day was breaking. Adria didn't know how long she had lain there by the couch afraid to look at her mother. And now she would never see her again. Not unless she went to glory.

She ought to want to go to glory along with her mother and father and Eddie. They were a family. Her mother said that all the time, and then she would pick up Eddie and pull Adria close to her in a hug at the same time. If Daddy was there, he'd put his arms around them all and make what he called a family sandwich with his children in the middle. That always made Adria giggle. She liked being in a family sandwich, and now that was gone. Unless she went back and lay down beside her mother to let the bad air get her too.

But she didn't want to do that. She was glad the big man was carrying her away from her house. Away from the bad air. She thought she ought to be sorry about that, and she was sorry. Very sorry and sad her family was gone, but she wasn't sorry she was still breathing. She wanted to believe it was like the big man said. That the Lord wasn't ready for her yet.

She thought she should tell the man she could walk. She was way past carrying age, but the man wasn't breathing hard and it felt good to let him take care of her.

"I prayed," she said. "Did God send you to my house?" That wasn't what she'd prayed for, but she heard the preacher say once that sometimes the Lord knew what you needed better than you did.

"That could be." The man's chest rumbled under Adria's ear as he chuckled at her words. "I reckon the good Lord has his ways of makin' things happen, but fact is, the doctor's wife told me you'd been there to get the doctor."

"She wouldn't let him come."

"Well, he couldn't rightly make it, child. The cholera has done laid him low too. Could be he'll make it through, but he can't be no use to nobody else till he does." The man's voice was soft and deep, with nothing scary about it.

"Are you an angel?" Adria had never thought about angels having black skin and smelling sweaty. She always thought about them floating around with wings and white robes, but could be that was all wrong.

The man's chest rumbled again. "That's something I never expected anybody to say about me. But no, missy, I ain't no angel. I reckon I should've tol' you who I is to rest your mind a bit. I'm Louis Sanderson, Mr. George Sanderson's man. He owns the hotel here on Main Street, and when the cholera come to call, he give me his keys and told me to carry on with things best I could. He aimed to get as far from the cholera as he could and I'm supposin' he did."

"Daddy wanted Mama to go, but Eddie got sick and then she got sick too."

"The cholera is a terrible thing."

"Why didn't you go too?"

"There's some wonderin' 'bout that, but whilst I ain't no angel, the good Lord had a job here for me to do. Folks to take care of. He somehow kept the bad air from bothering ol' Louis and seemed to me he must have had a reason for that.

Somethin' he expected me to do. The Lord gives you a job to do, then I reckon you'd best do it. Ain't that right, missy?"

She tried to listen and understand what he was saying, but she couldn't hold all his words in her ears. "I don't know."

Louis patted her back as he carried her up some steps to a door with painted glass. "Well, don't you never mind about that. Right now you just think on gettin' better. Matilda and me, we're gonna take good care of you."

Acknowledgments

From the time I first fell in love with books, I knew I wanted to be a storyteller. As a young girl, I imagined living in a remote cabin in the mountains with three or four dogs to keep me company while I wrote stories. I thought writing had to be a solitary occupation. But I'm thankful the Lord saw a different future for me and sent me a loving husband who puts up with my trips down story roads with my characters. I'm blessed by the support and patience of my children who grew up to the clacking of my typewriter. I'm thankful for their families now that make life so good.

I'm grateful for the support and encouragement of my editor, Lonnie Hull DuPont, who helps make my stories better. Karen Steele and Michele Misiak are never too busy to answer my questions even when I forget which one I should ask what. Many thanks to Gayle Raymer for the eye-catching cover that looks so authentically Shaker. A special thanks to Barb Barnes for her careful editing to smooth out any bumps in my story words. I appreciate all the others on my Revell

389

team who move my book along the publishing journey and out to readers.

I am continually blessed by the unfailing encouragement of my agent, Wendy Lawton. When I wasn't sure I was headed in the right direction with this story, she offered to read my first few chapters and assured me that yes, the story did work. Thank you so much, Wendy.

And of course, I thank the Lord for giving me a gift of words and letting that little girl's dream of being a writer come true.

Last but not least, I thank each of you who read my stories. I often think of storytelling as a partnership. I write the words, but you read them and let them come to life in your imagination. Thank you. I hope you enjoyed going back to Harmony Hill for another Shaker story.

Ann H. Gabhart is the bestselling author of several Shaker novels—*The Outsider*, *The Believer*, *The Seeker*, *The Blessed*, and *The Gifted*—as well as other historical novels including *Angel Sister*, *These Healing Hills*, and *River to Redemption*. She and her husband live on a farm a mile from where she was born in rural Kentucky. Ann enjoys discovering the everyday wonders of nature while hiking in her farm's fields and woods with her grandchildren and her dog, Frankie. Learn more at www.annhgabhart.com.

She Longs for Peace—in Her Land and Her Heart—but Can It Truly Be Found at Harmony Hill?

At the close of the Civil War in the Shaker village of Harmony Hill, Carlyn Kearny must come to terms with a personal tragedy and find a way to open her heart to love again.

"Characters are written with depth. . . .
Ann Gabhart knows
her Amish and Shaker history."
—*RT Book Reviews* ★★★★

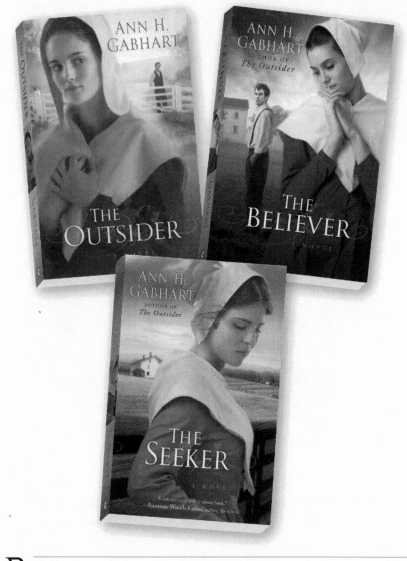

"Fascinating history from a sect that has almost completely vanished."
—CBN.com

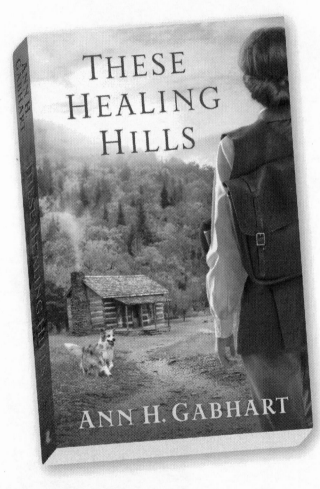

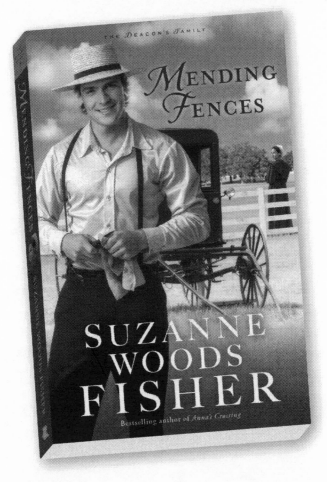

Meet
Ann H. Gabhart

Find out more about Ann's newest releases, read blog posts, and follow her on social media at

AnnHGabhart.com

Printed in the United States
By Bookmasters